## By
## ANN YIHYANG KIM

### Novels
### EYES OF AWAKENING
*Eye in the Blue Box*
*Tree of Eyes*

### Short Stories
"The Train"
"Half Open"
"The Lilies"
"Two Lines"
"Harvest"
"Memory"
"Whistle"

# TREE
# OF
# EYES

# TREE
# OF
# EYES

Book Two of
EYES OF AWAKENING

**Ann Yihyang Kim**

BLUE WOLF & EYE PUBLISHING • SAN DIEGO

For all those who need the warmth of another world
to survive in reality.

# CONTENTS

# SYNOPSIS

Welcome to *Tree of Eyes*, the second book of EYES OF AWAKENING.

In the first book, *Eye in the Blue Box*, James Mun, a twenty-five-year-old lover of instant ramen and slow mornings, falls asleep on a calm evening after work. He enters a strange dimension and follows the cry of a stranger, whom he wishes to help. He discovers a mysterious, blue box and within it, a pulsing, red eye, which he consumes.

From then on, he wakes up in the Flowering each time he falls asleep. He returns to Reality only if something jars him from his sleep or if something in the Flowering pierces his watch. For reasons unknown, his watch remains stagnant instead of tracking the hours passing in Reality, an alarming abnormality as all humans in the Flowering must remain there at least eight hours each night or die as a penalty for failing to stay long enough.

Moaning and groaning about his lot in life, he follows Crew Blue throughout the Flowering's shifting planes. He begins to regard Bloom and Lux as his friends but remains on rocky grounds with Honey and, in particular, E, who forces him to battle moulded citizens. The healing abilities humans gain each time they enter the Flowering ensure that James won't die despite the many injuries he sustains, but he grows bitter of his life in the Flowering nevertheless. Reality no longer proves to be easy, either, as he flounders both at work and in his graduate studies.

He finally explodes on Thanksgiving during a vehement argument with Heri, his sister. That night, he severs call and response with Crew Blue, only to walk straight into the trap of a fearsome moulded citizen.

He manages to defend himself until Crew Blue rescues him. They reconcile and, at last, begin to work as one.

All is well until a family of Hunters attempt to capture Bloom. In the chaos that ensues, James's watch changes. He sees a dark purple orb, which contains a monstrous beast in the form of a calf dripping with blood. One of its eyes is closed in slumber. The other is missing from its raw socket. On its forehead is a golden eye, which unfurls to reveal a vision of a young woman, whose strange, blue eyes are blind.

The crew escapes from the Calf's hungry darkness, which chases them through the plane. E, driven by rage and vengeance, tricks the Hunter, Blood Crow, into initiating call and response and becoming Crew Blue's prisoner. Along with the Roamer, Phoenix, they embark on a perilous journey to the City to find the woman James saw in his vision, Snow, the Twelfth Shaman.

Shamans, though blind, are the most powerful humans in the Flowering, for they can read the memories of any human they touch. The Third, the most notorious of the twelve Shamans, learns that the crew has seen the Calf almost as soon as they step foot in the City. He imprisons them in the Tower, but Snow's Guide, Zilch, manages to smuggle her and the crew into the Market.

The crew learns that the Third desires, above all else, the Red Calf's golden eye as he believes that it can restore the Shamans' sight. He also wishes to capture the Red Calf, which legends say was the most powerful citizen to have ever walked the Flowering, and wield its powers as his own. The crew discovers that Snow, too, ate of the eye in the blue box and that she and James are connected to each other and the Red Calf. They conclude that James's watch is counting down to the Calf's return to full strength.

The crew makes a harrowing escape from the City with the help of Kit, an ambitious Jackal who was once E's lover. The last the crew sees of

Kit is him fighting the horde of Merchants trying to capture them. They are forced to abandon both him and Zilch during their escape.

Now the crew must find a way out of No Man's Land, the dangerous territories surrounding the City, while evading the Third's men, and they must do so quickly, for they must hunt down the Red Calf before it can return to the Flowering.

# PART I
# UNRAVELING

# CHAPTER 1
# PARTNERSHIP

James rushed into his apartment and slammed the door shut. He didn't know why he had even bothered going to work today when all he'd managed to do was stare at the screen and barely contain his anxiety! The group had escaped from the Doors thanks to Kit, but Bloom was bound to be stuck in No Man's Land, still searching through those treacherous territories for the right exits, and the Merchants at the Doors had surely reported everything that had happened to the Third by now.

How far had Bloom managed to navigate through No Man's Land on his own? How many of the Third's men were out there searching for the group? And what about Kit and Zilch? The group couldn't possibly go back for them tonight. But they couldn't just leave them trapped in the City either!

He filled a pot with water then stood at the stove and tapped his foot as he waited for the water to boil. After a few seconds, he cast the water into the sink, tore open an energy bar, and grabbed his sleeping pills. He closed all the curtains before shoving himself under his blankets. He forced his breathing into deep inhales and controlled exhales. He had to clear his mind for now. He had to fall asleep. There was no use staying in Reality for even a second longer. He had to regroup with the others and figure out what to do. Minutes ticked by before drowsiness began to overpower him.

His eyes blinked shut then opened.

Bloom, Honey, and Lux stood next to one another, tense and silent. A few feet away, Snow stood shouting and pleading with E as she paced back and forth.

"We have to go back for Zilch, E, please!"

"I said be quiet! We're still in No Man's Land."

E stopped and glanced at the dark, verdant jungle which loomed several yards away from the group. The wide stretch of dirt on which they currently stood separated the jungle from tall, dry weeds covering half of a vast field. Beyond the field, yellow hills leaned against a blue sky.

"E, please. I'm begging you," said Snow. "They'll catch Z. They'll take him back to the Tower. We have to go back, E, please!"

"Shut up!" E roared.

Snow stiffened. Her wide, blank eyes stared into space for several moments.

"Are you really going to abandon Kit like this?" said Snow.

E turned toward her, her eyes glinting like blades unsheathed. James and Bloom took a few steps forward. Blood Crow appeared next to Bloom then stumbled back as E drew her dagger.

"Are you really going to abandon him? Do you really think he could have escaped?" Snow continued. "They'll catch him, and they'll take him to the Tower. They'll do whatever they need to do to make him talk, and they'll break him just like they break all the others. We need to go back tonight if you want to save him."

"E," James warned, walking toward her with quickening steps. "E, don't do it!"

She hurled her dagger into Snow's stomach. James groaned and clutched his head. All the anxiety that had built up within him throughout the day suddenly left him like air rushing out of punctured a balloon so that only his frustration and exhaustion remained. Snow exhaled softly, gathered her pale fingers around the hilt of E's dagger, and collapsed onto the dirt.

"Shut up, and let me think!" E shouted. "If we go back now, they'll imprison us all! We might not get another chance to escape. I ... I need to think."

Lux scrunched up his face, struggled, then blurted, "But E, she's right! Kit and Zilch are totally screwed if we don't go back right now."

"Kit knows how to take care of himself," E snapped.

Lux gave his head a slight shake then stared at her as if he'd never really seen her before. His face sank with disappointment.

"You're really going to abandon him like this? After everything he did last night? He risked everything for us. For you! We can't just–"

"Stop it!" she screamed.

Lux recoiled. His disappointment twisted into disgust. Phoenix appeared next to Bloom then did a double take at Snow curled up and bleeding on the ground.

"What's going on here?" he demanded of E.

She flashed him a piercing look then resumed pacing back and forth.

"E and Snow were arguing," Lux mumbled. "Snow wants to go back for Kit and Zilch, but E says it'll be too dangerous."

Phoenix stared at E as she continued stomping around. Blood Crow lifted her nose high into the air and walked over to Snow. Bloom and Honey joined her as she tended to the wound E's dagger had made. James rubbed the inner corners of his eyes and dragged his feet over to Lux and Phoenix. Phoenix stared at E a moment longer before turning to Lux.

"E's right," Phoenix said. "I've been thinking it over all day. We should get out of No Man's Land first. The Third's men are sure to be crawling all over the territories already. Once we're safe, we can think about what to do, who to rescue, and how. It's no use arguing right now. We need to get out of here."

"But what about Kit and Zilch?" Lux said with a pained expression.

"Kit doesn't exactly seem weak or stupid to me," Phoenix said. "And he's a Jackal. He said he'd get Zilch out, so let's see if he can. If he does, it'll be all the better if we can get out of here now."

Lux clicked his tongue and kicked at a few rocks embedded in the dirt. "I still think we should go back," he muttered. "E's just being stubborn again, and she's abandoning Kit even though he's bending over backward for her."

"Don't judge her like that. You don't know what's happened between them before."

Lux continued kicking at the rocks. James let out a deep sigh and buried his face in his hands. Phoenix was right. Going back to the City right now would be tactical suicide. But James agreed with Lux about E's behavior. E. She really could be so difficult. Rejecting Kit flat then kissing him so passionately and now flinging around daggers at a blind girl while screaming for all of No Man's Land to hear! He was growing so tired of her unpredictable storms of emotion and double standards. She could be so calm and controlled one moment then unstable and nearly unhinged the next. Why did she have to act like this?

"Phoenix ... do you ... are you jealous?" said Lux.

James lifted his face from his hands.

"Jealous," Phoenix repeated.

"Well, yeah. Kit was right, wasn't he? You like E too? You don't want her going back and finding him, right? I mean, I know she's playing hard to get and everything, but you saw how they were making out."

Lux shook his head and sighed. "Sorry, man. I don't know how else to put it. I shouldn't have brought it up."

"Any feelings I have for E are irrelevant. We need to survive right now. This is no time for my feelings or anyone else's feelings to get involved. If going back right now were the best thing to do, I'd have no problem with it."

"Yeah, sure. Okay," Lux mumbled. Then he clicked his tongue again. "Man, you're just making stuff up and being jealous!"

"Lux," James groaned. "Just drop it!"

"Don't tell me to drop it! You know it's true. He's just making things up because he doesn't want to admit that Kit is right and that he doesn't want to go back."

"Don't accuse me of being petty like that!" Phoenix retorted. "You're not thinking straight, and you're not making any sense right now, so just stop!"

"W-Well, maybe it's about time I snapped a little! I'm sick of traveling every corner of every plane every night. Last night was so crazy, and Reality is hard as it is. Work really sucked at the shop today, you know? And if you think your sister is difficult, James, you should meet mine! Everyone is being so ... so...."

Lux struggled then threw his arms over his head as if he wanted to shut out the entire world and find just one moment of peace. He scowled and flung his arms back down before walking away. Phoenix hesitated then followed him. James didn't bother. He wasn't in the mood to deal with any of this.

"Hey," said Honey as she walked up to him.

"Hey. How's Snow?"

"Good. Or at least good enough. Looks like E wasn't aiming for anything too important. Snow is a pretty slow healer, though. Slower than me if you can believe that. I don't think she's had much of a chance to practice, being cooped up in the Tower every night, but anyway. You want to look after her for a while? I wanted to chat with E a little."

"About what? You don't agree with Snow and Lux, do you? I know E's being difficult, but we can't go back right now."

"No, no. Not about going back. Just something between us girls."

"Huh?" he said. Honey and E weren't exactly the "girl talk" type of girls.

She eyed the look on his face then chuckled. "It's just about her and Kit. You noticed it too, didn't you? Even Blood Crow saw it."

"You're calling her by her name now?"

"Can you stay on topic? I know there are about a million other things we need to worry about right now, but I've had my fair share of bad boys in the past, so I know how distracting those kinds of boys can be. Blood Crow knows too, and we both agree that we can't have E being so distracted right now."

James's heart tightened at the thought of Blood Crow kissing another man as E had kissed Kit. "What do you mean?" he demanded.

"I just mean … I don't know. My tingly senses are all going off, and well, I'm really worried about E to tell you the truth, even with all the fighting and the battles and all that aside. Blood Crow is worried too, as a fellow woman and everything. She came up to me, and we talked about it back at Kit's place, and we both agreed that something feels really off."

E stopped pacing.

"We need to get out of No Man's Land for now," she told the group. "We need to escape from the Third, find the Calf, and kill it before it regains its full strength. We'll come up with a rescue plan afterward. Phoenix, do you think Alex might have a post nearby?"

"I'll check. There might be one in the jungle."

"Take Bloom with you. He might be able to pick up on her scent. If you can't find anything within a few yards, come back, and we'll try finding a post somewhere else."

Phoenix nodded then set out into the jungle with Bloom at his side. Lux glanced at E before following them.

"Blood Crow, Honey, go and stand guard. Look out for any search parties," E commanded.

Blood Crow nodded and marched off to keep watch.

"Wait. E," said Honey. "E, can I talk to you?"

James hurried over to Snow. Whatever Honey wanted to talk to E about, he did not want to be around when she said it. In her agitated state, E was bound to explode sooner or later, and he did not want to take needless shrapnel tonight.

"You okay?" he asked Snow as he helped her sit up.

She winced. Her hands sprang to her bandaged stomach.

"Yeah, I know how that feels," he said, giving her a sympathetic pat on the shoulder as, sure enough, E snapped at Honey from behind him.

"What is wrong with her?" Snow said with an angry sob in her voice. "A dagger? Really? That was so unnecessary! Is she always so abusive a- and rude?"

James looked up at the sky. Memories of E yelling at him and stabbing him swirled together with images of her rescuing him from citizens and a falling boulder.

"She's just trying her best," he ended up saying.

Snow shook her head. "How can she just abandon them like this? Even if it's not for Z, she should go back for Kit, shouldn't she?"

He felt a twinge of pity as he saw the desperation on her face. He wondered what Snow's day must have been like and how much her thoughts must have tortured her. He tried to imagine how he would feel right now if a member of Crew Blue were still stuck at the Doors.

"Snow," he said, keeping his voice low and gentle. "I know you want to go back, and I've been thinking about it all day too. But I think E's right. We'll all get caught if we go back now. Everything will have been for nothing. You know that, and Zilch will know that too. He's smart. And who knows? Kit really might get him past the moonlight. They weren't that far from the Blue Border."

Snow began rubbing her knuckles. James sighed.

"Let's try talking about something else," he said. "Try to take our minds off of things, at least while we wait for Phoenix. Focusing on the negative isn't getting us anywhere right now."

She continued rubbing her knuckles but did not protest.

"How ... how did you and Phoenix become friends? He found you as a newborn, right? What was that like? Tell me all about your first night from the beginning," he said, taking a stab at the first topic that came to mind.

"O-Oh! Well, we, um...."

Maybe Kit had rubbed off on him, but James thought he sensed something more than friendly feelings in the blush that darkened Snow's pale skin. His suspecting gaze wandered from her cheeks to her eyes. Thin, black lines webbed her irises like light playing on an ocean floor. He suddenly realized that the blue of her eyes matched that of the stone box they had found in their awakening dreams. The lines, too, matched those that had been sprawled across the box's surface.

"Well," she said as her hands slowly relaxed, "that night was pretty awful. At least until Phoenix found me. You know how scary things are when you're born. And eating the eye. And then I found out that I was blind. It was a lot to handle. A little too much."

"Yeah," he said. Being born into the Flowering had been chaotic enough even without eating the eye. He couldn't imagine adding sudden blindness to it all. "Yeah, I bet that was pretty crazy."

Her troubled expression softened. "I was born into a desert, or at least I think it was. I remember the ground being really dry and jagged, but I think there was some vegetation or something too because I tripped over some roots. There was this really strong smell there too. Actually, it's that smell you can smell right now."

"What smell?"

"That smell," she said, as if referring to the obvious. "That lavender smell that's coming from over there."

He stared in the direction toward which she had turned her nose but saw nothing except for the full moon and yellow hills. A few whiffs brought only the scent of fresh air and moist earth. Maybe Snow's vision wasn't the only sense that had something wrong with it.

"I ended up falling through what I think was an exit. Phoenix found me right after," she continued. "I was so lucky he found me. It could have been so bad if he hadn't. Imagine what could have happened if one of the moulded had found me first. But I didn't know how lucky I was in the moment. I yelled and screamed and said all sorts of mean things to him. But he was so great about it. He really saved me that night in more than one way. He was so caring and patient."

Now he definitely knew that she had more than friendly feelings for Phoenix.

"He calmed me down. Gave me clothes. We tried walking, but I kept falling over, so he carried me all the way to the City. He taught me to create and trained me a little with weapons too. Enough to protect myself, at least. He even named me Snow."

James smiled as she beamed.

"I see," he said. "Any reason in particular for the name?"

"There was white dust all over me when he found me. He said it almost looked like I was covered in snow. And when I told him that I really didn't want to be called Twelve for the rest of my life, he said, 'How about Snow, then? I think it suits you.' It was really sweet of him.

"When he had to leave me in the Tower, he didn't even ask for a reward. He just asked if he could see me for free whenever he wanted to. Him and any friends he might bring along. He promised to try and visit me at least once a year and maybe bring the Runner who had helped us so that I'd have more than one visitor.

"I knew he was just saying it to cheer me up, though. I didn't think he'd really come. You know how hard it is getting to the City, and him being a Roamer and all. But it was a really sweet gesture. Even Three was impressed with how nice and polite he was. And, well, I guess it gave me some hope and something to look forward to just in case he actually did end up coming back. And that hope got me through some difficult nights. Phoenix is a real gentleman."

James's stress slowly released its hold on him as he stared at the puppy-like infatuation glowing on her face.

"I'm glad he took good care of you. I think he's a good guy too, like you said. And, uh … it's cute how much you like him."

He smiled again as she blushed.

"Is it … can you tell I … is it that obvious?" she whispered.

"You might want to tone it down a little if you don't want everyone to notice," he advised.

She began rubbing her knuckles again. "James. Phoenix *doesn't like* E, *right? Like* Kit *said? I could hear everything from inside the* cart," she whispered.

James knew she was using Korean intentionally to block as many of the others as she could from accidentally eavesdropping, but it wasn't the fear of being overheard that made him hesitate before answering her. His honest answer was that Phoenix probably did have some sort of crush on E, but too much fear lay in Snow's eyes for him to dash her hopes based on a mere assumption. Besides, she had enough to worry about with Zilch.

"Does it matter if he does?" he said. "I know you couldn't see them, but E wasn't exactly pulling away from Kit when he kissed her at the Doors. I don't know what's going on between them, but I wouldn't be surprised if he ended up winning her over in the end. I mean, they were really kissing. Like, a lot. And the way they took down those Merchants together, it wasn't just ordinary teamwork. They've got chemistry, and they know it."

Uneasiness stole into his heart as he spoke. Though E and Kit's relationship had been shunted to the bottom of his growing list of worries, thoughts of them had flitted through his mind throughout the day. If they got back together, E wouldn't choose to leave the crew and join Kit in the Market permanently, would she? She would still want to stay with the crew and rescue the marked and slay the moulded like she always had, wouldn't she? His uneasiness sank into sadness as he imagined the crew traveling through different planes and battling the moulded without her. As difficult as she could be, she was still E.

He suddenly realized that E and Honey had grown quiet. He turned around to find them deep in conversation. E sat still with a far-off gaze as Honey whispered to her with alternations of slight and furious shakes of her head.

"What's that?" Snow said, tensing suddenly.

"What's what?"

"That sound."

E's head snapped up. She, James, and Honey sprang onto their feet and unsheathed their blades. Snow fumbled with the hilt of her knife. The sound of stumbling drew near. James spotted the top of Blood Crow's head gliding toward them through the sea of weeds.

A fawn tumbled into the clearing.

"*Help!*" the fawn cried out. "*Help! He's going to mould with me!*"

James saw the mark, red as blood, on the fawn's back then Blood Crow's raised spear. He launched himself forward, snatched up the fawn into his arms, and rolled across the ground as her spear flew past him.

"*Let it go!*" Blood Crow shouted as she drew her knife.

"It's done nothing to you!" he yelled, shielding the wriggling fawn with his body.

"*It's going to mould!*"

"It just said it's running away from the moulded. Seriously. How long are you going keep this up? Stop being so blind!"

The appearance of E's machete silenced them both.

"Keep. Your voices. Down," she growled. "Blood Crow, drop your knife."

She pursed her lips then let her blade fall to the ground. Honey sheathed her knife.

"*You,*" said E, pointing her machete at the fawn.

It froze in James's grasp.

"*What are you talking about? Is there a moulded citizen that's after you?*"

"*Y-Yes! One of the Ancients of old,*" the fawn said. Tears began dripping down from its large, black eyes. "*I know I should've listened to Forest. I know I shouldn't have left, but I ... I....*"

James shushed and cradled the fawn as it broke down into sobs.

"*Where did you see it last? The citizen that's chasing you?*" E demanded.

"*I-I lost him over the hills over there. But he's coming. And he's with others, with humans!*"

The fawn's eyes bulged as Bloom hurried out of the jungle with Phoenix and Lux.

"*You! It's you! You're Forest's brother!*" the fawn cried out, straining its neck toward Bloom and wriggling again.

Bloom halted with one paw cocked and lifted.

"*But that means it's all of you! The humans said that they were searching for a group that was traveling with a blue wolf. They're after you. They're after all of you. We need to run!*"

Snow drew a sharp breath. James recognized that look on her face. It was the same look that had gripped her whenever she'd heard enemies approaching in the Tower. After several moments of strained concentration, he heard it too. Engines were revving in the distance. He rose to his feet, still clutching the fawn, and looked toward the hills.

It was the monster. The monster the group had met on the rickety dock. The one that had chased them across No Man's Land and up to the Blue Border. It was bounding down the hills toward them, leading several large SUVs full of Bodyguards between shifting pieces of land. James could just make out Certus sitting at the helm of one of the cars. Though the number of men riding toward them were far fewer than that of the Merchants at the Doors, the combat skills which these Bodyguards had honed through their grueling training would, he was sure, make up for their smaller number.

"Phoenix, what was the land like in there?" E barked.

"Not good. It almost got us. We definitely need a Runner, but I couldn't find one of Alex's posts."

E's eyes darted from side to side before she looked at each member of the group. Determination flickered then blazed into life within her black gaze, hardening her expression and relaxing her shoulders. Another machete appeared in her hand. She walked to the middle of the land separating the jungle from the field then faced the hills.

"We have no choice, then. We stay here, and we fight. Get ready for battle! We slay them here. We might as well send them the message now. They will not keep hunting us. Not without a fight!"

The others' fierce expressions matched E's as they rushed to spread out on either side of her. James didn't join them but instead, grabbed Snow. Blind and slow at healing, she wouldn't last a moment in battle. He slung her over his shoulder, tucked the trembling fawn under his other arm, and hurried over to the edge of the jungle. He dropped her into the cover of lush fern and shoved the fawn into her arms. He threw large sheets of stray bark over them to hide them both.

"*Stay here, and don't move,*" he told them.

He aimed the spear that formed in his hand as he ran back to the group and positioned himself near Blood Crow. Adrenaline coursed through him, burning away his anxiety and fatigue. E stood at the forefront of the group, her black blades at the ready, a proud and fearsome leader, a deadly weapon in human form. James only had to glance at her once to know that he, too, was ready to fight.

The monster jumped into the weeds and began galloping toward the group. The nostrils of its flat, bat-like nose flared with each breath. Its wide grin glistened with the satisfaction of a predator that had succeeded in tracking down its prey. James and Blood Crow made to throw their spears.

"Hold fire!" E commanded.

The monster burst out of the weeds and continued running headlong toward the group. Only a few yards lay between them and the monster's feet when the monster suddenly crouched down, leapt up, and sailed over them. It skidded around as it landed and stared at them as the dust settled, its four black eyes glittering above its widening grin. It crawled backward until it reached the perimeter of the jungle then crouched low to the ground. It clearly had no intention of allowing them to escape from their approaching enemies. The cars finished plowing through the weeds and slowed to a halt at the border of the field.

"*What did I tell you, human? My nose did not fail me,*" the monster rumbled.

"*I apologize for doubting you,*" Certus said as he stepped down from the car.

He began walking toward the group then stopped as E crossed her machetes together and walked forward. As she halted, she uncrossed her blades in a single, swift motion as if she were slicing apart an invisible opponent. He beheld her with a regard that had been absent during the group's stay in the Tower. He must have heard what had happened at the Doors.

He snapped his fingers. The Bodyguards moved noiselessly without their bells as they poured out of the cars and spread out behind him, forming a wide semicircle that blotted the hills. Their wandering eyes betrayed their apprehension of the enormous, smiling creature crouched at the jungle's edge. James doubted any of them had ever talked to a citizen before, never mind teamed up with one. He masked his surprise as he spotted Marcus, the old friend whom E had greeted at the outskirts of the Tower.

"Under the Third's command, you are all hereby summoned to the Tower for interrogation!" Certus declared.

He paused as his eyes skimmed over the group. His gaze rested on Bloom, whose fur bristled as he glared back.

"Well, I see the wolf that the Merchants were all so excited about. But where's the Twelfth? I know she's with you too."

"Then you'll know all about me hacking off the heads of all those Merchants at the Doors," E snarled. "Take one more step toward my crew, and I'll take your head too, Certus!"

His expression hardened into the look of one who had decided to accept an unavoidable fight. A large sword appeared in his hand. E responded with a humorless smirk then scanned the Bodyguards. Several of them fidgeted as her burning eyes passed over them.

"*I know you recognize me because I recognize your coward faces!*" she shouted. "*You may have been safe in the stands, but we're out in the planes now! If you want to meet the same fate as all of my other opponents, then come at me and fight!*"

Pride swelled within James. The Bodyguards glanced at one another. A few weapons drooped as several pairs of feet crept backward. The corner of Marcus's mouth twitched. E spread her stance wider and lifted her machetes higher.

"*Fine. If you won't come to me,*" she said, "*then I'll come to you!*"

The eyes of the Bodyguards widened as she sprinted toward them. James bellowed a wordless battle cry as he charged forward with the others.

"*Bring them to the Tower!*" Certus shouted.

E picked up speed as the semicircle of Bodyguards folded in and rushed forth from either end.

"Spread out!" she yelled.

James and Blood Crow veered toward the group funneling in from the left and clashed their spears against their enemies' weapons. The blows and cuts from Honey's tomahawks and Lux's katana halted the group spilling in from the right. The monster crouched lower, ready to spring into the fray, then froze as Bloom dashed forth and challenged it with bared fangs. It continued to grin as Bloom prowled toward it.

E sliced off a woman's head with a speed that blurred her machete then sprayed arcs of dust as she spun across the dirt and slashed through a man's neck. Certus led the remaining Bodyguards forward as he ran toward E with his massive sword. Phoenix flew past her to intercept him.

Surprise flashed across Certus's face as he parried the bombardment of strikes that Phoenix rained down on him with his double-bladed sword. Cold, hard focus overtook his surprise as he answered Phoenix's strikes with blows so powerful that each swing seemed to rip apart the air before colliding with Phoenix's blades.

E sped past the dueling men and began drawing blood and screams from the remaining Bodyguards before they could come to Certus's aid. Though their thick, black vests protected their torsos from the full wrath of her strikes, the fear in their eyes told friend and foe alike that they could not keep their necks away from her forever.

James continued fending off the Bodyguards attempting to encircle him and Blood Crow with vicious swings and sharp stabs of his spear. Marcus scrambled from one side to another at the back of the group, a dagger lifted and ready to throw. But no matter how many opportunities appeared to throw his blade at James or Blood Crow, his dagger remained glued to his hand.

Panic flashed through James as a woman dodged his swing, slid to the side, then closed the gap between them. He cried out as she landed a crippling kick to the leg that made him buckle onto one knee. She spun away from his aim as he jabbed at her with his spear. As she lifted her blade high above her head, he gripped his spear with both hands, ready to block her blow. He shielded his face from a splash of blood instead as Blood Crow sliced off the woman's head with her broadsword. The determination to keep fighting, to keep up with Blood Crow, to beat the odds against them, boiled the hot battle rage pumping through his veins as Blood Crow screamed, "*Get up,* James*! Get up!*"

As she continued swinging her sword, he forced himself back onto his feet and began spearing feet, arms, and legs. He cried out again as a Bodyguard's sword pierced his thigh. He speared the arm holding the blade. As he spun and whipped his spear in a wide arc, he caught sight of

Honey and Lux sprinting toward them. Several Bodyguards were pursuing the two from behind. One of the men lifted his knife then hurled the blade at Honey. The knife skimmed past her ear. The man lifted another knife and aimed carefully.

"Duck!" James screamed at her.

She dropped onto the ground. Blood Crow threw herself at his opponents, keeping them at bay with ferocious swings of her broadsword as he broke away from the fight. His determination to honor Honey's trust fueled his strength as he dashed forward and threw his spear with all his might. Honey sprang back onto her feet and resumed sprinting as behind her, James's spear shot through the Bodyguard's vest, chest, then out his back. As the man fell to the ground, his comrades glanced at him. Lux made them pay for their distraction by leaping up, spinning around midair, and throwing a dagger at them. He landed on his feet again and kept running as his dagger flew into a Bodyguard's eye. James hurled a fresh spear into a man trying to stab Blood Crow as he ran back to her. He pierced several arms with the point of his spear then rammed the butt into a man's throat as he fought alongside her once more.

Gasps suddenly rose up from the Bodyguards surrounding E. James caught a glimpse of her as her opponents scrambled back. She held up a decapitated head for all to see as she screamed insults at the Bodyguards. With a final curse, she flung the head at a man, who squealed as it bounced off of him. The Bodyguards pursuing Honey and Lux pulled away and began running toward their comrades as they pressed in on E once again. Honey skidded to a halt.

"Come back over here, you little rats!" she shrieked. "Don't you turn your backs on me!"

She hurled her first tomahawk with such force that James heard it chopping through the air before it landed in the back of her victim's skull. The second slammed into a woman's thigh and sent her face-down into the dirt. A man spun around and dashed back toward Honey. He dodged every tomahawk that she threw at him then raised his sword. Lux's katana sang a clear, metallic note as he skidded in front of her and blocked the man's blow. The power of the clash sent the man stumbling back. A fountain of blood spurted up from the man's face as Lux swept up his katana again. Honey rushed forward and brought her tomahawk down onto the man's skull before she and Lux turned and sprinted across the final stretch separating them from James and Blood Crow.

The hope of victory burned brighter within him as Blood Crow cut into a woman's arm and Honey swung her tomahawk into a man's groin. Lux slashed and slashed and slashed again until he cut off a Bodyguard's hand. James speared a man through the leg then did a double take as all the Bodyguards fighting E began running toward them instead. Horror struck his hope a chilling blow as he caught sight of her. Two Bodyguards had speared her through the stomach. Though she had managed to keep standing, she had dropped her machetes to grip the shafts of the spears. A woman cut across James's arm, opening a deep gash and forcing him to tear his attention away from E.

The Bodyguards joined to form a large circle around James, Blood Crow, Honey, and Lux and fell upon them with the ravenousness of flies descending upon carrion. Spears and swords slashed and jabbed at him from all sides. He ducked, dodged, and weaved as daggers and knives began whirling through the air toward his head and neck. Honey screamed as a knife shot into her side.

"Honey!" Lux cried out.

He lifted his katana then doubled over as a Bodyguard speared him in the stomach. Blood Crow lifted her sword against Lux's attacker then jumped back with a cry of frustration as a man slashed at her waist. James screamed out her name as a sword pierced her leg. He slit open her assailant's throat with his spear before stabbing others and blocking weapon after weapon, blow after blow. But no matter what he did and no matter how hard he tried, their ring of enemies continued pressing in, closing in, squeezing them all like a snake bent on strangling the last bit of breath out of its prey. Another sword cut across his arm, taking away another chunk of flesh.

E plunged into their ring of enemies.

She had healed her stomach completely. The Bodyguards who had speared her were now lying on the ground, headless. The fire burning in her eyes embraced the anarchy of battle and fueled the skill that swore to subdue all her enemies so that both chaos and control swirled together into a perfect storm within her. Her machetes glinted white beneath the sun as she sliced through limbs. Her shadow fell black upon the dismembered bodies of her victims as she leapt over them. With spinning kicks and flying knees, she began breaking necks and smashing in noses before slicing off one head after another.

The monster let out a deafening roar, making weapons pause and waver. It thrashed and stomped about as it whipped Bloom from side to side in a futile attempt to loosen his teeth from its neck. Snow lay curled up among scattered pieces of bark with the fawn held tightly against her chest. She yelped as the monster's tail whipped over the inch of air above her head.

"James, go!" E shouted.

She charged at the Bodyguards closest to him and began carving out a narrow passage for his escape. He dodged flying weapons and threw his spear into one last Bodyguard before breaking free of the ring and sprinting toward Snow with the speed and focus he'd honed through all of Crew Blue's rescue missions.

Someone suddenly tackled him from behind. The monster's tail whooshed over their heads.

"No!" Marcus hissed, gripping James's wrist as he raised his knife. "Save the Twelfth! Go!"

He flung himself backward as if James had struck him. James scrambled onto his feet, ran to Snow, and threw her over his shoulder. She hugged the fawn tightly as he fled deep into the jungle. He shouted as branches sharp as spears burst up from the ground and forced him to skid to a stop. Heavy footsteps approached in rapid thuds, pounding the ground like war drums. He dove into a hollow groove beneath the roots of an enormous tree. He clamped his hands over Snow's and the fawn's mouths. The footsteps slowed. Twigs and leaves rustled beneath the monster's slithering tail. A deep growl rumbled out of its throat.

"*I can smell you, little one,*" it said. "*And you humans too. The roots ... will not save you!*"

They screamed as the monster's tail slammed into the trunk of the tree. A second blow, and the roots wrenched up, spraying them with soil. The monster leapt in front of them to block their escape. James jumped in front of Snow and pointed his spear with a cry that refused to acknowledge surrender or defeat. The monster's black eyes suddenly widened.

"*What?*" it breathed.

James hurled his spear. The monster dodged with a twitch of its head then crouched low and peered at Snow. James pointed another spear.

"*The Twelfth,*" it growled.

James prepared himself for a vicious attack as its face screwed up with fury. Confusion and suspicion joined the adrenaline pulsing through him as the monster flung its head back and boomed out laughter instead.

# CHAPTER 2

# DREAMS

The monster continued to laugh as it lumbered back several steps. The ground shook as it sat down on its haunches.

*"My, my. These two nights have been quite nostalgic,"* it said. *"To see those blue eyes again. Though, of course, they weren't blind when I saw them last. A pity, really. I always considered the Twelfth's eyes to be the most stunning out of all the Shamans."*

Snow stumbled as she drew herself up onto her feet. She continued clutching the struggling fawn as if it were her firstborn. James threw his spear. The monster dodged with another flick of its head. He created another spear. He had to get them all out of here!

*"Oh, humans,"* the monster drawled. *"Always leaping into battle without so much as a conversation. How the eras have eaten away at your inferior minds. Such little decorum."*

*"I-If you would like to converse, I am happy to oblige!"* Snow shouted as James made to launch his spear again.

"What? Snow!" he hissed. "Are you crazy?"

*"I am the Twelfth Shaman as you have stated!"* she pressed on. *"Do you know my eyes? I'm afraid I do not recognize your voice."*

He tried to fight down his panic. Then his breath caught in his throat as he spied a patch of blue fur and short, black hair creeping through the tall fern. Realization swept aside his panic. Had Snow heard Bloom and E? Was that what this really was? A distraction? The monster cocked its head to one side as it contemplated Snow.

"*Yes, child,*" it murmured. "*I know your eyes. There once walked a powerful Twelfth Shaman known as 'the Last' many eras ago. We clashed in many battles during my partnership with the Third. He grew quite skilled at cutting off my tail. Quite an irritating habit, actually.*"

"*The Third?*" said Snow. "*How is it possible that you've conducted business with him? I haven't known him to ever step foot outside of the Abode.*"

"*Ha! Not the current Third, my child. Not that weakling, no. The Third with whom I had partnered lived many eras ago and stands as the greatest Third of all. He held sway over the largest kingdoms the Flowering had ever seen, ones that would put that pathetic Market you now have to shame. Yes, those were nights in which the moulded could truly run free. The powerful joined with the powerful, and humans were well worth my while. As a matter of fact, this night is the first in many eras that I have stooped to partnering with such weak, plebian humans. Vengeance really does taste as sweet as blood, though, I must say. You could say that it is a weak spot of mine. The crew protecting you right now gave me quite a few injuries in my last battle with them, and I've always had a dislike for Castaways.*"

"*Castaways? I'm afraid I don't know that term,*" said Snow.

Fresh beads of sweat broke out on James's back. Even if the monster had failed to see Bloom and E, it would surely smell them any moment now. Snow's ruse would not last much longer.

"*Ah, how the Shamans have fallen,*" the monster said. "*Castaways, my dear child. Castaways! Just like that blue wolf who runs with you. They are citizens who have been blessed with the gift of immortality, though that does not mean that they are quite as powerful as citizens such as myself. I have moulded countless times and will not be humble about the fact that I am now quite prodigious in skill and strength and thus, nearly as immortal.*

*"I will, however, admit that I am quite jealous of Castaways. Because they have been spared from amalgamation, they can pass through the moonlight of Lapis Lazuli, and of course, they can stay in the Flowering without a mark for as long as they please. Ah, but you do not know of the other dimensions nor of our origins. Ignorant humans. How dare they forget where we citizens come from,"* it muttered to itself before addressing Snow again.

*"My child, my dear Twelfth. Citizens are born from human thoughts. We noble citizens are born from the thoughts that occupy the Seeding, which is that polluted dimension you humans call 'Reality.' When human thoughts travel from the Seeding and enter the dimension known as 'the Growing,' various human thoughts amalgamate with one another, and it is through this amalgamation that we citizens are conceived. We are then born into the Flowering, and of course, our mark later signals when our time has come."*

*"Time has come? For what?"* Snow asked.

A sharp-toothed grin split the monster's face as it rose onto all fours. *"Time for us to leave the Flowering and enter a human dream, of course. Which is why I choose to mould ... and never leave!"*

The monster lunged. Bloom leapt forth. The monster whipped its tail, swatted Bloom aside, and dodged James's spear. E sliced through the monster's shin. It let out a ground-shaking roar. James grabbed Snow and pulled her to the side of the fallen tree. The monster. It had smelled Bloom and E all along.

"Stay here!" he yelled to Snow.

White pain enveloped his watch.

He felt his knees collide with the ground first before he landed on his back. His hand broke and cracked and splintered into a thousand burning pieces, setting his arm then his entire body on fire. Snow's voice reached out to him from far away. Gravity pulled down on his fist as if his hand had turned into an iron mallet. He heaved and tugged his watch up to his eyes. The minute hand was slowly falling from three to six o'clock, tattooing his skin black in its wake. His hand jerked back down onto the floor. He felt Snow fumbling around his body. Her hand found his.

Everything disappeared.

James and Snow stood hand in hand within a boundless, black space. They watched together as something squirmed in the dark. Crimson blood dripped out in dollops from a broken, purple orb suspended in the middle of the darkness. A long, sickly leg slid out from the orb. The head of the Red Calf appeared then the rest of its blood-drenched body. The Beast flopped down onto the invisible ground and lay still. Its golden eye shone upon its forehead. Blood trickled out from its empty, raw socket. Its dark eye swiveled then fixed upon James and Snow. They let go of each other.

"*Heal,*" a voice whispered to him. "*Heal the–*"

James rolled onto his stomach and vomited on the jungle floor. The monster shrieked and squealed as if its body were on fire. E shouted Bloom's name, her voice full of alarm. James dragged his shaking hand across the ground and slapped his palms onto dried leaves.

His watch. Half of his watch had blackened. It now read six o'clock.

He reeled himself onto his feet and vomited once more. His eyes swept across the jungle even as he struggled to clear the shock numbing his mind. The Red Calf had regained more of its strength. It had broken out of the purple orb. Would it appear here in this jungle and chase them all with its darkness as it had back in the tunnels? He lifted his watch hand in a pathetic attempt to protect the others. He continued searching for the Calf.

But he saw nothing.

He covered his ears as the monster roared again. His eyes fell on Snow, who lay shaking on the ground beside him. The fawn stood over her, trembling as it guarded her body with its own. He pushed it aside and shouted her name. Her blank eyes stared up into the leafy canopy as she continued shaking.

The monster leapt onto the trunk of a towering tree and clawed its way up onto a thick branch. E ran forward and glared up at the monster. Bloom shook out his coat then prowled forth with bared teeth.

"*What is that thing?*" the monster shouted. Its wide eyes were full of fear and repulsion as it stared at James.

"*Come back down here! Come back down here and fight!*" E raged.

James let go of Snow and advanced with another spear. The tip vibrated in front of him as his arms continued quivering. He shook his head to clear the last remnants of his shock.

"*I see,*" the monster rumbled.

"*I said come back down here!*" E shouted.

"*This is not the moment for a paltry squabble!*" the monster roared back. "*That boy and the Twelfth have seen the Beast. I felt it as did your Castaway. I am correct, am I not, boy?*"

James tightened his grip. How had it known?

"*Yes. I see, I see, I see! So, the Last still lives,*" the monster murmured to itself. "*And you, young warrior,*" it said to E. "*I now know why your scent is so familiar. You are a blood descendant of the Last.*" It glared at her for a moment longer before snorting with a look of disgust. "*Well, it's very obvious that you've inherited his love for swordplay, though you'll need to practice more than that if you'd like to cut off my tail, or any part of me for that matter, like he used to do. But it seems that he's left some of himself in*" *these two as well,*" it said as it eyed James and Snow with a look of suspicion.

"*Shut your mouth and fight! Or are you too much of a coward to face me?*" E yelled.

"*Don't you speak to me of cowardice, human!*"

The monster kneaded the branch with its feet as if it wanted nothing more than to jump down and rip her to shreds. It snorted again and shook its head as if to calm itself.

"*You must take them to your pack,*" it told Bloom.

Bloom only lowered himself into a deeper crouch in response.

"*You must put aside personal differences and lead these humans to your pack! Take them to the Keep then slay the Beast as the Last once did with your father. But do it for good this time. And our battle here is finished for tonight, young warrior!*" the monster said before E could shout again. "*There is not a moment to spare. I will not risk being devoured by the Beast's darkness for a fight with you. Follow the wolf, and go to the place they call 'the Keep.' There is an old, gray wolf there whose name is 'Father.' He will tell you what you need to know in order to defeat the Beast. And defeat it you must! For we will all be doomed if you fail.*"

The monster curled up and turned around on the branch. It paused then craned its head around to look at Snow.

"*A parting gift to you, my Twelfth, for the sake of eras gone by and as thanks for our discourse tonight. You are a Shaman. Your sense of smell is superior to that of any other human and even that of many powerful citizens. The scent of lavender will lead you back to Lapis Lazuli and the scent of jasmine, away. The scent of burning indicates a coming shift in a plane. Use these scents to flee the Iris as quickly as possible. There are many who are searching for you.*"

It glared at E once more.

"*This is not farewell,*" it rumbled.

It leapt from the branch and vanished midair. Bloom sheathed his fangs. E lowered her machetes. They both glared at the invisible exit through which the monster had escaped before hurrying over to James.

"Are you all right?" E asked.

"My watch," he said. "E, my watch. It changed again. Snow and I saw the Calf. It's regained more of its strength."

She glanced at Snow shivering on the ground then stared into the jungle.

"We'll talk about it later," she said. "Let's worry about the war once we've survived the battle. Can you walk? Can you fight?"

"Yeah. What about the others? Are they okay?"

"I got most of the Bodyguards. Phoenix was handling Certus. Let's go."

The fawn jumped into Snow's arms as James slung her over his shoulder again. They ran through humidity and mist until the field and hills appeared along with the bodies of the slain. Blood gushed out of Lux's many wounds as he dragged himself toward Honey, who lay gasping among headless Bodyguards. Blood Crow shrieked as she sliced off a woman's head then collapsed. Dust rose from the ground in steady, low clouds as Certus and Phoenix continued dueling. James ran toward the fern to hide Snow again. E and Bloom sprinted toward Phoenix as he grunted and parried another blow from Certus.

"Marcus! Back up, now!" Certus yelled as Phoenix's sword razored past his throat.

Marcus swayed as he stood up, the last Bodyguard still in one piece. He created two silver machetes as he ran up from behind Certus. Phoenix and Marcus swung their blades. E and Bloom skidded to a halt.

Certus's head slid slowly off of his neck before both his head and body toppled to the ground. Marcus continued gasping for air as he glared down at the body, his blades dripping with Certus's blood. He cast aside his machetes. Phoenix whirled his sword then plunged one end into the dirt. James leaned on his spear and released a sigh of relief.

They had won.

"Thanks. He was a tough one," Phoenix said between labored breaths.

"Don't mention it," Marcus said, pressing a hand against a wound on his hip. He broke into a twitching smile as saw E staring at him. "Looks like I finally got to pay you back, E. And I'm not talking about all those beers you got for me either."

She dropped her machetes, walked, then ran up to him. She threw her arms around his neck and buried her face into his shoulder.

"Ah, now don't get all soft on me, E," Marcus said, patting her on the back before holding her out by her arms. "My wife and I even put an 'e' sound at the end of our daughter's name so she'd grow up strong like you."

"You shouldn't have done this. When the Third reads Certus...." She ended with a small, wordless sound of despair.

"I know I'm in trouble. Don't worry. I'm ready to take the consequences. Hopefully, the Third will see how much good you've done for me in the past and understand. He can actually be pretty merciful for the most part."

"But what if he's not? What if you're stripped of your title?"

"Then I'll figure it out from there. This was a risk I was willing to take. That, and my wife would've killed me if I'd told her that I just stood by and did nothing when you needed my help. But anyway, enough chitchat. It'll be obvious that I helped you guys if I'm not chopped up like all the others, so if you don't mind doing me a favor and making it quick," he said, shifting his gaze back to Phoenix, "that would be great. I'd rather have only the Third and Certus knowing about this. Bodyguards and their gossip, you know?"

He wore a grim smile as he stepped away from E.

"Marcus. Marcus, thank you," she said. "Thank you for everything. I never got to tell you just how much your friendship—"

"It's fine, it's fine. I told you not to get all soft, didn't I? But hey, we will get a drink again one of these nights. No one can stop us now," he said, pointing a stern finger at her.

E closed her eyes and nodded as she stepped aside.

"Go for it," Marcus told Phoenix.

Phoenix's blades sliced through the air. Marcus's head and arms fell to the ground along with his body.

"James," Snow said suddenly.

He spun around. "What? What is it? What's wrong?"

"I can smell it. I can smell the jasmine."

# CHAPTER 3

# JASMINE AND LAVENDER

Y ou can smell the jasmine? It's really there, like the monster said?" James exclaimed.

"It is," said Snow. "It's ... I think it's always been there, but I just never...."

Phoenix inhaled sharply before collapsing onto one knee.

"James, help the others!" E commanded before rushing over to Phoenix.

"Oh! Don't worry about it, E," said Phoenix. "Don't waste your creations. I'm fine. I'm totally fine, really."

She swatted away his protests then helped him to sit down. His eyes swiveled between her face and her hands as she created bandages. He blushed as she touched his bare skin. Snow released her grasp on the fawn as James slung her over his shoulder again. The fawn bounded toward Bloom, who lowered his head and quivered his nose in front of the fawn's.

James kept Snow at his side and used the bandages that appeared in her hands as he wrapped everyone's injuries. He didn't want to deplete any more of his creations than he had to. Certus, as the Third's Guide, was bound to have been leading the largest and deadliest search party, so winning this battle had definitely bought the group some safety for now. But the Third had plenty of other men, and they were, no doubt, scouring No Man's Land, still searching for them.

"One more," he said as he held down a bandage on Lux's chest. He grasped Snow's hand, expecting more bandages.

"I-I can't," she stammered.

"What?"

"That was my sixth creation. Shamans only have six per night. D-Didn't you know?"

He muttered a curse. "I think E might've mentioned it a while back."

"I'm sorry. I really am. I know it's super annoying."

"Don't be sorry. It's not your fault. I'll just use my own creations."

"Here," Blood Crow said, pushing herself onto her feet. "I can help."

"Hey! Stay down while you're healing," James said.

He ran forward and caught Blood Crow as she collapsed. He sighed. She didn't look as bad as Lux or Honey, but still. So much blood had splattered over her face that he could barely make out her freckles. He laid her down on her back with slow and steady care. He hesitated then gently brushed a few strands of hair away from her face. She blinked and continued staring up at him.

"E," Honey wheezed. "E, where do we go from here? What should we do?"

"Snow can smell the jasmine," James interjected. "Just like that citizen said."

He quickly described to the group what had occurred in the jungle and all that the monster had told them.

"One thing I don't get, though, is why the Red Calf didn't appear and chase us with its darkness like it did in the tunnels," he said. "I searched the jungle for signs, but there was nothing."

"It's because we weren't near the Beast this time," said E.

"What do you mean?"

She tied a final knot around Phoenix's leg and paused as if to reexamine her thoughts. Certainty fell across her face once more as she said, "You saw Snow before even though she was in the Tower. Now you saw the Red Calf where it still is. Back in those tunnels where we first found it. I'm sure of it."

"So, what does that mean?" asked Lux.

"It means we should stay away from those tunnels," Honey muttered. She winced as she forced herself to sit up straighter. "At least for now. We can't go near that thing while we're all injured like this."

"You said the Beast still looked weak?" E asked James.

"Yeah. It couldn't even stand up. It's getting stronger for sure, and it's gotten itself out of that purple orb, but we still have some time before it comes back to full strength. When my watch hits midnight, though, that's when we'll really be in trouble."

Bloom pawed at E's waist. He opened and closed his mouth then shook out his fur in frustration. She let out a small sigh as he continued to struggle for words. James knew that she, like him, wished yet again that Bloom could talk or that they could somehow read the words trapped within his mind. Bloom snorted and pawed at his muzzle as if he were exasperated with the uselessness of his own mouth.

"The monster said we could find answers about killing the Calf in that place, right? The Keep?" said Lux. "It said we should use Snow's nose to get out of here then go there for answers?"

"Can we really trust that citizen?" Phoenix asked.

E exchanged a worried look with him before asking Bloom, "Do you know if that citizen was right about Snow? Can she really get us out of No Man's Land using her nose?"

Bloom nodded with an intense vigor that both surprised and reassured James. Fresh flames of determination sprang up in E's eyes.

"Okay. Then let's get going. Snow, you focus on getting us out of here. Bloom, focus on smelling out any more of the moulded and any other humans. The Third's bounty on us is still active, and news about it has probably spread far and wide by now. We should steer clear of all humans and not just the Bodyguards. James, can you carry Snow?"

"Of course."

He suppressed his desire to remain with Blood Crow and hurried back to Snow. He made to throw her over his shoulder again then stopped. Now that he thought about it, hanging her over his shoulder was probably more than a little uncomfortable for her, and it didn't exactly make carrying her easy either. He knelt down and ushered her onto his back as Zilch had done before. She clung to him with a firm grip that surprised him as he stood up. He leaned forward and hitched her up higher on his back as he adjusted his hold on her legs.

"All right, Snow. Just tell me what to do. Tell me where to go," he said.

"It's—"

She fell silent, her finger suspended midair. Her arm slowly slid into a tighter coil around his neck as her legs squeezed his body. E stood up, her eyes glinting. She began walking toward them.

"It's that way," Snow said, pointing to their left. "The jasmine smell is stronger over there."

E gripped Snow's ponytail and wrenched her head to the side. A swift kick dropped James into the dirt. Snow yelped and flailed as E dangled her by her hair. Phoenix and Bloom hurried over to them.

"The jasmine smell is stronger over there, is it?" E snarled, giving Snow's head a sharp shake. "Are you really going to lie to my face like this? You dare put my crew in danger?"

Snow whimpered.

"E, stop!" said James. "Just calm down!"

She forced him to kneel with another kick.

"Tell me the truth! You're leading us back to the City!" she yelled.

"I'm sorry, I'm sorry!" Snow said with tears in her eyes. "E, I'm sorry. I just can't handle abandoning Z like this. You have no idea how cruel they can be in the Tower. He's better off dead if they do their worst to him!"

"You're hurting her!" James yelled as she shook Snow again.

Bloom nibbled on E's boot. Phoenix raised his hands in a sign of peace as he stepped closer to her.

"I'm not letting go until I get some kind of assurance that you won't lead us back to imprisonment and death," E snarled. "Are you insane? Huh? Are you crazy? If you think this battle was bad, think of what it'll be like if we go back to the Tower right now!"

"Snow," said Phoenix. "Snow, please listen. I know you want to go back for Zilch, and we will. But E's right. Let's get out of here first and try to find the Keep."

Snow drew a shuddering breath, held it in her chest, then said, "I'll agree to lead everyone out of No Man's Land on the condition that we go back for Z within a week."

"You little–"

"E," Phoenix said. He laid a hand on her shoulder and gazed into her eyes.

James stared at E. E glared at Phoenix. James waited for her to stab Phoenix or, at the very least, throw his hand aside and continue shouting at Snow. Instead, she looked at Bloom. He shuffled his paws, licked his chops, then stared at her with large, glistening eyes. She threw Snow onto the ground.

"Hurry up, and get us out of here," she snarled before turning away.

James tilted his head back and heaved a sigh as his patience battled with exasperation once more. He ushered Snow onto his back again.

"Are you okay, Snow?" Phoenix asked.

Tears spilled down her cheeks as she nodded. "I'm sorry. I know you're right, but Z is my Guide."

"We understand. It would be weird if you didn't want to go back for him."

"I won't do it again, I promise. Please. Please don't lose your trust in me."

Phoenix smiled. "Oh, come on, Snow. I still remember when we traveled to the City together and all the ways you helped me. I wouldn't even have my sword right now if you hadn't read me back then and dug up that memory. I was so young when I touched the sword, remember? I owe it all to you, and it's going to take a lot more than this to make me lose my trust in you."

James felt happiness radiating from her as Phoenix patted her arm. She wiped away her tears and smiled before squirming up an inch or two on James's back. She exhaled then sniffed the air once, twice. She drew in a deep, long breath on the third.

"That way."

Bloom sniffed the air for humans and citizens alike as Snow directed the group back into the jungle. James followed her pointed finger and whispered instructions as he placed one hesitant foot in front of the other. Every twig that snapped and leaf that crunched seemed like an omen of shifting land, a moulded citizen, or a new horde of Bodyguards.

Lux moaned and grabbed his bandaged head as he swayed and stumbled. E slung his arm over her shoulders then struggled to reach Honey as she began sinking onto her knees. Phoenix took hold of Honey's arm and supported her instead. E gave him a grateful look.

Blood Crow yelped as she tripped over the white roots of a colossal tree. Bloom shoved his head under her before she could fall and helped her to stand up again. They gazed at one another. Then they continued walking side-by-side behind the rest of the group. The fawn stopped trailing after Snow and bounded over to Bloom. Blood Crow only glanced at it as she kept walking.

"Wait!" Snow screeched.

James dropped onto his hands and knees. The group scrambled to a halt as the ground in front of them shot up in a rush of dirt and roots like a small mountain forming out of a clash of tectonic plates. He stared at the newly formed mass, shaking and gasping, before daring to stand up again.

"Th-The burning smell," said Snow, who had managed to maintain her hold on him. "It's everywhere here. It's so hard to tell. I'm sorry. The land must be really unstable. Could you please go slower, James?"

"Okay," he said as the group composed themselves. "Okay. You're doing great. You're doing great. Just keep focusing. Are there any humans nearby, Bloom? Or any of the moulded?"

Bloom shook his head then continued sniffing.

The group progressed from the stuffy mists of the rainforest to the clear, fresh air of a pine forest. Snow led them through an exit that stood next to a giant tree trunk, across an invisible strip of land that stretched across a teal lake, then through another exit on the side of a colossal, ivy-strewn boulder. The longer they traveled, the more her instructions grew from tremulous whispers bordering on a question to surer statements that carried authority. James, too, gained confidence. His steps, which had padded across the ground like that of a man wandering in the dark, began to find firm footing. His pace quickened as well.

The group stepped into a yellow bamboo forest.

"We're back," E whispered.

"This is the same forest, right?" said James. "The one we met Alex in?"

She nodded. Her eyes wandered among the leaves as a light wind rustled past. Kit had said that he'd found E as a newborn, which meant that they had met somewhere here in this forest....

The trees suddenly shuddered as if the forest were a giant beast whose spine had been stroked by an invisible finger. The yellow of the bamboo transformed into green.

"Don't worry. It's pretty stable here," said Snow as the group murmured with surprise. "I think we're close to leaving No Man's Land. The jasmine smell is super strong."

Bloom froze.

"Stop. I hear something," Snow whispered.

James unsheathed his knife. Blood Crow and Bloom flanked him as the others readied their weapons as well. Tall grass shook and swayed in front of them. The group lifted their weapons higher.

"Wait," E commanded. She squinted at the rustling grass.

Two humongous wolves, one red and the other dark green, emerged. Bloom's eyes widened. The red and green wolves lifted their heads. Their golden eyes grew round as they stared back at Bloom.

"*Brother!*" the green wolf cried out.

# CHAPTER 4

# TERRAIN AND FOREST

Blood Crow tugged James aside as the green wolf dashed forth and tackled Bloom. The two wolves rolled across the leaf-strewn floor as a giant ball of blue and green fur. After several moments of scuffling, they untangled themselves from one another. Tears welled up in the green wolf's eyes. He whined and yelped as he began sniffing, nudging, pawing, and licking Bloom. He emitted a frenetic energy, which charged every spin of his windmilling tail. His intimidating size, which was slightly bigger than Bloom's, clashed with his playfulness.

"*Brother! It really is you. We've found you! After all these eras! I barely recognized your scent,*" the green wolf cried.

Tears gathered in Bloom's eyes as well. He stood up and buried his face into the wolf's neck. The wolf, in turn, nuzzled him then continued writhing with excitement. E lowered her machetes. The group glanced at her before lowering their guard too.

"What's going on?" Snow whispered, prompting James to mutter a description to her.

"*Terrain! Didn't I tell you? Didn't I tell you, Terrain? I knew we would meet Brother again,*" the green wolf said.

The red wolf slunk forth. The color of his fur, his large, furry ears, and the keen glint in his eyes made him look more like a humongous fox than a wolf. Bloom stepped back from the green wolf to stare at the red. Unspoken words seemed to pass between them, carrying both pain and joy. The red wolf sighed before drawing close and pressing his neck against Bloom's. The green wolf trotted over to the fawn.

"*And we have found you as well, little one. I am so glad to see that you are safe.*"

"*I'm sorry for running away, Forest,*" said the fawn as it lowered its head in shame.

Forest licked the fawn then trotted over to E. She held out her hand for him to smell. Forest's nose vibrated in front of her fingertips. His head snapped back. His tongue flopped out of the side of his mouth as a wide smile stretched across his face. His shaggy tail began flailing from side to side. He knocked E onto the ground and began licking her face. She laughed and held up a hand to stop the group as they lurched forward to defend her.

"*You've found his child, Brother! The Last's child. He lives on within her!*" Forest cried.

E gently pushed him away then stood up and rubbed her hands into his neck in deep circles. His eyes widened before his eyelids drooped. A low croon rumbled out of his throat as his hind leg rose and scratched at empty air.

"*Did you say 'the Last's child,' Forest?*" the red wolf asked.

His nostrils flared as he trotted up to E and sniffed her too. He drew back abruptly and stared at her with something like wonder.

"*Indeed. There is no doubt about her scent. This girl is a direct descendant of our old friend. But he also lives on in these two, it would seem.*"

Blood Crow pointed her knife as the red wolf crept toward James and Snow. His eyes slowly widened as he stared at Snow.

"*The Twelfth,*" he whispered.

"*The Twelfth? Did you say 'the Twelfth,' Terrain?*" Forest said, scrambling away from E to join him. He gasped. "*It really is him! I mean, not him. But him too. But not him!*"

"*Brother,*" Terrain said to Bloom. "*How is it that you've come across these three, and where have you been all these eras? We heard rumors that you were still keeping to the old ways. Why did you not come back?*"

Bloom's ears flattened as his head drooped. Terrain sighed.

"*Still mute, even after all these ages?*" he said with a look of disappointment.

"*It's not his fault that he can't talk,*" E said. "*You can call me E, by the way. Are you both members of Bloom's family?*"

"*Bloom? Oh, you mean Brother!*" said Forest, laughing.

"*You let a human name you?*" Terrain said, sneering at Bloom.

"*Is there a problem with that?*" E growled.

Terrain's sneer remained curled on his face even as he lifted a paw and leaned back in surprise. "*No. No problem at all. My name is Terrain, and this is Forest. Brother is a member of our pack, but we haven't seen him for many eras. We were only tracking the fawn, so it is quite a surprise to find Brother here as well. But where are my manners? What can we call each of you?*"

"*I'm afraid introductions will have to wait,*" said E. "*There are others who are hunting us right now. We must leave the Iris as soon as possible.*"

She began explaining to the wolves about the bounty the Third had placed on the group. Though James remained alert for any signs of approaching danger, sadness still managed to slip past his wariness. The fact that Bloom had had a family and a whole other life before Crew Blue should have been obvious. He'd always sensed that Bloom was much older than he appeared, and E had mentioned her suspicions about him having issues with his family in the past as well. Yet, he couldn't help but feel a little sad at the thought that Bloom had belonged to a group other than their own. Would he eventually leave the crew to return to his real family now that he had reunited with them? Would Crew Blue lose Bloom and E both?

"*There is an exit out of the Iris this way,*" Terrain said as E finished explaining. "*Let us hurry before danger finds you once again.*"

The two wolves turned away on quick, soft steps and led the group deeper into the forest. The bamboo trees disappeared as the group dashed through an exit and into a vast, manicured garden, where giant hedge animals stood on either side of a wide walkway. Each animal was larger than the last and led to a pair of humongous rabbit-shaped hedges in the distance.

"*This way!*" said Terrain as they ran past a hedge in the form of a large, snarling tiger then another in the form of a fleeing deer. "*Let us place more planes between us and the humans searching for you.*"

James rushed after Terrain through an exit that lay within a python's open mouth. He entered a dark, empty room, where dusty floorboards groaned and cracked beneath his boots. As the rest of the group ran into the spacious room as well, the anxiety clutching his heart began loosening its grip. There was no way the Third could find them now. He looked at the wolves as they sniffed the air feverishly.

"*I do not smell any danger here,*" Terrain announced, causing James's anxiousness to loosen its hold further. "*No other humans. None of the moulded.*"

"*We can rest a little now if you'd like,*" Forest said, staring at the group as they panted with exhaustion.

"*Thank you. We'd appreciate that,*" said E.

"*Forest!*" the fawn said, bounding toward him. "*There's something I need to tell you. Something important.*"

"*Something important, little one?*" Forest said, turning toward the fawn with a smile.

"*Yes, yes! Forest, we have to get these humans to the Keep. I was being chased by one of the Ancients, but these humans and your brother saved me. But the Ancient One. The Ancient One said that the Beast. Forest, he said that the Beast is returning!*"

Terrain sprang forward and pinned the fawn onto the floor with one massive, red paw. E held up her hand in a silent command for the group to stand back as they stepped forward.

"*Don't you dare joke about such a thing!*" Terrain snarled as the fawn cycled its legs futilely.

"*I'm not joking!*"

"*Terrain,*" Forest pleaded. He nudged him with his snout.

Terrain slowly removed his paw as the fawn began describing the battle with the Bodyguards and all that had occurred in the jungle. By the end of the tale, Forest's eyes had widened into two round, golden discs, and his tongue was dangling long and loose from his slack mouth. Terrain stared at the fawn with a fearful look before rounding on Bloom.

"*Is this true? Is the Beast truly returning?*" he demanded.

Bloom snapped his head from side to side in vehement denial. He stared at his brothers with an earnest expression as if to assure them that the fawn was somehow mistaken.

"*But the Ancient One said that it was!*" the fawn cried. "*The Ancient One felt it, and so did your brother!*"

Terrain and Forest exchanged grave looks.

E gave Bloom an apologetic look before saying, "*Perhaps we are wrong, but we think it is as the fawn says. We think that the Red Calf from the Hunters' legends is returning and that* James's *watch is blackening with its growing strength. The monster–this Ancient One the fawn is referring to–said that we could find answers to defeating the Calf if we went to a place called 'the Keep' and spoke to a wolf named 'Father.' Do you know anything that might help us find the Keep, and if so, could you tell us how we might get there?"*

Terrain cocked his head, narrowed his eyes, and began circling James. He halted by his watch and sniffed. A growl erupted out of his throat as he bared his fangs.

"*There is a foul scent coming from this boy's watch,*" he snarled.

Forest pointed his snout at Snow's face. "*Yes, and the same scent surrounds the Twelfth's eyes.*"

"*What scent?*" said Snow.

"*The scent of death,*" said Terrain. "*If I didn't know any better, I would say that you carry the scent of the moulded.*"

"*It is very faint, though,*" Forest reassured the group as they glanced at one another with worried looks.

Terrain turned around with a swish of his red tail. "*Come. That's enough rest. The sooner we start our journey, the better,*" he said.

"*Where are we going?*" said E.

"*To the Keep, of course. It would be our pleasure to lead you all there.*"

"*The Keep is our dwelling place,*" Forest explained.

"*Yes, and it is where we will find Father,*" said Terrain.

"*Father is the leader of our pack.*"

"*Father helped the Last to defeat the Beast long ago. Of all those who live in the Flowering, he holds the most knowledge about the Beast. He may also know something about your scents too,*" Terrain told James and Snow. "*It will take several nights for us to reach the Keep, so we should start our journey now.*"

Bloom remained still as Terrain and Forest began leading the group toward a wide, wooden staircase, which descended to a lower floor.

"What is it, Bloom?" E asked.

"*Oh, don't worry, Brother. It has been so long now. Father will be happy to see you!*" Forest said.

"*I'm not so sure about that,*" Terrain said with a low, wheezy cackle. "*Brother and Father had quite the argument before he left our pack, you see, though they never did get along even before then,*" he told E. "*Come, Brother. You have to face him again one of these nights. You've already delayed it for far too long.*"

Bloom stepped back and glared at Terrain. Terrain's sneer slowly disappeared, giving way to a solemn expression.

"*I know you don't want to, Brother, and I know that Father will be difficult, just as you anticipate. But there is a very real chance that the Beast may have broken free from Mother's heart.*"

Alarm spiked Bloom's fur as he jumped.

"*You ran off before you could hear the whole story, so I can see why you would have thought it impossible for the Beast to return,*" Terrain continued. "*But Father has anticipated its return to power for many eras now. So come, Brother. You cannot hide any longer.*"

He turned away again and ushered the others down the stairs. James remained near E as she waited for Bloom. Bloom's eyes flickered from side to side before fixing on her. She walked up to him and stroked his head.

"What is it? Why are you so worried?" she asked.

Determination slowly creased Bloom's face as he continued gazing at her. He reared up onto his hind legs and slung his forearms on top of her shoulders. She chuckled as he licked her cheek and nuzzled her black hair. He settled back down onto all fours and smiled at her with a love that promised to do anything to keep her safe. He licked her arm before trotting after the others.

They climbed down the stairs into another empty room, this one larger than the last. Forest glued his nose onto the dusty floor and roved about before traveling down the room in a straight line.

"*Is something the matter, Twelve?*" Terrain asked as the group followed Forest.

"*Oh! No, it's nothing,*" Snow said. "*It's just that the smell of jasmine is gone now, and it feels strange. I guess I've already grown used to chasing after it.*"

"*Well, yes. Of course it is gone. We are no longer in the Iris,*" said Terrain.

"*I can still smell burning, though,*" she said, frowning as she lifted her nose higher. "*It's really small, but it's still there. It's coming from over there.*"

She turned her face toward a far corner of the room. Terrain followed suit.

"*Ah, yes. Yes, I can smell it too. It is faint, though, as you said. Nothing to worry about. The plane is quite stable if the smell is this weak,*" said Terrain.

Forest led the group down another staircase, the fawn bounding along at his side. Terrain grinned and shook his head.

"*You Shamans. I'd forgotten how good your noses are. Your sense of smell outdoes even our own at times. The jasmine and lavender, for example, aren't nearly as strong to us Castaways as they are to you. A bit frustrating on the rare occasions we do venture into the Iris, but it has always been so. We can smell the marks of citizens, though, and we can smell if they are one of the moulded. You Shamans can't do either of that. You are aware that you can smell exits too, aren't you? Not just within the Iris but in any plane.*"

"*No, I didn't know that. I don't think any of the Shamans know about any of this!*" said Snow.

"*Well, that is not surprising,*" Terrain said with another sneer.

"*The smell of peonies will lead you to exits that both humans and citizens can use,*" said Forest. "*Roses are for exits only humans and Castaways can use, and lilies are for exits that only citizens can use. It can be difficult to distinguish, though, so you'll need to practice. But we can help you. Actually, the next few nights would be wonderful to use for your training.*"

The group listened intently as Forest jabbered on about the Shamans and their powers, and as he and Terrain sniffed out exits and led them through numerous planes, they learned not only about the Shamans but also about the Flowering as a whole. They did not reach the Keep that night or the next, but with each passing night, the wolves revealed more of the Flowering's many secrets.

# CHAPTER 5

# THE OLD WAYS

The Flowering was as old as human thought, the wolves explained, for everything in the Flowering was created from human thoughts. Human thoughts traveled from Reality, or "the Seeding" as Ancient citizens called it, to a dimension called "the Growing." The Growing combined these thoughts into citizens, objects, and planes that were then birthed into the Flowering.

The group also learned that Shamans had once been great warriors whose eyes had been free of blindness. In those ancient eras, Shamans had only to look into another human's eyes to read memories, and each and every memory the Shamans read remained perfectly preserved within their minds. They had also held the power to remember all faces from Reality during the night as well as those they had seen and even read in the Flowering when they arose in the day. They had been able to create twelve creations, just like any other human, and whatever objects that the humans they read had touched in Reality were objects that they, too, had been able to create once they saw those objects in their readings.

Using these powers, the Shamans had served and instructed all human crews in their unified mission to vanquish moulded citizens. In the past, just as now, many citizens had been afraid to move on and enter the unknown realm of human dreams. But in ages gone by, all humans had considered it their duty to free, protect, and comfort the marked as well as any citizen that would cry out to them when injured or in need.

Crews had also traveled to the Abode, which the Shamans had used as their headquarters, to seek the Shamans' advice and so, improve their abilities to fight for the weak. There, the Shamans had freely drawn upon their vaults of innumerable memories to share wisdom, news, and creations with all those who had sought them. They had also encouraged those who struggled with time in Reality to stay within the borders of Lapis Lazuli for as long as they had need. Thus, the Shamans had interchanged their nights between Lapis Lazuli and the planes of the Flowering, working in harmony with each other as well as numerous Castaways to assist brave crews and protect citizens.

Greed, however, slowly began creeping into human hearts. As eras passed, humans began to desire the comfort of their creations, not their utility. They no longer wished to toil both in the day and in the night. The greedy began to overpower those who held to the old ways, and soon, greed swallowed the Shamans as well. Using their gifted sense of smell, they began seeking out stable and even stagnant planes, and upon such planes, they built vast kingdoms in which they and their followers indulged in whatever creations their hearts desired. The Shamans' ability to read and their legions of followers ensured that the Shamans could hunt down any enemy in both the Flowering and Reality so that all who opposed them were punished under the wrathful gaze of their eyes.

Quarrels turned into battles and battles into wars as the Shamans and their vassals vied for the stable planes they found most desirable. Humans began striking partnerships with the moulded and employed those with prodigious strength to fight in their wars and protect the planes they claimed as their own. They even fed innocent citizens to the moulded to strengthen them before unleashing them upon enemy kingdoms. Thus, the cruelty of humans grew, and the moulded were allowed to prey upon the marked with unbridled freedom across all of the Flowering's planes.

However, an era came when a righteous Shaman was born. He became known as the Last, for even in his own era, humans and citizens had both sensed that he would be among the last to hold fast to the good ways, the old ways. He was a Twelfth Shaman, a Shaman with eyes the color of lapis lazuli, who refused to partake in the greed of the other Shamans and instead, fought alongside his loyal followers to slay the moulded and free the marked as in nights of old.

Among his followers, one called the Brave stood as his most trusted warrior, and though most Castaways had long ago turned away from humans in dismay and wandered into the edges of the Flowering, a pack of Castaway wolves had remained at the Last's side. These wolves helped the Last and the Brave to battle not only the moulded but also the other Shamans and their followers, who persecuted the Last with intense ferocity as he continued felling the moulded citizens they called partners.

With dagger and sword, the Last defended himself and his friends against their enemies. But the greedy far outnumbered those who kept to the old ways. Thus, Lapis Lazuli, which had long been abandoned, became the haven to which the Last and his followers would often flee in retreat. They sought sanctuary within the Abode, which contained secret passageways, rooms, and exits that allowed him and his followers to escape the humans who hunted them.

However, unbeknownst to him or any other, a monstrous evil had been born in the far reaches of the Flowering. The negligence and greed of humans had taken their toll over the ages. A creature of unspeakable horror had begun to mould, gaining power in the shadows as humans quarreled over planes. Later, humans and citizens alike would whisper that the Beast had moulded primarily with the Dead, for it seemed to have no sense of identity or self. Neither did it have any motives or desires. It simply traveled from one plane to another, a lone creature dripping in its own blood, a monstrous citizen in the form of a deformed calf. The only thing the Beast did seem conscious of was its insatiable hunger, which it pursued relentlessly by unleashing a black emptiness that swallowed everything and anything in its path.

The Flowering began to change. News spread of the creature as citizens and humans met their end within the Beast's darkness. Soon, the Beast came upon the kingdoms of the Shamans and wreaked havoc as it fed upon the hundreds of humans who had long ago forgotten how to fight. The Shamans, discovering that they were no match for the Beast, remembered Lapis Lazuli and the protection of the moonlight. They hurried to the Abode with their surviving followers, and there, they found the Last waiting for them.

"*We were all there with the Last when those Shamans crawled into the Abode with what remained of their pathetic followers,*" said Terrain on the seventh night of their travels together. "*Those Shamans. They would not stop quarreling among themselves even in the midst of so much death and destruction. Nor did they stop after the Last and Father had defeated the Beast.*"

The group listened closely and responded as they had on previous nights as Terrain continued telling them tales of the Shamans' greed and cowardice. Snow gasped in horror or in awe. Lux shook his head and mumbled, "Man." Honey scoffed and rolled her eyes, full of indignation for the past. E and Phoenix asked questions or requested clarification before falling behind the rest of the group with Bloom and discussing their findings. James remained silent for the most part. He was too busy wrestling with the different emotions clashing within him to say anything more than "whoa" once in a while.

He definitely felt satisfaction and even a strange sense of peace in finally understanding what exactly the Flowering was and the purpose behind humans' existence in this dimension. He also felt proud that Crew Blue had been fulfilling their purpose all along by helping the marked and slaying the moulded as humans were meant to do. But he also felt a deep bitterness toward those in the past who had corrupted the Flowering. The Beast had the power to kill so many, both humans and citizens alike, and it had been born because of what? Greed? Such a simple yet twisted thing? Would the Beast have been born at all if humans had simply kept to the old ways and protected the marked as they had been sent into the Flowering to do?

Disappointment weighed down on his heart each time he answered his own question. No. The Beast would never have been born if humans had simply focused on helping the vulnerable instead of abandoning them, neglecting them, and even worse, preying on them.

Blood Crow, like James, remained mostly silent. He had expected her to deny every story and refute every claim the two wolves had put forth during their journey to the Keep, but to his surprise, she had neither interrupted them nor shown them the least bit of hostility. She had even been forthright with the wolves about her identity as a Hunter early on, stating that she didn't want to deceive them. Terrain had simply sneered at her in response and given her assurance that her identity troubled him very little. He'd asserted that even if she were to lead a family of Hunters to the Keep, they would have quite the time penetrating the Keep's defenses. The glint in his eyes had suggested that he would have even welcomed their attempts. His only request had been for her to tuck her ruby necklace out of sight so as not to perturb the Keep's citizens, a request she had honored without protest.

Most surprising, though, was Blood Crow's relationship with the fawn. The fawn, who had apparently forgotten all about Blood Crow's attempt on its life, had grown a strange attachment to her. The group had eyed her warily one night as she had suddenly stopped walking and stared at the fawn, which had simply smiled up at her in response. Much to the group's shock, she had stooped down to give it a few gentle pats on its bottom.

Ever since then, the fawn had spent every possible moment bounding along at her side, rubbing against her legs, or resting in her arms. James had also caught them engrossed in whispered conversations on more than one occasion. He knew little of Hunter culture but couldn't imagine that her family would find her bond with the fawn–or even her growing relationship with the wolves and Bloom, in particular–to be permissible. She was clearly changing with each passing night, but what did that mean for her future?

"*I'm glad Bloom taught us the old ways,*" E said as Terrain finished speaking. "*I'm glad that we've been helping the marked and slaying the moulded, just as the Last did.*"

"*I am glad as well,*" said Terrain. He fixed E with a sincere look as he said, "*It is a great pleasure to meet humans in this era who care about the well-being of those who are vulnerable.*"

"*We are grateful for you all!*" said Forest. "*It truly is wonderful to take humans such as yourselves to the Keep. I can't wait for all of you to see it and tell us what you think.*"

"*I'm sure it'll be to our liking,*" E said.

Terrain and Forest had explained during their journey that they used the Keep not only as their dwelling place but also as a haven for any marked citizens they had rescued.

"*As you already know, there are many among the marked who, for one reason or another, are afraid to move on to the dimension of human dreams,*" Forest had explained. "*We try to help such citizens by bringing them into the Keep so that they can rest and think without the risk of being preyed upon. You'd be surprised at how just a bit of rest and compassion can help a citizen to do the right thing.*"

Terrain had also explained that much of the hungry darkness the Calf had unleashed throughout the Flowering had disappeared upon its defeat at the hands of the Last and Father. However, some of its emptiness had remained. The wolves had discovered one of these remnants, which had taken the form of a giant ring, on a stable plane. They had then sniffed out safe paths into the ring's center and named their new dwelling "the Keep." All the marked citizens they rescued and brought to the Keep remained safe from the moulded as long as they remained within the confines of the black ring.

"*This is the final exit!*" said Forest, his tongue lolling out of the side of his mouth as he beamed. He bounded down the empty laboratory through which the group had been walking and halted in front of a glossy, white door. "*The Keep is just beyond here.*"

James exchanged hopeful looks with the others, relieved to have reached the Keep at long last. Forest and Terrain slipped one after the other through the closed door. James hitched up Snow on his back, stepped through the exit, then froze.

A towering mass of the Calf's darkness stretched to the left and to the right like a great, black cloud. Whisps of fog swirled about the emptiness, dissipating then reappearing in continuous cycles like ghosts striving to be seen.

James had visualized what the Keep would look like throughout the group's journey, yet the sight of the Red Calf's emptiness still paralyzed him. He thought of how the Beast had flopped out onto invisible ground. He remembered the hunger in its dark eye as it had stared at him and Snow. He heard again the Hunters' screams before they had met their end in the tunnels.

"James," Snow said gently. "Are you okay? What's happening?"

"We're here. It's just like Terrain said it would be. The Calf's emptiness is like a giant cloud. I-It's just kind of overwhelming. Sorry."

"*Hey.*"

He jumped and stared at Blood Crow.

"*It's all right,*" she told him. "*I know it's scary, but it's all right. The wolves will lead us in there and then we'll find out how to kill the Calf. We'll find some more answers about your watch too. I'm sure of it.*"

"*Make sure to follow our lead exactly,*" Terrain warned the group. "*These paths are treacherous if you are not acquainted with them. You know what will happen if you touch the darkness.*"

Blood Crow nodded at James. He swallowed and gave her a firm nod back. Together, they followed the others as they made their way toward the Keep.

# CHAPTER 6

# THE KEEP

A black river stretched forth in front of them. The Calf's darkness encased the river like a giant tunnel. James stumbled to a stop at the river's bank. Like the others, he was drenched in sweat and heaving deep breaths.

Navigating through the Keep's fortress of darkness had proven to be a terrifying ordeal even with the wolves' help. Sharp turns had brought them face-to-face with gaping emptiness. The dirt road had plummeted suddenly into gut-shrinking nothingness. Floating expanses of oblivion had forced them to crawl for miles.

James had found the journey doubly harrowing with Snow on his back and felt immensely grateful for the abundant space that now separated the group from the darkness. He tightened his hold around her legs, leaned forward, and hitched her higher up on his back as she slipped slowly out of his sweaty grip.

"*We are through the worst of it now,*" Forest told the group with a smile. "*This way!*"

The group followed him and Terrain onto a giant, wooden raft swaying to the cadence of the river's slow waves. The raft glided out onto the river as the last member of the group stepped on board. James wandered toward the sound of splashing at the front of the raft, peered over the edge, then jerked back slightly. A large, red creature swam just beneath the surface, pulling the raft forward as it pawed through the dark water with clawed feet. Only the top of its head, a raw-looking thing with long tentacles that drifted like hair, bobbed above the surface.

"*Don't be afraid,*" Forest assured the group as several of them peered as well. "*Our friend here has helped transport passengers into the Keep for many nights now.*"

The creature turned its head and stared at the group with empty eye sockets. It turned around again as the fawn and the wolves gave it a polite bow.

"*Please sit. The river is quite long. You should rest,*" said Terrain.

Low groans broke out as the group sat down. Honey rested her head on Lux's shoulder as E and Phoenix leaned their backs on Bloom. James crouched slowly so that Snow could slip onto the floor. He sat down next to Blood Crow and stared at the black upon black reaching on into the distance. Wisps of fog continued floating by overhead.

The fawn placed one hoof then another over Blood Crow's outstretched legs. She crossed her legs to create a small cavity in which the fawn promptly curled up. It closed its eyes as she stroked its head. James couldn't help but smile a little at the gentleness of her touch.

"*Tell me more about the current Third,*" Terrain said suddenly.

"*What more do you wish to know?*" E asked, breaking away from a discussion with Phoenix.

"*Anything,*" said Terrain as his tail swished back and forth across the floor.

"*Terrain is always interested in learning as much as he can about the current Third,*" Forest told E with a tongue-dangling smile. "*Isn't that right, Terrain? Ever since the Last's era, you've always had an interest in the Thirds.*"

"*I suppose,*" Terrain said, lifting his snout and shuffling his paws.

"*The Third during the Last's era was notorious for the many kingdoms he built. He was always trying to engage Terrain in a partnership to help expand the reach of his power,*" Forest said. He added in a loud whisper to E, "*I think that they were friends. It is very rare to find a natural connection with a human, and Terrain definitely had one with that Three. Even more so than he did with the Last!*"

Forest yelped as Terrain snapped his jaws at him. Bloom smiled and shook his head as Forest whined.

"*I never accepted any of his offers! The mere lure of power cannot tempt me,*" Terrain declared.

"*I never said that you did,*" whimpered Forest.

"*The current Third is a great man, one to be feared and respected,*" Snow said in a weary voice. "*He's a builder too. I'm sure he would have built as much as the ancient Third you speak of had he been born with his sight. He's done much for the Market and will be remembered for many ages to come.*"

"Don't be so respectful, Snow," said Lux. "Not after all the crazy crap he's put us through. Even Zilch said before that—"

Honey shushed him. Snow bowed her head, looking crestfallen. The group had hoped that Kit would have rescued Zilch by now and that Zilch, in turn, would have extended call and response to him so that they could both rejoin the group. But neither of them had appeared even as the nights had gone by. The group held on to the possibility that the two had used their collective knowledge of the Tower and the Market to evade the Third's grasp, but James knew that the others, like him, were growing increasingly worried. Snow, of course, continued to worry most of all.

"*The Third's accomplishments are many, but he does seem to be as greedy as the Shamans of old, unfortunately,*" Phoenix said, speaking up on Snow's behalf as she remained silent and dejected.

"*Well, that is no surprise. But I think there might be a bit of selflessness in him too,*" said Terrain.

"*What makes you say that?*" said E.

"*The Third, my acquaintance*"–he threw a sharp look at Forest as if to dare him to call him his friend again–"*came to regret the kingdoms he had built after losing his sight to the Beast. His dying hope had been for one of the future Thirds to make amends for his crimes. I remember you mentioning a few nights ago that the current Third saw the golden eye in his awakening dream. I wouldn't be surprised if that was my acquaintance's doing. Perhaps he revealed the golden eye to the Third because he saw something in him, something good, something selfless. Something that would help fulfill his dying hope. After all, this Third did turn away from the doors to save his son in his awakening.*"

"*Ha! I doubt there's anything good about this Third,*" said Lux. "*This Third is selfish, greedy, and old! His awakening doesn't mean anything. He's just crazy.*"

"*I'm inclined to agree with Lux,*" Phoenix said. "*Selflessness doesn't seem characteristic of him, especially when it comes to the golden eye. I think it's safe to say that there isn't a price he wouldn't pay to get his hands on it. At least, it seemed that way from the way he was pursuing us.*"

The conversation continued then petered out until only the river spoke in gentle splashes. James couldn't help but steal a glance at E and Phoenix as they began whispering to each other again. Phoenix, ever the gentleman, had interacted with E purely within the boundaries of friendship during the past several nights. Not once had he flirted with her. Yet, James could still see the softness in Phoenix's eyes every time he looked at her, and he knew that when a guy looked at a girl like that, it only meant one thing. He saw her as a woman. And not just any woman, but the only woman. The woman who dwelled within his heart.

As for E, he got the feeling that she had very little idea of Phoenix's affection for her. Either that or she was too preoccupied with everything that was happening each night to spare a thought about it even if she had noticed. As expected, she had said nothing in regards to her relationship with Kit and had remained silent during conversations revolving around his and Zilch's rescue. But James had often noticed her staring into the distance with a troubled look as if worry and sadness were eating away at her one small bite at a time. He could only assume that she was thinking of Kit in such moments. Though he felt bad for Phoenix and still dreaded E leaving the crew for Kit, for Snow's sake he hoped that things would work out between Kit and E, for E and Phoenix's whispered discussions throughout the nights had not gone unnoticed by Snow.

For seven nights now, James had carried Snow on his back. Together, they had shared laughs, admitted fears, and wondered about the Flowering's history. Their bond now felt like one between close siblings rather than one grown from mere circumstance. As a result, he could read Snow's emotions and thoughts almost as if he were a Shaman himself. A twitch of her arms told him whether she was surprised or nervous. An inflection in her tone revealed underlying desires or insecurities.

So, he knew without even asking that she was fast losing hope that a night would soon come when Phoenix would consider her as more than a friend. Most concerning, though, was the hardening James could see taking place in her heart. With each passing night, she'd grown colder toward E and now answered with either silence or one-word answers every time she spoke to her. When E had mentioned receiving a large bonus at work, only Snow had failed to congratulate her, much to James's disappointment. Still, he was hopeful. He and E had had their differences in the beginning too, but they had still become good friends.

"James," Snow said suddenly. "Did you want me to read you now? While we have the chance?"

"Oh, yeah! Sure."

Two nights ago, Snow had expressed frustration over the fact that she couldn't read like the other Shamans and that her readings usually left those she had read in a weakened or confused state. James had found it difficult to empathize or even to carry the conversation as he had no idea what it was like to read or be read. So, he'd asked her to read his memories once they had reached the safety of the Keep's interior.

"You're going to read him? Now?" E said.

"Yeah, I just want to see what it's like," James replied, knowing that Snow would answer with something terse or nothing at all. Scooting closer to Snow, he took her hands into his own.

"This is probably going to be really uncomfortable, like I said before," said Snow.

"Don't worry. I'm ready."

She exhaled then nodded. He placed her hands on either side of his head. Her face, the group, the river. All vanished. He became a still, invisible being floating within his own memories.

He saw himself hunched over his desk in his dormitory, poring over a textbook under the bright light of a solitary desk lamp. With one hand, he scribbled into a margin "assumes steady state conditions." With the other, he brought a wobbling plastic bowl full of freshly-microwaved instant ramen to his mouth. His past self felt a deep sense of contentment while sipping the hot broth. And so did he.

Something within him seemed to skip like a spinning record under a faulty needle.

"Für Elise" played in simple, mechanized notes from the speakers of an ice cream truck. He saw himself again but much younger. He had round cheeks and a black bowl cut. He stood on his tip-toes and leaned against the truck as he passed quarters to a man. The man handed him ice cream in return. The thin, blue packaging crinkled in his hands as he received it. Happiness flooded his heart. He opened the packaging and passed the ice cream to Heri. Bright pink rubber bands held up her hair in pigtails that stuck out of her head like small, floppy antlers.

The record skipped.

Another cleaver appeared in his hand. He swung it down and cracked open the hard shell of the creature's tail. The white coils of the snake woman loosened. He dropped into a free fall. Nails clattered across the floor. Bloom sailed through the spotlights to catch him.

The record skipped.

He sat naked on the lush, green grass. Smoke continued rising from his body. A young woman with short, black hair burned him with the intensity of her coal-black eyes. He lowered his gaze.

The record skipped.

Hunters were shouting. Honey was screaming and swearing. James stood in a puddle of his own vomit, trembling as he stared at a cracked orb of dark purple in which a bleeding calf bore a golden eye that unfurled to reveal a young woman who turned to stare at him with milky eyes of ocean blue–

James gasped as Snow tore her hands away from him. They tumbled backward. The fawn leapt across the raft with wide eyes as Blood Crow lunged forward to catch James. E and Phoenix jumped to their feet. Honey and Lux shouted as the raft threatened to capsize. The wolves howled and tossed their heads in agitation. The creature in the river floundered then pulled. The raft smacked back down onto the water's surface. Blood Crow held James in her arms as he continued gasping for air.

"*What did you do to him?*" she demanded of Snow.

"I'm sorry," she replied, panting quick and shallow breaths like James. "I'm sorry. I can't read like the others."

"Calm down. Blood Crow, calm down!" Phoenix shouted as she placed her hand on the hilt of her blade. "It's fine. This happened before when she read me too."

James pressed his hand against his chest as he tried to steady his breathing. He felt as if Snow had dug her fingers into his mind and lifted up memories that had long ago sunk to the bottom of the murky past. He'd seen himself as if he were a different person yet had felt all the emotions and known all the thoughts of his past self so that he had both observed and experienced his own memories.

He hadn't realized that he had stood in his own vomit while staring at the Red Calf or noticed how he should have brought down his cleaver with more arm and less wrist. He definitely hadn't known how happy he could look while eating ramen. And how could he have forgotten about that ice cream truck? Heri had loved that vanilla ice cream with the chocolate shell and nuts! He had probably bought her that thing every week for at least two months. He'd only stopped because his mother had forbidden it out of fear of Heri getting diabetes.

Heri. Heri! He had seen her face!

He searched his mind, frantic to remember her again. But it was no use. A flesh-colored smudge had obscured her face again not only within the unearthed memory of the ice cream truck but in all others as well.

But Snow would know. She would know now what his younger sister had looked like. And what he looked like. And that he was studying engineering in Reality.

For the first time, he truly understood why humans feared the Shamans. If Snow had rifled through just a few more memories, she could have discovered everything from his bank account number to what university Heri attended to where his parents lived. She would have obtained everything she would ever need to blackmail him. And to think that the Shamans of old had been able to remember every single memory they had ever read perfectly and had remembered them in both Reality and the Flowering. With such powers, they could have easily hunted down anyone, no matter the dimension. No wonder their reigns in the past had been so terrible and so great.

He breathed a sigh of relief as he reminded himself that amnesia now plagued the Shamans just as it did any other human. They wouldn't be able to remember any of the faces they saw once they returned to Reality, nor could they remember any faces from Reality when they were in the Flowering. At least that safeguard existed.

"You okay, James?" Lux said. "Say something, man!"

He suddenly became aware that everyone was staring at him. He sat up with a jolt as he realized that he was still curled up against Blood Crow's chest.

"I'm fine, I'm fine. Sorry. It's just that … that was really–"

"Crazy," Snow finished for him. Her shoulders drooped.

"Yeah. I can see what you mean now about your reading skills." He thought of how both the Third and Snake Eyes had remained totally composed during their reading in the Tower.

"It's not just the physical side effects, though," Snow said, looking pained. "I can't read chronologically like the others, and no matter how hard I try, I can't keep focused on one memory. It just keeps skipping and skipping even when I don't want it to."

"It's fine," Phoenix said. "We talked about this in the Market. It has something to do with the eye you ate. It's not your fault."

The raft floated out of the black tunnel and into an enormous, rugged passageway where clearer waters splashed. At the end of the river stood a massive stone stairway amidst soaring, rocky walls. As the creature pulling them submerged itself completely, the raft slowed and bumped up against the bottom of the stairway.

James knelt for Snow, who climbed onto his back with practiced ease. He whispered descriptions of their surroundings to her as the group climbed up the many stairs. The last step evened out into a long path of hewn stone. A pair of colossal, arched doors stood ajar at the path's end. James squinted as he followed the wolves into the red-gold light spilling out from the gap between the doors. The group stepped out onto a cliff.

"*Welcome to the Keep,*" said Terrain.

A low, red sun loomed just above the Calf's black ring of emptiness. A silent city of gray high-rises stood far below within the center of the ring. The fiery glow of the sun colored the high-rises in slanted, red slices. Several of them stood unfinished so that rusted steel beams crisscrossed at their tops. Bright yellow light colored a few of the buildings' rectangular windows, and puddles of pale light surrounded the bases of the streetlamps standing on the empty streets. The majority of the Keep, though, rested within shadows.

"*Come! This way. Father resides in the center of the Keep,*" said Forest. He bounded down a long, sloping path hugging the side of the cliff.

"*Don't be so nervous, Brother. I'm sure Father will be delighted to see you,*" Terrain said sardonically. He let out a low, wheezy cackle then followed Forest.

Bloom responded with a flat look that was all too accustomed to Terrain's taunting. He smiled as E drew him closer to herself.

The group traveled down the path and into the dark and empty streets. They walked in and out of shadows as they passed by one streetlamp after another. The hollow windows of the surrounding buildings stared at the fixed sunset like black eyes. James had anticipated the Keep to be teeming with life, but maybe that had been a mistake on his part. Forest had explained that the marked citizens they rescued usually decided to move on not long after their arrival in the Keep. Plus, even if any of the marked were within their vicinity, they were likely hiding from the group, who were, after all, human strangers wandering about within the safety of their city.

The wolves halted with perked ears as the sound of clopping hooves slowly approached. Two massive horses rounded the corner. James blinked as his brain struggled momentarily to understand what he was seeing. The horses were incomplete. Their bodies ended halfway in tatters like worn rags and gradually disappeared so that they stood only on their forelegs with half a body. They snorted and tossed their glossy manes before approaching the group. The mark stood out on their long necks, red against their black coats.

"*Good evening, gentlemen,*" Terrain said.

"*Evening, Terrain, Forest,*" said one of the horses. "*We are glad to see you've both returned.*"

"*Yes, Sleet was beginning to worry about you,*" said the other horse.

"*And about the fawn as well. But I see its retrieval was successful.*"

The fawn trembled against Blood Crow's leg as the horse lowered its head and stared at it with glowing, red eyes.

"*You have caused Terrain and Forest much trouble, little one,*" the horse said.

"*Oh, it is nothing. We found him in the end, and that is all that matters,*" said Forest.

Terrain's expression stiffened as he sniffed and shuffled his paws.

"*If I may, though, why have you brought these humans with you?*" the horse asked.

"*Yes, we trust your judgment, of course. But I'm not so certain about bringing humans into the Keep.*"

"*Oh, but before that, please do introduce us to your friend,*" said the horse, looking at Bloom.

"*Oh, yes, of course. Where are our manners? Welcome to the Keep, my friend. What is your name?*"

Bloom smiled sadly as he stared at the horses in silence.

"*This is Brother, the long-lost member of our pack,*" said Terrain, stepping up to Bloom's side.

The horses gasped.

"*And this human here is a direct descendant of the Last,*" Terrain said, looking at E.

The horses gasped again.

"*And this is the Twelfth. Out from Lapis Lazuli at last!*" said Forest.

The horses reared back on invisible hind legs and whinnied.

"*If you are headed to where Father is, we would be pleased to escort you!*"

"*Yes! It would be an honor to escort the Last's descendant. And the Twelfth too, of course. I assure you it will be much faster if you ride upon our backs.*"

James stared. There wasn't much of a "back" to ride on.

"*Don't let our looks deceive you,*" said the horse, smiling at him. "*We can easily carry at least two humans.*"

"*Yes, I assure you that you will find us quite up to the task.*"

After receiving a nod of approval from E, James hoisted Snow onto what existed of the horse and helped wind her fingers into its mane. He placed his hands on the horse's sleek coat then slid them sideways. To his surprise, he felt a warm, sturdy body against his palms though he saw nothing. Leaping up, he settled himself behind Snow. The fawn jumped up into Blood Crow's open arms once she and Phoenix had seated themselves on the other horse. The others climbed onto the wolves.

James threw his arms around Snow's waist as the horses suddenly reared up with a whinny. They galloped down the street with the wolves in their midst. He didn't know what was stranger, seeing half a horse running down the street or seeing nothing below him as his body bounced up and down and forward and backward. A few citizens peeked out of windows and doorways as the group sped deep into the heart of the Keep. Snow maintained a strong and steady hold on the horse with her hands and legs. She clearly had experience riding. James unglued his arms from around her and grabbed the horse's mane. He followed her example and forced his body to move in sync with the horse's galloping until he felt himself riding with the horse instead of struggling against its every movement.

The horses' hooves clattered to a halt in front of an enormous high-rise towering up into the bloodshot sky. Rows of giant, hollow windows reached down the building, forming rectangular entrances that lined all four of its sides. The vastness of the structure added to its aura of abandonment.

The group dismounted and thanked the horses, who snorted and nodded in response. They eyed E and Snow with palpable curiosity as the group followed Terrain and Forest deep into the building. Darkness obscured depth inside so that everyone seemed to stay in place yet glide across the ground. They turned at an opening in a wall and stepped into a long room, where the smell of metal coated James's tongue like the faint taste of blood. Rectangles of dim light fell through dirty, plastic tarp hanging from the rafters. A tall, wooden platform stretched down the length of the wall facing the group. Cobwebs draped the dusty lamps, worn furniture, and cans of used paint piled on top of the platform. Terrain glanced at Bloom then stared into the darkness beneath the platform. James knew who lay there in the shadows even before Terrain spoke.

*"Father, we have returned."*

# CHAPTER 7

# FATHER

Two golden eyes glinted as they opened in the dark. A deep growl rumbled forth. A great, gray wolf emerged from beneath the wooden platform. His weathered face and shaggy fur gave him the appearance of one who had endured harsh battles and lived to see ages rise and fall. Anger drew back his lips to reveal his massive fangs as he prowled toward the group.

"*What have the two of you brought into the Keep?*" he snarled.

"*Father,*" Terrain began solemnly. His eyes widened as Forest hopped in front of him.

"*Father! We have brought Brother back. He has returned to us at long last!*" Forest said.

His tail flagellated the air as if it were trying to put out an invisible fire then curled between his legs as Terrain threw him a scornful look. Father's growl diminished into silence. E hesitated before stepping aside to reveal Bloom. He stood with his teeth bared, ears back, and fur standing on end.

"*Father!*" a voice called, making the group spin around. "*I heard Terrain and Forest had returned with the Last's descendant!*"

A wolf of pure, soft white skidded to a stop. He stared at Bloom with wide eyes that, like his, were golden. A plush tuft of fur encircled his neck like a ruff, giving him a wise and elite appearance. The manner in which he stood, with his head held high and his chest thrust out, added to the look.

"*Brother*," said the white wolf.

Apprehension flashed across Bloom's face before settling into sadness. His hackles relaxed as the white wolf walked up to him with halting steps. After sharing a long, earnest stare, the white wolf rubbed his neck against Bloom's. Bloom licked his snout as they broke apart.

"*Allow me to introduce the final member of our pack*," said Terrain as he shuffled his paws with palpable unease. "*This is Sleet. He is second in command next to Father.*"

Father's eyes remained fixed on Bloom as Sleet exchanged greetings with the group. Bloom glared back at Father in response.

"*Father*," Terrain resumed, "*these humans have some very important–*"

Father turned around and began lumbering back into the shadows. Terrain sighed and shuffled his paws again. Forest whimpered. Sleet glanced at Bloom.

"*Wait*," said E. "*Wait, we need to speak to you.*"

She reached toward Father. A snarl ripped out of his throat as he snapped around to face her. Bloom leapt in front of her, his eyes full of rage. E stood her ground and signaled for the others to stay back as Father began prowling toward her. His nose suddenly quivered. Wide-eyed wonder replaced his snarl as he slowly raised his head and gazed at E.

"*It is he*," Father whispered.

"*Yes*," said Terrain, looking relieved. "*Yes, Father. This is the Last's child. His line has survived these many eras, it would seem.*"

Father continued gazing at her. Terrain cleared his throat and began telling Sleet and Father of the group's journeys. Sleet jumped to his feet in alarm as Terrain described the Red Calf's appearance in the tunnels. The grooves lining Father's face deepened, but he remained stoic otherwise. As Terrain finished speaking, both Father and Sleet approached James and Snow. They, too, erupted into growls as they sniffed his watch and her eyes. They backed away, still growling.

"*Father*," said Terrain. "*You have always suspected that the Beast would return. Tell these children what you know so that we can kill it once and for all. Let us partner with humans again as we did in those eras of old.*"

Father breathed a deep sigh that seemed to carry the weight of memories buried long ago but never forgotten. He sat down and gazed at the group with a solemnity that added to the ages already engraved upon his face.

"*The eye which* James *and the Twelfth consumed in their awakening dreams ... the eye within the box made of lapis lazuli stone. That eye was the eye of the Beast. Its evil changed* James's *watch and impaired the Twelfth's ability to read. It is why the scent of death lingers upon them both.*"

There was a quiet moment of shock before vertigo slammed into James's head. An image of the Calf's raw, empty socket flashed across his mind. Its missing eye. He and Snow had eaten its missing eye. That was the eye in the blue box!

Lux shouted as James's knees gave way. Snow's arms unraveled from around his neck. E caught him before he collapsed onto the floor. Lux ordered him to breathe as the group pressed in on them and asked anxious questions. E made everyone step back with a trembling hand and gestured for silence.

"*The Beast's eye?*" she said, her voice barely above a whisper. "*But h-how is that possible?*"

"*When the Last and I battled the Beast many eras ago, I tore out one of its eyes,*" Father said. "*The Last, upon defeating the Beast, consumed that eye, and that consumption caused his death. As he was dying, a part of him left the Flowering in a manner that I had never seen before. It resembled a cloud, a mist. He must have used his remaining strength to pass on the eye to the two of you.*"

"*Wait,*" E said. "*Wait. I don't understand. Consumed the eye? Why?*"

"*Why?*" Father growled. He jumped to his feet. "*Why? Because of the Shamans, that is why! The Last knew the Beast's eye still held much of its power. He knew that if any of the other Shamans found the eye, they would use it for their kingdoms. He could have returned to the Abode and traded the eye for comfort and riches. He could have kept its powers for himself! But instead, he chose to consume the eye even though he knew it would kill him. He sacrificed himself for the safety of the Flowering and died fighting the greed of humans, the greed that had grown so grotesquely for so many eras!*"

The group stared at Father in silence as he trembled with indignation. After several moments, he shot out a sharp sigh through his nose and sat down again.

"*During the eras when Shamans could see, they were able to share their powers with one another. When a Shaman borrowed another Shaman's sight, he could see all the memories of not only the lender but also of those whom the lender had read, and he could create anything that had been touched in Reality within those memories. The borrower also gained six more creations with every sight he borrowed, and his physical sight was enhanced with each sight as well. Of course, there were negatives to such powers. Until the borrower returned his sight, the lending Shaman lost his ability to see, and his creations dwindled to a maximum of six. He also suffered from amnesia just like any other human, and he was forced to rely on physical touch to access a human's memories.*"

"*It was an ancient form of partnership used to enhance a Shaman's ability to comfort and protect both humans and citizens who had particular needs or more complex circumstances,*" Sleet said. "*And, of course, such powers helped them to defeat more of the moulded with greater success. It was a partnership that was forgotten by the Shamans as they fell into greed and warfare.*"

"*Yes. And I revealed my knowledge of it to those greedy cowards in an attempt to help the Last, who was determined to defeat the Beast,*" said Father. "*I convinced all eleven of those quarreling fools to lend him their sight. How else could they hope to save their kingdoms, I argued. The Last was the only Shaman who had had enough practice hunting the moulded to be able to stand a chance against the Beast and the only Shaman they could trust to return their powers, for he was known for his selflessness and had never built a single kingdom. In the end, all eleven of those greedy cowards agreed to lend him their sight.*"

"*We were all sure that, with the powers he had borrowed, he would succeed in killing the Beast. But we were wrong,*" said Sleet. He sighed and shook his head. "*I regret it still, Father. We should have gone out with you into battle that night. We should have fought alongside you.*"

"*No! We suffered enough losses that night. Your presence would not have made the slightest difference. And,*" Father said. He closed his eyes briefly. "*And it was what Mother had wanted.*"

Bloom walked away from the group.

"Bloom?" E said.

Terrain rushed forward and fixed himself in his path.

"*You must stay, Brother. If you loved Mother, you will do her the honor of learning what exactly occurred that night.*"

"*Let the coward leave!*" Father snarled. "*Abandoning his pack is what he does best, after all.*"

Terrain blocked Bloom as he made to walk away again. Sleet stared at Bloom with an expression that carried both pity and disapproval.

"*Mother and Brother had a very close bond,*" Forest told the group in a quiet voice. "*Her death was very difficult for him, as it was for all of our pack and for the Brave.*"

"*The Brave,*" Father growled. "*That stubborn child does not deserve such a title. We told him to stay behind, but he refused. He declared that he would rather die than let the Last face the Beast on his own. And of course, Mother ... Mother refused to stay behind as well.*"

"*Mother was the Brave's anchor. They were partners and close friends,*" Sleet explained. "*They always rode out into battle together, and the battle with the Beast was no exception.*"

Forest began to tremble with stifled sobs. "*She had the most beautiful black fur. So loving and so caring. So strong and courageous. The fiercest Castaway to have ever lived!*"

Phoenix hesitated then said, "*I'm sorry, but I thought that Castaways were immortal.*"

"*We are immortal, but only if we choose to be,*" said Sleet. "*It is our heart, you see. We can choose to give up our heart as a weapon. Anyone who wields a Castaway's heart can use it to trap any one thing or being of their choice for all eternity. All one must do is touch the heart against the target and desire it to be trapped. It was a last resort that Castaways and Shamans used during ancient eras to defeat the most powerful of the moulded. But removing our heart causes our death. It is the only way we can die. That and the Beast's darkness.*"

"*We were sure that we could find the Beast's mark and kill it,*" Father said. "*But we discovered in battle that the Beast is an abnormality. It can instantly move the location of its mark to a different part of its body. We had never encountered such a thing before, and no matter what we attempted, no matter how hard we fought, the four of us could not find a way to deal the death blow. Even the powers the Last had borrowed from the other Shamans proved insufficient. And so, Mother gave up her heart before any of us could stop her. It was the only way."*

The cracked, purple orb materialized in James's mind. The orb. The purple orb in which he had seen the Calf. It was the heart of Bloom's mother. The memory of the ram eating the black wolf in the tunnels washed over that of the orb. Bloom's mother had been a black wolf too.

*"So, you and the Last battled the Beast with powers borrowed from the other Shamans,"* said E. *"You tore out one of its eyes, and the Last used Mother's heart to trap the Beast. Then he chose to eat the eye in order to keep it away from the other Shamans. But then how is it that the Beast is returning? You said a Castaway's heart would imprison what it touches for all eternity."*

*"It all happened too quickly,"* said Father, shaking his head. *"As Mother's heart touched the Beast's flesh, the Beast looked upon the Last. Had it not been for her heart, the Beast would have surely taken his life, but instead, it managed to take only his eyes. I saw the golden eye form upon its head, and after Mother's heart had closed, the Last and I heard the Beast promise that it would return. Such a thing should have been impossible. Nothing can escape a Castaway's heart, not even a voice. But it was there. A voice. And a promise. And I have waited all these long eras for the Beast to fulfill that promise."*

*"But that still doesn't explain how the Beast managed to break free of her heart,"* E said.

*"It is the golden eye,"* said Father. *"When the Beast took the Last's eyes, it stole nearly all of the powers which the twelve Shamans had given him, and it retained those powers in the golden eye which formed upon its forehead. It is the Shamans' powers within that eye which give the Beast a living connection to the Flowering, a connection that extends beyond*

*Mother's heart. It is a connection that has allowed it to eat away at her heart throughout the ages."*

James tried to catch the myriad of thoughts that had begun whirling around in his mind, but each thought that he grasped struggled in his hold before springing free and flying about once again.

*"Was it you?"* he managed to say as he saw the purple orb in his mind again. *"Were you the one who hid her heart in those tunnels?"*

"Yes," said Father. *"The Last instructed me to hide her heart in a plane outside of the Iris so that when the Beast returned, humans would have an opportunity to escape into the safety of the moonlight, for out of all that exists in the Flowering, only the light surrounding Lapis Lazuli is impervious to the Beast's darkness."*

Father lumbered up to James and Snow. James gazed into his golden eyes. They were so similar to Bloom's, yet they carried a hardness that Bloom's lacked. He was surprised to hear the gentleness that softened Father's voice as he continued.

*"The Beast dwells within you both, but it is not the only thing. Remnants of the Last's powers which the Beast was not able to take live on in you as well. What powers remained in the eye of the Beast and the Last's body the night of his death have now passed down to the two of you. I do not know exactly what powers you have been bestowed or how those powers will manifest. They will have intermingled within the eye you both consumed so that your powers are neither purely of the Beast nor solely of the Last. But I am sure the unique powers you have been given will be wondrous.* James's watch is but one example."

*"Wondrous?"* James repeated. He couldn't help but give a hollow laugh. His watch was nothing but a curse. A horrible thing counting down to the end of everything. A black mark that tied him to the Red Calf.

"*Yes,*" said Father. "*Your watch has acted as a vital warning for us all. It tells us how much time we have left and will inform us of when the Beast's return is, at last, complete. It is a gift as much as it is a curse.*"

James stared again into Father's eyes. He wished he could believe him.

"*The Last was the most powerful Shaman I have ever known,*" Father said. "*His dying wish was that any strength left within him would pass down to aid those worthier than him, those who would be able attain the peace he had fought with all his might to bring back into the Flowering. He used his remaining strength to pass down great powers to the two of you, and those powers will help us to attain the peace which he so desperately sought. I am certain of it.*"

The group jumped as Blood Crow let out a sharp sob. She seemed to crumble as she buried her face in her hands. Even in his shock and despair, James felt a twinge of pain at the sight of her crying. The fawn nuzzled her arm.

"*How? How could everyone, all Hunters, all humans!*" she cried. "*How could everyone have forgotten about the old ways, about all of this?*"

"*I am afraid more than one human is to blame for that,*" said Sleet with a grim smile. "*Much confusion followed the defeat of the Beast. Truth was muddied, and false legends arose.*"

"*It was chaos reorganizing the Flowering once the Shamans were blind,*" Terrain said. "*Of course, the Shamans did very little to help with all the chaos. All they cared for were their riches and spending their nights mourning over the loss of their eyes.*"

"*But the Brave!*" said Blood Crow. "*He survived the battle with the Beast, didn't he? He must have done something during all that chaos. He was the Last's most loyal follower!*"

"*On the contrary, the Brave complicated matters significantly,*" said Sleet. "*The Last's death and witnessing all the destruction caused by the*

Beast made the Brave increasingly wary of citizens. It all came to a head when one night, a moulded citizen in the form of a great, white serpent killed his daughter in battle. He became completely mad with grief after that, and his grief quickly transformed into rage. He accused Father of murdering the Last and cut ties with us. Yes," he said, nodding at the group's scandalized expressions, "*his madness amounted to an unshakeable paranoia in the end.*

"*He was not with the Last in the final moments of the battle, you see, for the Last and Father forbade him to fight once Mother had died. Later, in his madness, the Brave convinced himself that it had actually been Father who had killed the Last. He turned against us all and founded the Hunters' way, which added to the on-going chaos.*"

"*He kept our motto of 'protect,' though,*" Terrain said as he wrinkled his snout and shuffled his paws. "*And he passed that motto down to all his Hunters. They still use that motto to this very night.*"

"*Let us not forget that the First Head Merchant came into power too and created a stir by trying to overthrow the Shamans,*" said Sleet.

"*There were many newborn humans to account for as well,*" said Forest. "*The Beast had killed many humans, and each one that died meant that another was born in their stead. Everyone was scattered, much was forgotten, and even more was twisted into stories and myths. Everything started over, although, of course, some remnants of the past do remain.*"

"*Yes. Remnants of kingdoms still exist in some planes,*" said Sleet. "*And, as you can see, not all of the Beast's darkness disappeared with its defeat. There are pieces of it, such as the ring surrounding the Keep, but more often, you will discover black orbs of its darkness. The Beast used to fire those orbs at its victims at such a speed that few escaped its attacks.*"

James remembered the wasteland which the crew had stumbled upon and the black orbs that had littered it. That wasteland must have been one of the Shaman's kingdoms built upon a stagnant plane, a kingdom ruined by one of the Beast's ambushes. That night, he'd felt a strange familiarity which had moved him only toward disgust. The part of the Beast within him had recognized itself within those orbs, but the Last's powers within him had sensed an enemy.

"*There is also a black tree in the Iris that bears twelve eyes,*" Sleet continued. "*It stands where the Last passed away and grew from the blood that spilled when Father took the Beast's eye.*"

"*The Desert was born from that blood too. Before the Beast's defeat, that territory had flourished with trees and grass and sea,*" said Terrain.

"*What will happen?*" Snow said suddenly. She had remained so still that James had forgotten she was sitting next to him. "*What will happen if we can't kill the Beast before its return to full strength?*"

"*There is no way for us to stop the Beast from returning now,*" said Father. "*From what you have told us, it is clear that the Beast intends to remain in the safety of its darkness until it can return to full strength. Its darkness has likely consumed most of that plane by now, or at the very least, all the tunnels that would lead us to it. We must wait until it steps out into the open to eat again then meet it in battle near Lapis Lazuli. The Last and I made the grave mistake of meeting the Beast out in the open all those eras ago. This time, we will use the Blue Border as our shield to secure our victory.*"

"*And I must join you when you go out into battle,*" Snow said softly. "*The Last was a Twelfth Shaman, so only another Twelve can restore the Shamans' sight. That means only I can retrieve the golden eye, doesn't it?*"

"*Yes,*" said Father. "*We have no other choice. You will accompany us into battle so that we can take the golden eye and cut off the Beast's connection to the Flowering. Once we have severed its connection, we can kill it and put an end to its ravenous eating once and for all. Otherwise, it will destroy everything in both the Flowering and Reality.*"

James gave his head a sharp shake. The others stirred as well.

"'*Destroy everything in both the Flowering and Reality,*'" Honey repeated. "*What does Reality have to do with any of this?*"

"*All dimensions are linked to one another,*" Father said. "*The Flowering creates everything that passes on to the dimension of human dreams. The dream dimension, in turn, allows what you humans call 'sleep' to exist, though, of course, you humans are foolish enough to think that it is sleep that creates dreams. The more the Beast swallows the Flowering, the more the dimension of dreams will disappear. The more the dimension of dreams disappears, the more sleep will disappear from Reality. Without sleep, it will not be long before humans begin to die, and the more humans die in Reality, the less citizens will be born into the Flowering. Everything will disappear, and in the end, we will all perish together.*"

Horror overtook James in a slow, cold wave. If they didn't stop the Beast, they would all die. His family. Crew Blue. All humans. All citizens. Everyone would die.

E's voice wavered as she broke the group's stunned silence. "*What must we do now?*" she asked.

Father jumped up onto all fours and shook out his fur. "*We must first evacuate the Keep, and we must do so immediately. Who knows when James's watch will change again and how the Beast's darkness will react when it does? Sleet, Forest, Terrain! Go and gather–*"

He lay on his back, suspended in a peaceful limbo as warmth and comfort bathed him. A few moments passed–or perhaps it was many–before awareness began stealing over him. He began to struggle within his immobile body. He didn't have the luxury of lying here like this. Who was he? Why was he here? Why did the tranquility confuse and disorient him so? As he continued rising through the air, his confusion began to fragment and break away. His identity began to form.

James ... James ... his name was James!

He gasped as he lurched forward and sat up in his bed. He fumbled with his screeching alarm clock before silencing it. He sat still, listening to the ticking of the clock, then grabbed his laptop and began typing away at an email that called in sick for work. He already knew it would be useless to try working today. There was no way he could focus. The Beast was gathering more of its strength with every passing moment, and when it was ready, it would come to consume everything and everyone both inside and outside of the Flowering.

# CHAPTER 8

# ON

As ten PM struck, James sat down on his bed and stared at the wall. He remained lost within his thoughts even as the mattress bounced up and down beneath him. He'd spent most of the morning processing everything he'd learned from Father. In the afternoon, feeling anxious and at a loss for what else to do, he'd sat down to study. Several hours later, he'd tossed his pencil onto his desk, slammed his textbook shut, and cursed himself for wasting so much of the day reading and re-reading the same few pages over and over again before trying to study once more. By nightfall, he'd given up completely and spent the rest of his time analyzing his thoughts and memories of the Flowering while shoveling down ramen. He wiggled deep into his blankets as he reviewed the night ahead.

The pack would finish evacuating the Keep then lead the group out as well. Then they would begin their journey back to the City so that they could use the moonlight as their main defense in their battle against the Calf. But then what? How long did they have until the Beast regained its full strength? Once the group returned to the safety of the moonlight, how would they stay hidden from the Third? And how would they lure the Beast into battle once it did return? What if it roamed endlessly through different planes, eating everything in its path, before finally arriving at the Blue Border? Would there be anything left to save?

He stomped out the anxiety ballooning in his chest and beat down the questions multiplying within his mind. He reminded himself that he could not succumb to panic or freeze up under the pressure of everything. The group had Father now, and they could discuss all the details with him once they left the Keep. For now, he would simply have to stay calm, regroup with the others, and wait. He took a deep breath and closed his eyes. Several more minutes passed as drowsiness softened his consciousness.

He opened his eyes in the Flowering.

The group stood in front of a small shop with boarded windows and a faded, striped awning. Tin cans, metal pipes, and wooden beams littered the floor inside.

"*We are almost complete with the evacuation,*" Sleet was telling the group. "*Please wait for us here. I will come for you once we have finished.*"

James touched Snow's arm and knelt down in front of her, prompting her to climb onto his back. Broken glass crunched beneath the group's boots as they filed into the store. Sleet blocked Bloom as he made to follow.

"*Come, Brother. The children are all here now, so you can come with me. Let us continue helping Father and the others.*"

Bloom's head and tail sank. E sighed.

"*Can't Bloom stay with us? That Father of yours isn't exactly kind to him,*" she said.

"*Our pack's teamwork will play a key role in defeating the Beast,*" Sleet replied, fixing her with a cool gaze. "*Brother must practice collaborating with us as much as possible before the battle. Too many eras have passed since we ran together as one.*"

Bloom side-eyed Sleet with an annoyed look and sighed through his nostrils. He made to turn around with Sleet then stopped and looked at E as if to ask if she would be all right without him. James raised an eyebrow, unsure of where Bloom's concern was coming from. Bloom was well used to leaving her on her own when the occasion called for it, and the occasion definitely called for it! E lifted her chin, paused, then nodded. As Bloom continued gazing at her, she placed her hands on either side of his face.

"Go," she said. "Your brother is right. I'll be okay."

He gazed at her a moment longer before licking her hand. Together with Sleet, he ran down the street, turned the corner, and disappeared from sight.

Honey scowled. "You'd think he could have given us somewhere a little better to stay," she said, tossing a hand up at the dilapidated room.

"There's no use complaining about it," said E. She tore her eyes away from the spot where Bloom had disappeared. "Let's rest while we can. We probably have another long night ahead of us."

Honey continued grumbling as the group picked their way across the room. Phoenix lowered an empty, wooden bookcase face-down onto the ground and sat on its back. E swept her boot across the floor, curled up next to the broken storefront window, and stared again at the corner where Bloom had turned. Honey and Lux wandered to the end of the room, peeked behind a closed door, then began exploring the space beyond. Blood Crow sat down with her back against a wall and secured the fawn in her arms. James made to sit down with Snow then stopped, lowered her down next to Phoenix, and seated himself a few feet away from them instead. Maybe a few moments alone together would give her a better chance with Phoenix. James smiled as Phoenix struck up a whispered conversation with Snow.

"*Do I really have to go?*" the fawn asked Blood Crow.

Phoenix looked away from Snow and stared at the fawn instead. James groaned inwardly. Just when they were about to make some progress!

"*Yes, little one,*" Blood Crow said. "*We've discussed this before. All citizens must move on after receiving the mark, and you have received yours.*"

"*I know, but....*"

"*But?*" she said, stroking its head.

"*But I wanted to see my mama again. She had red fur, just like you. Did I mention that?*" it said with a sad smile.

"*Yes. Yes, you did.*"

Its smile faded. "*I thought that if I could just find her again....*"

"*But we discussed this too, little one. It wasn't your fault. She made the decision to join the moulded. You could not change her then, and you cannot change her now.*"

"*But if I could just—*"

"*No,*" Blood Crow said. She stroked the fawn again as it began to tremble. "*No. You cannot find her now. You cannot go back to her. You will only become part of the moulded yourself. It is too late, little one. But sometimes, that is just a part of life.*"

Tears rolled down the fawn's face. It lowered its head onto Blood Crow's lap.

"*I still wish I could have said goodbye.*"

The fawn closed its eyes, breathed a soft sigh, and disappeared.

Blood Crow lowered her hands onto her empty lap. James's heart filled with the sadness he knew was flooding hers.

"Are you all right, Blood Crow?" he asked.

She didn't answer but instead, pulled out her necklace from under her tee-shirt. She smirked as she rolled the two rubies between her thumb and index finger.

"I became a Hunter because I wanted to protect humans. A good friend of mine ran out of time because of a moulded citizen, and this is all I have left of her," she said, holding up one of the rubies. "I thought I was doing the right thing, but my life ... the Hunters' way ... it's all been a lie. I've been idolizing a madman and slaughtering the innocent. There were so many that begged me to spare them. Even my namesake–" She choked on her tears.

Another wave of emotion swelled within James as her tears spilled down her cheeks. He thrust aside a sudden desire to throw his arms around her and reminded himself that now was not the moment. She wiped her tears away and drew a deep breath.

"All Hunters are named after their first kill. Mine was a crow. Everyone thought its red eye was just a red eye, but I knew better. I knew its pupil was its mark. It tried to escape, but it couldn't fly. It just kept hopping around, dropping feathers and blood and screaming. It was screaming for its children, and I killed it with my spear."

Tears streamed down her cheeks again. This time, she did not wipe them away. James sat in silence, paralyzed as he struggled to find the right words to comfort her.

E rose to her feet. Cans rolled and glass crunched as she walked over to Blood Crow. Blood Crow continued shaking with suppressed sobs as E knelt down in front of her. For several moments, she gazed at Blood Crow. Then, with the gentleness of a mother, she drew her into an embrace.

Blood Crow stiffened. Sheer surprise seemed to stop her tears before her shoulders began to jerk and quiver. She drew a sharp breath before gripping E and burying her face in her shoulder. She began to sob.

E didn't shush her. She didn't try to cheer her up with forced words. She didn't ask her to talk or do anything. Instead, she simply held her in her arms and rocked her back and forth with an ease that both did and didn't surprise James. After all, this was the E who he knew lived beneath the savage exterior, the E whom he tried to bring back every time her rage threatened to consume her, the E who was his friend.

Many moments passed before Blood Crow grew quiet and limp. Only then did E speak.

"Leaving something you love and are loyal to is never easy. But sometimes, it's the right thing to do." She stared up at the ceiling and sighed. "It's the only thing you can do. But you're welcome to join Crew Blue permanently if you'd like. You both are," she added, looking at Phoenix.

"Thank you," he said. "I'm ... I'm honored to accept."

"Me too," Blood Crow whispered.

Joy exploded within James. She was staying! She was staying with the crew forever! He'd get to see her every night for the rest of his nights! He cleared his throat and made sure not to smile too widely as he nodded at Blood Crow.

"But my family," she said. "They'll need to know that I'm leaving and that I'm still alive."

"We'll get word to them somehow," E assured her.

Something shattered in the back room. The crew unsheathed their blades as they jumped to their feet. Honey shouted indiscernible words before she and Lux burst into the room. Her arms were folded and her lips, pursed. Lux wore an irritated expression that clouded the sparkle which usually danced in his eyes. He avoided the crew's stares.

"What's going on?" E demanded as they stopped in front of her.

"Ask Lux," Honey spat.

He only rolled his eyes then shifted his gaze from the floor to the wall.

"Well?" E barked.

"Lux is being stupid!" Honey shouted.

"No, I'm not. You're the one who's being stupid!"

"How am I the one who's being stupid? You're the one who's being stupid! You're being crazy!"

"What's so crazy about wanting some peace and quiet?"

"Both of you. Calm down. Now!" E snarled.

They fell silent.

"What is going on? Is there something we need to worry about, or is this just another one of your stupid fights?" said E.

"It's nothing to worry about," Lux muttered as he kicked at bits of broken glass on the floor. "I was just telling Honey that I liked the Market."

"And that you wanted to leave us and live there," Honey said.

"I didn't say that!"

"Well, you might as well have!"

"I said that I liked the Market and that it wouldn't be so bad to live there!" He looked at E with an expression that shone with both defiance and shame. "I'm sorry. I know you hate the Market, but you know about my family. You know how tired I am these days, and every day that passes, every night, I just feel myself getting more tired. There's been a lot more drama at the shop these days, and my dad's health just got worse. My family is being difficult, and now everything with the Flowering. It's been a lot lately." He sighed. "I was just saying it'd be nice to take a break. Maybe take Kit up on his offer and tour the place for a few nights after all our stuff with the Red Calf is over."

"How can you even think like that?" Honey said. A suppressed sob made her voice quaver. "Did you not see that red-light district? What the Merchants were like and the Shamans?" She struggled then shouted, "Crazy! You're crazy!"

"I'm not crazy, Honey! I'm just tired."

"We're all tired."

"I'm different. You know how hard-pressed my family is."

"Stop," E said.

Lux tried to look at her before glaring at the ground again.

"Lux," E said.

She paused. Her expression was, to James's surprise, devoid of anger and instead, tinged with apprehension.

"Lux," she said, "if you want to go to the Market, I can't stop you. You aren't a prisoner to Crew Blue. None of you are. You know what I think about Hedonists and Merchants and all the rest of them, so I won't nag you about it. You know that I would never give you over to the Market out of my own free will. Ever. That place is evil, even if it doesn't seem like it at first. But if that's the path you want to choose, then I won't keep you chained to the crew. I won't say it's the right decision, and I wish you'd believe me when I say that it's not. But I'm not going to make you stay with us against your will. Just promise me that you won't do this out of desperation."

"E," Lux said. "Don't. I wouldn't ever leave you. I wouldn't ever leave any of you guys. That's not what I meant." He shook his head as shame twisted his expression. "I'm sorry. I won't bring it up again. I just thought that since you and Kit are–I mean!"

A small sigh escaped from her. She took a step back from him.

"I-I'm sorry." His mouth opened and closed. For a moment, he looked as if he would simply fall silent. Then he balled his fists, looked E in the eye, and squared his shoulders. "It's just that you two really seemed to like each other, and if you guys got back together, you'd stay in the Market, right? At least for a little while? Because Kit's a Jackal? Then we could all stay with the two of you, and we'd be happy and still together. It'd be nice."

"E can do better than Kit," Honey snapped.

"He's not that bad of a guy."

"Oh, because you know him so well!"

"Well, you don't know him that well either!"

"I don't have to. I know his type. Boys like him can never really love a girl."

"What are you talking about? He's crazy about E. He literally used his own body to protect her back at the Doors, he risked his position to smuggle us out, and the way he looks at her. You just know!"

"Oh, don't give me that crap. 'The way he looks at her.' Ha! Open your eyes. You're only saying that because you always trust everyone we ever come across without ever thinking about it twice. You're like ... you're like a stupid puppy, Lux!"

"Well, it's better than being paranoid of everyone like you, Honey!"

"Paranoid? You really think I'm being paranoid right now? Kit is bad news! You're just too much of a fanboy to see it. E can do way better than Kit because he's nothing but a player!"

E hurried out of the shop. She broke into a run before turning a corner and disappearing. The group stared at the corner in silence. Honey rounded on Lux.

"Great. Now look what you've done!"

"I didn't do anything!"

"Did you really have to mention Kit?"

"Well, somebody had to! And come on, you all admit it. You guys have been wondering about them too."

No one replied in the guilty silence that followed.

"Come on," Phoenix said after a few moments. "We should go after her."

James ushered Snow onto his back again before following the others out onto the street. After a few more moments of explosive shouting, Honey banished Lux from the group. He threw his hands into the air and walked away by himself, grumbling about Honey, E, and all women in general. Phoenix mumbled that he searched best when he was alone before running on ahead. Honey and Blood Crow joined James and Snow as they made their way down the street.

"Hey," Honey said, looking all around. "Where's the fawn?"

She and Blood Crow fell into a solemn conversation. Snow's arms slowly tightened around James's neck.

"What's wrong?" he asked, knowing this to be a sign of anxiety rising within her.

She laughed. "You read minds better than me now, James."

He smiled. "Did you want to talk about it?"

"It's just Z. As usual."

"We don't know that he's been caught yet."

"I know. But whenever I think of 'what if,' I start imagining him being dragged back to the Tower. And then I think of the Tower and everything that place has put us through." She squirmed up higher on his back.

"It's really bad in there, isn't it?" he said as he adjusted his grip on her.

"It is. I guess it's kind of ironic, though. It's only because the Tower is so bad that Z and I were able to become friends. He really didn't like me at first."

"Really? Why?"

"He and my predecessor were really close, and he was not happy with someone new swooping in and taking the old Twelve's place without so much as a memorial service. He knew it wasn't my fault, but still. Poor Z. He was so young when they brought him in, and the Twelfth was one of the few who treated him kindly. Almost everyone else used to bully him, especially the Bodyguards. They even named him Zilch just to remind him that they saw him as nothing. They used to beat him up a lot too. That's actually the main reason he ended up finding all those passageways in the Tower. He needed to find ways to avoid everyone or escape from them if they were hunting him down for fun. It wasn't until I defended him from two of the Bodyguards that a lot of them finally started leaving him alone."

"You defended him from Bodyguards?" said James, his tone wavering mid-sentence as he tried to hide his surprise. He didn't want to offend her, but Snow couldn't even aim a knife properly with the way her eyes were. He couldn't imagine her fighting off two Bodyguards on her own. "How did you do that?" he asked.

She hesitated then said in a quiet voice that betrayed both shame and pride, "I tricked them. I waited until I knew that they were standing in a corner. Then I kind of leapt for them and clung on to them and read them. They didn't dare touch Z after that. It ... it was a dirty trick. I'll admit it. But I've had to learn that sometimes, that's what it comes down to."

She sighed and wrung her fists.

"If only I could see. Then both Z and I wouldn't have to deal with the Bodyguards or the Shamans or any of it. We could just leave the Tower and join you guys and help you out on your rescue missions. I wouldn't have to burden you like this either. I know it's not easy carrying me around everywhere."

"You're not a burden," he said quickly.

It was a lie, of course. Or half a lie. He really didn't mind helping her and enjoyed many of the intimate conversations carrying her had made possible. But he had to admit that carrying her slowed him down significantly and made him more vulnerable to attacks. He'd managed to carry her all the way to the Keep because the group had strived to stay safe and reach the Keep as quickly as possible, but he couldn't imagine carrying her like this once they began embarking on rescue missions again. As much as he didn't want to part with her, he knew that, eventually, she would have to return to the Tower.

She chuckled. "Thanks for saying I'm not a burden, even though it's not true. It's kind of you, James. I'm glad to have a friend like you in the Flowering. I'm glad the Last chose someone with compassion to pass his powers on to. It's a relief to be going into battle against the Calf with a good guy like you."

Unsure of how to reply to such a compliment, James simply chuckled as well. If he was honest with himself, though, Snow's words weighed down on him as much as they touched him. He still didn't know why the Last had chosen him to help defeat the Calf. Snow was the Twelfth Shaman, but he was just a normal human. Had he really been chosen to inherit the Last's powers, or had it all just been a fluke? Shouldn't all of his powers have gone to Snow? Or if the Last had really wanted to split his powers, shouldn't he have chosen E instead? She was ten times the fighter that he was and the Last's direct descendant too. What could he possibly do that she couldn't do on her own? His focus returned to Snow as she squirmed.

"You know," she said, "as angry as I am with the Third for hunting us, I have to admit I understand where he's coming from. If we had our sight, we'd be free." She hesitated then said slowly, "James, you don't think there's a way to keep the golden eye, do you?"

He flinched.

"I know we have to take it out of the Calf," she added hastily. "But that doesn't mean that we have to destroy the eye once we have it, right? Maybe we can keep it and restore the Shamans' sight."

Uneasiness made him cock his head from one side to another. "I don't know, Snow. I mean, I want you to have your sight too. Trust me, I really do. I don't want you to go back to the Tower. But the Beast was born because humans got greedy, and the Shamans were the ones who made it possible for all that greediness to grow the way that it did. They only stopped because they lost their sight and were confined to the Tower. If they could see again, well, I mean, I'd trust you with your sight and your powers, but I'm not so sure about the others or even the Twelfth who would come after you. I'm not so sure that history wouldn't repeat itself. I mean, just look at the Market."

She inched up higher on his back. Denial and acceptance were warring within her, he was sure of it.

"What if," she said, "what if I could get just my sight back, then? Just me? Like you said, I would never abuse any powers I had. What if there was a way to get back my sight and then before I die, lock it away somehow?"

"Snow," he said, shaking his head. He hated to kill her hopes like this, but this wasn't even a hope. It was a pipe dream. A desperate and unhealthy wish. "Snow, even if there was a way to do that, I don't think it would be a good idea. And I think you know that deep down too."

"There!" Blood Crow said, pointing at a window high above them.

James glimpsed E's back before she disappeared from view. They rushed into the building and up several flights of metal stairs before emerging at the far end of a long room. Identical, rounded strips of fiery light spilled in through tall, arched windows embedded along the length of the right wall. Numerous water fountains, each carved out of an enormous lump of rough rock, stood throughout the room and filled the space with the sound of flowing water. Endless fathoms lay beneath each rippling surface. Underwater lights revealed black sharks, colorful koi, and glinting schools of fish swimming within the fountains' depths. Blood Crow pointed toward the middle of the room.

It was E. She was seated on the ledge of a fountain with her back toward them. She had abandoned her socks and boots on the floor. She dragged her calves back and forth through the water as she continued staring into the fountain's depths. Phoenix stepped into the light a few yards away from her.

Honey slapped her hand over James's mouth before he could call out to them. Blood Crow threw her hand over Snow's mouth as well. They pulled and shoved James behind a fountain then forced him to crouch down with them.

"What are you doing?" he whispered as he pried off Honey's hand.

"Don't interrupt their moment," she hissed.

"Yeah! Give Phoenix a chance," said Blood Crow.

Snow's arms tensed.

"Sh-Shouldn't we leave the room or something, then?" he asked out of concern for Snow.

"Are you crazy?" Honey and Blood Crow said in unison.

They gripped him and forced him to scurry from fountain to fountain with them before settling within listening distance of E and Phoenix. They peered over the ledge of the fountain. He rolled his eyes and cursed the curiosity of women before peering over the ledge too.

"E," Phoenix said.

She stared at him as he walked toward her.

"What are you doing here?" she asked.

"I wanted to make sure you were all right," he said. He stopped a few feet away from her, clearly wary of making her uncomfortable with proximity.

"Why?"

"Why? Because! You looked distressed."

"I'm fine," she said, dropping her gaze back into the water.

He took another step toward her but remained silent. Honey squinted as she leaned forward with palpable curiosity.

"You want some popcorn too?" James hissed.

She glared at him.

Phoenix sighed, nodded to himself, then walked up to E. "Look, I'm not trying to pry, but if you're worried about Kit, you shouldn't be. We'll be back in the City soon. We'll probably have some time before the Beast returns, so maybe a few of us can try rescuing him and Zilch."

"*Oppa* doesn't need rescuing."

"What?"

"*Oppa* doesn't need rescuing," E repeated in a weary voice.

"And by '*Oppa*,' I'm assuming you mean Kit."

"Sorry," she mumbled as she rubbed her eyes. "*Oppa* is an honorific in Korean. A title or a name or whatever you want to call it. It's what you're supposed to call any guy who's older than you by a year or more. And, well, it can also be used as a term of endearment. But anyway," she said, shaking her head. "He's the strongest man I've ever met and one of the sharpest. If anything, he might end up rescuing us again when we go looking for Zilch. But all that is beside the point. We need to stay focused on the Beast right now. We need to kill it. Otherwise, everyone will be doomed. I'm sure Kit *Oppa* is fine. Or, at least, I hope he is."

"E," Phoenix said. "E, if you need to talk about it, I can listen. The worst thing you can do right now is bottle up something that's upsetting you."

"I'm fine. Besides, what does it matter?"

"Oh, come on. You know it matters. We've talked so much over the past few nights. If you need to talk about something that's on your mind, I can listen. Let me be a good friend for you like you've been for me."

Confusion twitched on his face as she scoffed in response.

"Go be a good friend to someone else!" she said. "Go be a good friend to Snow. She's the one who's your girlfriend."

"What?"

James's stomach dropped. Honey and Blood Crow looked at Snow. Her arms grew rigid around his neck.

"I said, go be a good friend to Snow. She's your girlfriend, not me. Just go. I'll be fine."

"What do you mean 'she's your girlfriend?' She's not my girlfriend."

Phoenix jumped as E smacked her hand down on the fountain's edge. He backed away from her as she swung her legs out of the water. Her wet feet slapped onto the cement floor.

"Don't you play dumb with me!" she said, advancing toward him.

"I-I'm not playing dumb!"

"Yes, you are. You are! Don't just stand there and pretend like there's nothing going on between you two. What do you take me for?"

He gaped.

"I've been two-timed enough, and I know what it feels like, so don't you go playing that game with me! Flirting with her all the time, and now you have the gull to come here and be a friend to me? In the dark? Alone? And here I thought you were a good man."

She spun around and began walking away from him.

"No, wait!" He lunged with an outstretched hand then leapt back as she swiped at him with her dagger. "What do you mean flirting?"

"What do you think I mean flirting? Flirting. Talking. Liking each other. Call it what you want!"

"She's just a friend!"

"A friend? Oh, yeah, I'm sure. A friend who smiles every time you talk to her. A friend who blushes every time you say something nice. A friend you're always defending and looking out for. Yeah, sure. Friends. Just friends. It's all just business as usual!"

He stared at her, open-mouthed. "I...."

She walked away again.

"No! E–"

He dodged as she swiped at him with her dagger again. She cursed, flung the blade aside, and created a machete. He grunted as he parried her blow with the sword that appeared in his hand.

"I don't like her that way!" he shouted.

"How dare you come into my crew and start yo-yoing girls around! How dare you! Get out! Get out now!" she raged. She swung her machete around wildly.

"E!" he said, blocking each of her blows. "E. E, stop!"

He swung his sword in a circle and yanked out her machete from her grip. Her blade spun through the air then fell into a fountain with a splash. James's jaw dropped as did Honey's and Blood Crow's.

"E! Just calm down and listen to me," Phoenix pleaded as another machete appeared in her hand.

She lifted her blade. He flung aside his sword and raised his hands in surrender. Her blow stopped a millimeter away from his neck. She glared at him.

"I've always thought of her as a sister. A sister! I didn't know that ... I didn't know that she...."

Snow's breaths, though measured, now held a trace of a quiver. Phoenix rubbed his forehead then smeared his hand over his face.

"I'm a moron," he said.

E's blade faltered then slowly drifted down to her side. Her grip on the hilt loosened. Phoenix turned and walked away.

"Where are you going?" she said.

"I need to clarify things with Snow!"

Honey, James, and Blood Crow ducked behind the fountain.

"Oh, no! What do we do?" Honey squealed.

"Don't ask me," James snapped. "You're the one who wanted to eavesdrop."

They spun around at the sight of Phoenix. He did a double take.

"You guys! What are you doing here?"

He tensed as his eyes found Snow. E ran up to him. She stared at Snow too as she came to a stop at his side.

"Snow," said Phoenix. "How long have you been there?"

Her arms loosened around James's neck. "I heard everything, Phoenix," she said. "And, well, it is what it is."

Pity twisted James's heart as he heard a sad smile in her voice.

"I am so sorry," Phoenix said. "It was totally moronic of me, Snow."

"It's fine. It's really fine."

Again, that sad smile.

"I'm just glad I know now," Snow continued. "And it's not like I was really expecting anything anyway. And it never would have worked out. I need to go back to the Tower, and you're part of this crew now. Which I'm really happy about, by the way! I remember what you told me before, about how you gave up on finding a good crew because you got so sick of running into bad ones. I'm happy you don't have to Roam anymore and that you're able to trust some humans again. So it's fine. Please, don't worry about it."

Blood Crow and Honey stared at the ground. Phoenix continued staring at Snow. E stared at Phoenix. James tried to stare at anything but Phoenix as he hitched up Snow on his back and slowly stood up. Honey and Blood Crow followed his lead and stood up as well.

Blood Crow cleared her throat. Throwing her arm around Honey's shoulders, she steered her out of the room and down the stairs. E's eyes darted from side to side. She glanced at Snow again then walked back toward the fountain on which she had been sitting. James followed her, barely aware of what he was doing. The supreme awkwardness of the situation had wiped his mind clear of everything except for a vague desire to get Snow away from Phoenix as quickly as possible. He stopped in front of E as she picked up one of her boots. She paused.

"Snow. I'm sorry," she said.

Snow shifted toward the sound of her voice. James could feel Phoenix still staring at them. Why couldn't he just go away?

"It's fine," Snow said. "It's ... let's just ... if we can just start searching for Z as soon as we get back to the City–"

E threw down her boot. Snow flinched as the shoe hit the floor.

"Snow," James said, trying to insinuate with his tone that she should shut up.

"We have been through this enough times," E growled.

"B-But it's like Phoenix said! We might have some time once we get there. And we made a deal. We made a deal that if I got us out of No Man's Land, we would go and rescue Z."

"We made no deal. Stop lying to me!"

Snow's breath quickened. E continued glaring at her then sighed. She closed her eyes as she tilted her head back. She gritted her teeth as if to hold back a torrent of angry words. James winced, expecting her to explode at any moment. Instead, her machete clattered onto the floor, and she sank down onto the ground. With her eyes still closed, she threw her back against the fountain.

"E. E, are you all right?" James asked.

He signaled for Phoenix to stay back as he made to approach. E suddenly looked so tired, so much so that James knew that if she were to open her eyes, he wouldn't see the fire of determination that always burned within them. But that was impossible. This was E. That fire could never go out. At least, not completely.

"Just leave me alone," she murmured.

He didn't know what to do. Maybe it would be best to leave her alone. Phoenix had failed to get her to open up, and instinct told him that his luck wouldn't be much better. Maybe, in this moment at least, solitude really was the best thing for her. And she really did look like she wanted to be alone.

He turned to leave.

"No!" Snow cried out. "No, James. I can't leave like this. If I lose Z, I lose everyone I love in the Flowering. You have your crew, but I only have the Tower! I need to know when we're going to rescue him. I can't stand this anymore!"

"Shut up," E said. "Shut up. Shut up!"

Her bare feet slapped against the floor again as she jumped up. Snow recoiled on James's back.

"Shut up, and stop being so selfish! We're going to rescue him eventually. What more do you want? And stop acting like Zilch might have been the only one who was captured. He's not the only one who risked everything. Kit *Oppa*–"

She snapped her mouth shut, looking frightened, angry, and sorrowful all at once. Snow began to shake. For a moment, James feared that she might burst into tears. Then he felt something build within her like steam in an engine. Her breaths grew deep and steady. E's palms and feet slapped against the floor as she sat down again. With a sigh, she closed her eyes once more.

"Let's get out of the Keep first and see what the wolves say once we get out," she mumbled. "We'll rescue Zilch as soon as we can, but we need to stay focused on the Beast. There's just too much at stake. We can't let personal feelings get involved."

James knew that the conversation was over. Whether Snow protested or not, he needed to get her, Phoenix, and himself out of this room and leave E alone. He signaled for Phoenix to go then bent his knees and leaned forward to hitch Snow up on his back.

Snow heaved her weight upon him.

He teetered, surprised by the sudden force. Snow's words from earlier in the night echoed through his mind: "It ... it was a dirty trick. I'll admit it. But I've had to learn that sometimes, that's what it comes down to."

He saw Snow reach out her hand and realized what she was about to do. E opened her eyes. He flung out his hand to stop Snow as he fell forward. Their hands touched E in unison.

The room disappeared.

James found himself next to E, watching her, both himself yet not himself, a bystander holding hands with Snow, an all-seeing eye connected to E's every thought and emotion.

He joined Snow as she began reading E's memories.

# CHAPTER 9

# E

E stood alone, a girl too old to be a child and too young to be a teen. She jumped as her mother slapped her father across the face.

"*Do you really want to see me kill myself?*" her mother shrieked in Korean.

Howling and crying, her mother pinned her father against the side of the doorframe. She kicked him, punched him, slapped him, then kicked him some more. Her father took the blows with an empty expression that gazed past the floor and into a place only he could see. The other woman at the door continued tapping her foot before expelling a sigh of impatience. She gripped E's father by the arm, pulled him across the threshold, and began leading him toward a parked car. He followed like a dog on a leash. Her mother continued to scream.

E took one step back then another. Her back hit the wall. She slid down onto the floor. Her unblinking gaze strayed away from her wailing mother to her own hands clenched around her arms. She released her white grip, slid one hand onto her shoulder, the other over her ribcage, and cradled herself.

Something seemed to skip like a record. But not under a faulty needle as when Snow had read James. This time, the needle glided and pinpointed the next memory.

Terror seized E's thin body as her father stormed toward her. The instinct to flee shot through her as he pounded on the screen door. He screamed and spit like a rabid animal. He accused her of fault and denied any of his own.

Anger cracked open within her. Sparks glowed then raged into a fire that purged her of all fear. She marched forward, slammed her fists onto the screen door, and shrieked back into her father's face.

The record skipped.

"*What was that sound?*" her mother said.

Deadly silence filled the kitchen as her mother's eyes darted from E's trembling hands to the broken glass on the floor to E's wide eyes.

"*You little bitch! How many times do I have to tell you to hold on to things tighter?*"

"It's just glass, *Mom*," E pleaded.

"*What? 'Just glass.' Do you know how many hours I have to work every night? If it's 'just glass,' you go out and work, and you go out and earn money for all the things you've broken! You're just like your father. Always breaking things. Always being so clumsy!*"

The embers of rage stirred in E's heart, slowly eating away at her fear.

"Don't say that I'm like Dad," she growled.

"*You little! Are you really going to speak to your mother like that? You disrespectful, little–*"

She smacked E across the head, first with her palm then with the back of her hand. She stormed out of the kitchen. E stood still as the remnants of the blows pulsed across her skin. Several minutes passed before she knelt down to pick up the broken pieces of glass. Her thoughts strayed away from her mother and wandered through a numb fog of resignation before finding an image of her father.

He didn't know that she'd been accepted into one of the best universities in the state and on full scholarship, no less. Instead of embracing her with tears in his eyes and bragging to all his friends about her, he was probably sprawled out in a random gutter somewhere, drunk and without a single thought about her or anyone else.

She drew a deep breath and smoothed her expression into one of dignified stoicism even as tears rolled down her cheeks. She hated her father, but she also hated herself for wishing that he were here. She hated herself for wanting a father.

The record skipped.

Smells of vomit, cigarettes, and instant ramen hit E as the door creaked open. She grimaced then sighed. She already regretted coming back to visit her mother for spring break. Now she regretted venturing out to see her father too. When would she learn?

She waded past cigarette butts and crushed cans and found him lying on his side on the floor. She sighed once again and shook her head. At least she didn't have to worry about him choking to death on his own vomit.

"*Dad*," she said, shaking him gently. "*Dad*."

A four o'clock shadow and crusted eyes appeared as he turned his head toward her. "*Oh, Meehae. You're here.*"

She helped him to sit up. He rubbed his eyes then his nose and mouth. The familiar stench of stale alcohol floated out from between his cracked lips as he sighed.

"*Meehae. When did you come back?*"

"*On Saturday.*"

He gave his head a sharp shake then sighed again. He stared at her.

"*What is it, Dad?*" said E. She shrank away from his gaze despite herself.

"*You've grown so much. Jeez, you really have grown. My daughter's grown up into a young lady. A beautiful young lady.*"

E swallowed. She didn't know why his nonsense still made her emotional after all these years. He always babbled like this when he was hungover. She lowered her gaze. Her eyes were dry. It was a good thing she had forgotten how to cry long ago. She conjured up soothing words as she helped her father to stand up.

The record skipped.

She gripped the pew in front of her. Her ears were raw from the sounds of sobbing and wailing. Her father's portrait stood behind his ashes, surrounded by white lilies.

He was an idiot. A complete and utter idiot! Driving in the rain at night. He was hardly sober even in broad daylight. What had he died for? For what? To give her a Christmas present? She couldn't even wear earrings! It was so typical of him. So typical! Always ruining everything! She was graduating college next semester, and now, he wouldn't even be there for that. He had never been there for anything in her entire life, but now she couldn't even hope that he would be. He'd taken what little she had clung on to, even in his last moments!

For the first time in years, tears welled up in E's eyes. A pained, weak sound crept out of her mouth before growing into a howl. Her mother clasped her against her chest. E sobbed into her shoulder. A dull realization floated through her foggy mind. Her mother's health had deteriorated too much. She barely managed to work part-time with her body the way that it was, and now, with her father gone, there was no one to give her mother money, no one to provide for her. E's dream of going to grad school was now only that. A dream. When the coming semester ended, she would have to find work to help her mother.

The record skipped.

She gasped as if she had broken through an ocean's surface. Wind rushed through yellow bamboo leaves. Her shaking hands fumbled over her naked body and bare scalp. Steam rose from her as if she were a fallen star. Where was she? What was happening to her?

She gasped again as a voice approached. She curled up and covered her chest with her arms. A young man stepped into the clearing ... the most handsome man she had ever seen....

The annoyance wrinkling his face melted away as his eyes locked with hers. A short exhale escaped him as he took a step back.

Even in her fear and confusion, she felt something white-hot spreading throughout her chest. It ensnared her heart and threatened to still its fierce pounding. There was something about this boy, and it wasn't just his looks. She could see his soul. It was bright and beautiful and terrifying. A thunderstorm crackling with fierce lightning.

"What ... what's your name?" he said.

She curled up tighter. "I-I'm Mee-ee ... Meehae. Meehae Kim. Please. Who are you? Where am I? What's going on?"

Her body began to shake uncontrollably.

"Whoa, whoa, whoa."

He approached her and knelt down with his hands raised in surrender. He extended an open palm. She recoiled as clothes appeared.

"It's okay. It's all right. You don't have to be afraid. You can join our crew. We'll take care of you. And I know I just asked you for your name, but that was a mistake, that was my bad. I shouldn't have...." He shook his head. "Just so you know, you shouldn't tell anyone else your real name from now on. Identity is pretty sensitive around here. Though it's kind of a shame." A crooked grin slowly lifted a corner of his mouth. "You have a nice name. *'Mee' for 'beautiful' and 'hae' for sea, right?*" he said in Korean.

"Kit!" a voice called. "Kit, where are you?"

"Daisy! Daisy, over here! I found a newborn."

"What? Whoa!" A young woman with short, dirty-blond hair reeled back as she stepped into the clearing. "It really is a newborn!"

"Yup. She is, indeed," he said.

She found herself falling into his soft, black gaze.

Daisy sniffed and cleared her throat. "So, what's your name?" she said, crossing her arms and glaring.

"Just call her E," he said, interjecting before E could respond. "And you can call me Kit, by the way. It's nice to meet you, E. *Welcome to the Flowering*."

The record skipped.

She stood at the edge of an expansive plateau, gazing at the giant full moon. The outlines of the Tower and the Market stood within the blue veil of moonlight.

She hoped tonight would be the night that the crew would finally make it all the way across No Man's Land. The last two Runners their leader had insisted on hiring had failed to Run the crew successfully. Of course, they could have avoided all the trouble had they simply listened to Kit. Kit had recognized Runners' attempts to con the crew even before the Runners had finished planning their ploys, and he'd found exits back to No Man's Land almost as well as he fought and healed.

E's gaze reverted inwards and focused on the first night she'd seen him battle a citizen. Eyes burning, he had sliced through the beast and saved her before the monster had had a chance to sink its claws into her. That night had been the first of many during which he had rescued her. She would have lost hours of time by now, maybe even a fatal amount, if it hadn't been for him.

"E, are you ready?" said Kit, jogging over to her.

"*Yeah, Oppa. Sorry.* I got distracted. The City is beautiful, just like you said it'd be."

"Yeah? Well, I don't know. There are other things that are more beautiful."

Her heart fluttered as he smiled at her.

"Come on. Enough wasting time. I want you to train harder. No more getting your watch pierced," he said, leading her away from the cliff.

"Yeah. And thanks again for saving me last night. I completely froze, and then my arm broke...." She sighed, disappointed in herself. "I wish I could heal as fast as you. That way you wouldn't have to save me so often."

He slowed to a stop and fixed a long, hard stare on her. His face creased with contemplation.

"W-What is it?" she said.

He glanced over at the crew sitting a few yards away then scanned their surroundings. He walked her back to the edge of the plateau.

"I've never told anyone this before, so I'm going to have to ask you to keep this to yourself too. But, well, I guess today's lesson can be about healing! So, the key to healing is this. It's all in the emotion."

"Emotion? What do you mean?"

"A lot of people think that healing is kind of like creating. You focus on it, you think about it, and it happens. But that's dumb. It's different. I mean, the focus definitely helps, but with healing, the more you feel the pain and the more you feel what the pain makes you feel, the faster you heal. I know it sounds kind of loose and crazy. But it works. Or at least it works better than just thinking about it and hoping for the best. But yeah, the key is emotion. And the best emotion is anger. Anger always works."

E's eyes swiveled from side to side as she digested the information. She never would have guessed that emotions could play such a powerful role. Sure, her healing seemed to speed up a little whenever she felt an overwhelming sense of desperation, but even then, she never would have thought to harness her emotions to push her healing even further. Nor would she have thought to try out different emotions to see which one worked best. It was a genius technique born from a totally out-of-the-box kind of thinking, and she was sure that few, if any, other humans knew about it. What a privilege it was, then, for her to know. And what a privilege it was to hold so much of Kit's trust. He never would have revealed his secret to her if he didn't trust her to keep her silence. He only ever grinned and shrugged whenever others asked him about his healing abilities. She swore to herself that she would take his secret to the grave.

"Thanks, *Oppa*," she said. "Thanks for telling me. But how did you figure all of this out? It's kind of genius."

Kit smirked. "Well, I have a lot of anger issues, so it came pretty naturally. And hey, you have a lot of anger issues too, so it'll probably be easy for you too," he said, laughing. "But still, you have a long way to go before you can catch up to me, so practice hard, okay?"

She nodded, determined to do so.

The record skipped.

"Harder! Faster!" he yelled.

She spun again and again, slashing with all her might.

"You're not doing it hard enough!"

For a split moment, she wanted to throw down the heavy swords in her hands and simply collapse. Then she saw the anger in Kit's eyes.

She ran and hurled herself into the air. She brought her swords down with a blow that forced him down onto one knee. She jumped up, kicked off his arm, and skidded across the dirt.

"Yes!" he cried. "Yes! E! That was–that's–that's my girl. That's my girl! Yes! Why didn't you tell me you were a gymnast?"

"H-How did you know? I mean, I took lessons up until we ran out of money but–"

"The way you moved, it's obvious! Man, forget the rest. What you lack in power, you more than make up for with moves like that. Use that agility, girl. Use it!"

His eyes burned with pride as he shook her by the shoulders. A small smile bloomed on E's face.

The record skipped.

He greeted her with a bright smile.

"E!" he said. "Finally. You want to–what's wrong?"

The words came tumbling out of her mouth. Her mother's mind was deteriorating, her depression worsening. Today, she had murmured a desire to take her own life along with E's so that mother and child could simply die together. E didn't know what to do. Daisy rolled her eyes as Kit led E away from the crew.

"It's all my fault," she said. She cursed herself for betraying tears. Before the funeral, she had been so skilled at holding them back. Why did she have to slide back into this damn, weak habit in front of Kit? "I'm not taking care of her enough. I killed my father, and now I'm going to kill my mother too!"

"Whoa," said Kit. He shushed her as he wrapped her in his arms. "Hey, now. Calm down. Let's not say things like that."

She buried her face in his chest and wept as he cradled her gently from side to side. When she had exhausted herself, she apologized for staining his clothes with her tears. He only shook his head and grumbled something about her mother. She couldn't tell if he looked more angry or upset.

The record skipped.

"Yup. Just remember that terror tactics work best if you're ever outnumbered by humans," said Kit as he led her down to the stream. "Personally, I prefer to rip their guts out. Can't fight if you can't heal enough, and there's no way you're going to heal enough if your guts are lying all over the floor. But it can be anything, really. Rip their eyes out, rip their heads off, throw their heads around. I don't care what it is, just do what you have to. I know that sounds brutal," he said, catching the wide-eyed look on E's face, "but I don't want you risking your safety. Humans aren't exactly known for fighting fair in the City, or anywhere in the Flowering, really."

As they reached the stream, they ventured deep into tall, swaying reeds that surrounded them like living walls.

"Damn Bodyguards," he muttered, looking around. "Like I said, they're supposed to be here guarding the storage units. Probably off screwing around with each other instead of doing their jobs."

"You don't think anyone's stolen anything from you, do you?" she asked. He'd told her how hard he had worked to gain the prized possessions he was about to show her.

"No, no. It'll be fine," he said, waving a hand. "Not a lot of humans know that the land here is stagnant. Actually, most humans don't know about here in general. A lot of Runners tend to miss it. But here we go."

He created a shovel and began digging. Plastic bags and boxes varying in size emerged from the earth. He removed a box of rich, red wood from a bag. He dusted off the lid then cleared his throat as he handed the box to E.

"This is ... uh," he said, scratching the side of his neck.

She waited with a small smile. He cleared his throat again then lifted his head high.

"I want you to have this. It's supposed to be priceless, and it's one of the best things I've got. Go ahead. Open it."

She pretended not to notice his furtive glances or the nervousness on his face as she opened the box. Her breath left her. Inside, lay a magnificent dagger. Large stones of deep blue studded the shining, silver hilt. The blade glinted like sunlight on the sea.

"It's quality silver, and the stones are made of lapis lazuli. I had a guy look it over before, and he said he'd never seen anything like it, especially the stones. They're supposed to be almost flawless. It obviously has some wear and tear on it but … do you like it?"

"It's beautiful," said E as her breath returned to her. "Thank you, *Oppa*. I love it."

His shoulders relaxed. "Of course you do," he said, crossing his arms and grinning.

He smiled as she continued examining the dagger. She ran a finger over the number twelve, which had been engraved onto the blade in Our Word. She lifted the dagger out of the box. Mischief glimmered in her eyes as she looked at Kit. She slid the tip of her finger across the dagger's edge and cut open her skin. Focusing on the pain and finding the fierce anger within, she healed her finger in an instant. She looked up at him again, hoping he would never regret all the nights he had spent training her.

His smile dissolved into a solemn stare. He stepped closer to her, hesitated, then raised his hand. She tried to suppress the shivers jittering throughout her body as his fingers traced her cheek then found the bottom of her chin.

"*Meehae*. I like you," he said. "Will you be my girl from now on, and my girl only?"

"Yes," she whispered. "Of course."

She continued to tremble as he leaned in and kissed her. Joy transformed into panic as his hand slipped under her clothes and caressed her bare skin.

"What's wrong?" he said, pulling away from her. "Do you not want me to?"

"No! I–"

"I won't do it if you don't like it," he said, pulling away further still.

"No, *Oppa*! I ... I like it."

He grinned then continued.

The pain began as a sharp jab then grew into a rough chafing. She tried to focus on his groans and the way he murmured her name as she held in the scream that would have told him to stop. Her body would heal, but she would never forgive herself if she ruined this moment.

She loved him.

The record skipped.

The Market's grandeur sparkled all around her. For the umpteenth time, she felt grateful to have Kit. He had put his foot down and ordered the whole crew, including their stubborn leader, to stop wasting so many nights on useless Runners and instead, leave everything to him. Within a week, he had scoped out a safe route to the City. A few jovial conversations and some well-placed bribes had then secured them an extended stay of a whole year in the Market. When she and Kit had severed call and response with the crew, the crew members had held back their objections in fear of angering Kit and losing their year-long stay.

"We'll find another crew later. We can definitely do better than them," he had told her before surprising her with keys to their new apartment.

Joy unfurled within E's heart. She was with the strongest, smartest man in the Flowering. How had she gotten so lucky?

"So, where do you want to go first?" he said. "Oh, hey! That restaurant is really good. *You want to eat together there?*"

She did a double take at the childlike happiness that had bloomed on his face. He flinched as if she'd caught him in an act of indecency. He erased his smile, set his shoulders back, and cleared his throat.

"*You want to eat together there?*" he said, his voice now gruff.

E stared then giggled then laughed.

"Why are you laughing?" he said, frowning.

"*You're cute, Oppa,*" she said, still laughing.

He rolled his eyes. She wiggled her way under his arm and peered up at him. A reluctant grin spread across his face. He planted a kiss on the side of her head.

"Kit!" someone shrieked.

They turned around to see Daisy pushing her way toward them.

"What is it?" he said. "You still worried about the deal? I told you, it's solid. You're good for a year."

Daisy swiped a knife at E's face. She dodged with ease then hurled a kick into Daisy's chest. With fists raised and stance spread wide, E contemplated her next move even as she wondered what had gotten into Daisy. She slowly lowered her fists as Kit stepped in front of her.

"What, exactly, do you think you're doing?" he asked Daisy in a low voice.

"You're really going to choose that thing over me?" Daisy shouted. "Just look at her! She's pathetic! Always going on and on about her screwed up family and–"

E jumped as Kit slammed his fist into Daisy's face. Teeth scattered across the cobblestone. Passersby hurried past. Bodyguards looked the other way.

"Did I ever say that we were together?" he yelled. "Did I ever tell you that I wanted you? Don't you ever come near me again! And if you raise so much as a finger against E, I'll cut you to pieces!"

Daisy lifted herself off the ground with quivering arms.

"Let's go," Kit told E.

She glanced back at Daisy as he wrapped his arm around her and led her deeper into the Market.

The record skipped.

People shouted and jumped out of the way as Kit raced the motorcycle down the street.

"Whoa! Off! Off!" he shouted.

He and E leapt from the motorcycle. The bike shot into the wall and burst into flames.

"E!" Kit said, scrambling off the ground and running to her. "E! *Are you....*"

A crooked grin slowly spread across his face as she rolled onto her back, laughing.

The record skipped.

They were panting, gasping, sweating, clutching. She wanted all of him, and she had all of him.

"*Meehae,*" he groaned. "*Meehae Kim!*"

The record skipped.

"Yup. When you wake up, just go to this website and pick one of the machetes they have." He handed her a piece of paper. "The bigger swords don't play to your strengths, and I don't care how good you are, there's only so much you can do with daggers and knives. I really think machetes will suit you best."

E unfolded the paper. "I like the black ones."

The record skipped.

Her face turned as red as the magnificent bouquet of silk roses he handed her. Passersby glanced with a jealous eye. She had never received flowers from a boy before.

He grinned at her before piercing his watch and vanishing from the street.

The record skipped.

She grinned down at him as he gripped her hips. He threw his head back and clenched his teeth.

The record skipped.

"I miss my brother," he whispered.

She slid her hand onto his shaking fist. He buried his face deeper into her lap and curled up tighter on the sheets. She stroked his hair as he continued to gasp and shudder. She let out a small sigh as tears dripped down her cheeks.

"We'll see our loved ones again someday, *Oppa*."

She felt so helpless, so useless. If only she could bear some of his pain. She couldn't even begin to imagine what it was like to lose a brother to suicide.

The record skipped.

She flinched as he slammed his fist down onto the table.

"He's giving everything away! And to bastards who didn't even do half the work that I did." He let out a long exhale and raked his fingers through his hair. He smirked. "That idiot doesn't even know that we've been staying this long in his own claim. So much for being watchful. Orion. He doesn't deserve to be Head Merchant."

The record skipped.

"Kit!" the Merchant screamed. "You backstabbing bastard!"

E's machete spun through the air like a boomerang and sliced off the Merchant's head. His body thudded onto the ground. Battle rage pumped savage satisfaction through her veins as she kicked another man in the head then plunged her blade down into his belly. She looked around at the puddles of blood and heaps of limbs before gazing at Kit. The brightness in his eyes seemed to illuminate the dark alleyway as he approached her. His fingers slowly traced her cheek then found her chin. He took her face into his hands and kissed her.

"When I take over the Market, you'll be my queen."

The record skipped.

"What?" said E.

"I entered you for a fight in the Arena. You haven't been practicing enough. You won't last in the City or out there in the planes at this rate. Only Bodyguards, Bits, and Merchants usually get to go into the Arena, but I pulled some strings for you."

The record skipped.

She stood over her opponent with the tip of her machete pointed down at his bloodied face.

"Pierce! Pierce! Pierce! Pierce!" the crowds chanted.

E looked at the referee, who nodded, then at Kit, who grinned at her from outside of the cage. All sorts of weapons already lay piled on the dais that bore her name, winnings from the bets he had placed on her. She did a double take as she spotted Daisy glaring down at her from the stands. She returned her focus to the young man at the end of her blade. He held up two shaking hands.

"Hurry up!" a man yelled, banging his fists on the cage.

Anger ignited within her. These Hedonists. They always scrounged for more time, yet they were always the first to demand that a fighter's watch be pierced. With her aim on the Hedonist's eye, she spun across the Arena floor then hurled the lapis lazuli dagger Kit had gifted her. The Hedonist screamed in pain as her aim proved true. The crowds roared with laughter.

E helped her battered opponent onto his feet before marching over to the Hedonist still twitching on the ground. Thrusting her arm through the fencing of the cage, she yanked him close, wrenched out her dagger, then stabbed him in the stomach for good measure. Someone cried out her name. She glared up at the stands as chants of "E" caught fire among them.

Her heart faltered.

Kit stood laughing and chatting with another woman.

A tap on her shoulder made her whirl around.

"Hey, thanks for that," her opponent said, still gasping for air as his wounds slowly sealed. "I owe you one."

"Don't mention it," she said, extending her hand. "E."

"Marcus," he said. He grasped her hand with a firm shake.

The record skipped.

Kit hurled his knuckles into the Merchant's mouth, drew him up, then pummeled him some more. The Merchant spit out blood and broke out in delirious laughter.

"Punch me all you want, Kit. You're just a failure with a cute girlfriend."

Kit threw his fist again as E shoved her machetes into the last man.

"No wonder Orion didn't promote you," the Merchant continued. "You don't have what it takes. Even when you go on your little stabbing sprees, you need your bitch over there to help you. I've seen her fight in the Arena, but what about you? I bet you wouldn't last a single–"

Kit thrust his dagger into the Merchant's throat then twisted slowly. The Merchant fell silent at last. E bounded over to Kit, expecting to share their usual kiss. Her smile faded as he pushed her aside and walked out of the alleyway.

The record skipped.

A girl hopped up and down in a futile attempt to grab a box of chocolates resting on a top shelf. E reached up on her tip-toes and retrieved the box for her. The girl's eyes widened. She began to shriek and clap and effuse praise about E's last win in the Arena, which she insisted had inspired women of all ages. She begged for E to sign the box. Kit shooed the girl away.

"You shouldn't be so nice to everyone. They'll take advantage of you. I thought I taught you better than that," he said.

Shame fell over E like a soft, gray shadow as Kit steered her out the door.

"When I become Head Merchant, you'll be right there next to me. If you're not as cut-throat as I am, we'll lose everything before we know it. Just ... stop doing all this nice stuff, okay?"

Her shame thickened into a suffocating, black cloud as she nodded. The confused apology that welled up in her mouth sank back down into her chest and congealed into something numb as Kit's eyes trailed after another woman walking down the street.

The record skipped.

"*Oppa*, where have you been going every night?"

"Just business stuff. You don't need to worry about it."

"But...."

"But what?"

"We haven't done anything together in a while. And I miss–"

"E!" he snapped, making her flinch. "I don't have time for this!"

She shrank beneath his burning eyes.

"I need to focus right now! Just ... stay here. We'll do something later."

She flinched again as he slammed the door shut.

The record skipped.

"That is some good beer," Marcus said as he brought the bottle back down onto the table.

"I don't know. I prefer the hard stuff," E said. She grinned before downing a shot of liquor.

"Oh, well, look at me. I'm Miss E, the undefeated champion of the Arena. I can handle anything!" Marcus said. He rolled his eyes and toasted her.

E chuckled. A group of Bits whooped and raised a fist to salute her as they passed by. She merely smiled then took another shot. Bits weren't so bad. Many of them, Marcus included, were forced to fight in the Arena as part of their training, or hazing, rather, as E often called it. They usually showed good sportsmanship, though sadly, that tended to change once they completed all their training and became Bodyguards.

"You're famous," said Marcus. He toasted her again then sighed. "I don't get it, E. I still don't understand why you're not signing up to be a Bodyguard. They'd kill to have you, and you'd climb the ranks without even trying."

"It's not my place," E murmured, thinking of Kit.

Marcus's gaze darted back and forth between her face and the table. E didn't like the pity she saw in his eyes.

"How's the girlfriend?" she asked.

"Well, way to awkwardly switch the conversation to another topic," he said with a laugh. "But we're doing fine, thank you. I'm, well, I'm actually going to propose to her next week."

"What? Marcus!" E said, setting down her glass. She hopped off of her stool and embraced him. "Congratulations!"

"Well, she hasn't said 'yes' yet, so let's not get too excited. But thanks. You know I owe a lot of it to you," he said, tipping his bottle toward her as she slid back onto her seat.

"What? What do you mean?"

He choked on his drink. "What do you think I mean?" he said as he coughed and thumped his chest. "You've helped me out so much! Sparing me that first time we fought in the Arena and all the training you've given me since then. When I become a Bodyguard, it'll be because of your help. I wouldn't have been able to get all the way here if it hadn't been for you."

E waved off his praises. Her smile drooped then disappeared.

"Aren't you scared?" she said.

"Of what?"

"Of enlisting as a Bodyguard. Being trapped in the City, maybe forever."

Marcus sighed and poured her another shot. She swirled the liquor around in her glass, wondering if she'd had too much to drink.

"Mm ... I'm a little scared," said Marcus. "But it'll be worth it. My life in Reality runs pretty tight on time, so even though being a Bodyguard might be tough, I won't have to worry about missing my eight hours a night. As troublesome as humans are, they'll never be as dangerous as citizens or the planes. Unless, you're Miss E, of course. Then we'd all have balls of steel and be wandering all over the Flowering on our own, ready to take it all!" he teased.

"Please. I wouldn't last two nights out there on my own."

She paused in her drinking as Kit strolled up the street. A group of laughing girls followed him like a cloud of buzzing flies. Marcus watched E as she took another shot. He bolted up from his seat and waved his arms at Kit.

"Hey, Kit!" he yelled.

Kit looked over at them and jerked up his chin in acknowledgement.

"Why don't you come over here? Have a drink with us?" Marcus shouted.

Kit laughed as he waved goodbye to the girls and jogged over to them.

"Sorry," he said, rubbing E's back. "Business. You guys drinking together again? How often do you guys meet up?" His eyes glinted even as he smiled.

E stood up and walked away.

"*Hey. Hey! Where are you going?*" He ran after her and grabbed her wrist. "*What's wrong? Why are you so annoyed? Is it because of the girls?*"

He smirked. "Don't be so paranoid. It was just some business and some laughs."

"Let go of me."

"E."

"Let go!"

She yelped as Kit tightened his grip. Marcus whipped out his gun and aimed at Kit's head. E stood still as Kit turned and glared at him. After a few endless moments, he smirked. Releasing his hold on her, he shook his head and walked away.

The record skipped.

Kit threw her onto the floor.

"I told you I'm trying to retake what's mine!" he roared. "What do I have to do? Give you a memo and ring a bell every time I want to go out and do something?"

"Stop yelling at me!" E raged back.

She yelped as he gripped her wrist. He dragged her to the bed then wrenched down on her arm and forced her to sit.

"Stop being so difficult," he told her. "And stop whining for more of my time. It's annoying."

She hated herself for trembling. She flinched as he slammed the door. Several moments passed in silence before she drew up her legs and hugged them. She bit down on her lower lip until pain turned into numbness. She held back the tears that gathered in her eyes.

The record skipped.

The Merchant towered over her, twice her size in both height and width. She glared at him as she wondered what dirty trick he would try to pull next. Like all Merchants, he fought without honor or integrity, but even in comparison to all the others she had battled, he was particularly brutish.

The Merchant's spear whisked past her ear as she dodged its tip. She backflipped across the floor. Daisy watched from her usual seat, her face alight with malicious hope. E didn't bother searching for Kit. He had stopped coming to her matches long ago.

The Merchant lunged. For a fraction of a moment, E knew she had made a mistake. Then a cry of despair burst from her throat as the Merchant's spear ripped into her stomach. The crowds erupted into a din of bloodthirsty ecstasy. Her machetes fell from her hands. She grasped the spear. She skidded and stumbled as the Merchant drove her across the floor and into the fencing of the cage. He grinned as he twisted his spear. Several spectators tossed up their hands in disappointment. The crowds joined the referee in a raucous countdown. Gasping and convulsing, E scanned the bulging eyes and spitting mouths surrounding her. They were all screaming at her as if she were a dog in its final fight. The memory of her father lying on the floor flashed across her mind. Would she soon be sprawled out like him?

*"My daughter's grown up into a young lady. A beautiful young lady,"* he had told her.

Fury ignited within her horror. The Arena, her father's death, her mother's insanity, Kit's wandering eyes. Everything consumed her in blinding, white anguish. As the Merchant twisted his spear once more, her rage spiraled into an all-consuming redness that erased logic, numbed pain, and fueled her will to fight, to win, to survive!

She lifted the machetes that appeared in her hands, brought down the blades, and broke the spear's shaft. The Merchant dodged the first machete she hurled at him. He stumbled as she threw the second into his guts. The crowds shouted and screamed. E dug her fingers into her belly. Her scream of pain transformed into a raw howl that thirsted for vengeance as she pulled out the head of the spear. Her flesh and nerves pleaded with her to stop, to rest. She focused on the anger within her pain, hating her body for daring to be weak. Gasps and cheers erupted in the stands as she sealed her wound with another cry of rage.

She dodged the Merchant's attack, ran, leapt up, and repelled her foot off the cage. New machetes formed in her hands as she twisted in the air. She cleaved the Merchant's arm from his shoulder. The crowds exploded, whooping, clapping, stomping, chanting her name. The Merchant's other arm soon thudded onto the floor. She didn't stop hacking away until she had cut him into countless pieces. She never noticed Kit watching from the shadows.

The record skipped.

Getting past the Doors had been as easy as she'd anticipated. Several of the Merchants had recognized her as "Kit's girl" and stepped aside without another word. She wasn't sure why she wanted to wander out into No Man's Land. A citizen could attack at any moment. The land could shift and tear her to pieces. But even with the risks, she'd found herself drawn to the grassy hills rippling under the winds. There was no Arena here. No eating. No smoking. No gambling, talking, laughing, or crying. Just the wilderness, the open sky, and survival. And yet, she couldn't help but think of him as the wind caressed her cheek. How long had it been since he'd wanted to spend more than a few moments with her? Would the moments in between grow longer and longer until he eventually left her?

Grass rustled. E drew the dagger Kit had given her, crouched down, and waited.

A citizen appeared at the top of the hill.

It was a blue wolf and an enormous one at that. He lifted his snout and sniffed the air. E lowered her dagger as he fixed his gaze on her. Even from a distance, she could see the recognition steeped within the wolf's golden eyes. This wolf knew her somehow. But there was something more. Something she, too, recognized and knew well. A few more moments passed before she realized that she saw pain in the creature's eyes. The wind traced her skin and tugged at her body as she continued to stare.

The wolf turned and disappeared over the hill.

The record skipped.

"Well, here we are at your humble abode once again, my lady," said Marcus.

He bowed to E with a flourish under the dim light of the gas lamps. She and the other Bits laughed at him as he stumbled. Someone shouted that he'd had too much to drink. After some scuffling, an explosive stream of vomit, and more laughter, the group departed. E waved them off then turned toward the apartment and opened the gate.

"Hey, E!"

"Hey," she said, stepping back out onto the street as Marcus ran up to her. "What's up?"

"Hey, uh … so I was thinking about it the other day. And I was even talking about it with my fiancé, believe it or not. And I don't know if it's my place to say it, but hey! I'm drunk, so why not?"

E chuckled and shook her head.

"See, the thing is … okay, so my fiancé and I are planning to have kids as soon as we get married, right? And in the process of that, we've been talking a lot about kids."

"Okay," E said, smiling as she tried to guess where this joke was going.

"And the thing is … ah, E. If you were my daughter or even my kid sister! I'd … I'd tell you to leave Kit."

Her smile slid off her face.

"I'm sorry. I know you love him. I see it. He sees it. We all see it! But as your friend, I just can't say it's all right. You're more than strong enough to make it out there as a Roamer. Or just find a new crew here in the Market. Find a new crew, and leave this place. You don't deserve to be trapped in the City forever or to be stuck in the Arena every night or to be treated the way Kit's always treating you. Just get out of here. Run away from all–"

Kit's fist slammed into Marcus's face and unhinged his jaw. Marcus collapsed onto the ground. Shock and horror wiped away E's ability to move, to think, as Kit positioned himself over Marcus's body like a lion readying to devour its prey. Across the street, an entourage of girls stared with their hands over their mouths. One broke away from the group.

"Kit, no! You'll get in trouble with the Shamans!" the girl shouted as she ran toward him.

"Wait," E said as the girl reached for his shoulder. "Don't–"

Kit's punch pulverized her face. Something cracked as the girl fell onto the ground. She remained face-down as her blood pooled on the street's black, polished tiles. Kit grabbed Marcus's collar. With his fist, he bashed his face into a pulp. He unsheathed his dagger and pumped the blade in and out of his chest.

"*Oppa. Oppa*, stop!" E screamed. She was terrified for Marcus's watch, his fiancé, their plans to get married, to have children. "Stop! Stop! Stop!"

Kit spun around, flung his knife aside, and gripped E by her shoulders. Her teeth chattered as he shook her.

"And you dare ask me what I've been doing every night?" he roared.

He gave her one last, dizzying shake before throwing her aside. She hit her head as she collided with the stone column of the gate.

"I'll kill you if you ever come near her again!" he roared at Marcus.

He spit on his broken face. The group of girls shrank away from him as he passed them. E placed a hand on the column as she tried to regain her balance. She sank onto her knees.

She couldn't stop her body from shaking.

The record skipped.

Waves of grass rippled in the wind as she walked alone through the hills. She had nowhere else to go, nowhere else she wanted to be. Ever since Kit's attack on Marcus, she and the Bits had reached a silent but mutual agreement to refrain from seeing each other. Their agreement didn't state when they'd all see each other again.

She stopped in front of a large cave and unsheathed her lapis lazuli dagger as footsteps padded across the dirt toward her. Golden eyes appeared within the dark. The wolf emerged, large and majestic. He stared at her dagger then leaned his snout forward and sniffed with his eyes half closed. She hesitated then sheathed her blade. Her heart thudded against her chest with rapt excitement as she stretched out her hand. His wet nose quivered against her fingertips. She jumped as he sneezed. He sat down, cocked his head to one side, and gazed at her.

Again, that recognition. Again, that pain that reflected her own. Her mouth parted in amazement as his face broke into a smile. He sprang forward and knocked her onto the ground. She yelped then laughed as he licked her face. Burying both hands in his soft fur, she pushed him aside. He laid down and twitched his tail. She suddenly realized that she hadn't laughed like this in many nights and many days. She paused then decided to try.

"*I'm E. What's your name?*"

She knew without a shred of doubt that he'd understood her, yet he remained silent. Maybe he wasn't capable of speech. Not all citizens were, after all. As she gazed into the wolf's eyes, red roses bloomed within her mind. She saw Kit handing her her first bouquet of flowers in the middle of the street. She remembered how she'd laughed and smiled so easily back then. Would such nights ever come back?

"*Bloom,*" she found herself saying. "*I'll call you Bloom. Is that all right?*"

A small, shaky smile formed on her face as he twitched his tail again. She stood up.

*"Can I come find you again tomorrow night, Bloom? Somewhere near the Doors?"*

She yelped again as he reared up onto his hind legs and slung his giant forearms on top of her shoulders. She laughed as he sniffed her black hair and licked her cheek.

The record skipped.

"I guess we're out of luck tonight, Bloom."

She'd had her doubts about these crazy rescue missions he always seemed so determined to set out on each night, but after two successful rescues, she'd realized that she much preferred using her battle skills for helping citizens than for entertaining bloodthirsty crowds in the Arena. The joy citizens expressed when she and Bloom freed them brought her an immense and inexplicable kind of satisfaction. They always seemed so happy to be liberated.

"If only I could be free too. Leave the Market. Wander the Flowering with you. I really hate the Arena and those humans," she told him.

The floor of dried branches crackled and crunched beneath Bloom's paws as he padded to a halt. He gazed at her.

"What is it?"

He doubled over. She jumped as he began choking and heaving labored breaths.

"Bloom? Bloom!" she cried as she grabbed his mane.

*"Ca ... ca...."*

She slowly released her grasp on his fur. He wasn't choking. He was speaking!

*"Call,"* he growled at last.

"*Call?*" Her breath caught in her chest as she realized what he was saying. "*Call and response? Bloom, are you saying we can do call and response?*"

He nodded.

A quivering laugh escaped from her as excitement flooded her and washed away all other thoughts and memories. This was it. Freedom. Freedom wasn't just an illusion, and it wasn't just for everybody else. She could have it too!

"*Hello,*" E said, jittering with adrenaline.

"*Hel ... lo,*" Bloom responded.

She released a short exhale. "Does this mean you're my anchor now?"

Bloom nodded. Twigs snapped as she sank down onto the ground. She could hardly believe it. With Bloom at her side, she was sure she could survive out in the planes. She was free of the Market, free of the Arena, free of....

"Wait. But what about my call and response with Kit *Oppa*? Do I have to break off call and response with him? It wouldn't matter with humans, but you're a citizen."

Bloom doubled up again. "*Hu ... mans ... first,*" he growled.

Her heart sank. Humans first. Her call and response with Bloom came secondary to hers with Kit. Regardless of her connection to Bloom or how far they wandered out into the planes, she would still wake up tomorrow night in the City at Kit's side. Of course, she could simply tell Kit "goodbye" and cut off call and response with him that way before fleeing the moonlight. But....

"I can't leave Kit *Oppa*, Bloom. I love him. And he's counting on me."

Bloom looked at her with pity in his eyes.

The record skipped.

"I don't want you wandering out there again," Kit said. "And stay away from that wolf. Hunters might be maniacs, but they're right about how dangerous citizens can be."

E lowered her eyes. Kit sighed.

"I'm saying this because I want to protect you," he said.

She remained silent. He sighed again, walked to the door, then stopped with one hand on the handle. He came back to her.

"*Here.*"

Her eyelids fluttered as he held out a paper envelope. She looked up to discover that blush had crept up his neck and into his face. Even his ears were red.

"Just ... burn it after you're done reading it!"

He rushed out of the room and slammed the door shut. E stared at the door then opened the envelope and unfolded a letter.

> Dear E,
>
> I've never written something like this before, so don't laugh if it ends up sounding dumb. First off, I wanted to apologize about what happened before with that Bit friend of yours. I haven't been able to stop thinking about it, and I shouldn't have done that to you. I snapped when I shouldn't have. I'm sorry. I'm really sorry.
>
> Second, I wanted to let you know that I may be a jerk, and I may be a flirt, but I'm not a cheater. I really have been away on business. I would never cheat on you, and I just wanted to put your mind at ease about that. I like talking to girls and whatnot, but even if I wanted to cheat, I wouldn't be able to get it up with someone other than you. My dick just dies!

But in all seriousness. None of the other girls have what you have, E. That fire in your eyes. The way you rain down vengeance. No other girl can do what you do. No other girl has ever made me feel the way you've made me feel. You're one of a kind. My warrior. My queen. You're my girl and mine alone.

It's been almost a year since I found you, and I've had the privilege of seeing you grow as a woman ever since. I've never really said this to you, but I'm sorry for everything you've had to deal with. Your father. Your mother. I wanted you to know that none of it is your fault. None of it. The things they've done to you are horrible, and I'm sincerely sorry that I forget everything you've gone through as often as I do.

It's crazy to me just how good you turned out, though. How caring you can be. How smart. How brave. How indestructible. And not just your fighting skills but your soul. Who you are right now is a testament to who you are on the inside and all that you've overcome, and I wish you'd give yourself more credit for that. You're worth so much more than what you give yourself credit for.

This past year has been crazy. For the both of us. But you should know that I've been happy ever since I found you. I'm grateful that we met. From the moment I saw you, I couldn't stop thinking about you. Every moment, even when we're arguing, has made me happy one way or another. And it's not just in the Flowering but in Reality too. Like I said, even when I want to turn to another girl, I can't. Not really.

Because no one has the fire that's in your eyes. The fire that only I can see. The fire that burns as bright as mine.

I love you, E. There. I said it! And you know I've never said that to any other girl before! But I do. You're my girl. And together, we'll take the Market. No one will stand a chance against us. They never do.

I want to meet you in Reality too, E, wherever you are. I want you with me in the day and not just in the night. I want you by my side now and always. Because you're my fire, my girl, my Meehae. And I'll love you forever. I swear it.

Your Oppa,
David Chunryong Kang

The record skipped.

They lay on red silk. His fingers grazed her arm as if she were made of delicate glass then traced her cheek before finding the bottom of her chin. His eyes were as black as space and as bright as the stars.

"I love you," said Kit.

She slid across the silk and nestled herself against his chest. He inhaled deeply as he wrapped his arms around her. He kissed her on the head then leaned his cheek against the spot he had kissed.

"I love you too," said E. "With all my heart."

He drew back slightly. A soft smile bloomed on his face. He pressed her palm against his chest and closed his fingers over hers.

"With all my heart," he said.

She closed her eyes as he kissed her deep and slow.

The record skipped.

She would make this quick. Bounding across the Arena, she flung herself into the air, twisting, turning, and slashing. The heads of her opponents rolled onto the floor. The crowds erupted once more. E tucked her machetes under her belt and waited for the doors of the cage to open. The number of times she'd had to fight in the Arena had steadily increased over the past few weeks, and true to her word, she hadn't left the moonlight to visit Bloom. As a result, something inside her had slowly started to strain to a breaking point. She wanted to leave the Arena as soon as possible so that she could ease whatever it was that was preparing to snap.

"*Round two!*" the announcer's voice boomed through the speakers.

"What?" E said, spinning around. "Plata, *what do you mean 'round two?*"

He covered the mic with his hand. "Kit *signed you up for three rounds total from now on. Sorry, E!*"

Three rounds total? The words seemed to rip through her like bullets. She looked around at the red-faced crowds then at her watch. Her time was almost up. The doors opened. Three women and three men stepped into the Arena. She backed away. It wasn't that she couldn't take them. She could, and she'd win too. But this was enough. She couldn't do this anymore. She wasn't just some dog to be put in a cage and ripped to shreds! Hadn't Kit himself told her that she was worth so much more than this? The crowds cheered as she ran forth.

"*Wait!*" Plata cried. "*The match hasn't started yet!*"

Anger and hatred burned bright within her as she brought down merciless slaughter. She sliced off the last head then threw a machete to jam the door.

She fled.

Daisy bolted up from her seat. "That's not fair! I paid for three rounds! Get her back! Get her back now!"

E slashed through the few humans foolish enough to stand in her way then sprinted into the streets. She pushed passersby aside and leapt over Merchants' carts. When she reached the Doors, she shoved past Merchants and ignored their shouts. Hope sprang up within her as she set her eyes upon the hills. Bloom sat there, waiting for her. Flinging aside her machete, she forced her aching, blood-splattered legs to run at full speed across the dirt and toward the Blue Border.

"E? E!"

She skidded to a halt and spun around to see Kit breaking away from a group of Merchants. She took a step back. Her body began to shake. She only had to take one more step to pass through the moonlight.

"What's going on? What happened?" Kit said.

He did a double take and skidded to a stop as he saw Bloom. Bloom's lips curled back as he bared his teeth. Kit's face slowly gnarled. A bright hatred began to glow in his eyes.

"There! She's over there!"

Kit turned around. Daisy appeared at the edge of the warehouse with a mob of Arena spectators behind her. He scanned them all with glinting eyes then smirked. His large, curved swords grew from his hands. He positioned himself in front of E and blocked her from the mob's view.

"I thought I told you to stay away!" he shouted at Daisy.

"Kit! You backstabbing bastard!" she yelled back.

"Yeah, yeah, yeah. Whine all you want! Either come here and fight me or go back to your gambling. There's nothing to see here!"

"She escaped from the Arena!"

"Well, good for her!" Kit yelled, much to E's surprise.

Daisy balled up her fists, shaking with stifled sobs. "Kit! How could you do this to me?"

"Get over it already!" he roared. "I never even liked you!"

E clutched at her chest as she began gasping for air. Flashes of memories were flooding her, drowning her, killing her. Kit stepping into the bamboo clearing, Daisy's teeth scattering across the cobblestone, the towering Merchant in the Arena, Marcus lying in a bloodied heap, a dagger gifted to her by the stream, his tight grip around her wrist, his fingers tracing her cheek, Bloom's golden eyes, the letter.

Suddenly, E understood. She loved Kit, and she loved him with all her heart. But the time had come to leave. She had to leave. It was over. It was all just a cycle on repeat. It would never really change.

"*Oppa.*"

"Not now!"

"*Oppa!*"

"I said not now!"

"Kit!" she shrieked.

"What?" he roared, spinning around.

The rage gripping his face slowly released its clutches as his eyes found the lapis lazuli dagger pressed against her watch hand. He stared at her as she stepped back and slid out of the moonlight.

"*Thank you,*" she said. "*And I'm sorry.*" Her heart shattered even as she spoke. "*Goodbye.*"

"No, wait–"

She saw Kit's heart break in two as she plunged the tip of her dagger through her watch.

The record skipped.

The full moon hung in the sky, giant and forlorn. Twelve eyes swayed on jagged, black branches above Bloom and E. She could barely make out the outline of the Market through her tears. She hoped that he would somehow hear her sobbing and come running to her. Bloom nuzzled her and licked away her tears. She threw her arms around him and continued to weep.

After several long moments filled with nothing but her sobbing, she raised the lapis lazuli dagger Kit had given to her so long ago. She brought the blade down into the arid ground. As she dug a hole among the tree's roots, she slowly regained her self control. With shaking hands, she piled dry dirt over the dagger. She pressed down on the last layer then stood up and turned her back to the City. White, cracked tiles stretched out into the horizon to kiss the dim sky. More tears fell from her eyes even as she wiped them away.

"Come on, Bloom. Let's find a Runner. It won't be easy, but I think I've learned enough tricks from *Oppa* to bribe them from talking about us."

The record skipped.

She slumped down in the pouring rain, unable to take another step forward. Pain sat on her chest like an anvil, suffocating her and slowly breaking her heart into pieces.

She wished he were here next to her.

Bloom licked her cheek then wrapped himself around her. His touch comforted her as Kit's arms once had. She grasped his wet coat and buried her face in his neck.

The record skipped.

E couldn't help but smile as Lux and Bloom gamboled through the tall, golden wheat. She had been terrified of inviting another human to join her and Bloom, but in the end, she hadn't been able to bring herself to abandon a newborn. Lux would have met a terrible fate if they hadn't taken him in, and even if another crew had miraculously come across him, she had not wanted this boy falling into the wrong hands as she had. He was vulnerable.

The sunlight warming the wheat seemed to dim as she thought of Kit's black eyes. She bowed her head as the words "I love you" echoed through her mind. Then she thought of how those eyes had strayed. She thought of the cheers and stomping of the Arena. Her memories injected anger into her heart, and she felt her pain numb, if only for a little while.

The record skipped.

"Please!" the girl cried. "If you really don't like me after a few weeks, just sever call and response and I'll Roam! But please. I can't stand being in that crew anymore. I can't be lonely for one more night. Not for one more night!"

E glared at her. Was it wrong to be suspicious of this girl because she had dirty-blond hair like Daisy? Lux and Bloom turned toward E with round, glistening eyes. She pushed away the memory of Kit stepping through the bamboo forest as Lux pleaded on Honey's behalf.

The record skipped.

E couldn't believe how little it took for James to give up. No matter how much she pushed him, he simply didn't show the will to fight, to win, to survive! He would die within the month at this rate. Swearing to herself that she wouldn't let that happen, she stabbed him in the side for what seemed like the thousandth time. She would never forgive herself if she let anything happen to her crew. They trusted her, and she would not let them down. She would not allow the Flowering to hurt them. The Flowering would not take them away from her!

The record skipped.

Crew Blue sat in a circle, shivering as seagulls cawed and ocean waves crashed. E wondered how she had become so cruel, so cold, so ruthless. So much so that James had felt compelled to sever call and response with the crew. Had she always been like this?

The record skipped then rewound then skipped again. Something was changing. A scream. Someone was screaming ... and pulling away....

E watched with wide eyes as Phoenix leapt from the monster's back. He soared through the air, his blades flashing like talons, his eyes blazing like the sun. He landed on the Desert's white floor. The monster fled from him as he stood ready to protect the crew.

The record skipped.

"It was only a matter of friendly conversation, so I'm uncertain where your concern is coming from," Phoenix told the Third.

Behind the fearless expression she wore, E was relieved that Phoenix was with them. His ever-calm demeanor as well as his battle skills and good heart helped soothe some of her fears. Was she foolish to start trusting him?

The record skipped.

Bloom, E, and Phoenix walked behind the rest of the group as they followed Terrain and Forest. An endless series of soccer fields stretched on before them beneath a sparkling night sky. She smiled as Bloom licked her arm. He had been careful to stay at her side ever since meeting Kit in the City, and she felt grateful for his concern. He understood how much her heart was hurting.

"You were saying about your mom's side of the family?" she said to Phoenix.

"Oh, yeah. Well, my mom's side is mainly French, Italian, and English. Oh, and German, I think," he said.

"I see. And your dad's side?"

"One hundred percent Chinese."

"Really? Never would have guessed."

"I'll take that as a compliment. Not that I'm ashamed of being Chinese. Or Asian!" he added hastily as E raised an eyebrow. "I-I'm proud of my heritage. It's just that I'm not a huge fan of my dad. I wouldn't want to look like him. I wouldn't want to be anything like him, actually. Looks, personality, all of it."

She stared at the shadow of bitterness that had fallen over his face.

"Why?" she asked.

"He's a workaholic. And a negligent husband, negligent father. My grandma's the one who raised me for the most part. My mom did as much as she could too while juggling everything. But my dad. Good ol' Dad."

He forced a smile that she didn't return. He lowered his gaze and said, "I'd rather die than be like him."

"Do you think you are?" she said.

"What?"

"Do you think you're like him?"

"I try not to be."

"That matters."

Phoenix lifted his eyebrows and twisted his mouth into another smile. He chuckled as he sighed.

"You shouldn't live chained to your father like that," she said. "You should do what you do because you want to and because you believe it's right, not because you're fighting against someone or even something all the time. Don't be more about what you're against than what you're for, if that makes sense."

She didn't know why it mattered so much to her to say this, but it did. Her focus latched onto Snow as she burst into laughter and continued chatting with James. Phoenix stared at her as well. E supposed Snow and Phoenix made a good match. They were both gentle, after all.

The record skipped.

"I'm a moron," Phoenix said.

She suddenly realized that he was the first real gentleman she had ever met. He turned and walked away from her.

"Where are you going?"

"I need to clarify things with Snow!"

The record skipped.

"I love you."

The record skipped.

"And if you raise so much as a finger against E, I'll cut you to pieces!"

The record skipped.

David Chunryong Kang

The record wobbled before skipping once more. The screaming grew louder. She was screaming. She was screaming, "No...."

Merchants' heads, limbs, and guts lay scattered across the warehouse floor. Zilch remained curled up on the ground, trembling but unharmed. Kit turned to face her. She gazed into the fire within his eyes, that unquenchable fire.

He stepped closer to her. They stood still for a moment, simply looking at one another. Then he tossed his blades onto the floor and slowly raised his hand. His fingers traced her cheek before finding the bottom of her chin.

"I was so.... The thought that you might be dead.... I regretted so much of what I did after you left. I sent men to find you, but they always came back empty-handed. I even stooped to asking Marcus if he had heard anything, and I nearly got fired in Reality because I was so.... But you're here now, just like before. And E. I still love you. You know I do. I promised you!"

Her heart dissolved within her chest.

"I love you. I should have told you more often. I should have told you every night. I'm ... I'm sorry. I'm sorry."

He hesitated for a brief moment before gathering her face into his hands and kissing her gently. Her body seized up. She warred with herself, trying to find the will–the strength–to push him away.

Then her machetes clattered onto the floor. Her hands slid onto his chest as she leaned in. His arms wrapped around her, protecting her and comforting her as they once had. And for a brief, black moment of bliss, she was home.

They broke apart slowly.

He kissed her on the forehead then wrapped her in his arms again. He leaned his cheek against her head.

"I know you have to go right now," he said, "but please … come back to me."

The record shattered.

"NO!"

E's scream pierced James's ears as she wrenched herself away from him and Snow. The three of them toppled onto the cold floor. James clutched his head as E's memories bombarded his mind in flashes of colors, expressions, gestures, and words.

"E? E!" Phoenix shouted. He ran toward them.

"Phoenix, no!" Snow yelled, thrusting out her arm.

For one wild moment, James thought that she was trying to stop Phoenix out of jealousy. Then he saw the tears in her eyes and the anguish on her face and knew that E's memories had horrified her just as much as they had horrified him.

"Just leave her alone!" Snow cried.

E stumbled away from them. The sun of the Keep threw its golden bloodlight over her, accentuating the panic on her face. She clutched at her chest, gasping for air just as she had the night she had told Kit goodbye. She gripped her head. Tears began dripping down from her bulging eyes.

"E," James said. "E."

She drew a shuddering breath then screamed. James rushed over to her, barely aware of the tears streaming down his own face. He wrapped her in his arms and refused to let go as she sobbed and tried to fight him off. After several moments of vicious struggling, she finally collapsed onto his chest. They sank down onto their knees together.

James didn't let go of her as she wailed. Nor did he let go of her as her wails gradually diminished into quivering sighs. He would hold her and comfort her forever if he had to.

E. Oh, E. Her body simply wouldn't stop shaking.

# CHAPTER 10

# MIDNIGHT

E lay cradled in James's arms. Her breathing had calmed now, though an occasional tear still slid down her cheeks. The peaceful cadence of the fountains' rushing waters clashed with the anger that had begun to seethe within him. He continued rocking her gently back and forth as he glared at the endless strips of red-gold light stretched against the wall.

Kit. That bastard. That bastard! The Arena. All those fights. E would have died ten times over had she been any other human. And he'd had the nerve to look at other girls. To cheat. After all she had done for him! She had stayed with him, fought for him, comforted him, and loved him even as he had used her, neglected her, endangered her, manhandled her, and even.... James wiped away fresh tears as images of Kit shoving himself into E by the stream replayed within his mind.

Why? Why hadn't she listened to Marcus sooner? Why had she stayed with Kit for so long? How could she have loved such a man and love him even still?

Red roses unfurled in James's mind. Kit stepped out of the bamboo forest and offered E clothes. He burned with pride as he taught her the ways of warriors. He slashed through a citizen that leapt toward her. He stood between her and the mob that Daisy had led to the Doors. He wrapped his arms around her as she wept. He took a blow to the neck that was meant for her. He handed her a letter.

Had Kit really loved E? Was he telling her the truth when he'd said that he loved her still? No. No, of course not. How could James even think that Kit could love her after seeing all the horrors he had put her through? He'd done so many terrible things to E!

But ... he had also protected her. And cared for her. And he'd gone out of his way to do so. He'd held her close and shown her parts of himself that he never, ever would have shown another human. And as horribly as Kit had treated her, James had to acknowledge that E had been different from the other girls. Kit's eyes had held a softness when looking at her, and James knew that when a man looked at a girl like that, it only meant one thing. He saw her as a woman. The only woman. The woman who dwelled within his heart.

James desperately wished it could all be clear-cut and simple. Kit had treated E terribly. Therefore, he didn't love her at all, and she should have left him without so much as a second glance. Anything outside of the box that this line of thinking created should have been illogical and foolish on E's part.

But James now saw that it wasn't that simple. Kit and E and all the memories they shared were a painful mix of terrible and wonderful bleeding into one another. There were no black or white lines that delineated where the bad started and the good ended. There was only a mass of nebulous gray. And as much as James wanted to deny it, a small part of him continued to whisper that Kit, with all his flaws, his lies, his pride. Kit had and still did love E.

It was love, but it wasn't love. It wasn't true love. It wasn't right love. But it was love. It was history. It was the past leaking into the present and coloring the future. And if love still remained, even as a shred of what it had once been, wasn't it a worthy and even noble pursuit on E's part to try and stay until the bitter end? To pursue that love even now?

But in the end, whether Kit loved E or not, James knew that it didn't matter. Love couldn't be the single, defining factor in their relationship. Not when it manifested itself in such a warped way. Because E was right. It would never really change. Kit would never really change. His actions would never align with the love he professed. She would be forced to live out nights and days that stretched on and on in suffering. She would never be able to live the life for which she was truly destined, the life of a leader, a protector, a friend. No matter how strong she was, serving each of Kit's selfish needs would either break her or cause her to fade into a ghost of herself over time. She could not survive on Kit's love alone. It was more complicated than that.

But E. Why hadn't she said anything? Why hadn't she ever told him or the others about any of this? He couldn't help but feel angry at her for her silence. She must have been dying on the inside when Kit had led the crew through the Market, and yet, she had borne it all for their sakes and for their safety.

Why? Why did she always have to do that? Why did she always have to push them out of danger and take the pain in their stead? She was always taking care of them! Just as she'd taken care of her crazy, ungrateful mother and her drunk, good-for-nothing father.

James hated himself for failing to ask more about her parents. But she'd simply told him that her mother was "difficult," that her father had died on Christmas Eve, and that she hadn't been able to go to grad school. She hadn't said anything at all about the pain and the messiness.

But then again, how could she have told him? How could she have explained any of this to anyone? James himself couldn't begin to articulate all the memories he'd just seen, so much so that if someone had asked him to describe E's life, he wouldn't have even known where to start. And even if E had somehow miraculously managed to tell him everything that had happened to her in perfect detail from start to finish, would he have understood? Or would he have simply listened and turned away?

He pressed E against his chest and continued rocking her back and forth as he admitted to himself the awful truth. He wouldn't have understood because he wouldn't have tried to understand. E could have spilled her heart out to him, but her words would have only penetrated so deep before falling away as a passing thought. Because what had happened to E hadn't happened to him, and because it hadn't happened to him, he wouldn't have felt a burning need to remedy all the pain within her. He would have been too busy with his own thoughts and his own life, and E would have been left utterly alone as she had always been. Her bouts of rage, what she had said about her parents, her behavior around Kit, all of it. James loved E like a sister, but he had never stopped to consider, even for a moment, what all the pieces added up to.

"James, Snow, I'm not leaving until someone explains to me what's going on!" Phoenix shouted.

James ignored him just as he had ignored all of his other attempts to get an answer out of them. It wasn't that he didn't understand Phoenix's concern. He just didn't care. The last thing E needed right now was Phoenix pestering them all with questions and making her relive everything. Plus, she had enough drama in her life with Kit. She didn't need Phoenix too!

"Phoenix. Please. Just leave," Snow said for what felt like the hundredth time. She was still sitting in front of the fountain where she and James had read E.

Phoenix shook his head in exasperation. His boots tapped across the cement floor as he began marching toward them. He looked angrier than James had ever seen him.

"Leave!" Snow shrieked.

He stopped.

"Leave! Leave! Leave!"

She threw her hands over her ears then dug her fingers into her hair. After a moment of struggling, she broke down and began crying in earnest. James recognized the guilt in Snow's cries, but he didn't pity her. She had mercilessly torn into the frail stitching E had managed to sew across her broken heart. He might have found forgiving Snow easier had she hurt E for a good reason or even a grand one, but she had pulled her dirty, little trick out of petty jealousy and injured pride.

He hoped that she felt her guilt in this moment. He hoped that her guilt would fill her soul and transform into remorse so that the memory of this night would brand itself onto her heart and kill the temptation to do anything like this ever again. He scrubbed away his tears then lifted E off of his chest.

"E, can you say something? How do you feel?" he asked. He knew the stupidity of his own question but was at a loss for what else to say.

Tears trickled down from her eyes. Though she stared at him, he knew that she saw only the memories which Snow had forced her to relive. He bit back another sob. After a few deep breaths, he yanked together the pieces of himself threatening to fall apart and cut off a strip of his shirt. He dabbed E's cheeks, all the while searching for even the slightest glimmer of that fiery determination that always seemed to burn in her black eyes.

"James," she whispered.

"*Yes? What is it? What do you need? What can I do for you?*" he said in Korean. Words of comfort had always sounded more caring–parental, even–in Korean to him. He tried to smile as he wiped away more of his own tears.

"*How did you do it?*"

*"Hm? Do what?"*

*"How did you read me?"*

*"I...."*

E's memories had shocked him so much that he'd completely forgotten that only Shamans were capable of reading.

Blinding pain split his hand.

His mouth fell open into a scream. The pain traveled up his arm and tore his body apart in an explosion agony. His head tilted back and hit something hard. A voice shouted his name as he struggled to breathe. He pulled up his left hand. The minute hand of his watch scraped his skin black as it slowly traveled up from six o'clock toward nine.

Everything vanished. The pain disappeared.

James smothered the breath that returned to his lungs then scrambled onto his feet. He scanned the quiet, black emptiness in which he now stood.

"James."

He spun around to find Snow standing a few paces away from him.

Her eyes. They were different. Less milky.

She pointed at the space behind him.

The Red Calf lay on its side in a glistening pool of its own blood, twitching and struggling. Blood trickled out of its gaping, raw socket so that it seemed to weep red tears. It raised itself onto one knee, trembled, then collapsed.

*"My eye,"* the Beast groaned.

James ran to Snow.

*"Heal,"* a voice whispered. *"Heal the–"*

He gripped her arm.

"James!"

His eyelids flew open. He drew a long, strangled gasp as the ceiling zoomed back into focus. The sound of flowing water returned to his ears. He flipped onto his stomach and vomited. E stretched his tee-shirt as she tried to sit him up then fell back down onto the ground. James slapped one trembling hand then the other onto the floor before lifting himself onto his hands and knees.

"James!" E repeated.

They stared at one another before their eyes jumped down to his watch.

The time now read a quarter to midnight.

The strips of red-gold light on the wall disappeared as a black shadow overtook the room. James gripped E's arm, held out his watch hand, and sat still, ready to protect her at the first sign of danger. For a few moments, only the wavering glow of the fountains' lights illuminated the darkened space. Then the shadow receded like a wave pulled back into the ocean and began washing in and out of the room.

"James," E whispered.

He spun around and stared out the windows. The fortress of black emptiness surrounding the Keep blotted out the sunlight at uneven intervals as it rose and fell and undulated. The Calf's darkness, which had lain dormant for so many centuries, remained still no more. Phoenix ran to Snow and threw her over his shoulder.

"Run!" he shouted.

E pushed herself off the ground. James swayed as he stood up then ran with her down the room. He skidded to a halt as she collapsed.

"E!" Phoenix cried.

She gave her head a sharp shake and pressed her hand against her temple. James glanced at her bare feet then scooped her up into his arms. He ignored her mumbled objections as he ran with Phoenix down the stairs and out into the street.

Streetlights flickered as if possessed. The shadows covering the barren sidewalks and the faces of the high-rises stretched and shrank and moved from side to side. In the distance, the darkness continued to rise and fall in waves that slowly climbed higher into the red sky.

"Honey! Blood Crow! Where are you?" Phoenix yelled.

"Over here!"

They ran to one another.

"What the–" Honey exclaimed. "What's wrong with E? And where's Lux?"

"I don't know. Let's get back to the shop first," said Phoenix.

They sprinted down the street and turned the corner to find the wolves running up to the store where Sleet had left them. The two horses made of half bodies galloped in their midst. Bloom halted in his tracks at the sight of E then ran up to her. He frantically sniffed and licked her limp body.

"*We must leave the Keep!*" Father shouted.

"*We can't find* Lux!" Honey cried.

"*I'll find him and track you down. Go on without me!*" Sleet said. He dashed away before anyone could stop him.

"*Hurry! Onto our backs!*" the horses shouted.

"*And ours!*" said Terrain.

Blood Crow helped James seat E on one of the horses as Phoenix hoisted Snow then himself onto the other horse. Honey continued searching the street for Lux as she climbed onto Terrain. As Blood Crow jumped onto Forest's back, James leapt up onto the horse, secured E between his arms, and gripped the horse's mane.

"*This way!*" Father shouted.

The group ran after him through moving shadows and flashing lights. They dashed into an empty high-rise filled with the smell of dust. Only their panting and the galloping of hooves disturbed the silence as they sped past cement columns and whisked through still shadows. They leapt out of the building through a giant window then dashed across an open plaza where fountains splashed. Hollow windows stared down at them from surrounding buildings as they flew down abandoned streets. The Calf's darkness continued to rise and rise.

"*Here!*" Father shouted.

He shot into an alleyway, where clotheslines crisscrossed a long slice of crimson sky. Air whistled past James's ears as hooves and paws pounded over loose dirt. E's head began to loll. She slumped forward then slid sideways. James shoved her back into place with his arms.

"Stay with me!" he cried.

Father swerved left as the alley diverged into two paths. The group veered and hurtled after him.

"*Wait!*" Snow cried out. "*An exit! I smell a closer exit!*"

"*Where?*"

"*That way!*"

"*Lead us!*"

She spun the horse around then urged it forward with a prick of her heels. The group ran after her as she led them down an alleyway, where brick walls forced them into a single-file line. E jerked her head up. James dared not loosen the barricade he had formed around her even as she tightened her hold on the horse's mane.

The group spilled out onto a wide street. The darkness lapped up the last bit of sky. For a moment, the darkness stood as a black dome that encompassed the entire city. Then a thick torrent of black spilled down and began flowing into the Keep. The horses whinnied and galloped faster. The wolves strained and panted. James shouted for the group to hurry. He knew that the Calf's emptiness was rushing throughout the streets in search of living things to devour.

"*Over there! There!*" Snow shouted.

She pointed to a chain-link fence blocking the street several yards ahead.

"*Forest, you first!*" Father yelled.

Swiftness blurred Forest's paws as he outstripped the group. He leapt toward the fence with Blood Crow still seated on his back. They both disappeared.

"*Terrain!*" Father shouted.

"Wait! Lux!" Honey screamed. "Where's Lux?"

They vanished through the fence.

"E! James!"

Panic seized James as the horse galloped toward the fence. Had Sleet found Lux? Would he be able to smell the group this far away? He lurched forward as E yanked on the horse's mane and forced it to skid to a stop. Bloom careened around to a halt as well. Father crouched down and struggled to slow his paws. Phoenix leapt off of his horse. It whinnied with surprise before disappearing into the fence with Snow still seated on its back.

"*What are you doing?*" Father shouted.

"I'm not leaving without Lux," E mumbled.

"There! Look!" Phoenix yelled.

Sleet burst into view from one side of the street as the Calf's emptiness spilled out from the other. Lux clung to Sleet's white fur as he raced toward the group at full speed. The darkness rushed closer to Sleet's heels. James grabbed E as she tried to jump off the horse.

"Lux!" she cried out.

James flinched as Phoenix zoomed past them in a convertible. The car shrank into a miniature of itself as it sped down the street. The darkness reared back as if to leap forward. Phoenix swerved in a screeching circle. Sleet jumped into the car. The car hurtled back toward the group as the darkness lunged forth and gave chase.

"*Into the exit! Now!*" Father yelled.

James tightened his grip on both E and the horse as it ran toward the fence with Father and Bloom at its heels. Behind them, Sleet, Lux, and Phoenix leapt out of the car and sprinted after them. The horse ran through the exit.

"Whoa!" James cried.

The horse gave a shrill cry as it dodged a white pedestal holding a delicate sculpture. It continued galloping down the long, spacious hall they had entered. Paintings hung on the white walls of the hall. Roped-off statues and curious shapes in glass boxes stood in a circular lobby at the hall's end. High above, a peaceful night sky sparkled beyond a vaulted, glass ceiling. A shout, a yelp, and the crack of breaking stone announced that Lux had knocked over the pedestal and slammed into Father and Bloom as he safely entered the new plane with Sleet and Phoenix.

"*No,*" the horse moaned as it slowed to a stop. "*No! The Keep. Destroyed!*"

"*I'm sorry,*" James said as it began to weep.

The horse continued to mourn as it walked back to where the group stood recuperating. E swayed, nearly falling off the horse again. James gathered her up into his arms. Pity squeezed his heart as he stared at her half-closed eyes and pale cheeks. Phoenix and Blood Crow ran up to him.

"Is she okay? What's wrong with her?" Blood Crow demanded.

James only shook his head and allowed the horse to continue walking.

"James!" Phoenix shouted. "Stop ignoring me, and tell me what happened!"

Anger blazed up within him. "You're bothering her," he growled. "Just shut up!"

Phoenix and Blood Crow stood still as the horse continued walking. Up ahead, Honey stood with her arms wrapped around Lux and her face buried in his shoulder. Snow was still seated on her horse. Next to her, the wolves were arguing.

"*You coward,*" Father snarled at Bloom. "*You let your brother go after the boy!*"

"*There wasn't a chance to think, Father,*" Terrain objected.

"*Silence!*"

Terrain shuffled his paws. Forest whimpered and lowered his head. Sleet stared at the floor with a neutral expression. Bloom glared at Father.

"*You are more familiar with the boy's scent,*" Father continued. "*At the very least, you should have gone with Sleet! And for all your love for the Last's child, you could do nothing for her. Even after all of these eras, you are still a disappointment!*"

A red fury seemed to cloud Bloom's eyes. He began to choke and heave. "*M-Me? M-Mother. You ... k-killed!*"

"*Brother, stop,*" Sleet said. "*You know Mother gave up her heart willingly.*"

Bloom's eyes bulged with outrage. His entire body began to shake. "*H-Him. Sh-Should ... been.*"

"*How dare you,*" Father rumbled. "*How dare you! You, who abandoned your pack. You, who can barely fight the moulded half your size!*"

"*Father, please!*" Forest said. "*You are always blaming Brother for everything. I know you have high expectations for your only blood son, but you are too hard on him. You have always been too hard on him!*"

"*That is because he is weak!*"

Forest's voice trembled as tears rolled down his face. "*No, Father. It is because you are hard on him. Did you not see the anguish on his face the night that Mother died? He was in so much pain he couldn't even listen to the details of the battle, and when he left, you stopped us from running after him. How can you say that he abandoned us?"*

*"I remember nothing of that night except for this excuse of a Castaway shouting that he hated me. It was the only full sentence he has ever managed to say without his pathetic stuttering!"*

*"Don't you dare,"* E growled.

James pinned her against his chest and grabbed her wrist as she made to draw her dagger. Embarrassment swam within Bloom's eyes as he gazed at her. The crew stared at E in disbelief as she continued struggling against James in vain.

*"I don't care if we need your help, and I don't care if you're Bloom's father! If you keep insulting him, I'll cut you to pieces!"* E shouted as tears sprang up in her eyes.

Father snarled and bared his fangs.

*"Father, stop! This is not the moment for a quarrel,"* Sleet said. *"We are a pack. A team!"*

*"Let him do what he wants!"* E cried. *"I'll fight him right here, right now!"*

Everything muted.

James shook his head and blinked. A tingling sensation erupted in the middle of his watch and rippled over his hand in pulses. As he shivered, the sensation sank into his flesh and spread until every cell within him seemed to quiver. His body turned cold as if his watch were drinking in his blood.

He had always expected the last stroke of his watch to bring an excruciating pain that would put the agony of all the other strokes to shame. But he continued to feel only tingling as the minute hand of his watch crept steadily across his skin toward twelve o'clock.

"James," Snow whispered.

Together, they looked up at the vision James knew that only they could see. The empty air above them had ripped open like a patch of canvass torn from a painting. The Red Calf slowly raised itself onto all four of its hooves then crouched down so that its stomach hovered just above the invisible ground of its darkness. The abnormal length of its thin legs was more apparent now that it was standing. Its body, too, was larger than the innocent creatures that James called "calves" in Reality. Its skin clung to its ribs so that it looked starved and emaciated. But the sides of its belly also bulged so that it looked full and gluttonous.

It lifted its head and inhaled deeply as if to savor the full power of its lungs. It pumped its bent legs up and down as it turned around in its nest of darkness and faced James and Snow. Its gaping socket was as wet and raw as ever, and its golden eye shone upon its forehead, bright and unstained. Its single dark eye held a voracious hunger that yearned to take back the powers Snow and James had swallowed in their awakening dreams.

"James," Snow thought.

"It's coming for us," he answered.

Eyes of lapis lazuli opened within his mind.

"*You must heal the darkness!*" the Last shouted.

The rip in the air closed like a window slamming shut. The Red Calf and its darkness disappeared from sight. James continued staring up at the night sky then looked down at his watch. A black circle lay embedded in his skin like a dead full moon.

It was midnight.

E gripped him as he slid to the side. His weight pulled her down with him as he fell onto the floor. Snow's horse shouted as she dropped onto the ground as well. An image of the Calf's dark gaze remained branded onto his mind as footsteps rushed toward him. He heard the Last's command again as hands propped him up. The Last had asked him to heal the darkness. But what did that mean? Phoenix and Blood Crow pulled Snow upright as the group began bombarding her and James with questions. They fell silent as he held up his watch.

His mouth seemed to move on its own as he said, "*The Red Calf has returned.*"

The group fell silent. One of the wolves took a few steps back. E took James's watch hand into her own.

"When did this happen? It wasn't like this back at the Keep," she said.

"Right now. It happened right now."

"Right now?" several in the group exclaimed.

James nodded. "The Beast has regained its full strength, and it's coming to hunt me and Snow. It won't stop until it finds us. It wants its powers back. It wants the powers we inherited in our awakenings."

"*Then we must go to Lapis Lazuli as quickly as possible,*" Father said. "*We must cross the Blue Border before the Beast finds* James *and the Twelfth.*"

"*Wait,*" said Phoenix. "*What are we going to do about the humans in the Iris?*"

"*What do you mean?*" said Sleet.

He swallowed then said, "*There are Runners in the Iris and humans traveling in and out of Lapis Lazuli. How will we keep them safe from the Beast when it comes for us and when we battle it?*"

"*And the Hunters,*" Blood Crow said, her eyes widening with realization. "*They're all at Lapis Lazuli for the Solstice right now too. When they see the Calf, they'll all run out to hunt it!*"

"*All the better,*" Father growled.

"*No!*" she shouted. "*We can't just let them run to their deaths like that. There must be another way!*"

"Whoa! You guys, time," Lux said, waving his watch. "We're out of time tonight."

"It doesn't matter if we're out of time," James said as fear tightened its grip on him. "We need to get to the City as soon as possible. The Beast is coming for us, and it's coming for us now! We need to get to the moonlight before it finds us. We need to win this battle!"

"But we can't just keep sleeping forever," Honey protested.

"And we need to keep our sleep schedules normal until the battle," said Phoenix. "Who knows how long it'll last? I don't want to risk waking up in the middle of it."

"*We can assist,*" said Sleet. "*We will travel through the planes as quickly as possible while you are in Reality. You can ride upon our backs once you return. Leave it to us, and return to Reality for now.*"

"*Okay, that works for now, but what about the Third and his men?*" said Lux. "*How are we going to stay hidden from them once we do get back to Lapis Lazuli?*"

"*And what about all of you?*" Phoenix asked the pack. "*There will be Bodyguards everywhere, and with all the Hunters at the Solstice, it'll be too dangerous.*"

"*There is no other way,*" Terrain said, rolling his eyes. "*We must go to Lapis Lazuli regardless of whether or not the conditions are perfect. We will find a way to hide ourselves once we are within the safety of the Blue Border!*"

"*Hey! Don't you give us attitude when we're just trying to look out for you,*" said Honey.

"*I am simply stating the truth,*" Terrain growled.

"*Then say something useful, and help us figure things out!*"

"*Let us not quarrel,*" said Sleet. "*We must not be difficult with one another.*"

"*Honey isn't the one being difficult!*" Lux retorted.

"Quiet!" E roared.

James caught her as she doubled over. Bloom shoved his head under her arm. They helped her to stand up.

"Everyone, quiet! The wolves can start traveling to the City while we return to Reality, but we need to figure out a plan for everything else. The Bodyguards, the Third, the Hunters, Zilch." Her face twisted before she cried out, "And *Oppa*. Kit *Oppa!*"

Snow balled her fists and bowed her head. The weight of regret sank James's heart. If only the crew hadn't gone to the City. E never would have met Kit again, and the goodbye she had told him years ago would have stood as a permanent farewell. Now that goodbye meant nothing. Her escape had been reduced to a reprieve. They had to rescue Zilch and Kit from the Third, and James knew that when they did, there was a chance that E would be lost forever.

Of course, he no longer personally cared about rescuing Kit after everything he'd seen in E's memories. If anything, he would have preferred to have let him rot in whatever dungeon the Third was likely holding him in. But they needed to rescue Zilch, and Kit was likely imprisoned alongside him. Plus, the group needed all the help they could get to win the battle against the Calf. E and Kit's teamwork would surely double their chances at winning and play, perhaps, a pivotal role in determining whether or not all the dimensions would survive. They needed Kit. It was the cold, hard, and hateful truth.

"We're out of time tonight, and we won't have the luxury of planning while we're running back to the City. Not with the Beast hunting for us," E continued. Small flames of determination flickered to life within her eyes. "We need more time to think. We need to get everything right."

She hesitated.

Then her determination grew into a fiery blaze.

"I propose that we meet in Reality. I want us to stick together and talk in the day so that we can be coordinated in the night."

The gravity of her words struck James. Meeting in Reality was the ultimate form of trust. The crew would find out information about each other that otherwise only a Shaman could ever discover. Yet, James didn't need to think twice about his decision. In fact, he only regretted that they hadn't done this sooner.

"I trust you, E. And I trust all of you," he told the group. "My name is James Mun. I'm in San Diego, California. It'll be great to finally meet all of you."

Honey bit down on her lower lip then nodded. "My name is Sarah McIntosh. I'm in Davis right now. Davis, California. And if there's a chance of us all dying soon, I want to meet in Reality at least once before we do."

"Javier Gutierrez," said Lux. "But my friends call me Javi. And man, James, no wonder we're in the same time zone. I'm in S.D. too!"

"Paul Wu," said Phoenix. "I'm in Palo Alto. It's a little crazy, but I'm actually flying down to San Diego in the afternoon for family."

"Rose Miller," said Blood Crow. "I'm in L.A. I'll drive down as soon as I wake up."

"Meehae Kim," said E. "And believe it or not, I'm in San Diego too."

"So we were all up and down the same state this whole time. Well, that explains why we're all in the same time zone," Lux said with a smile.

James followed E's line of sight as she stared across the room at Snow. One by one, the others turned to stare as well. If Snow revealed her identity, her powers as a Shaman would be rendered useless against Crew Blue. She would never be able to hold the upper hand over any of them for as long as she lived. If anything, they could use her identity to hold an upper hand over her. Snow took a deep breath. Her knuckles turned white as she tightened her fists.

"My name is Sophia Han," she said in a firm voice. "I'm in Orange County."

A slight pause ensued.

Then Blood Crow said quietly, "We can drive down together. I'll pick you up."

James's heartbeat quickened with excitement even as his fear of the Calf continued digging into his chest. He would finally be able to remember the faces of his friends no matter the dimension or the time. Crew Blue would now survive together or die together whether it be by day or by night.

"Quick. Everyone get in a circle before we wake up," said E. "Write down your number, and hand it to whoever is on your right. James, you call me first as soon as you wake up, then I'll call Lux and so on and so forth."

"*And we will begin the journey back to Lapis Lazuli,*" said Father.

He and E nodded at one another. In their silence lay the understanding of a truce. The urgency of the moment demanded that they set aside all animosity and instead, focus on their mission to kill the Red Calf. They had to finish this battle, this battle that had begun so many eras ago.

Bloom rubbed his face into E's hand. "I'll see you when you return," his eyes seemed to say. He followed Father, the horses, and the rest of the pack as they ran down the hall. The crew created pens and paper and scribbled furiously. Silence followed as numbers were crammed into memories.

"I got it," James said. He stuffed the paper with E's phone number into his mouth and swallowed. "I'm going now before I forget. I'll wait ten minutes before I call you."

"I'll talk to you soon," said E.

James drew his knife and pierced his watch. His eyes snapped open in Reality. He threw aside his blanket and ran to his desk. He grabbed the first pencil he saw and scribbled E's number down into the margin of an open textbook. He gripped the edges of the book, sat down, and began shaking his leg. After ten minutes, he snatched up his cell phone. Blood pounded in his ears as he listened to the steady ringing of the line.

The ringing stopped.

"Hello?"

James's heart leapt up into his throat. "This is James Mun. Who am I talking to?"

Silence then, "Meehae. Meehae Kim."

# PART II
# COLLIDING

# CHAPTER 11
# REALITY

James was seated in his cubicle, shaking his leg and staring at the clock. Three o'clock struck. He grabbed his backpack. The office's worn, gray carpet muted his steps as he rushed down the hallway and threw open the door. He ran toward an empty elevator then sprang inside before it could close. He jabbed the button for the lobby in rapid succession and ignored the disapproving looks of oncoming people as the doors clapped shut in their faces. As the elevator clunked into a slow descent, he reviewed the plan Crew Blue had formed through their texts throughout the day.

He and E would leave work early then carpool to the airport to pick up Phoenix and Honey. Phoenix would then call Lux, who, in turn, would feign sickness and make his brother take over the auto shop for the rest of the day. Lux would call Blood Crow, who, as promised, had picked up Snow and arrived in San Diego. They would all then meet at Phoenix's home, which Phoenix had offered up as headquarters for the crew.

The elevator dinged. He rushed out into the lobby, where the cold, winter air made him grimace. He fought against the wind as he pushed open the tinted front door. He ran to the colossal building that stood on the other side of the parking lot then doubled over and wheezed for air. He stared up at the building.

He still couldn't believe that E worked here. Right here. This whole time! And for none other than the company he had cursed months ago for swooping in and stealing all the parking spaces in the lot. How many times had he and E passed each other without even knowing it? Which car was hers, and what did she look like?

Large, glass doors slid open for him as he approached. His skin tingled in the lobby's warmth as he walked swiftly across a polished, marble floor. After throwing himself into one of the many elevators available, he pressed the button for the highest floor. A soft melody played as the elevator ascended. A digital number transitioned from one to two to three....

James's heart hammered with anticipation. He crossed his arms and shook his leg as the numbers continued to climb. He didn't know why he felt so nervous. He saw E and the others every single night. Yet, the prospect of meeting them in the flesh and in the life they had first been born into filled him with an eagerness that bordered on panic. Today was the day he would finally see their faces. Today, he would meet them as they were outside of the Flowering.

The doors opened. He rushed toward a large reception desk draped in silver tinsel. A young woman wearing a flashing necklace in the shape of Christmas lights greeted him with a smile.

"Can I help you with something?"

"Hi, yeah. I'm here to see E-Esther," James said, merging his words together at the last second.

E had commanded the crew to refrain from using their Flowering names in Reality. Though James wholeheartedly agreed with taking this safety precaution, he was still getting used to shaking off their Flowering names from his tongue. To make things doubly confusing, E used an

English name in her professional life. Too many people butchered her Korean name too often, and she'd grown tired of having to perform linguistic gymnastics so that coworkers could correctly pronounce a name that was, in James's opinion at least, simple enough to pronounce.

"Oh, yes! Of course. She mentioned someone would be coming to see her. Just down the hallway to your right. You'll see her name next to her door."

He mumbled his thanks before hurrying down the hallway. His heart seemed to pound a dozen times with each step he took. He turned the corner and sped past several doors. He slowed down as he spotted a gilded name plate that read:

Esther M. Kim
Executive Assistant to Vice President Phillip M. Wu

He stared at the plate as he continued panting for air. He swallowed and shifted his backpack on his shoulders. After a final, deep breath, he stepped in front of E's open door.

A young woman was seated at a desk. Her eyes were fastened on a clock, and her fists were pressed down on her lap. Her long hair covered her back like a sheet of black silk. She snapped her head around to look at him. Her pale, drawn face carried an aura of exhaustion as if her body constantly struggled to bear the weight of countless invisible burdens. But her eyes. James knew, somehow, that the fire within her black eyes burned as brightly in Reality as it did in the Flowering.

He smiled. She blinked. A small smile formed on her face.

"Good. You're on time," she said in a voice that was rough with fatigue.

She stood up from her chair. She was much less muscles and blades and much more bones and edges in Reality. Though her blazer, blouse, and skirt gave her a neat and professional appearance, the thinning fabric and faded hues betrayed that she had long outworn the worth of her outfit. Her bangs were uneven as if she had tried trimming them herself. James wondered if she had any money at all to spend on herself or if all her income always went straight to her mother.

She smirked. "Do I really look that awful?"

"No! No. I just...."

His memory rewound and stopped on the moment he had first met E. Had he really resented her once? This woman, who had saved him in so many ways on so many occasions? This girl, who had gone through so much and whom he had grown to care for like a sister? Pain stung his heart again as he remembered a younger E cradling herself as her mother screamed. Flinging decorum into future nights that would likely end in death and destruction anyway, he walked over to E and hugged her. He tightened his hold as she stiffened. She laughed softly then returned his embrace.

"Um ... thank you, by the way," she said.

"For what?"

"For last night. Holding me and everything when I was so–oh, Phillip!"

A balding man had appeared at the doorway. He wore a dark navy suit, a festive, red tie, and a bemused smile. His dark eyes twinkled as they flitted back and forth between E and James.

"Esther! I am so sorry to interrupt. I just came by to ask for something, but it's nothing urgent, nothing urgent at all. Please. Carry on. I don't want to be that old fogey who interrupts Christmas time for young lovers," he said, chuckling as he turned to leave.

E stared at James. James stared at E. Understanding struck them simultaneously.

"Whoa! He's not my boyfriend. He's not my boyfriend!" she cried as they sprang apart.

James shook his head and waved his hands frantically from side to side.

"This is James," she said as the man reappeared at the doorway. "He's just a friend. James, this is Phillip. He's my boss."

"Oh!" said Phillip. "Oh, I see! Well, that's my mistake, then. I'm Phillip Wu. It's such a pleasure to finally meet one of Esther's friends."

"James Mun. Nice to meet you too," he said, sweating as they shook hands.

"Here," said E, who looked as red as James imagined himself to be. She fumbled around her desk. "Might as well give this to you now since you're here."

Phillip's smile fell as she thrust a leather portfolio at him. He took the folder with two fingers then wrinkled his nose and stuck out his tongue as if he despised the contents within.

"And make sure to be on time this time," said E. "Last time was the third time you were late, and people were pissed off enough as it was."

"Oh, don't worry. Those morons will be angry no matter what time I show up."

"Phillip!" E said, her eyes flashing.

He hung his head and stared at the floor, looking cowed.

"You are the vice president. If you screw this deal up, the whole company will suffer."

"My dear Esther, please. No one is going to screw up anything. I am an adult. An adult!" he said, clutching the folder and throwing back his head with a pained look. He muttered to James, "She's always yelling at me like this. I sometimes wonder who the real boss is around here."

"I am doing my job," E snapped as James laughed.

"Yes, yes. And you do it while being frank and direct and never giving a word of flattery. Not a single one! And now that I have my briefing, I'll be on my way. And escape before she can chastise me some more," he added in an undertone to James.

Though James laughed again, an uneasy fear for E's job security stole upon him as she growled in wordless disapproval. To his surprise, though, Phillip gave her a warm smile.

"Don't worry, Esther. I won't let the company down. I know how to deal with these sharks. It's what I do best. Besides, what do I have to worry about when I have you to prepare my briefings for me?"

E rolled her eyes. He chuckled again.

"Well, at any rate, I know you're leaving early today, so if I don't see you again, please have a wonderful holiday break. And James, it was a pleasure. Please do make sure to stop by more often. This one desperately needs a bit more fun in her life."

E growled again as Phillip grinned and walked away.

"Do you guys ... uh ... always talk like that?" James said once Phillip had disappeared down the hall.

"Like what?" E grumbled as she pulled out a purse from a drawer and led him to the door.

"I don't know. Like, so casually."

He didn't know how else to intimate to her that the manner in which she spoke to Phillip seemed a bit out of line. Sure, he seemed like the type of man who encouraged people to feel comfortable around him, and the way he talked inspired an air of familiarity, but he was her boss and the vice president too.

"Of course I talk to him so casually. How else am I going to keep him on track with everything? I swear, if he's late to that meeting again, I'll really give him something to complain about. He'll be the laughingstock of the entire company if he keeps this up."

Caution made him answer slowly. "But he's your boss. And he seems to treat you really nicely."

He shut his mouth as she glared at him and pulled the door shut behind her.

"I talk to him like that precisely because he treats me so nicely. I need to keep him on track with everything, and things get done more effectively with him this way. It's either this or letting the company burn to the ground because he's being a moron!"

James swallowed the rest of his concerns as they hurried down into the lobby then out into the parking lot. At least she was back to her full fiery self again, though he doubted that she was as well as she appeared to be. How could she be after everything Snow had forced her to relive last night?

"It's that one," E said as she led him to an aging sedan.

Like her clothes, the seats of E's car, though worn and faded, bore the cleanliness of careful maintenance. As James climbed into the passenger seat, he swore to himself that he, too, would take better care of his car. They set off toward the airport and discussed the impending trip back to the City as they wove through piling traffic. The more they spoke, though, the more hope and despair battled within him. His hope sprang from the thought of meeting the rest of the crew and strategizing all together. His despair spawned from his and E's inability to discover any solid plans even as they spoke.

"Call Sarah," E commanded as they exited the highway.

James put Honey on speakerphone as she answered.

"We're almost there," E said.

"Okay. Paul's going to call Javi right now, then," said Honey. "We're out front by the palm trees. Paul is in a red sweater, and I'm wearing antlers."

"Antlers," E repeated.

"Yes, antlers! Haven't you ever heard of Christmas spirit? Plus, it'll be easier to spot us."

And sure enough, at the end of a packed terminal stood a young man wearing sweatpants and a cardinal red college sweater and a young woman, whose headband sported antlers. James leaned out the window and waved his arms at them. Honey swatted Phoenix on the arm. He promptly picked up the bags lying at their feet and hurried after her.

Honey's hair was longer in Reality and her body, plumper. Her playful antlers and glittery Christmas sweater clashed with James's memories of her shooting moulded citizens and spraying Hunters with bullets. As for Phoenix, he looked as tall as James remembered, but the glasses perched on his long nose created a bookish aura that he had never associated with him before. His sweater, which revealed that he was a graduate student at an extremely prestigious university, added to his bookishness, though in a more intimidating way.

Honey broke into a run as James and E climbed out of the car. She shuffled to a halt in front of them and stared at them with wide, brown eyes. She lunged forward and threw her arms around E. E's face wrinkled with emotion as she hugged her back. Honey began jabbering away about her flight as Phoenix set down their bags. He hesitated then extended his hand to James.

"It's nice to finally meet you, James," he said with a lop-sided smile as they shook.

James smiled back and glanced at Phoenix's midriff, which lacked the pudge rimming his own. Phoenix's large, doe-like eyes strayed toward E then back to James. Though he said nothing, his anxious expression clearly asked if E was okay.

James made sure that she wasn't listening then muttered, "I'll tell you about it later. I promise. Just let it go for now."

He'd anticipated that Phoenix would still be worried about her and had finally decided earlier on in the day to divulge at least some details about her breakdown to him. Keeping him in the dark would only breed more suspicion and worry, which, in turn, would lead him to question E. Plus, it definitely wouldn't hurt to have at least one more crew member be aware of the danger that Kit posed to her.

James jumped as Honey threw her arms around his neck and smacked a kiss onto his cheek. The faint smell of cigarettes clung to her hair and sweater.

"Nice to meet you, mister James," she said. She gave him a devious grin that felt all-too familiar.

For a few seconds, he simply stared at her, dumbfounded by her kiss. He chuckled and shook his head. He supposed his friendship with Honey had come a long way too since they had first met.

"It's really nice to meet you too, Sarah."

As James began loading Honey's bags into the trunk, Phoenix gave E a sheepish smile, which she returned with a small one. Honey stared at them, raised her eyebrows at James, then climbed into the car. The four of them dove into discussions regarding the nights ahead as they drove out of the airport and onto roads infested with red taillights. Hopeful suggestions and elaborate solutions sank into loaded silences and frustrated groans. The blue of the sky began dissolving into a cocktail of yellows, pinks, and oranges. Dusk had cast its silver shadow by the time E returned to the parking lot and pulled up next to James's car.

"We'll meet you at Paul's," she told him.

He nodded and tried to use his body to hide the crumpled receipts and unopened mail strewn around the seats of his car. He drove behind E across the freeway then through quiet streets. Phoenix's address had forewarned him that he would be entering an affluent neighborhood, but he still couldn't help but marvel at the size and fanciness of some of these houses.

He slowed to a stop and parked behind E as they arrived in front of Phoenix's multi-storied home. Spotlights lit up several stocky palm trees on a manicured lawn. A paved walkway wound toward a large, arched entryway and a wooden door decorated with elaborate ironwork. He counted four garage doors as he grabbed his luggage and joined E and Honey. Both of them stood with their mouths slightly open as they continued staring at Phoenix's mansion. Phoenix seemed completely oblivious to their awe.

"Sarah! Meehae! You guys!"

A thin, young man ran toward them from down the street. He had thick, black hair and a wide, radiant smile. His eyes sparkled like fireworks. Honey let out a shriek of joy and ran to Lux with outstretched arms. Lux flung aside his duffle bag and laughed as he caught her and spun her around. He gazed at her as if she were his long-lost twin. Then his eyes locked on E. She took a step back. He dashed toward her.

"No, Javi, wait, no!"

E expelled a grunt as he tackled her with a bear hug. Honey cackled as E squirmed in the clutches of his lean, muscular arms. He released her only after she had managed to extricate one hand and pat him on the back. She stared at him then pulled him into a soft embrace. Honey tilted back her head and fanned away her tears as Lux wrapped his arms around E again.

"If only Bloom were here," she murmured as they drew apart.

Honey laid a gentle hand on her shoulder as Lux turned to James and Phoenix.

"James? James, is that you?"

James could only smile back at him as a rush of affection stole away all the words he wished he could say, the words that could express just how glad he was to meet, at last, the first real friend he had ever made. The callouses on Lux's palm and fingers scratched against James's skin as they clasped hands. He yanked James into a tight hug before reaching for Phoenix as well.

"Meehae?" a voice called.

E squinted. "Rose?"

James's heart seemed to lurch forward within his chest as he spotted two young women hurrying toward them. Blood Crow's wild, red hair seemed to carry the warmth of the sun that had set. She wore large, black-rimmed glasses and a tired smile. Her chest was a bit bigger and her thighs, thicker than they were in the Flowering. James sucked in his stomach and for the millionth, inexcusable time, punched himself mentally for failing to go to the gym. As she stopped in front of him, he gazed at the constellations of freckles on her face. Her eyes were gray like the remnants of dusk dissipating around them. She blushed as she smiled at him. She hitched up the duffel bag hanging from her shoulder and held up several grease-stained, paper bags.

"We got dinner for everyone," she told the crew.

"Oh, yeah. Dinner! I forgot about dinner," Lux said, echoing James's thoughts.

The petite, young woman next to Blood Crow held up several bags as well. Her skin was pale like the full moon. Her stylish hair ended at her shoulders. Her oversized jacket accentuated her thinness. Her eyes, which were such a light shade of brown that they appeared almost yellow, carried the heavy weight of guilt.

Snow looked at James then at E, who refrained from giving her so much as a glance. James, too, avoided her eyes. He was with E on this one. Though he knew Snow felt sorry for what she'd done last night, he wouldn't soon forget how E had sobbed and screamed in his arms because of her.

Phoenix took some of the paper bags from Blood Crow, reached out a helping hand to Snow, then drew back. The crew tensed. Snow exchanged swift looks with Blood Crow before smiling.

"B-Boy! That L.A. traffic. We thought it would be okay early in the morning but guess not," said Snow. "Could you help me with these, Paul? They're way heavier than they look."

"Oh! Sure. O-Of course."

A relieved smile spread across his face as he helped her. Blood Crow made a loud comment about the drive down from L.A, prompting them all to break out in conversation. As Phoenix led them to the door and asked everyone to take off their shoes, Lux slunk up to James's side.

"Sarah told me about the whole rejection thing with Sophia and Paul," he whispered. "Is she okay?"

"She'll be fine," James said flatly. Snow's boy problems were nothing in comparison to all of E's real problems.

After setting down their bags in an immense living room, the crew followed Phoenix down a long hallway. Lux stopped to laugh at a collage of framed photos that had captured Phoenix at various stages of life. One showed him as a chubby-faced toddler in the arms of a woman with whom he shared the same long nose. Another showed him in a cap and gown and with one arm wrapped around an elderly grandmother, who was seated in a wheelchair and was wearing a gentle smile.

The crew turned into a kitchen that was as large as James's whole apartment. Copper pots and pans dangled above a huge island with a glistening granite countertop. E helped Phoenix set out dinner on a dining table made of heavy, dark wood while Lux led the others in grabbing cans of soda and sparkling water from a well-stocked fridge.

James resisted the temptation to drink soda and instead, chose flavored sparkling water in hopes of finally embarking on the diet he had long promised himself he would start. He sat down at the dining table with his drink and waited for the others to join him so that they could continue their discussion of the night ahead.

# CHAPTER 12

# WHAT LIES AHEAD

Drinks snapped open. Paper bags were ripped and ruffled. The crew plunged into discussion. As James emphasized the need to reach the moonlight as soon as possible, Snow suddenly proclaimed that she would use her sense of smell to lead them back to No Man's Land within the night. Everyone, except for Blood Crow, immediately expressed their doubts. After all, it had taken them more than four nights to reach the City before, even with Bloom's help.

Minutes ticked by, and Snow continued to argue with such persistent passion that by the time the crew had finished their burgers and fries, they had given up fighting her and assumed that, as a Shaman, she would be able to lead them to the City in a minimum of two nights. They could only hope that the Calf wouldn't find them before then.

Lux dug through the fridge for a second round of drinks as they transitioned into a discussion about whether they would rely on Snow's nose or Alex to cross No Man's Land. They unanimously agreed to hire Alex again so that they could warn her about the Calf and bring her into the safety of the moonlight. She would also know more than Snow about the whereabouts of the Third's men as well as the paths that humans keen on collecting the bounty on the crew would most likely take. The crew had managed to escape from No Man's Land without running into other humans before, but they couldn't count on their luck holding out this time. Not when the Third was bound to have sent out even more Bodyguards since the crew's battle with Certus.

Next, they agreed that they had an obligation to warn not only Alex about the Calf but also all the other humans in the City and No Man's Land, from the other Runners to the Hunters to the Merchants and anyone else coming into and out of the moonlight. Now, they concurred, was a time to set aside differences and prioritize human life, not quibble over who deserved to live or die based on group association. How they would manage to warn everyone and do so without getting caught by the Third, though, remained an unsolved problem despite further discussion.

As for Kit and Zilch, everyone was in favor of setting out on a rescue mission as soon as they reached the City, though James and, somewhat to his surprise, Snow were reluctant to agree to the plan. But in the end, he had to accept once again that Kit would be a powerful ally in their battle against the Calf and agreed to the rescue, as did Snow. Zilch could also help spread word of its return. The crew disagreed on how they would proceed with the rescue, though. Lux and Honey wanted to stick together and search the City as a group. Phoenix and Blood Crow wanted to split up so that some of them remained near the Blue Border to keep watch for the Calf. James and Snow argued that Phoenix and E should stay at the Blue Border while the rest of the group set out on the rescue. Phoenix and E, they said, were the crew's best fighters and would be best prepared to intercept the Calf if it arrived, though James was sure that Snow, like him, had ulterior motives for trying to leave E behind while they searched for Kit.

After nearly half an hour of arguing, E declared that she would save everyone the trouble and set out alone to search for Kit and Zilch once they reached the moonlight. Protests broke out in response. Escalating voices, frustrated pleas, and boiling tempers culminated in E snarling for silence then calling for a break.

James leaned back in his chair and rubbed the inner corners of his eyes. Honey laid her forehead down on the table with a dull thud. Snow, Blood Crow, and Phoenix cleared the remnants of the crew's dinner as Lux disappeared into a walk-in pantry. E gathered apples and a paring knife from the kitchen and began peeling away. Blood Crow glanced at Snow, who nodded.

"So," Blood Crow said, "going back to what I was saying about the Hunters last night. Sophia and I had an idea about how to deal with them while we were driving down."

"You really think they'll run out of the moonlight like maniacs to kill the Calf when they see it coming?" Lux yelled from within the depths of the pantry.

"Definitely," said Blood Crow. "It's the Hunters' way."

Lux stuck his head out from the pantry. "But they ran away in the tunnels when the darkness chased all of us. Won't they just run away from the Calf's darkness again and stay within the Blue Border when it starts attacking?"

"I don't think they knew that a citizen was responsible for the darkness," Blood Crow replied with a grim look. "I thought the darkness might be related to a citizen at first, but when I didn't see anything around, I figured it was just a weird part of the plane or some kind of shift and ran for it. Trust me. If the others had known that it was a citizen that was causing the darkness, they would have kept trying to hunt it down. I definitely would have."

"Well, then," E said as she passed around a plate of apple slices. "What's the idea you came up with?"

"Well," said Blood Crow. She glanced at Snow again. "Sophia and I were both thinking that I should enter the Tournament."

E frowned.

"What's the Tournament?" James asked as he took a slice.

"It's an event that happens at the Solstice. The Solstice is a tradition that the Brave passed down to keep all the Hunters bonded and unified," Blood Crow added, catching his blank expression. "Every year during the winter solstice, Hunters all gather in the City. We share a two-night meal called 'the Feast' before we have the Tournament. We hire Runners to bring a marked citizen near the moonlight, and each family that wants to compete sends out one member of their family. Whoever kills the citizen first, wins, and whoever wins the Tournament wins the right to lead the Meetings afterward."

"What happens during the Meetings?" asked Lux as he sat down at the table with multiple bags of chips in hand. "I've heard about it, but I don't know much about it."

"It's basically what it sounds like. Hunters announce things that have happened throughout the year and bring up concerns, and everyone discusses them. It usually takes multiple nights to go over everything, but the one who wins the Tournament leads everything and has the final say, which is why I want to enter and win. I can warn all the Hunters about the Calf and make them stay within the moonlight when it comes. And outsiders aren't allowed to bother Hunters during the Solstice, so as long as we get into the Feast, and especially if I become the Lead, the Third won't be able to take us. We won't have to worry about where to hide once we reach the City."

"I don't care about traditions or laws," E growled. "The Third can force his way in, and the Hunters can rebel against you even if you do become the Lead."

"Having the pack with us won't help either," said Phoenix.

"We can't bring the pack into the City when the Solstice is happening," said Honey. "They'll just have to wait outside."

"No," said E. "We don't know when the Calf is coming. I won't risk them being eaten by that darkness."

"But then what are we going to do?" said Lux. "It's like Paul said last night. How are we going to hide them with all those Hunters and Bodyguards crawling all over the place?"

"If I become the Lead, I can tell the Hunters to keep away from the pack. I can make them stop any Bodyguards from taking them too," said Blood Crow.

E scoffed. "And you really think they'll listen?"

"They'll have to."

"Well, if you're going to have that much power, you should make them help us out with the battle too," said Lux.

The crew answered him with a smatter of "huhs" and "whats."

"Guys. They're Hunters," said Lux. "If there's anyone who can help us kill the Calf, it's them, and there'll be like a million of them at the Solstice. Sure, we need to warn them about not running out of the moonlight all recklessly and getting eaten by the darkness and stuff, but once we get them to calm down and explain everything, there's no reason they can't fight with us, right?"

The crew fell into a contemplative silence before E spoke.

"If Rose becomes the Lead and really can control them, we'll consider it. But I'm willing to bet that they won't listen. Hunters always try to fight before they listen. It's just the way they are. No matter what you say, they'll run out to hunt the Calf the moment they see it and keep trying until it's too late. They'll keep trying to hunt the wolves too."

"Well, okay," said Lux. "But then what are we going to do when we do go out into battle against the Calf? I mean, we need the pack to help us during the battle, especially Father. Then all the Hunters will see the wolves and the Calf, so what are we going to do about that?"

E sighed. "I suppose it means that we have no choice but to have Rose win the Tournament so that she can try and control the Hunters as their Lead."

"Wait," said Phoenix. "Hasn't the cut-off for the Tournament passed already? I thought you had to reach the City by the end of the winter solstice, and that was already two nights ago."

"Lion Paw will vouch for us," said Blood Crow. "He's the head of my family and a good man."

E smirked. "He didn't seem like that good of a man when he ran away from me in the tunnels."

"Well, you were trying to take off his head," Blood Crow said, looking annoyed. "Look, I know none of you guys like him, but Lion Paw is like a father to me. He's always looked after me, and he's never been late to the Feast before, so as long as we can find him there, he can say I made it in with him by the deadline and put my name on the roster for the Tournament, and that'll let me qualify no matter how late we are. It won't be a problem."

E's frown deepened as she took back the plate of apples from Phoenix. James agreed with what he knew she was thinking. This wasn't much of a plan, though it did seem to be their only option for now.

"Well," said E, "maybe I can go search the Market for Kit and Zilch while you guys are taking care of everything with the Tournament, then. At least get that out of the way. It'll save us some time and energy."

"None of us agreed with you going into the Market on your own. It's not safe," Phoenix said. "And when we reach No Man's Land, I really want to try and–"

Something clattered onto the floor. James twisted around in his chair then jumped with surprise. Phillip stood at the entrance of the kitchen with one hand on the door frame. His briefcase lay on the floor where he had dropped it. His eyes darted from E to James to Phoenix.

"Phillip?" E exclaimed as Phoenix said, "Hey, Dad." They looked at one another.

"You know my dad?" said Phoenix, jerking his head back.

"Phillip is your dad? Wait–what–Phillip! This is Paul? This is your son, Paul?"

James's mind reeled with revelation. So Phillip was the negligent, workaholic father whom Phoenix resented so much? He found himself exchanging glances with Snow.

"Wait, how do you two even know each other?" said Phoenix.

"H-He's my boss."

"Your boss?" he exclaimed.

"J-James," said Phillip. "And Esther. What ... what a pleasant surprise. Paul! You mentioned you'd be bringing friends over, but I never imagined they'd be my friends as well."

"You know James too?" said Phoenix.

"He came to my office today, remember?" E said.

"Yes," said Phillip, picking up his briefcase and striding over to them. "I had the pleasure of meeting James earlier today. But never mind all of that. Where are my manners? What are your names?"

As Phoenix introduced each member of the crew, Phillip shook hands with them and welcomed them into his home. Though he smiled, he still looked pale with shock.

"I'm guessing you came home early because a meeting got canceled?" Phoenix said.

James thought he heard a hint of annoyance in his voice. He wondered how late Phillip usually came home if he considered this to be early.

"Well, yes. My last meeting did get canceled, as Esther well knows! But I also wanted to come home a bit early because you were arriving today."

"Oh," said Phoenix.

Phillip's weak smile faltered further as silence bore down on them all. He cleared his throat.

"I don't know if you saw your mother's message, but her flight has been delayed. She'll be landing tomorrow at the earliest. You know how airports are around this time of year. But how was your flight?"

"Great," Phoenix said.

Another unbearable silence began to descend upon them all. As James considered excusing himself from the table and dragging the others out with him, E suddenly thrust the plate of apple slices toward Phillip.

"D-Did you want one, Phillip? There's plenty."

"Oh! No. No, thank you. But thank you very much for the offer."

"I'll have one. I love apples!" Snow proclaimed before silence could strike again.

Phillip stared at her as her fingers scrambled around the plate. She shoved a slice into her mouth.

"Does anybody else want one?" she asked, spurting out coughs as she choked on the juice.

"Well," said Phillip as E passed around the plate to an overly enthusiastic crew. "I see that you're all busy eating and conversing. I'll leave you to it, then. Please let me know if you need anything."

He nodded at Phoenix and avoided E's troubled gaze as he hurried out of the kitchen. His footsteps shuffled down the hallway before disappearing. The crew munched on apples as they stole glances at Phoenix. He pushed his glasses back up onto the bridge of his nose then resumed discussing back-up plans for hiding the wolves. Intense conversation and heated debates failed to lead to any definite solutions even as ten PM neared. The crew groaned as they rose to face what was sure to be another long and treacherous night.

"We're just going to have to wing some of it, you guys. There's no way around it," Lux said as he emptied a cascade of trash into a garbage can.

James grunted in agreement. He would have preferred not to wing the fate of the dimensions and all the lives within them but didn't know what other choice they had.

"Wait. Meehae, James," said Snow. "Can I talk to just the two of you for a second?"

Blood Crow loudly wondered where the bathroom was then herded the others out of the kitchen. James crossed his arms. E glared at the kitchen island. As Snow rubbed her thumb over her knuckles, James decided that he wouldn't stop E from doing or saying whatever she wanted to do or say to Snow.

"Meehae," Snow began. "Meehae, I am so sorry about last night. It was so wrong of me to do what I did."

E scoffed and rolled her eyes. Snow rubbed her knuckles.

"Does it make you happy to know so much about me now?" said E, still glaring at the island.

"No! No, of course not."

"Use whatever you want. You can threaten me, blackmail me. I don't care. I lost everything when I lost my father, and I lost everything again when I left Kit *Oppa*. I'm not afraid of losing anything anymore, so take what you want!"

"No! Meehae!"

Snow grabbed E's arm as she made to turn away. E's leg twitched. Snow flinched. James placed a hand on E's shoulder. On second thought, maybe it would be better to stop her from dealing out any potential kicks.

"I would never, ever use your past against you," said Snow. "I know my word doesn't mean a lot right now, but I do give you my word. I'm going to take all of this way more seriously, and I'm going to stop being so self-centered. I'm going to think about the big picture. And you know who I am now. If I ever try to trick you again or do anything to you, you can reveal my identity in the Market."

Snow recoiled as E finally looked at her.

"You really think I would do that to another human?" E said. "You really think I'd stoop as low as a Shaman?" Pain swam in her eyes as she said, "I may have helped Kit *Oppa* with his dirty work, but I never killed anyone!"

"I know you didn't!" Snow cried out, looking mortified.

E wrenched her arm out of her grasp then stopped mid-step. "*If you ever tell anyone else about Oppa's name or about his brother, I'll never forgive you,*" she said in Korean.

James stopped himself before his sadness could make him sigh. Even in Reality, E was careful to protect Kit and his identity. A tearful expression scrunched up Snow's face as E marched out of the kitchen. James looked away from Snow as she stared at him.

"I don't know what to say to you right now," he said.

"James, I'm really–"

"I can't believe you would do something like that! To E! To me!" he said, his voice rising along with his temper despite his will. "Did I carry you around all these nights just so you could figure out how to trick me and stab E in the back and make her relive all of her worst memories?"

"No! No, James. No. That's not it at all. I messed up. I really messed up. I was just so scared. I'm still so scared!"

"We're all scared, but we don't turn on each other!"

Snow drew a trembling breath then exhaled. "I have no excuse for what I did to both of you last night. All I can say is that I am so, so sorry. I get it now, and I'm all in. I'll put the crew first. I'll put the Flowering and the dimensions first. I'll take the Red Calf more seriously. I was being petty and immature, and I'm going to stop now."

James shook his head as an image of E pale and limp in his arms flashed across his mind. Then his mind skipped to the night he had abandoned the crew. E had sighed and looked away from him before forgiving his betrayal amidst the cold, teal waves. He rubbed the inner corners of his eyes as he pushed the memory away.

"Oh ... and ... one other thing," Snow said. "If you don't want to talk about it right now, I totally understand. But while we have the chance, I did want to say that that's the fastest I've ever managed to read. And the most."

James glanced at her downcast face. "Yeah, I was thinking about that on and off today. You couldn't read chronologically before, either."

"Do you think it's one of those gifts Father talked about? One that came from eating the eye?"

James uncrossed his arms. "I do. It's the only explanation. And besides, we both ate the eye. Half of it is in me. Half of it is in you. We were touching each other and E when we read her last night, and two halves combined mean–"

"Mean a stronger whole."

"Yeah. A stronger whole." Several seconds passed before he said, "What you did was really messed up."

"I know."

"But I forgive you."

She stared at him, her expression still heavy with remorse.

"I'm forgiving you because you freaked out and because I know it can be hard to understand where E's coming from. But never again."

She nodded fervently. He sighed.

"And be ready for E. It might take a while for her to trust you again."

"I'll find a way to make it up to her. I'll earn back her trust."

"Yeah, well, good luck with that." He grasped the back of his neck with both hands and groaned as he stretched out his back. "Come on. Let's get ready for bed. E won't be happy if we're running late. She might not be able to stab us in this dimension, but she can still kick us. Or slap us, at least."

He gave her a reluctant smile, which she returned with a grateful one. They walked out of the kitchen side-by-side.

"By the way, I was thinking about explaining things to Paul. Not everything, but just enough to stop him from bothering E. I'm not going to tell the others anything, though," James said.

"It's not our place to tell the others," said Snow. "It's the Shamans' code to keep all memories private. Or at least it's supposed to be. I did tell Rose a little about what happened when we were driving down, but I only talked about me messing up and not anything we actually saw. And Paul." She clicked her tongue and flipped her bangs to the side, looking irritated. "He really needs to leave her alone. I don't understand why he can't just drop it. I've told him so many times now. *Why is he so tactless?*"

They climbed up a large, curving staircase and followed the muffled sounds of the crew's voices down another hallway.

"What? What is it?" he said as Snow slowed to a stop.

"What are we going to do about Kit?"

James didn't answer. What were they going to do about Kit, indeed? The question had attacked his mind at random times throughout the day, but he'd failed to reach an even mildly satisfactory answer.

"I don't know," he said finally. "I don't know either. I want to talk to E about him, but I don't know how. I just know that when we do end up finding him, we have to stop her from going back to him."

"But she'll try to go back to him. You know she will!"

"We won't let him take her!"

"But how are we going to convince her? I ... I broke her trust, James. It doesn't matter that I know everything now. I broke her trust. Whatever I say won't matter."

"Well, then, I'll say something or team up with Phoenix or have Honey talk to her again or something! Look, I don't know what we need to do to convince her, but I am not going to stand around and let that monster take her again. I can't. I can't just watch her go like that. Not without a fight!"

# CHAPTER 13
# BETRAYED

James slipped into his sleeping bag and flopped around until he found the most comfortable position. Phoenix tossed and turned and shifted about in his sleeping bag. James could tell from his restlessness that his thoughts were needling him. In the privacy of a locked bathroom, James and Snow had finally explained to him that they had read E. They had also revealed that Kit had been abusive and that they feared E would eventually return to him. Phoenix had remained silent throughout the whole conversation before simply opening the door and walking away. James had known then and there that he would forever refrain from questioning E about her breakdown. The knowledge had given him and Snow a brief moment of relief.

James squirmed around again. He hoped the sleeping pills he'd snuck from Phillip's medicine cabinet would soon take effect and overpower the anxiety electrifying his nerves. What plans the crew had managed to create tonight were shaky at best, and if even the best-laid plans always went astray, how much more would shaky ones? He wormed around a final time as he reminded himself that he did not have the luxury of obsessing over "what ifs" and possible failures. He had to remain focused and take one step at a time.

Drowsiness began spreading throughout his mind, muffling the sounds of the others shifting about within their sleeping bags. His eyes began to blink shut. The girls lay clustered together on the other side of the room. Snow had poked her nose over the edge of her sleeping bag and was staring at E's turned back....

"*Halt!*" Father shouted.

The wolves and horses skidded to a stop then regrouped around James and Bloom. James raised his knife and scanned the plane. A lone streetlight stood beneath a giant slice of a highway bridge next to him. The ring of distant mountains surrounding him stood side-by-side in a succession of neat, oblong lumps as if a child had drawn them into being. The sidewalk beneath his feet began and ended abruptly beside an asphalt road that stretched forth and draped itself over one of the mountains like a black ribbon.

No signs of danger. No signs of the Calf.

He sheathed his blade and checked the size of the full moon. He hadn't expected the wolves to reach the City in a single night and knew that he should be grateful the crew even had the wolves to help them at all. But still, he couldn't help but wish that the moon looked just a little bit bigger.

He grabbed Snow's arm as she appeared. Bloom shuffled his paws and looked at each crew member with wide, expectant eyes as they appeared as well. His face split into a smile as E appeared last. He smeared kisses on her face then swirled around her. She smiled and ruffled his mane. Father's lips parted to expose his many fangs.

"*Like a common dog,*" he growled in disgust.

E threw him a sharp glare then swallowed as if to hold down a wave of threats.

"*We have been fortunate,*" Sleet said, stepping up to her as she yanked on the boots and socks that appeared in her hands. "*We encountered very few obstacles during your absence. We are not yet halfway to Lapis Lazuli, but we are still much closer than we had anticipated.*"

"*Thank you for your help while we were away,*" E said as she climbed onto Bloom. "*We discussed our plans for the nights ahead and agreed that Twelve should lead us to Lapis Lazuli from here on out.*"

Snow's face fell at E's refusal to use her name then quickly hardened into a look of resolve that stirred pride within James. E explained to the wolves the rest of the plans which the crew had formulated in Reality.

"*And you are absolutely sure that this Runner can be trusted and that she will not simply sell us all to the Third?*" Father asked as she finished speaking.

"*Positive,*" she growled. "*Why? Do you have any objections?*"

The pack stiffened as they glanced at Father. He stared at E for several moments.

"*No. I have no objections,*" he said at last. He turned around. "*I trusted the Last once, and now I will trust you. Castaways were meant to assist humans, not lead them, and we no longer have the luxury of simply standing here and quarreling. We must reach the moonlight without further delay.*"

The pack relaxed. James and Lux raised their eyebrows at one another. So, Father was capable of getting along with others after all, though, unfortunately, Bloom clearly remained a target of his condescension.

"*What a joy to be following the nose of a Shaman again. After all these eras!*" said Forest.

His tail flailed about as he welcomed Blood Crow onto his back again. Terrain and Honey glared at one another, clearly still sore about their argument the previous night, before snorting in unison. They gave each other a cordial nod before Honey climbed onto his back. Sleet gave Lux a solemn stare and crouched down for him. Phoenix jumped onto one of the horses. James lifted Snow onto the remaining horse and seated himself behind her.

Snow lifted her nose and inhaled deeply. The group waited in silence as she sniffed. Moments passed, but still she continued sniffing, so much so that James began to wonder if she smelled anything at all. Were they too far away from the City? Did she lack the skill to guide them all the way back to the moonlight?

"Snow," he ventured after several more moments. "Do you smell anything?"

She snapped her head toward the full moon. Leaning forward, she gripped the horse's mane.

"*Everyone, get ready,*" she commanded. "*I'm going to go as fast as I can. We will reach the Iris within the night. I give you my word. I will not let the Calf catch us.*"

James's breathing eased. More than one crew member let out a sigh of relief as well. The wolves crouched down as the horses pawed the ground and snorted. Snow exhaled like a runner on the verge of starting a race. She yelled and kicked the horse's sides. It reared up with a whinny. The group took off at a gallop and sped down the asphalt road until they reached the foot of a mountain. They strained and panted as they ran up a steep slope.

"*Exit ahead! Get ready!*" Snow shouted.

The mountains disappeared. Dishes broke as the group burst into a bustling sushi restaurant. People screamed and jumped out of the way. Large fish heads mounted on the walls yelled like bewitched taxidermy. Snow steered the horse toward a blank wall.

"*Exit!*" she yelled.

The group sped through the wall, one after another. They slammed into each other in a humid apartment, where soil carpeted the ground and plants grew as if in a jungle.

"*There!*"

She pointed to a closed window covered in mold and vines. The horse reared up and leapt. The room disappeared, and the group charged single-file through an orchard, where bees hummed around bouquets of white flowers. The full moon grew larger as Snow led them through another exit and another and another.

They ran through a cool, dark forest, where a white-bearded wizard brandished a wooden staff at them; through a house, where a boy sat alone at a desk, muttering to himself in one of countless rooms; across a hilltop, where a dog lay tethered to a pole at a gas station and a woman stared at them from across a neighboring hill; through a musty Victorian home full of floating furniture and beaded lamps; through an empty deli shop, where raw carcasses hung from the ceiling; across a sprawling zen garden in a quiet meadow; through a boundless, white space, where metal chairs stood in an infinite row and a phone rang and rang....

Water sprayed as Snow pulled on the horse's mane. The group halted in a long, empty hallway. Rain fell through a solid ceiling and flowed in curved sheets down a slanted, wooden floor. Closed doors lined the walls. Snow turned her head this way and that. She inhaled deeply before pointing to one of the doors.

"*It's here. The Iris is beyond this exit.*"

The group murmured in amazement. The wolves nodded approvingly. James grasped her shoulder. She had done it. Despite the group's doubts and even his own, she had led them back to No Man's Land within the night. Determination blazed in E's eyes as she drew her dagger. The others unsheathed their blades as well.

"*Keep quiet, and be ready for anything,*" she commanded.

She leaned forward on Bloom's back as he crept through the closed door. James prodded the horse with his heels. It walked through the exit and into a forest of thin, white trees, where moisture dripped and pattered onto leaves the color of autumn. He remained seated on the horse with Snow, ready to protect her, as he scoured the surrounding mist for the glint of an enemy's blade or the thick, black fabric of a Bodyguard's vest. The others dismounted and spread out with cautious steps. The wolves roved about as they sniffed the air and ground with vibrating noses.

Something snapped. The crew turned in unison with their weapons pointed. They waited. After a long silence, Bloom nodded at E.

"*We are alone,*" Sleet confirmed.

James relaxed the aim of his knife but not his grip. Snow remained tense between his arms.

"*Bloom and I will go find* Alex's *post,*" said Phoenix.

He gave E a firm nod then disappeared into the mist with Bloom. E commanded the group to stand in a circle and keep watch. Snow inclined her head in what James knew was a concentrated effort to hear any sounds that would signal a threat. Long moments passed, filled with nothing but the sound of dropping moisture. Snow jerked her head to the side. The wolves lifted their snouts. The crew raised their weapons higher.

"*What is it?*" E whispered as the wolves sniffed feverishly.

"*They have returned. I assume the new scent is the Runner,*" Father said.

Vague shadows materialized in the mist before shaping into Alex, Phoenix, and Bloom.

"Phoenix told me everything," Alex said as she clasped hands with E. An anxious expression sat in place of the cheerful smile with which she had previously greeted them. "Follow me. No need to keep formation for now. Let's move before the Bodyguards come this way."

They hurried after her into the woods. Though Father maintained a fixed, suspecting gaze on Alex, he remained silent.

"Word's been out about you guys," she said as they weaved between the trees. "The Third wants Snow and James back at all costs. It's good to see you again Snow, by the way, even though I wish it were under different circumstances! But yeah, everyone wants to find you guys and get the Third's reward. He's been sending a lot of men after you, and he sent out even more earlier tonight. He made an announcement that he'll pay a crazy amount to anyone who finds just E and Phoenix too."

Dread swooped into James's stomach.

"Just me and Phoenix? Why?" said E.

"Who knows? Obviously, he wants all of you, but the priority is on Snow, James, Phoenix, and you right now, so if we end up getting surrounded, you guys need to escape first. Who knows what he'll do to you if he captures you?"

James didn't have to guess what the Third would do. He would force them all to retrieve the golden eye then keep the Calf alive "in the name of research," as Zilch had put it. As for the new bounty on E and Phoenix, he'd always known that the two of them shouldn't have spoken so aggressively to the Third during their meeting in the Tower. Especially E! She never should have mouthed off at him like that. Now the Third wanted to take her and show her who was boss. He tried not to think of the naked women in Lavender and the leering men. Maybe the Third wouldn't use E to get to the Calf. Maybe he had some other sort of punishment in mind for her, a punishment worse than death.

"Do the Hunters know about the bounty on us yet?" asked E.

"I don't think so. They've been too busy with the Solstice to care about anything else, and the Third's men haven't really been able to talk to them because of the whole don't-interrupt-the-Solstice thing. But he'll get news to them soon one way or another, you mark my words. It's the Third we're talking about here."

Alex stopped, raised one hand, then put her finger to her lips. She sprinted ahead, leapt into the air, and disappeared. The group jumped one after another through the exit. Icy snow crunched under hooves, feet, and paws as the group landed on a cliff jutting out from the side of a black mountain. Alex frantically signaled to them as a band of Merchants trudged into view on the cliff below.

"Follow my steps exactly!" she whispered.

The group followed the trail she made for them as she sidestepped shifting plates of stone. They scurried behind the cover of black crags which grew out of the ground as they neared. James yanked his shirt over his nose and covered Snow's mouth with his hand to conceal their white breaths. The group trembled in the searing cold until the crunching of the Merchants' footsteps faded away.

Alex peered out from behind the crag then motioned to the group again. They rushed after her along the brink of the cliff and through another exit. They splashed into a swamp filled with humming and the strange cries of hidden citizens. Reeds rustled, and voices sounded. Alex commanded the group to submerge themselves. James grabbed Snow and slipped off of the horse as the voices approached. Moss swiftly crawled over the water's surface as he laid down with her in the murky water.

The voices grew louder. He watched the horses through patches of clear water as they pretended to drink. He continued wrestling with his need to breathe until slowly, the voices turned away and descended into silence. The group stifled their gasps as they resurfaced. James ushered Snow onto his back and waded after Alex with slow movements to ensure that he made as little noise as possible.

The group continued to mimic Alex's every move and rushed to obey her commands as she led them from one territory of No Man's Land to another. Under her guidance, they evaded dozens of Merchants and Bodyguards, all of whom conversed among themselves of the Third's reward, the missing Twelfth, and most of all, the famed E of the Arena, who slaughtered humans with her black machetes and now commanded a fearsome blue wolf that helped her in her campaigns.

Sunlight and a gentle breeze warmed James's mud-stained body as the group rushed out onto yellow hills. His stomach jumped up into his chest as he saw the City, at last, in the distance below. The vast land separating the Market and the Tower, which had been empty during the crew's last visit, now glittered with the lights of the Feast. Swarms of Hunters stirred so that the land seemed to jitter.

Alex swiveled her head from left to right then plunged into the tall, rippling weeds in front of them. The group followed her in a single-file line down the hill and into the refuge of swaying poplar trees.

"You guys can drive straight into *Lapis Lazuli* from here," Alex said, panting. "The land won't shift, so you should be good. Make sure to really step on it, though. I don't know when the Bodyguards will come this way again."

"You're not coming with us?" said Phoenix.

James, who had already begun running over to the giant car that Lux had created, paused along with the others as Alex shook her head.

"I'm going to go warn the other Runners about the Calf," she said.

"But that thing could come at any moment," said E.

"I can't let the others get blind-sided. Me and the other Runners can try to warn as many of the crews traveling within *the Iris* too, save as many as we can. You guys go ahead and take care of the Hunters."

E and Phoenix exchanged worried looks.

"I'll be all right," Alex assured them. "I'll just have to move fast."

"*If it is a matter of speed, we can assist you,*" said one of the horses.

"*Yes! You will travel much faster with us, and we can help transport other humans back to the moonlight too.*"

Alex looked at one horse then the other. *"Actually, that might not be such a bad idea."*

*"Then we shall go with you. It is decided."*

*"Which means our long friendship has come to an end at last,"* said the horse as it turned toward the wolves.

Realization then sadness settled upon James. Both of the horses were marked. They had no reason to remain in the Flowering any longer. The Keep was gone, and they would not be able to pass through the moonlight, for they were neither human nor Castaway. They would only risk falling prey to the moulded or the Calf if they failed to move on to the dimension of dreams soon, which meant that helping Alex would be their last mission.

Forest burst into tears. Terrain rubbed his eyes with his foreleg.

*"I cannot tell you how thankful we have been for the two of you throughout the ages,"* Father said as Alex jumped onto one of the horses.

*"Yes. Overseeing the Keep would not have been possible without your help,"* said Sleet. *"We shall miss you terribly, my friends."*

*"Oh, well, I'm sure you won't miss having to scold us for losing track of some of the little ones,"* the horse said, chuckling.

*"Or for letting them play in the fountains!"* said the other.

Father smiled. *"It was truly an honor,"* he said.

He led the pack in stooping their heads in a bow. E commanded the crew to assemble and bow to the horses as well. The horses snorted and pawed the ground as they withheld their tears. Alex gave the group a final nod. The horses smiled at the wolves, broke into a gallop, and disappeared beyond the trees.

"Let's go," E said after a brief silence. "Blood Crow, you drive. You'll need to take the lead and do all the talking once we get there."

The group rushed toward the car. Lux opened up the back to reveal a large trunk space. After the wolves piled in, James squished Snow into the middle of the pack and covered them all with a massive blanket. Even if someone were to peer in through the tinted windows, their lumpy shapes would easily pass for miscellaneous cargo in the trunk. Satisfied, he ran to the front passenger seat, climbed in, and slammed the door shut. Blood Crow stepped on the gas. The car burst out of the trees and zoomed toward the City.

"Just remember that you're supposed to hate all citizens," Blood Crow told the crew as the engine revved. "We need to wipe out all of the marked ones and keep all humans safe, no matter the cost. I'm known for being a hardcore Traditionalist, so if a Hunter from the other faction—they're called Contemporaries—start asking you about what methods you endorse, just yell about how you can't ever endorse torture.

*"Oh, and use only Our Word. That's a thing with Traditionalists. It's supposed to keep us all united and closer to our roots and the Brave and all that. Contemporaries speak in Our Word too, especially if they need to get past any language barriers, but they usually speak in whatever language they feel like using because it emphasizes that they have the freedom to do whatever they want. So stick to Our Word only, and don't use any other language. Everyone will assume you're a Traditionalist that way."*

James sat up straighter in his seat as they continued hurtling toward the moonlight. Blood Crow gripped the steering wheel as the engine revved fit to burst. They were so close to the Blue Border now. The lights of the Feast sparkled brighter as they neared. The full moon glowed huge above them. Anxiousness accelerated James's heartrate to full throttle as he searched the land around them for signs of the Third's men and the Red Calf.

They shot through the moonlight and into the City.

He let out a moan of relief. Lux clapped then punched the air. Honey closed her eyes as Phoenix and E continued scanning their surroundings. Blood Crow smiled as she decelerated. At the very least, they had made it into the moonlight before the Calf or the Third could find them. Now they had to focus on sneaking into the Feast and signing up Blood Crow for the Tournament.

The sounds of booming music, clashing swords, and raucous laughter grew in a crescendo as they neared an expansive line of Hunters guarding the festivities. Blood Crow slowed the car to a stop as one of the Hunters broke formation. She left the motor running and jumped out to greet the man. They embraced and exchanged muffled words. James slid his hand toward the hilt of his knife, ready to defend her should the man show any signs of aggression. He knew even without turning around that the others had gripped their blades as well. Several more moments of conversation passed before she hugged the Hunter again and ran back to the car.

"*Okay, we're in,*" she said as she locked the doors. She continued beaming and nodding at the Hunters as they parted to make room for her to drive through. "*We'll find a place to park first and then we'll find Lion Paw. And try to look happy you guys, jeez! You're Hunters at the Feast, remember? This is supposed to be one of the best nights of the year.*"

James slapped on his best, office-appropriate smile as Blood Crow steered the car through the human wall and drove along the circumference of the Feast. Speakers pumped out bass-heavy music that made the windows of the car shudder to the beat. Screens and strobe lights flashed inside large tents interspersed throughout the crowds. Countless Hunters sat on the ground, gorging on piles of food laid out on endless rows of thick plywood covered with golden tablecloths. Polished silverware and bejeweled goblets sparkled in the light of patio lamps and bonfires. Droves of families raised their drinks and shouted toasts of "for life" and "protect" over bursts of laughter. Just as many argued and yelled threats.

"*You need clean cuts! Clean cuts and clean kills!*" a Hunter shouted.

"Don't you compare me to those dirty Merchants! I took those weapons because I needed them!" another yelled.

James stared straight ahead as a family eyed the tinted windows of the group's car. Another family smashed in the windows of a parked car and began looting its contents. James glanced back at where the wolves and Snow lay hidden then at Lux's watch. They didn't have much time left in the night. But who would guard the car when they returned to Reality?

"*Wait*," Blood Crow said. She squinted then gasped.

James shouted with surprise as she slammed on the brakes. She leapt out of the car and ran into the crowds.

"*Blood Crow!*" E yelled.

Her red hair continued traveling deeper into the multitudes.

"*Everyone, stay here and keep guard*," E commanded. "James, *you're the fastest, so you run with me. What is she thinking?*"

He dashed into the crowds alongside E. They dodged drunk Hunters, sped past laughing families, ran through clouds of smoke, and leapt over sumptuous dishes of food. They called out to Blood Crow, but she only continued running.

"*Lion Paw! Steel Heart!*" she shouted.

A horde of squabbling families streamed out into the path ahead, forcing James and E to skid to a halt. James swore then crouched and stood and swayed from side-to-side as he tried to catch sight of Blood Crow again. Beyond the clamoring families, he saw Lion Paw turn. His sapphire eyes widened as he saw Blood Crow. Beside him, Steel Heart, the black-haired teen who had tried to protect James from the snake woman, turned as well.

Steel Heart uttered a cry of joy before running to Blood Crow and wrapping her in a tight embrace. Lion Paw continued staring at her, pale and speechless as if he were looking at someone who had risen from the grave. He took one step forward then another before running and throwing his arms around her and Steel Heart both.

E growled with frustration as the bickering families blocking their way broke out into an open fight. Spears began soaring through the air. Dust rose from the ground. James rolled his eyes.

"*Come on. Let's get through to her,*" E grumbled.

They stepped into the fray, James with his knife and E with her machete. They evaded screaming Hunters and the haphazard swings of various weapons. Blood Crow broke away from Lion Paw and Steel Heart and began speaking to them. A large Hunter slammed into James from behind. Instinct made him shove the Hunter back. He cursed himself for his lack of self-restraint as he dodged the man's blow. E kicked the man's legs out from under him then stabbed him in the stomach. James hurled his knife into a Hunter who ran toward her. E sliced off the arm of a woman who raised her sword against James. James jumped closer to E and threw the spears that appeared in his hands as she slashed apart those within close proximity.

Heads began to turn. The families' animosity toward one another disappeared as they closed in on James and E instead. Blood Crow grabbed Lion Paw's arm. He pulled out of her grasp and stepped back with a look of disbelief.

"*All right, all right. Break it up, break it up! I've had enough of this,*" someone said.

The Hunters whirled around then dropped their weapons as a man marched toward them. He wore copper-colored contacts and a necklace that boasted two rubies. It was that cocky Hunter who had argued with Blood Crow back in the tunnels! The one who had run away from the crew at the fiery chasm and carried the teen girl who had lost her leg to the Calf's darkness.

"*Copperhead!*" a Hunter exclaimed.

"*Yes, it is I, Copperhead. I have come to break up this annoying fight that's re-broken four times now even though I warned all of you to stop last night! Now, do you want to go your separate ways nicely, or do I have to take away your Tournament privileges? Which one is it going to be, huh?*"

"*I'm sorry. It won't happen again. At least, not with my family,*" said one of the Hunters.

The families threw glares at one another. A few hands began wandering toward the weapons lying on the ground.

"*Now, did you really have to put it that way?*" said Copperhead. "*Just for that, I'm going to ask the heads of each family to shake hands. Go on! Shake hands! I know you can do it.*"

He crossed his arms as they grumbled and complied. The families continued muttering among themselves as they stalked off in different directions and blended back into the crowds. Copperhead dragged his hands down his face with a loud groan before turning to E and James. Suspicion sprang up within James as he greeted them with a wide smile.

"Miss Fearsome! And Yelling Guy. Never thought I'd see the two of you here. It's so great to see you! How have you two been?"

James and E looked at each other then glared at Copperhead again. What was this guy playing at? Had he heard about the Third's bounty on the crew? Was this some pathetic attempt to capture them all? James prepared to strike with his spear at E's signal.

"I've been great," Copperhead said as if they'd asked. "Just busy here with the Feast and everything. Still fulfilling my role as the Lead from last year. You know the drill. But, um ... hey, I know this is a little random, but you don't happen to know where that furry, blue friend of yours might be right now, do you? You know, the one who saved Red Rock from falling into the fire? Because if you do—whoa! Hold it!"

He sprang back, barely missing the swipe of E's machete. James aimed his spear at Copperhead's eye as another machete appeared in E's hand. Copperhead flung up his hands in surrender.

"I'm only asking because I wanted to say thank you!" he said.

"*Go waste someone else's time with your lies,*" E growled.

"I ain't lying, Scary Lady! I don't know what would have happened to Red Rock if your friend hadn't saved her from that fire. And it sniffed out that exit for us too!"

Copperhead closed his mouth and swallowed. James tried to decipher the change in his expression. Was it fear that he saw or determination? Copperhead slowly lowered his hands and continued in a hushed voice.

"None of my family members who were taken by that weird darkness in those tunnels returned after that night, and Red Rock's leg never regrew. She says it's paralyzed in Reality, and none of the doctors she's gone to know how to fix it."

He paused, looking torn again. Then he sighed and said, "Okay, look. I was asking you about the wolf because I thought it might know something about that darkness. I've never run into something that humans couldn't heal from. Your wolf friend was on the same plane as that darkness, and citizens tend to have a better understanding of the planes. I thought it might be willing to help Red Rock again if I thanked it for last time and begged it for its help. Maybe it knows how to find the rest of my family too. Or maybe you guys know something? You knew that darkness was dangerous, right?" he said, looking at James. "You kept yelling that we had to run for it."

James remained silent. The desperation in Copperhead's eyes made him wonder if he wasn't out to capture the crew, after all. Regardless of whether or not he was telling the truth, though, there was no way that James was about to trust him with information about the Red Calf or its darkness. They couldn't risk any information leaking out before Blood Crow won the Tournament.

"Please," said Copperhead.

He took a step closer to them. E's machetes flashed. He remained still as she pressed her blades against the skin of his neck.

"I know I did you guys wrong before, but please," he said. "I'm the head of my family, and I need to find out what happened to the rest of them. Or at least help me help Red Rock. She's just a kid, for crying out loud. I've tried everything to get her leg to heal. Everything. But nothing's working. I bribed a Merchant to make her a Hedonist for now, but she can't stay like that forever."

"*Does everything we've been through mean nothing to you?*" Blood Crow screamed.

James's focus snapped onto her. She continued shouting as Lion Paw shook his head and walked away. Steel Heart glanced back and forth between her and Lion Paw before murmuring something to her and running after Lion Paw. E glared at Copperhead a final time before lowering her machetes.

"*Let's go before she runs away again,*" she told James.

They rushed over to Blood Crow. Copperhead hesitated then followed them.

"*What's happening?*" E demanded. She pointed her machete at Copperhead's face to keep him at bay.

"*He won't believe me!*" said Blood Crow.

She gripped E's shoulders and shook her slightly. Tears were streaming down her face, and her eyes were so wide that they seemed in danger of popping out of her head. She didn't even seem to notice Copperhead.

"*He won't believe me about the Red Calf, about anything!*"

"*Whoa,*" James said, glancing at Copperhead, who frowned. "*Maybe we should talk about this someplace else.*"

"*And he won't put me on the roster for the Tournament,*" Blood Crow continued. "*He says he won't call me family anymore if I don't want to hunt. He doesn't want anything to do with me anymore!*"

"*You told him you don't want to hunt?*" E hissed.

Copperhead jumped. "Wait. That darkness," he said. Realization widened his eyes. "*The Red Calf?*"

James suppressed a groan of frustration. Great. Lion Paw had disowned Blood Crow, and now Copperhead knew about the Red Calf. What else could possibly go wrong? Blood Crow let go of E and clutched at her own hair.

"*I wanted to tell him the truth. I wanted him to know the truth. About me, about everything! I don't understand. He's like a father to me. He's always been like a father to me. We all swore a blood oath that we'd die for each other!*"

"Wait, wait, wait, wait, wait," said Copperhead. He checked their vicinity before whispering, "The Red Calf. Is that darkness related to the Red Calf? But how? How?"

E sighed and lowered her machete from his face. She pinned him with a black glare again as she scrutinized him for several moments.

"*The Red Calf has returned, and it's coming here to Lapis Lazuli,*" she told him.

Had E lost her mind? James made to protest, but she held up a hand to silence him. Shock transformed into dismay on Copperhead's face as she summarized the crew's journeys as well as everything they knew about the Calf.

"*The Third will use us to retrieve the golden eye and capture the Calf. And once he has his sight and the Calf's power, he'll destroy the Flowering with his greed like the Shamans of old. We came to the Feast because we wanted Blood Crow to enter the Tournament and become the Lead, but now....*" She looked at Blood Crow then sighed, looking more exasperated than angry.

Blood Crow swallowed. "*I'm sorry, E. I really thought Lion Paw was loyal.*" She glanced at Copperhead then grimaced as if she were kicking herself for saying too much in front of him.

"Well, if it's a matter of getting on the roster, don't worry about that. I'll put you under my family, and you can enter the Tournament that way," said Copperhead.

Blood Crow snorted and shook her head. James cleared his throat, shifted his weight, and adjusted his grip on his spear. He looked at E pointedly, but she continued staring only at Copperhead.

"Look, bad news is I can't enter the Tournament for you guys because I won last year," Copperhead said. "Good news is I won last year, so I'm still the Lead until someone else takes over tomorrow night. I'll just put you guys under my family, and if anyone says anything, I'll pull rank."

James rolled his eyes with the type of impatient skepticism that would have made Honey proud. "*You really expect us to believe that after everything you did to us in the tunnels?*" he said.

"You really think I'm not going to help you guys after what the Red Calf did to my family? I want that thing dead! Because if what you're saying is true, it killed my family members. Killed! Do you understand? They're dead now because of the Calf! And I'd rather die too before I let any more Hunters inside or outside of my family end up like them or Red Rock. Red Rock." His face wrinkled under the crushing weight of an unwanted truth. "She's crippled for life now."

James couldn't help but pity Copperhead a little as he turned his face away from them to hide his grief. His mind replayed the dying screams of Copperhead's family. He sighed then mentally scrolled through the crew's options. They had counted on Lion Paw to get them on the roster, and now, with his refusal to help Blood Crow, they had no way of entering the Tournament. Maybe taking Copperhead's offer was their best bet. It wasn't like they had any alternatives. He exchanged looks with E again.

"*Fine*," she said. She tucked her machetes under her belt. "*Get us into the Tournament, then.*"

"Done," said Copperhead. "And if you need anything else, just tell me. I'll help. We need to work together from here on out."

Blood Crow simply glared at him before walking away.

"Hold it there, Miss Fearsome," Copperhead said, stopping E and James as they made to follow. "I need your names if I want to put you all on the roster. Oh, and drop the Our-Word-only thing, you guys. You're Contemporaries now."

E rattled off the crew's names as Copperhead pulled out a notebook.

"Hold it, hold it! Okay, yeah. So that's not going to work. We need Hunter names for you guys. Phoenix is all right, but how about...." He tapped his pen against his lips. "Lux can be Deadly Sunshine. Honey can be Golden Bee. You can be Dark Watch. And you, of course, are Black Fang."

"Name us whatever you want. I don't care," E growled. She turned to leave then stopped.

"What is it?" James asked as she stared into the distance.

"All right. What is it? Come on. Spit it out. What do you need?" said Copperhead.

"We have cargo in the car that needs guarding, cargo that'll help us defeat the Calf," said E. "We can't have any of the Hunters seeing it until Blood Crow wins the Tournament."

James knew that E wouldn't listen to any of his protests, so instead, he struggled to keep his expression blank as he wondered, again, if she had gone crazy. Trusting Copperhead to get Blood Crow into the Tournament was one thing, but entrusting the safety of the wolves to him was another thing entirely!

"Cargo?" Copperhead repeated.

"The cargo is blue."

"What?" he exclaimed. "But how?"

"If you care about saving your family and everyone else here, you'll guard our car with your life. We need that cargo no matter what. And there's more than one. They came in a pack, and we need all of them to win the battle. Oh, and Miss Blue Eyes is in there too."

Copperhead's mouth opened and closed, opened and closed. He swallowed then said, "It's done. My family will guard it. A lot of them are in different time zones, so they can guard it at all times. I'll forbid them from looking inside too. It won't be a problem. But man. This really is some crazy sh–"

"Just shut up and follow me," said E. "Oh, and I'm assuming you remember our fight in the tunnels?"

"I remember. And I get it! If I do anything to endanger the 'cargo'"– he used air quotes–"I'll go ahead and stab my watch every night until I die. It'll probably be better than waiting for you to come and hunt me down, Miss Black Fang."

"*Do really you think it's a good idea to trust him with the wolves?*" James asked E in Korean as she began leading them through the crowds.

"*There's no other choice.*"

"*Well … wouldn't it be better just to keep sleeping? We can guard the car.*"

"*I agree with what* Phoenix *said before. Who knows if the battle with the Calf will last for a moment or for nights? We can't afford to mess up our sleep cycles until then.*" She sighed. "*I don't know about the other Hunters, but I think we can trust this one for now.*"

*"Why? What's so different about him? He's a Hunter! Have you already forgotten what he did to* Bloom*?"*

*"Of course I haven't,"* she growled. *"But he's a leader who genuinely loves his family. If it's for his family, he'll do whatever he needs to do."*

*"You mean that's what you would do. This Hunter is different than you!"*

*"Don't you remember how he took care of that girl after she lost her leg? And when they were hunting* Bloom*, he asked* Lion Paw *to hunt all together. He knows how to join forces with his enemies if he needs to. He knows how to set aside his ideals to look at a bigger picture."*

As they approached the car, Blood Crow's mouth formed the words "what now." She and the others jumped out with their weapons drawn. Copperhead raised his hands with a resigned expression. E stopped the crew from marching up to him. Their aggression slowly transformed into uneasiness as she explained the situation. After several moments full of objections and Copperhead swearing upon his honor that he would keep their car locked, guarded, and safe, the crew obeyed E's command to get back in the car.

Copperhead walked toward the front passenger seat as Blood Crow took her place behind the wheel. James leapt into the front seat and slammed the door in his face. The seat next to Blood Crow was his and his alone! Plus, he'd never appreciated just how much attention Copperhead always seemed to give Blood Crow.

"Hey! What gives?" Copperhead exclaimed.

James ignored him. Copperhead grumbled as he climbed into the seat next to Honey instead. Though she wrinkled her nose and looked him up and down, she didn't object to his presence, and after one more glance, she scooted over to make more room for him. She introduced herself and Lux in a low grumble then continued conversing with him as

Blood Crow drove around the crowds. She even smirked at one of his jokes as they pulled up next to his family.

"I'll let them know you guys are a part of our family now. And I know, I know!" Copperhead said as E glared at him. "I won't tell them any details. I'm not stupid. Sheesh."

Blood Crow scowled and locked the car as soon as Copperhead had jumped out. He ordered several Hunters to surround the vehicle then gave E a thumbs up.

"Time, you guys," said Lux.

"Let's go back, then," E said. Still facing forward as if she were speaking to the crew, she told the wolves, "*Please don't make any movements. Hunters will guard you for now. We'll be back.*"

"*Hunters?*" Terrain exclaimed.

One of the wolves shushed him.

"*We will be waiting for you,*" Father growled.

James unsheathed his knife. He resisted the temptation to turn around and check on the pack one last time before he pierced his watch.

He rolled over onto his side and opened his eyes.

Phoenix had already woken up and wandered off somewhere. Lux groaned and stirred beside him. The girls shifted in their sleeping bags.

A cry of rage ripped apart the morning. James and the others flailed about before sitting up. The shouting continued from down the hall.

"Paul?" E said.

She was right. One of the voices—the angrier one—was definitely Phoenix. The other sounded like Phillip. James squirmed out of his sleeping bag as the others hurried to stand up as well. The doors of the room burst open.

It was Phoenix. His face was flushed, and he was heaving deep breaths. Every trace of his usual calm demeanor had disappeared. He staggered to one side and shoved his fingers into his hair. Phillip ran up to him.

"Son," said Phillip, his eyes flickering between Phoenix and the crew. "Son, calm down."

"Don't tell me to calm down!" he screamed. "E! You guys! It's him! It's him! How could I have missed it? How could I have missed it for all these years?"

What was Phoenix thinking, using E's name in Reality like it was nothing? As the words "shut up" boiled up into James's mouth, Phoenix thrust a shaking finger toward Phillip as if he were identifying a criminal.

"E, this is him! It's him! He just told me himself. He's Three!"

# CHAPTER 14
# RECOGNITION

James couldn't move, couldn't speak. Phillip couldn't be Three. He couldn't possibly be Three. The Third was the evil, power-hungry Shaman who was hunting the crew. He couldn't be the same man who had allowed E to scold him in her office. The man who had chuckled and tried to give her and James privacy when he had caught them in an embrace. And he was Phoenix's father. How could Phoenix's father be the Third?

E dropped down onto her knees. Honey and Blood Crow lurched forward to catch her as she slumped over onto the floor.

"E!" Phoenix cried.

He outraced James and Lux as they all ran to her. He skidded onto his knees, grabbed E by her shoulders, and called to her in a voice that struggled to suppress panic. Phillip stepped forward.

"Stay back!" Phoenix shouted. "Stay away from us. Don't you dare come near us!"

Phillip stopped and placed a shaking hand over his eyes. Lux muttered, "I'll get some water," and ran out of the room. Blood Crow and Honey exchanged a stunned look before staring at James. He shook his head then looked at Snow. Out of everyone in the crew, she alone had remained rooted to where she'd been standing. All the blood had drained from her skin so that she had gone from pale to white. She continued staring at Phillip with a stricken face.

Everyone flinched as James's phone began to ring then again as Lux flew back into the room. He passed a cup of water to Phoenix. He took E's hand and wrapped it around the cup. She nodded then began to drink. Phoenix jerked closer to her as she choked. Honey thumped her on the back as she coughed. E waved away the crew as they pressed in around her. James's phone fell silent. E heaved several deep breaths. She pierced Phillip with a black glare.

"Esther," he said. "Esther, please listen to me."

"How long have you known?"

He breathed a small sigh of defeat. "How long have I known what?"

She began with a growl and ended in a scream as she said, "How long have you known who we are?"

She threw the cup onto the floor. Water splashed in all directions as the cup bounced and rolled across the carpet. Phillip covered his eyes again.

"I didn't know until last night. I swear it. I walked into the kitchen when you and Paul were speaking about the Market and No Man's Land, and that's when I realized you were both a part of the Flowering. But I must confess, I was only able to realize who you really were because of James's name."

Understanding swallowed James whole. It was because of him. His name had been the missing link that had allowed the Third to connect their identities in Reality to their identities in the Flowering. This was all because he had refused to change his name in a fit of impertinence during his first night. His pride had betrayed them all.

"Why didn't you ever tell me?" Phoenix said through clenched teeth.

"I think I should be asking you the same question," Phillip replied.

James's phone burst into melody again. He looked at E, uncertain of what he should do, but she ignored him. She stood up slowly and waved away the crew again as they leaned in to help her.

"The Red Calf is coming to the City," she told Phillip. "It'll be at the moonlight soon."

Phillip frowned. Crew Blue exchanged looks of alarm. Snow's hands slowly balled into fists. James's phone fell silent once more.

"Business is always first, right? So, let's talk business," E said. "You were right about the Calf. It was trapped out there in the Flowering, waiting to return, just like you had hypothesized, and it's broken free now. It's back with its full strength, and its darkness has already killed several Hunters."

Phillip's face smoothed into a mask-like expression devoid of emotion. James glanced at Lux, who responded with his own look of panicked confusion. Why would E tell the Third this information after all the trouble they had gone through to keep it and themselves out of his hands? But then again....

But then again, who other than the Third possessed the power to keep all the humans in both No Man's Land and the City safe? No one. Not the Runners, not the crew, not even the other Shamans. No one had power like he did. Only the Third could truly ensure that each and every one of the hundreds of lives at stake could be kept safe, and now that he'd found the crew in Reality, E had taken her chances and told him about the Calf's impending arrival.

But the Third had imprisoned the crew and set a man hunt on them. He was the greedy Shaman who hungered for the golden eye and the powers of the Red Calf. He was the man who could very well cause the crew's demise as well as that of the Flowering and Reality. The crew needed his help, true, but they could not dare to trust him. James tried to channel a silent warning to E with an unblinking stare. She glanced at him before speaking again.

"I know you want that golden eye, Phillip, and I know you want the Calf alive. But you haven't seen the Calf. You haven't seen what its darkness can really do. It's almost killed us twice already."

Phillip glanced at Phoenix.

"The Red Calf can't pass through the moonlight," E continued. "So please. Forget about capturing the Calf, and forget about its golden eye. Focus on using your influence as the Third to command all the humans in and around the City to stay within the moonlight. Humans will die otherwise. I can guarantee it."

Phillip drew a deep breath and lifted his head high. "If that is what will save lives, then that is what I will do. I give you my word," he said.

James stiffened with surprise. He hadn't expected the Third to comply so easily! E, on the other hand, though clearly relieved, reflected very little surprise. Maybe the Phillip she knew wasn't as greedy as the Third.

"I will give the order tonight," Phillip said. "I will gather all of my men and have them round up everyone in No Man's Land. I will enforce a lockdown on the Market and the Tower as well. Once everyone is safely within the moonlight, I'll send the full strength of my forces to the Solstice to contain the Hunters and prevent them from doing anything rash. As you can imagine, they'll be more difficult to control, but hopefully, with the amount of men I'll send, they will comply."

James's heart dipped into the fear that swelled within him. If the Third sent his men to infiltrate the Solstice, he would, at last, capture the crew and the pack.

"We have a plan to hold back the Hunters," E said after glancing at James again. "Just focus all your efforts on the Tower, the Market, and

No Man's Land. Leave the Hunters to us. We'll let you know if we really can't handle it. We'll take care of the Calf when it comes too."

"What do you mean you'll take care of the Calf when it comes?"

"I mean we know how to kill it, so we are going to kill it," E growled.

"I understand that," he said, sounding impatient with her for the first time. "But you can't expect me to simply sit here and allow all of you to go gallivanting around when you just told me that the Red Calf is coming to the City at full strength? No. No, I will not allow it. You will all return to the Tower immediately. The whole reason I revealed my identity to Paul was because I wanted him to know that I mean no harm!"

He threw Phoenix an annoyed look before sighing and shaking his head. "But perhaps it is better this way. Now that you know who I am, surely you must believe me when I say that I do not mean any of you any harm. Please, come back to the Tower. I do not want any of you out there risking your watches and facing the dangers of planes and citizens every night, and I doubly do not want you out there now that the Calf has returned. Come back to the safety of the Tower. You will have the best room and board the City can afford, and I will deploy my best Bodyguards to take care of everything."

"No," said Phoenix.

Phillip blinked rapidly. Phoenix swept past E and placed himself in front of her so that his body shielded hers.

"This is all just another one of your tricks to get what you want. You just want us to come to the Tower so that you can lock us all up and use whatever we tell you to get to the golden eye and capture the Calf!"

Phillip sputtered and scoffed. "What? Paul—I—lock you up? Do you really think I would imprison you? I only want you somewhere where I can keep you safe every night! And what is all this about capturing the Calf? What kind of moron do you think I am? We must kill it!"

James exchanged startled looks with the others again. Phoenix, however, remained stoic.

"And what about its golden eye?" he said.

Phillip struggled then said, "Of course I will retrieve the eye. We might as well salvage what we can."

"No!" Phoenix shouted. "See? This is what I'm talking about. You already have the City in the palm of your hand. I won't let you have the eye too. You'll destroy everything with your greed. Your blindness is barely holding you back as it is!"

Phillip stared at him open-mouthed. "You cannot be serious," he whispered. An ugly redness spread over his cheeks. "Paul, I must retrieve that eye. I must retrieve my sight! It is my sight. My sight! I cannot spend the rest of my nights trapped in the Tower like this. The depths to which I've had to sink in order to survive. Years and years of it. I am at my wits' end with it all! Why do you think I stooped to conducting all those pathetic experiments on No Man's Land, and believe me, I know how pathetic they are. But if I could be free of the City and all of its sordid affairs even for a moment! If I could step outside of the moonlight on my own without fear. This is the opportunity I've been waiting for, Paul. I must take back the sight of the Shamans!"

"Yes, Three," Snow said. She rushed up to Phoenix's side. "You'll take back the sight of the Shamans, and then you'll keep it all for yourself. You'll use me and James to retrieve the eye for you even if it means risking our lives!"

"I will not be risking anyone's lives, Twelve," Phillip snapped. "You all must come back to the Tower!"

"We are not going back to the Tower!" Phoenix shouted.

"I won't allow you to face the Calf! You will come to the Tower, and you will stay with me where I can protect you!"

"Protect us?" Phoenix said. He let out an incredulous laugh. "Protect us? Don't act like you care about us! Snow's right. You'll send her and James to their deaths. You'll send all of us to our deaths. Me, E, all of us!"

"What?" Phillip breathed. "Paul. Do you really believe that? Do you really believe that I would risk your life? You are my son. I'm your father!"

"I don't care if you're my father," Phoenix said. "You didn't raise me, *Nainai* and Mom did. And what else do you expect me to believe? All you've ever cared about is yourself. Nothing's ever been enough for you."

Phillip gaped at him. E placed her hand on Phoenix's arm and gently drew him back. James's phone began ringing again. Honey let out a groan of frustration. E glared at James then flicked her chin toward his luggage. He ran across the room, shoved his hand into his backpack, and pulled out his phone.

It was Heri.

"Sorry. It's my sister," he muttered. "Hello, Heri? Sorry, but I'm in the middle of something."

"Where are you?" she raged. "And why haven't you been answering my texts?"

"What do you mean, 'where am I?' Look, I told you I'm in the middle of something!"

"James, you promised!"

"Promised wha...."

His stomach dropped. He looked at the date on his phone then whispered a curse as he realized that it was Christmas Eve.

"'Promised what?' Are you serious? You said you'd help out with cooking today. I thought you were being serious this time!"

"Heri," he mumbled. "I'm really sorry. I really did mean it. It's just–"

"Just what? You always do this. You always give me some stupid, made-up excuse!"

"I'm not giving you an excuse! Look, it's literally life or death, okay?"

"Oh, life or death now, is it? That's a funny way of saying 'I'm too busy stuffing my fat face with thousands of calories worth of instant ramen to keep my promise to my little sister!'"

"Heri," he said through gritted teeth.

He cringed as Honey held up an imaginary phone to her ear then hung it up. E's eyes glinted with a wordless warning. James gestured to them that he understood even as his mind flailed about in an attempt to make up a reason that Heri could understand and, hopefully, accept.

"Heri, I ... I have a project at school," he improvised. "It's a group project, a-and it came up last minute."

"Oh, really? Tell me about this imaginary group project, then. I want to hear all the imaginary details!"

"It's a sleep project. A group sleep project! We need to ... we need to sleep for eight hours a day. And record a bunch of stuff. And if we don't, we fail the entire class, and we're just tied up with a lot of details right now, and there's nothing I can do to control it. But look, I'm really sorry for not picking up. It wasn't intentional, I swear, and I will call you back! Now, I have to go. I'm sorry."

An ominous silence ensued.

"Wait. Heri? Uh ... Heri? Wait, hello?"

"You're part of the Flowering."

Shock snatched away James's ability to speak. For a second, he struggled to breathe. He choked then forced out, "What?"

"I said, is this eight-hour-a-night-project thing actually the Flowering?"

"Wait," he said. What was happening? First Phillip and now Heri? Was every single person he knew in Reality a part of the Flowering too?

He glanced at Phillip before saying in Korean, "*What are you talking about? How do you know about the Flowering?*"

Snow jumped. E held up a hand as Honey made to speak.

"It is the Flowering. You're a part of it," Heri said, sounding awestruck.

"*Heri, will you please answer the question? Are you part of the Flowering too?*"

"No, of course not! Have you ever seen me keep a sleep schedule? I have friends who are. They've had to crash at my place once in a while when they were desperate for sleep and—wait. James. James, are you running low on sleep?"

The panic in her voice somehow eased his own.

"*No. Not yet,*" he said.

"What do you mean '*not yet*?'"

"*It's a really long story. We're having a really hard time right now,*" he said.

"And by '*we*,' you mean your crew?"

"*Yes.*"

"How many of you are there?"

"*Seven, including me. Why?*"

"Where are you guys all sleeping tonight? And where are you right now? I'm guessing you're trying to speak in Korean because it's not safe to speak in English."

"Uh...." He highly doubted that the crew would want to stay in the Third's house tonight. They needed to get out of here.

"If you guys don't have a good place to stay, just come here to Mom and Dad's. I'll convince them to let you stay the night."

"*We can't do that. There are too many of us! It's fine. We'll just go to my apartment or something.*"

"Oh, like seven people are going to fit in that dirty, little craphole of yours. Are there any girls with you?"

"*What? Yeah. Why?*"

"Good. Mom will try to set you up with one of them. It'll make things easier. Are there other guys too?"

"*Heri–*"

"Are there any guys?"

"*Yes, but–*"

"Good. She'll probably try setting me up with one of them too. She'll love having all of you over. And you guys can help cook while you're at it."

"*We can't–*"

"Just come, James! I'll let Mom and Dad know that you guys are homeless, and they won't be able to refuse. But it all makes sense now," she said as amazement overtook her voice again. "No wonder you were so pissed off at me on Thanksgiving. You really did have a lot going on!" She scoffed then said, "You could've just told me the truth. I would've understood! Whatever. We'll talk more about it when you get here. Just get here soon. We need to start cooking, okay? See you soon. Bye."

"*Wait, Heri–*"

The line went dead. James hung his head. He turned around to find the crew staring at him with expressions that varied in their shades of annoyance and confusion.

"My sister," he mumbled. "I promised her before that I'd help her out with Christmas Eve dinner, and now she wants us all to help out too. She says she'll talk to my parents so we can sleep over at their place."

Phillip gave Phoenix an imploring look. Phoenix only glared back before nodding at E. Pity formed into a helpless expression on her face as she looked back and forth between father and son.

"Let's do that, then," she said. "We'll stay at James's house for tonight. Let's ... let's all pack up."

Phoenix turned on his heel and began gathering his things. Phillip stood still as the crew rushed around and threw their belongings into their bags. Determination pushed aside the sadness on his face. He marched toward Phoenix.

"Son. Son, listen to me. Stay here. Stay home."

"I hate you," Phoenix said.

The pain in Phillip's eyes went past his heart and into his soul. James avoided looking at him as he finished stuffing his sleeping bag into its case. He swung his backpack onto his shoulder and hurried out of the house with the rest of the crew. Phoenix slammed the door shut once they had all stepped out into the cold.

"What was all that about your sister and the Flowering?" E asked James.

"Wait, what? She knows about the Flowering?" Lux exclaimed.

Honey slapped him across the shoulder and shushed him before jerking her head toward the door. James shrank away slightly as he stared at the peephole. He suddenly found it unnerving to think that they were all still standing on the Third's doorstep. And to think they'd been sleeping under his roof the entire night. He made sure to whisper as he recapped his conversation with Heri. The howling winds made the crew shiver as they listened.

"I think staying at your parents' home really is the best solution we have for now, then," E said as he finished speaking. She rubbed her arms and grimaced as another gust streamed past. "Let's hurry up and get going. I don't want us to catch colds. And make sure to change once you're in the car."

James did a double take. They were all still in their pajamas. The wind shuffled through the trees as the crew hurried to their cars. Soon,

James was leading everyone down the freeway. Alone in his car and listening to the white noise of the winds rushing past, he lost himself within his thoughts.

Could they really trust Phillip to use his influence as the Third to protect everyone in the City and No Man's Land? He had seemed sincere enough when he'd said that he would. Plus, it was in his best interest to save as many humans as possible. After all, he'd be powerless if there weren't any humans left to hold power over. He had also seemed intent on killing the Calf instead of keeping it alive as the crew had thought.

Had the crew jumped to conclusions? Had they been wrong all this time to assume that the Third would take his greed that far? Now that James thought about it, the Third had never struck him as power-hungry to the point of madness. It did seem more likely that he would take the golden eye and get rid of the Calf and any danger it posed to himself and others. Did that mean the crew had wrongly assumed his motives for trying to capture them? Would he really keep them all safe once they were in his grasp?

Images of the Tower and their meeting with the Third flashed through his mind.

No. Maybe the Third wasn't crazy enough to keep the Calf alive, but the crew couldn't trust him to keep them safe. Phoenix was the Third's only child, so the chances of him sending out Phoenix on as dangerous a mission as taking back the golden eye were slim to none. James could also see him sparing E, his prized assistant in Reality. But the Third barely knew James or the others, and Snow was the only human alive who could take back the eye. The Third had no reason to show them any mercy.

But did that really matter now? The crew was determined to kill the Calf, and they had long ago accepted the dangers of their mission.

Maybe it would be better to join forces with the Third if they were going to battle the Calf anyway.

But the golden eye. If the Third got his hands on that eye, the Shamans would regain their sight. Or maybe he'd find a way to keep the Shamans' sight all to himself, like Snow had said. Either way, it would be the eras of greed leading up to the birth of the Calf all over again. The crew had to stay away from the Third's clutches, James was sure of it now. They couldn't let him take the golden eye.

His car shivered to a halt in front of his parents' home. As the others parked and unloaded their luggage, the door to the house creaked open. Heri poked out her head. Her face split into a sunny smile as she bounded out to meet them.

"Hello! I'm Heri, James's sister. It's so great to meet all of you."

A small ray of pride warmed James's heart as he watched her shake hands with everyone. The crew's weary and burdened expressions began to fall away as she laughed and chatted with them all. Lux came up alongside him as she led the crew up the walkway.

"James, your sister isn't so bad," he whispered as Honey cackled at one of Heri's jokes. "I had a totally different girl built up in my mind!"

James merely grunted and took extra care not to say anything too nice about his sister. Heri opened the front door and continued babbling away as she led the crew in taking off their shoes. She motioned for them to follow her into the living room. Crisp morning light shone through the sliding glass door leading out into the backyard. The plastic Christmas tree, which James could only assume Heri had unearthed from the garage, stood in the corner next to the television. Dozens of mismatching ornaments, which she and James had made as kids, hung on the dusty branches. His grandparents were seated on the couch, watching a Korean variety show.

James dipped his head in a quick bow and hailed them with his usual greeting. E motioned to the crew before inclining her head in a deep bow and greeting them in formal Korean. Snow quickly followed suit. The rest of the crew swapped uncertain looks before mimicking their bows. James's grandparents chuckled and welcomed them in a mixture of Korean and broken English. James rubbed his arm, unsure if he should do something to help facilitate the conversation.

"Well, I'm guessing you're not the leader of your crew, James," Heri hissed.

Lux chortled. Heri smiled at him. James's mother wiped her hands on her apron as she shuffled out of the kitchen. She stopped in her tracks as she saw them.

"*Why are there so many of you? You're a regular herd!*" she exclaimed.

"*I told you there were a lot of people, Mom,*" Heri said.

E stepped up to the forefront of the crew and bowed deeply to James's mother. "*We're very sorry to barge in on you like this so suddenly. And we're sorry to come empty-handed. Thank you very much for letting us stay the night.*"

A wide smile spread across his mother's face. "*My goodness. Who is this well-mannered young lady? And you speak Korean so well too!*"

James could practically see the imaginary four-by-six photos of future grandchildren flashing before his mother's eyes as she continued conversing with E. Heri cocked an eyebrow at him as if to say, "See? I told you so."

"*I wish Heri and* James *could speak Korean half as well as you do. No matter how hard I try to teach them, they just won't learn. Heri, you should grow out your hair too. Look how pretty her hair is. Straight hair, so black. Anyway,* come in, come in. Welcome! Put your things over there. *Yes,* over there. *Aigoo, why are all of you so big? I don't know whether or not there'll be enough food to feed all of you,"* she said as she bustled back into the kitchen.

*"Can we help you with something?"* said E.

*"No, no. Just go sit. Go sit!"*

*"But—"*

*"It's fine. It's fine. Go sit. Sit!"*

E strode into the kitchen. She wrestled and argued with James's mother until she surrendered a large, plastic basin full of Korean green chili peppers. Though his mother let out a low sound of disapproval and muttered a few inarticulate words, the glint in her eyes betrayed that she approved of E's behavior.

E gave her a small smile then turned to the crew and growled, "Be polite. Come and help."

Lux rolled up his sleeves. Heri trailed along behind him as he walked into the kitchen. Soon, James found himself crammed alongside the rest of the crew, washing, skinning, cutting, and chopping as his mother scurried about and instructed them all. Phoenix stood next to him, cutting away at a hunk of beef with swift, deft strokes. Though his expression had receded into his usual calm demeanor, a hint of anger still stirred within his eyes. James's heart swooped in a deep arc as Blood Crow squeezed herself in between them. He grabbed the basin of wet lettuce that she passed to him, hyper aware of her body against his.

This was so dumb. How could her touch make him feel this way when he'd battled alongside her and even wrapped her wounds so many times now? But then again, this was the first time they'd been this close to each other in Reality.

His eyes skimmed the rim of her glasses then the freckles on her nose and the contour of her cheeks. He smiled slightly as he reminded himself that he'd be able to remember these details from now on. He couldn't quite place his finger on why, exactly, he cared about these details, though. For that matter, he didn't even know why he liked her at all or when his attraction had started. But he supposed his feelings had something to do with how much she cared for others regardless of who they were. If she felt that another human needed her help, she was willing to fight for them. And when she had no longer been able to deny that she'd been using the wrong means to help others, she had been brave enough to change. Blood Crow was fearless in how much she cared for everyone, and he admired that.

Plus, she was cute.

He spun around as Heri burst into laughter behind him. She giggled and pushed Lux's shoulder. As she made to lift a large pot of water out of the sink, Lux lunged forward and hauled out the pot for her. She smiled at him. James narrowed his eyes.

"Heri, come help me with this," he said, spraying drops of water as he brandished a head of wet lettuce at her.

Blood Crow smirked at him as Heri joined them.

"What?" Heri hissed. "Did you eat so much ramen that you forgot how to wash lettuce now?"

"Just help me!"

"Says the person who almost forgot about today!"

"I told you! We're in a lot trouble right now, so stop giving me a hard time, okay?"

He snatched up a carrot and sent orange skins flying across the counter as he peeled with undue force. Heri's lower lip quivered then jutted out.

"You guys are okay, right?" she asked. "Is there anything else I can do to help?"

Remorse pinched James for his sharp words. He lowered the carrot with a sigh. Blood Crow glanced at him before clearing her throat and migrating toward Snow. That was another thing he liked about her. She was tactful.

"It's fine. Don't worry," he told Heri. "You've done enough by getting us a place to stay. Just make sure Mom and Dad don't wake us up by accident, and keep them away if we end up sleeping in."

"I will. Just leave it to me," Heri said with a look of fierce resolve. She glanced at the countertop then at James. "I'm really glad you told me, though. About how you're a part of the Flowering. I know it's a huge deal, telling someone in Reality, so it means a lot."

Her lower lip jutted out once more. He began peeling the carrot again, this time with a softer hand.

"I'm sorry I didn't tell you sooner," he said. "And I know I didn't really say it before, but I'm sorry I was such a dick to you on Thanksgiving. I should've told you everything then instead of getting all angry and immature like that. But it all sounds like crazy talk if you're not a part of the Flowering. I couldn't even believe everything at first, so I thought you wouldn't believe me either. I mean, it's no excuse. But that was what I thought at the time."

"No, I get it," said Heri. "It is pretty crazy. I actually did have a hard time believing it at first when my friends told me everything. But, well, when you have two different friends who don't even know each other telling you the same thing all the time and running around like maniacs trying to get eight hours of sleep every night for no reason, at a certain point, you kind of have to take them seriously."

"*Heri, come over here, and help me with this,*" James's mother said.

Heri gave him a grim smile before joining his mother at the sink. He finished peeling the carrots then took over the lettuce again. E squeezed her way toward the refrigerator.

"*Meehae, do you have a boyfriend?*" his mother asked loudly.

"*Mom!*" James said, dropping the lettuce.

E froze with one hand on the refrigerator handle. Snow paused in rinsing a bowl of seaweed.

"*Mom, don't ask her stuff like that! Just ... just ... leave her alone. That's private,*" James said, giving up on trying to find the right Korean words.

"*Why? I'm just asking,*" his mother said with an expression that suggested that James was the ridiculous one. She tucked her chin in and eyed him with a knowing smile. "*Why? Are you two going out?*"

"What–I–no! No! We are not dating!"

Lux spurted out laughter then coughed and continued washing vegetables. Honey shot him a disapproving look and threw a fistful of dried anchovies into boiling water. Phoenix's eyes darted between James and E before he continued slicing the beef.

"*Meehae,*" his mother said, "*what do you think about our son? I know he can do stupid things once in a while, but he has a good heart.*"

"*Mom!*"

"*What? You need a girlfr–*"

"*I-I'm sorry, but I already have a boyfriend,*" E said.

James and Snow snapped around to look at her. She avoided their eyes.

"*You already have a boyfriend?*" his mother said, her shoulders drooping a little. "*Aigoo, that's a pity. But, well,*" she said with a sigh, "*if a girl like you can't get a boyfriend, who can? But, well, I'm not saying that you two will break up, but if you do, how about you consider* James?"

He groaned. "Meehae, come on. Come here, and help me with ... with this." He seized a basin full of fresh beansprouts.

E grabbed a bag of garlic cloves out of the refrigerator and a cutting board and knife off of the counter. She hurried to the dinner table with James.

"Sorry about my mom," he mumbled as they sat down.

"It's fine," she said, still blushing.

She began mincing the garlic. Snow gazed at them with eyes full of concern before returning her attention to the seaweed. James stole furtive glances at E as he began peeling off the thin film covering each head of the beansprouts.

What did she mean, she already had a boyfriend? Had that simply been a lie to deflect his mother, or had she already made up her mind to go back to Kit? He had to ask her. Of course, he still didn't have the faintest clue as to how to broach the topic with her. But maybe finding the perfect wording didn't matter as much as simply saying something. He had to talk to her now before they found Kit again, before it was too late. He had to convince her not to go back to him, just like he and Snow had discussed. But how was he supposed to convince her?

"I really respected Phillip, you know," E said suddenly.

"Huh?" James said, breaking away from his thoughts.

"I know you're right. I know I talk back to him more than I should, but he's always been kind to me and respectful, even though he's so high up. He let me be more of myself at work and never took offense when I'd be rude or rough. I've learned so much just from working with him too. He really is smart. He's not the vice president for nothing. And when he found out about my mom, he looked out for me and made sure I got good raises and bonuses. I really thought he was someone I could look up to, but he's not. He's Three." She set down her knife. "Oh, James. Phillip is the Third!"

Her body began to shake. He laid a gentle hand on her shoulder.

"Why do I always trust the wrong person?" she said, her voice trembling with self-loathing.

"It's not your fault. None of us knew. Even Paul didn't know, and he's his son. If anything, I'm the one to blame. Me and my name and being so stupid and proud."

"But I let you keep your name."

"It doesn't matter. It was my choice."

She bowed her head. He sighed again, reached for her other shoulder, and turned her around in her seat to face him. She gazed up at him, looking weary and broken.

"Listen to me. There really was no way you could have known. We'll just have to do better from now on. That's all we can do. Maybe ... maybe I can start sticking to that Hunter name Copperhead gave me last night, just in case," he said as he tried to come up with some kind of practical solution that would comfort her.

She closed her eyes and nodded. Laughter burst out from the television set. His grandfather chuckled along with the audience in the show. His grandmother laughed and patted her knee. In the kitchen, Heri chatted away with Lux. His mother held out a red bag of gochugaru for Honey and Phoenix to study. Snow stirred a large pot on the stove with a look of intense concentration. Blood Crow scowled as she shook out two handfuls of dirty lettuce.

There was so much going on, so much to consider and to worry about. Who knew what would happen tonight with the Third? Who knew if any of them would even survive their impending battle with the Red Calf? But strangely enough, despite the chaos that lay parallel to this moment, James felt that right here, right now, with his family and friends all around him, this imperfect moment was somehow perfect. He wanted to protect everyone–no, he needed to protect everyone–so that such moments would return again and again for nights and days to come.

"You can't go back to Kit," he said.

E tensed. He tightened his hold on her shoulders and looked her straight in the eye.

"Meehae, listen to me. You did the right thing leaving him. I know you love him, and I know he did a lot for you, but you never deserved to be treated that way. Ever. You gave him everything and he...."

He knew that what he was about to say would be painful for her. But he had to do it. He had to do it gently, but he had to do it. He had to speak the truth, no matter how painful it would be for her and even for him.

"He used you, Meehae. He was abusive," he said quietly.

He had anticipated the pain that flooded her eyes, but it didn't make it any easier to see.

"I should go help the others," she said, pushing his hands away. "Your mom is growing suspicious of us."

James snapped around to see his mother grinning at them. E rose from her seat. He grabbed her arm.

"*Meehae*," he said.

"Let go. You'll make a scene in front of your mom."

"I'm not afraid of making a scene in front of my mom!"

He hesitated then pulled on her arm as gently as he could, terrified that she would fly away from him at any second. To his relief, she slowly sank back down into her chair and stared at the floor.

"I-I'm sorry," he mumbled. "I know it's not.... Look, it's like what ... it's like what Marcus said before," he said, grasping for an ally, any ally–present or not–to help him persuade her. "I wouldn't be a good friend if I didn't tell you what I saw."

She continued staring at the floor. Silence passed. Just as he began to wonder if he'd done the right thing to bring up the subject at all, she said, "I have this made-up dream about *Oppa*. And it's one I can never really let go of for some reason."

"O-Oh," he said. He tried his best to conceal the relief that had washed over him the second she had begun to speak. "What dream?"

She shifted her gaze onto the dinner table.

"It's raining in my dream," she said. "It's raining, and we're in the bamboo forest again. The one in the Mountains, where he first found me. You didn't see it when you read me, but we had a fight one time in that forest too. A big fight, but then we made up. It was raining that whole night. It was so cold, but it was that nice type of cold too. The type that you can only find in the rain. It almost feels warm after a while because it's so cold. He took me to a place in the forest that only he knew about, and we–"

She stopped abruptly and glanced at him. His eyes darted about, looking at random corners of the room, before he cleared his throat and nodded in understanding.

"W-Well, what I mean to say is that it was one of our good nights. And it's like that in my dream too."

James gazed at her as she hesitated.

"Go on," he encouraged her.

Her eyes remained fixed on the table as she took a deep breath.

"In my dream, we'd have an honest conversation. In that forest. In that rain. I'd tell him I never wanted to leave him. That I only left because I couldn't take it anymore. That I really did love him with all my heart and that I wasn't lying. He'd tell me that he'd change, and ... and he'd be telling the truth. We'd start arguing because we always argue, but then we'd see that it was real this time. And then we'd take one last look at the City before we'd leave for good."

She looked up as Lux laughed in the kitchen. James gazed only at E. She lowered her eyes again.

"He'd join Crew Blue, and we'd all be happy together. He'd rescue citizens with us, and he'd become the protector he was meant to be. The true warrior he was born to be. And even though it would be hard at first, he'd become more sure with every passing night that he had made the right decision. He would change and forget about the Market. We would meet in Reality like he promised in his letter. And we'd...." She lifted her eyes and looked at James with a hurting kind of desperation. "We'd get married, and we'd raise a happy family. I'd give him daughters because I know he'd want at least one. And we'd finally be together. Really together. In peace. At last."

Emotion wrapped its fingers around James's heart and squeezed. E shrank away from him. She shook her head, looking upset at herself.

"Sorry. It sounds so much dumber saying it out loud. But I just always wanted to hope...."

She sighed and shook her head once more. James grabbed her arm again as she rose to leave. He wanted to tell her. He wanted to tell her that it wasn't dumb at all and that it wasn't fair because she wanted all the right things. She just wanted to be happy with the man she loved, and there was nothing wrong with that. He wanted that for her too, but the problem wasn't her. It was Kit.

The urgency to speak screamed within him.

But all he could do was remain wordless and powerless as E slipped out of his grasp and walked away.

# PART III
# SACRIFICE

# CHAPTER 15

# THE TOURNAMENT

The crew sat huddled together on the floor of the living room. Snores rumbled toward them from down the hall. James whipped throw blankets off of the sofa and distributed them as the crew reviewed their plan for the night ahead.

They would assume that the Third would stay true to his word and protect all humans from the Calf's oncoming approach. Meanwhile, the crew would proceed with Blood Crow entering the Tournament as a member of Copperhead's family. Once she'd won and become the Lead, she would order the Hunters to stay within the moonlight and enlist their aid in battling the Calf.

Of course, there were about a million things that could go wrong with this plan. Blood Crow could fail to win the Tournament. The Hunters could refuse to listen to her even if she did win. The Third would likely ignore E's command to leave the Hunters to the crew, and they had no idea when his men would arrive at the Solstice, though thankfully, it would take his men a while to round up all the other humans in No Man's Land and the City first. Blood Crow could command the Hunters to protect the crew and the pack from his men if she did become the Lead, but again, everything depended on her winning. In the end, they were forced to accept that they had no choice but to "wing it" again when obstacles inevitably arose.

"You're all absolutely sure that you don't want me to compete in the Tournament instead?" E asked.

Everyone groaned.

"Yes, we're sure," Blood Crow scowled. "Could you please have a little bit of faith in me? It's not like I haven't won the Tournament before, jeez!"

"But–"

"Meehae, we have been through this enough times now," said Honey. "We don't know what's going to happen tonight with the Hunters or the Calf. We can't have you wasting your creations or your energy until you really have to."

"I know but–"

"No buts!" said Lux. "Rose knows about this Hunters' way crap way better than you anyway, so she needs to be the Lead, not you."

"All right, all right!" E said as the crew continued hurling objections at her. "I was just checking."

The Christmas tree lights clicked off. E glanced at the clock.

"Let's get going," she said. "And don't forget to use our Hunter names. Dark Watch for James, Deadly Sunshine for Lux, Golden Bee for Honey, and Black Fang for me."

"Man, why did I have to get stuck with the stripper name?" Lux complained.

Honey gave him a few sympathetic pats on the back as James led them upstairs. He raised his hand to knock on Heri's door then stepped back as she flung it open first. She welcomed the girls into her room with a bright smile. E thanked her as she entered. Heri, in response, began chattering away about how fun Christmas Eve had turned out to be.

Both fear and compassion had prevented James from talking to E about Kit again. But that hadn't stopped him from telling Snow about his failed conversation when the others had been distracted with helping Heri hang Christmas lights outside. Snow, unable to stand by in useless silence any longer, had pulled E aside and begged for her forgiveness once again in hopes of winning back her trust. She'd even gone as far as to try and get down on both knees to grovel. E had stopped her, of course, but James could have sworn that he'd seen something soften ever so slightly in E's expression as she had forced Snow to stand up again. But in the end, neither of them had spoken to her about Kit and instead, had kept a worried eye on her all day as she had continued helping his family around the house and leading whispered discussions with the crew.

She had looked so normal, so completely unperturbed, so much so that he wouldn't have been able to tell that a part of her was hurting so badly had their talk in the morning not occurred. Why was it still so hard for him to see past her armor of fearlessness and to understand who lived beneath? Should he have forced another conversation with her to pick up where they'd left off? Had he lost his only chance to convince her to do the right thing?

"James," said Heri.

"Hm? What is it?"

"Good luck."

He stared at the sincerity in his sister's eyes before forcing his mouth into a smile. As he ushered Lux and Phoenix into his bedroom, he heard her close her door and lock it. He made sure to do the same.

"You guys ready?" he asked.

"I was born ready," said Lux as flames of resolve danced in his eyes.

"Me too," said Phoenix.

They looked at one another with the grave determination of three men who knew that they were standing on the brink of a great battle. As they spread out and began unrolling their sleeping bags, James left his bed empty and took his place between Phoenix and Lux. It didn't feel right to take the bed and leave them on the floor, not with everything they would soon be facing together.

He wormed deep into the soft cotton of his sleeping bag. Warm in the comfort of his own room and still full from Christmas Eve dinner, which had, of course, consisted only of Korean food, he found drowsiness stealing upon him quickly. He burped, blew his breath into the cotton, then burrowed deeper.

Snippets of memory began swimming in and out of his fading consciousness. Heri was laughing with the crew, Phoenix was yelling at Phillip, Lux and Bloom were playing in a field of golden wheat, Kit was planting a kiss on the side of E's head....

James opened his eyes and looked at the others through the rearview mirror as they, too, appeared in their seats. Copperhead's family was still standing sentinel around their car. Tents, tables, and other vestiges of the Feast lay abandoned across the empty land. The wall of Hunters that had guarded the festivities had disappeared.

In the far distance, hundreds of Hunters swarmed around a stage and two giant screens that had been erected at the brink of the moonlight. Behind the stage lay the Desert, vast and white. On its parched floor stood a huge fence, which stretched out in a wide semicircle and ended at the Blue Border on either end. James squinted.

Something was moving in the middle of the fenced-in land.

"*How are you all doing back there?*" E asked the wolves as she appeared.

"*Never better,*" Terrain growled.

His tone made it clear that he wanted nothing more than to break free of the car's confines. The wolves shuffled restlessly about under the blanket as Snow's outline appeared as well.

"Let's go," E commanded.

Blood Crow honked the horn. Copperhead's family parted to let her drive forward then jogged alongside the car as she slowly weaved through the discarded remnants of the Feast. They encircled the car again as she parked away from the crowd. The crew jumped out and hurried toward the multitude.

Both of the screens flanking the stage showed one angle of the Desert for several moments before flashing to another. Through the different angles, James deduced that barbed wire wrapped the entirety of the fence and that dozens of Hunters stood behind the fence with their broadswords in hand, ready to cut the bundles of taut, black ropes that stretched out into the middle of the enclosed space. There, tied down by the ropes, writhed a large citizen.

It resembled a giant salamander with veined flesh. Large, black pores perforated random areas of its body. Sharp talons radiated out of its feet like huge sickles. Its long tail, which the Hunters had somehow managed to pin down with a humongous stake, ended in a lump that gleamed with dozens of sharp spikes. James cast a fearful look at Blood Crow. She was going to go out there all by herself to kill that thing?

"We need to get to the stage," she told the crew.

They dove into the laughing and chattering crowds and began making their way to the front. Copperhead climbed onto the stage, thumped his palm against a microphone, and cleared his throat.

*"Competitors! Calling all competitors! Come up now if you want to compete in the Tournament, or forever hold your peace!"* he called.

He gave the crew a knowing nod as they came to a stop near the stage. E responded with a firm nod of her own then grasped Blood Crow's shoulders.

"Be careful," she said. "But don't hold back."

"I won't," said Blood Crow.

The fierce look that she gave them promised that she would not fail. James wrestled with his anxiousness as she rushed up onto the stage. That citizen would be difficult to bring down even if the whole crew were fighting together. He didn't care if Blood Crow had won the Tournament before. That monster could rip her to pieces! He jumped as Honey put her hand on his arm. She stood up on her tiptoes and leaned into his ear.

"She'll be all right. Just hang in there, mister James," she whispered.

He stared at her, wide-eyed, as she winked and sank back down onto her heels. A weak but grateful smile formed on his face. He should have known that Honey would have detected his feelings for Blood Crow by now.

Honey hissed at Lux to give James space as he wandered closer to them. As the two began to quarrel, James took a deep breath and straightened his back. He didn't want Blood Crow looking over at the crew and seeing him like this. If he was this nervous, he could only imagine how she might be feeling. He glanced at the creature on the screen again before scanning the crowds in an attempt to distract himself. Several Hunters shook their heads as they studied the citizen. Others laughed and pointed as if they couldn't wait to see how the competitors would fare against such a creature. When Copperhead took up the microphone again, James wasn't surprised to count only fifty or so competitors assembled on the stage.

"*All right, all right. Three, two, one, and we will now start the Tournament!*" Copperhead announced.

The Hunters thrust their fists into the air as they shouted and cheered. James swallowed as the monster let out an impatient squeal that echoed across the Desert.

"*You know the rules!*" Copperhead said. "*The Hunter who pierces the mark will be the next Lead. No machinery or technology of any kind. Only spears and blades. No competing if you competed last year, one Hunter per family, and only the ones who came by the deadline can compete. All right? All right! Let's have all the competitors come this way!*"

"*Wait!*"

Murmurs broke out. Heads swiveled in every direction. Alarm quickened James's pulse as he spotted Lion Paw pushing through the crowds. Phoenix grabbed E as she made to step forward. Blood Crow maintained a blank expression as Lion Paw climbed onto the stage and stared at her.

"Lion Paw," Copperhead said, lowering the microphone. "What are you doing? You know there are no interruptions allowed."

He didn't answer but continued staring at Blood Crow.

"Lion Paw," Copperhead repeated. "I asked you what you're doing!"

"*I am sorry, Blood Crow,*" Lion Paw said. "*But I cannot let you do this. It is against our ways and our traditions.*" He faced the crowds and shouted, "*Blood Crow did not come to the Solstice by the deadline! Furthermore, she expressed to me last night that she no longer wishes to be a Hunter! She cannot compete!*"

Horror and rage exploded within James. Families whispered and looked at Blood Crow.

"Don't!" Phoenix said as E made to run onto the stage. "Making a scene right now will only make her look more suspicious."

"What do you want me to do, then? Just stand here?" she snapped.

Whispers grew into murmurs among the crowds. Copperhead glanced at Crew Blue then smirked at Lion Paw. He began to clap slowly. Lion Paw frowned.

"*Wow, Lion Paw. Wow. This is low even for you!*" Copperhead shouted into the microphone.

"*What are you talking about?*" said Lion Paw.

The Hunters quieted as Copperhead smirked again.

"*What am I talking about? I'm talking about how you're making up lies just to get back at me! Blood Crow is a member of my family now, after all. But hey, you knew all about that already. Because that's what this is all about, isn't it? You're just jealous that I took Blood Crow away from you!*"

Copperhead shook his head with a smug look of understanding as Lion Paw's mouth fell open with outrage. He continued speaking in Our Word at the top of his lungs, no doubt to ensure that the maximum number of Hunters assembled would understand him and, hopefully, side with him.

"*I get it, Lion Paw. I get it! But that's still no reason to sabotage her chances at the Tournament. That's low even for you!*"

"*I would never sabotage a fellow Hunter's opportunity to compete!*" Lion Paw said as boos rose up from the crowds.

"*Uh-huh. Yeah. Sure,*" Copperhead said. He raised his eyebrows with a sniff and a smile.

"Traditionalists always lie! They're always trying to sabotage us!" someone shouted from the crowds.

"*What was that? Come over here and say that again to my face!*" a man yelled back.

"*My fellow Traditionalists!*" Lion Paw shouted. "*Many of you can vouch for my character! I would never sabotage a fellow Hunter, even a Contemporary. And many of you know Blood Crow. You know that she*" *has always hated Copperhead. She would never join him! Copperhead is lying!"*

Several more voices sprang up from the growing clamor.

*"I saw Copperhead and his family at the beginning of the Solstice! Blood Crow wasn't with them!"*

"Shut up! What reason would Copperhead have to lie?"

*"What reason would Lion Paw?"*

Traditionalists continued yelling that Copperhead was lying. Contemporaries flung curses at Traditionalists as they defended both Copperhead and Blood Crow. Arguments multiplied as shouts became screams and threats joined curses. Soon, James couldn't tell which faction was which or what they were even arguing about.

*"Shut up! Everyone, just shut up!"* Copperhead yelled. *"I am the Lead, and as the Lead, I say Blood Crow is allowed to compete, and that is final! Lion Paw, get off my stage! This is just another one of your elaborate schemes to make Contemporaries look bad!"*

*"Don't you dare keep accusing me of sabotage, Copperhead! I would never lie about a Hunter, Traditionalist or Contemporary. Blood Crow did not come by the deadline. She arrived last night with them!"* Lion Paw pointed at Crew Blue.

Countless pairs of eyes latched onto the crew. James stood still, his heartbeat in his ears, his mind scrambling to catch up with the spiraling situation. Phoenix grabbed E's hand to prevent her from creating the machete James knew she would have created otherwise.

"Phoenix!" she snarled.

He didn't respond but stepped in front of her and gazed up at Lion Paw.

*"None of them are Hunters either!"* Lion Paw continued, still pointing at the crew. *"I fought them not long ago because they attempted*

to protect a citizen during a hunt. *They should not be allowed to stay here and partake in our traditions!*"

"*Of course you'd say that!*" Copperhead spat as more and more Hunters turned to stare at the crew. "*They're all part of my family too! You're just trying to slander us all!*"

"*That's right!*" Blood Crow cried out.

Lion Paw stared her in disbelief as she broke away from the rest of the competitors and rushed over to Copperhead's side.

"*I don't care how far back we go!*" she yelled with tears in her eyes. "*I can't let you keep slandering my family. This is exactly why I joined Copperhead. You're always throwing around crazy accusations! You're crazy. Crazy!*"

James snapped around at the sound of bones colliding. Shouts and curses rang out as two families clashed in a heated fistfight. Other Hunters jumped into the fray and ignored Copperhead's commands to stop. As a family began prowling toward Crew Blue with bloodlust in their eyes, E threw aside Phoenix's hand. Her machete appeared. James created his spear as Honey held up her tomahawks and Lux readied his katana. Phoenix ran up onto the stage and snatched the microphone out of Copperhead's hand.

"Phoenix!" E exclaimed.

"*My fellow Hunters!*" he shouted.

A few families turned toward him. Others continued diving into the expanding fistfight. James jabbed his spear forward in warning as more Hunters crept toward the crew.

"*For life! Protect! Is this not our way? And yet you constantly turn against one another!*" Phoenix cried. He slammed his fist over his heart as if the mere thought of it pained him. "*If Blood Crow's presence causes this much strife, then I will take her place!*"

More families turned to look at him. Several Hunters nodded and murmured to each other. The ring of Hunters that had surrounded the crew stopped and stared at him as well. Vindictive joy smirked within James as Lion Paw looked Phoenix up and down. Lion Paw had never seen Phoenix before. Phoenix had joined Crew Blue after they had escaped from the tunnels.

*"You can't switch places! That's not allowed!"* someone yelled.

*"I am the Lead!"* Copperhead shouted back. *"Me! Not you! And it is allowed! There are no rules against family members swapping places!"*

*"That's right!"* said Phoenix. *"There's nothing against swapping, so I'll say it again! I will enter in Blood Crow's place and compete for our family! I can no longer stand around and watch as you all keep fighting like this. And besides, we've wasted enough of this night!"* He thrust his finger toward the creature on the screen. *"Let's start so I can kill that thing already!"*

Lux began clapping and cheering loudly. Honey quickly joined him. A smatter of applause followed. James nudged E, and together, they started shouting pleas for the Tournament to begin, pleas which others began to echo. Whistles and shouts of agreement began to float across the crowds. Several Hunters cast annoyed looks at the families that were still brawling. Copperhead seized the microphone from Phoenix.

*"I said,"* he screamed, *"settle down!"*

James winced and groaned along with the crowds as the microphone screeched.

*"I'm going to keep screaming until you settle down, and whoever doesn't settle down, I'll skin them! I'll skin them, I'll skin them, I'll skin them alive!"* Copperhead raged into the screeching microphone.

Hunters leapt forth and pried apart the fighting families. A few more half-hearted punches and kicks followed before they drew back. The Hunters who had surrounded Crew Blue glared at them before receding into the crowds as well. Copperhead huffed then turned to Lion Paw as the crowds massaged their ears.

"*Do you have a problem with Phoenix too, or can we all move on with our lives now?*"

Lion Paw scrutinized Phoenix once more. "*No. I have no more objections.*"

"Good," said Copperhead. "Then get off my damn stage."

Lion Paw pursed his lips, glanced at Blood Crow one last time, then marched down from the stage.

"I'll take it from here, Blood Crow," said Phoenix.

She nodded and whispered something into his ear. A small part of James couldn't help but sigh with relief as she made her way back down and returned to the crew. She stared at them all, her mouth open with words she couldn't express. She bowed her head in shame.

"I'm sorry," she told them.

"Forget it. It was Lion Paw, not you," E said.

James, Lux, and Honey reassured her as well.

Copperhead sighed loudly, cracked his neck, then forced a grin. "*What's the Tournament without a little arguing, am I right?*"

Laughter rippled across the crowds.

"*All right. Contenders! First one to kill the thing wins! Let's go!*"

# CHAPTER 16

# PHOENIX

The crowds cheered as the competitors ran down from the stage and climbed into the cars waiting for them. Copperhead hurried down to Crew Blue as the cars zoomed past the moonlight and out into the Desert.

"Is it just me, or did they choose an extra tough one to kill this year?" he asked Blood Crow.

James planted his spear in the ground and watched the screens as the cars continued driving toward the creature. A horn sounded from the Desert. The Hunters behind the fence brought down their broadswords and cut the black ropes restraining the citizen. The cars swerved to a halt as the creature shook and shuddered. Phoenix created a spear, leapt out of the car, and began running headlong at the creature. The other competitors scrambled to jump out of their seats then bellowed battle cries as they rushed forward as well. Though they gritted their teeth and ran faster, Phoenix continued to outstrip them all.

The creature shook off the last rope and jumped onto all fours. It blinked and cocked its head at different angles like a bird. A forked tongue shot out of its mouth and dabbed its eye. It spun around and, with a swipe of its claws, uprooted the stake pegged into its tail before whirling around to face the competitors. It dabbed its eye again then pumped its head up and down as it shrieked. It crawled swiftly forth to meet them.

A hush stole over the crowds as the creature and the competitors charged across the Desert toward one another. James exhaled a quivering breath. Copperhead muttered "come on" over and over again. Honey and Lux gripped each other's arms. Blood Crow breathed hard through her nose as if she were running with the competitors. E tightened her grip on her machete.

Phoenix drew back his spear and hurled it. The creature jumped aside. The spear struck the ground. Phoenix dove aside and rolled across the floor as the creature began spinning swiftly toward the competitors in circles while swinging its spiked tail around like a mace. Its tail smashed into several competitors in an explosion of flesh and blood. The crowds erupted into cheers and shouts. Phoenix began army-crawling toward his spear as the creature dabbed its eye then continued spinning. Blood splattered across the white floor as its tail pulverized more competitors.

The citizen squealed with pain as spears flew into its body. It stopped spinning then twisted around and glared at the competitors who had thrown the spears. It whipped its tail. Spikes zinged through the air and thudded into heads, chests, and stomachs. The creature shrieked again before fleeing toward the fence. Phoenix pulled his spear out of the ground and gave chase. The other competitors hesitated before running after him.

The Hunters standing guard behind the fence picked up jagged pieces of earth from the Desert's floor and flung them at the fence. The citizen skidded to a halt as the fence crackled and sparked. It twisted around and stared at the competitors again as they continued to charge forth. It arched its back as it spasmed and twitched. Several Hunters in the crowd shouted with excitement and pointed at the screens.

"It's shifting!" someone yelled.

The creature's tail split into three, its legs and wrists grew thicker, and its claws shrank in length. It blinked and cocked its head at different angles before running toward the competitors with weighted steps, its body swinging from side to side with a heavy, metronome-like cadence. A volley of spikes flew from its flagellating tails. Phoenix dodged. Competitors behind him screamed as they were impaled. Still sprinting, Phoenix hurled his spear. The crowds burst into fresh whoops and shouts as the spear pierced the creature's throat. Another spear appeared in his hand. He sent it sailing into the creature's wrist then created his double-bladed sword as he came within yards of the citizen. It began swiping at him with its claws. He leapt aside and dodged again and again with swift and sure movements that made the Contemporaries cheer so wildly that they seemed to shake the full moon above.

"Phoenix! Is on! Fire!" Copperhead bellowed.

Honey and Lux hopped up and down, screaming and shouting. Spit flew from Blood Crow's mouth as she yelled and jabbed the air with punches. James remained frozen, too terrified and elated to do anything. E took a small step forward. She flinched as the tips of the creature's claws raked across Phoenix's side and sent him rolling across the ground without his sword. He drew daggers from his belt and flung them into the creature's face and neck, forcing it to scuttle back before it could crush him. He kicked up onto his feet, created two spears, and spun as he threw one after the other into the creature's hand. He leapt away with an infuriated look as it swiped at him. He created another sword as he continued evading its claws.

"No! So close. So close!" Blood Crow wailed. "Its mark!"

"What? Where? Where's its mark?" James said. His eyes darted about as he scoured the creature's body.

"Don't just look everywhere for it! Focus, James! Focus!" Blood Crow screamed, spraying him with spit. "If you don't see red right away, it might be in a crevice. If it's not in a crevice, it might be hiding in plain sight! This one is in a crevice. That hole in its hand! See?"

James mustered all his focus and forced his eyes to rest on the citizen's hand. His heart threw itself against his chest with painful rapidity as he saw the mark at last. Barely visible, it lay on a lump of flesh just inside one of the large pores covering the creature's hand. Hunters began pointing at the mark too. E took another step forward.

"Its mark is at a difficult angle," she said. "He's already used up half of his creations. He needs to cut off its hand."

She flinched again as the creature sent Phoenix tumbling across the ground without his sword once more. He sprang onto his feet, turned, and ran away. Contemporaries gasped in disbelief. Traditionalists guffawed.

"*Look at him! He's a coward!*" someone shouted.

The creature coiled up on its haunches and leapt forward with the greediness of a cat chasing a mouse. Phoenix stopped in his tracks, whirled around, and hurled a spear into its eye. The creature crashed onto the ground, squealing. Phoenix ran toward its mark, his face alight with the hope of victory.

A Hunter's blade flew into his ribcage.

He shouted as he stumbled then collapsed onto one knee.

"No!" E yelled as more competitors began throwing their knives and daggers at Phoenix.

Lux began swearing in a mixture of English, Spanish, Our Word, and even Korean, which he'd undoubtedly picked up from E long ago. Honey and Copperhead shook their fists as they shouted. Blood Crow screamed, not even bothering to use words. James's hand inched toward his spear. How he wished he could spear all the Traditionalists who were laughing!

Phoenix wrenched the blades out of his body, flung them at his opponents, then jumped aside as spikes shot toward him. He jerked his head to the side, narrowly missing a Hunter's spear, then ran with a new sword in hand. Both the citizen and the competitors chased after him across the Desert.

The citizen shrieked and skidded to a halt. Phoenix spun around. He watched with fury and terror in his eyes as the other competitors threw their weapons at the citizen's mark and cut away at its wrist with their swords. He began sprinting toward them as the creature ran toward the fence. Several competitors pursued it. The creature turned, leapt, and crushed the competitors beneath its claws as it landed with a ground-shaking boom. It shuddered then arched its back. Its three tails merged into one, and its legs and wrists grew thinner. Competitors rushed forth only to be dashed to pieces as the creature spun and swung its spiked tail.

As others lobbed their weapons at its hand and slashed at its wrist again, those who had stood further away ran toward Phoenix and surrounded him. He glared at each of them then spread his stance. He pointed his sword and let out a fearsome cry that made several Hunters in the crowd gasp with awe. His eyes blazed with determination as he flew at his opponents with his sword and began slicing off one head after another with a ferocity that was both terrifying and glorious to behold.

The citizen smashed the last of its attackers as Phoenix beheaded his last opponent. The creature turned and glared at Phoenix with its remaining eye. His spear still protruded from the other. Blood flowed from the many deep cuts the competitors had dealt upon its body. Its hand dangled from its wrist by a few chunks of flesh that continued creeping slowly over exposed bones.

For one eternal moment, Phoenix and the creature simply glared at one another. Then Phoenix spun his sword. With another mighty cry, he flew toward the citizen at full speed. The creature shrieked and whipped its tail. He darted from side to side, dodging the volley of spikes that thudded into the Desert's floor. As the creature whipped its tail again, he sprang to the side, skidded across the ground, and continued running. He threw a spear at its mark. The creature jumped aside. And in that split moment, as the citizen's gaze focused on the spear flying toward its hand, Phoenix leapt into its blind spot and hurled another spear straight into its other eye.

The creature's body seized up as it shrieked. The crowds yelled and stomped and shook their fists. Phoenix leapt up onto the creature's hand. His blades flashed as he sliced away at what remained of its wrist with deep, deft strokes. The creature stumbled as its hand separated from its wrist.

Phoenix raised his sword and, with a final cry, plunged his blade through its mark.

The citizen disappeared.

A long yell of triumph burst out of James's throat as the crowd detonated with cheers and screams. Blood Crow and Copperhead thrust their fists into the air as they let out a ululating cry of victory. Lux and Honey hopped around in a circle with their arms around each other. E took a few steps back and placed one hand over her chest.

Phoenix staggered then drove one end of his sword into the ground and leaned on it. He pressed his hand against one of the many wounds on his side as he struggled for breath. He turned to face the cars zooming toward him then sank onto one knee as one swerved to a stop next to him. The Hunters who jumped out shook him by the shoulders and thumped him on the back before carrying him into the car. They began binding his wounds as they sped back to the Blue Border.

Lux and Honey hurtled into James and squeezed the breath out of him with their embraces. Lux shouted for Copperhead to join them. He laughed and threw himself on top of them all. As Blood Crow jumped into the pile next, Honey squirmed to the side and pushed her into James's chest. He hesitated only for a moment before pressing her against himself and screaming with joy.

"E!" Lux shouted. "Come here, E! Join us!"

But E remained still and gazed only at the screen as Phoenix returned to the moonlight.

# CHAPTER 17

# BRAVE

Phoenix winced as he limped onto the stage, still armed with his sword. Copperhead strode up to the microphone stand with a blue, velvet box in his hands and a smug grin on his face. Traditionalists rolled their eyes as he cleared his throat pointedly and coughed loudly into the microphone. Contemporaries nodded in approval of his passive aggressiveness. He thrust his fist into the air.

"*The winner of the Tournament is Phoenix!*" he proclaimed.

Traditionalists remained stony-faced as Contemporaries exploded into cheers and stomped harder than ever. Copperhead lifted a ruby necklace out of the box and motioned to Phoenix. Pain spasmed across his face as he knelt in front of Copperhead. Silence rolled over the crowds as Copperhead raised the necklace high above Phoenix's head. James's heart beat like a drumroll. The moment had come at last. The moment for Phoenix to become the Lead and assume command over the Hunters.

"*Phoenix of the family Copperhead! I present to you this necklace as a symbol of our pledge. Our pledge to draw the blood of all citizens who pose a threat to humans! It is my duty, right, and privilege to pass on to you the responsibilities of the Hunters' Lead. Do you swear to maintain honesty and uphold fair conduct as you lead the remainder of this Solstice and resume your role at the next?"*

"*I swear it upon the name of the Brave,*" Phoenix declared.

"*And do you swear to lead with the honor, decency, and wisdom by which the Brave commanded us to lead and by which all the Leads preceding you have striven to uphold for these many eras?*"

"*I swear it again upon the name of the Brave!*"

"*And do you swear, above all, to live for the lives of others and to protect your fellow humans in the remainder of the nights given to you?*"

"*I swear it again and again upon the name of the Brave, upon my honor, and upon my very life!*"

"*What is your purpose, O Hunter?*"

"*To kill all marked citizens and to slay all threats!*"

"*For what purpose, O Hunter?*"

"*To defend our own and to protect the Flowering from darkness!*"

Copperhead lifted the necklace higher. "*Protect!*" he shouted. "*Protect our fellow humans from the dangers of the Flowering!*"

"*For life!*" Phoenix cried.

Copperhead gave him a solemn nod. Phoenix bowed his head as he slipped the ruby necklace around his neck.

"It's done," Blood Crow whispered to the crew. "Phoenix is officially the Lead now."

"*Then, my friend and brother, I hereby delegate to you–*" Copperhead did a double take then squinted into the distance.

Phoenix looked up at him as families frowned and murmured. E then the rest of the crew spun around. Icy dread flooded James's heart. An army of SUVs was speeding toward the crowds.

The Third's men had come.

"No," Blood Crow whispered.

An SUV was driving toward the crew's car.

Snow. The wolves.

"Get ready," E commanded.

The crew jumped closer to one another with their weapons raised. The piercing look that she cast toward Phoenix told him that he had to gain control over the Hunters now or never. He nodded and struggled to his feet as cries of outrage rose up from the crowds.

"*Do you see that?*"

"Bodyguards!"

"*There are Merchants too!*"

"*How dare they interrupt the Solstice!*"

"Phoenix, you're the Lead now! Do something!"

Phoenix yelled into the microphone for quiet and order. The crowds responded with more cries and demands. The Third's army began slowing to a stop around the circumference of the crowds. Several families gripped their weapons, marched forward to meet the intruders, then halted as Certus jumped out of one of the cars.

The crowds hushed.

A large group of Bodyguards and Merchants followed Certus as he began walking toward the stage. Shouts and curses sounded here and there before growing into a clamor again, but neither Traditionalist nor Contemporary dared to stop the Third's Guide. Instead, more of them turned to Phoenix and demanded that he stand up to Certus and expel the trespassers. They only yelled louder as he shouted more commands.

James bit back his frustration. If only the Third's men had come a little later. Phoenix had put on such an impressive fight during the Tournament that he might have been able to persuade the Hunters to do his bidding with a few moments of uninterrupted attention and an inspiring speech. At the very least, he would have convinced all the Contemporaries to follow his lead. But now, with the Third's arrival, everything had been upended. E shook her head as Phoenix continued shouting orders in vain.

"It's no use," she said. "We've lost our chance. They're not going to listen to him now. Not in this state."

James scanned the escalating frenzy then jerked forward as a man threw a rock at Phoenix. The man scurried back as Copperhead threatened to skin him alive. Blood Crow lowered her spear.

"This is all my fault," she said. "We never should have come to the Solstice. We're doomed."

"We are not doomed!" E snarled. "No one can fire guns this close to the moonlight. As long as they can't mow us down with bullets, we have a chance of cutting our way through!"

"That's right," said Lux. "We've won impossible battles before. This is just one more of them."

Honey adjusted her hold on her tomahawks with a grim look that accepted an immediate future fraught with pain and suffering. Blood Crow stared at E, swallowed, then lifted her spear again.

"What about stopping the Hunters from running out to kill the Calf?" James asked.

"We'll have to leave it up to the Third," said E. "He has the men and the power. He'll contain them somehow. We need to focus on getting Phoenix off the stage and get back to the car. We'll go back out into No Man's Land to escape from the Third and find a way to sneak into the moonlight again before the Calf arrives. James, you escape without us if it comes down to it."

"What?" he snapped.

"I'm not saying we're doomed," E said, glaring at Blood Crow again, "but we're clearly outnumbered a hundred to one. If any of us do end up getting caught, you need to get the pack and Snow and run for it.

You guys are the key that the Third needs to get his hands on the golden eye. We can't let him get to you."

James choked on his outrage. "No. No! We're all getting out of here. I'm not leaving without you guys!"

"James," E growled.

"Who knows what the Third will make all of you do if he can't get to me and Snow?" he said, knowing this would shut her up. "We all need to escape together!"

He refused to back down even as she continued glaring at him. She wouldn't be winning this argument. Not this time!

"Forget it, E," Lux said. "James isn't listening to you on this one. We're all in it together like we've always been, ride or die!"

Certus stopped in front of the stage and waved his hand at the Bodyguards and Merchants who had followed him. Crew Blue aimed their weapons as several of his men encircled them. The rest rushed up onto the stage and surrounded Copperhead and Phoenix. Blood spread across the bandages tied around Phoenix's wounds as he spun his sword and assumed a battle stance. Copperhead hesitated only for a moment before creating a broadsword and pointing the tip at Certus.

"*You dare defy the ancient pact between Hunters and Shamans?*" Copperhead shouted.

The crew looked up at him in surprise.

Copperhead glanced at them before yelling, "*The Third has enough power as it is! I won't just stand around as he tries to take even more!*"

He'd said nothing about the golden eye, but James had understood nonetheless. E had told Copperhead that the Third would use the crew to take back the eye and cast his power across the planes like the Shamans of old. Copperhead was refusing to stand by and let that happen. He wanted to fight alongside the crew. He wanted to help them escape.

"*No one, not the Third or any of the other Shamans, is allowed to interrupt the Solstice!*" Copperhead continued, shouting louder so that even more of the crowds could hear him. He drew back his sword like a batter ready to swing. "*I'd never be able to look at myself in the mirror again if I didn't give him the punishment he deserves! Isn't that right, Phoenix?*"

"*Absolutely!*" He raised his sword higher. "Certus! *I suggest you leave while you still can, or have you forgotten about our last battle already?*"

"I haven't forgotten," Certus said cooly. "Forgive the intrusion, but the Third has asked me to relay a message to the Hunters."

"*They're not in the mood to listen!*" Phoenix retorted.

Several Hunters in the crowd shouted in agreement.

"That is of little concern to the Third," Certus replied.

Anger blazed in Phoenix's eyes. "Think about what you are doing," he said, lowering his voice to address Certus only. "If you stop the Solstice now, the Hunters will never forget it. Does your boss really want that? Is the Third willing to risk all the relationships, the deals, the time, the energy he's invested in the Hunters?"

"The Third is aware that this may damage relationships for years to come, but he considers some things to be worthy of great sacrifice," Certus said with a knowing look.

James recoiled slightly. Phillip hadn't told Certus that Phoenix was his son, had he?

Certus plucked the microphone out of the stand. "*Good evening!*" he shouted. "*The Third sincerely apologizes for this sudden interruption, but he has learned of a great danger that will reach Lapis Lazuli at any moment! He kindly asks everyone here to seek shelter in the Market and to remain there until further notice.*"

"*What great danger?*" a Hunter demanded.

"We aren't going anywhere!" another shouted.

*"As an apology for this breach in our traditions,"* Certus continued as shouts and curses swelled, *"the Third will allow all Hunters to enjoy all restaurants and casinos in his claim free of charge until the danger passes. Additionally, he has partnered with the Tenth, who has agreed to give free access to many of his finest pleasure houses."*

James glared at the crowds in disgust as boos died and yells dimmed into rapid whispers and shocked murmurs. Some Hunters exchanged looks of interest, others of deep suspicion.

*"And what is this danger that merits such a generous gift from the Third?"* a man shouted, his voice loaded with irony.

*"The Third himself is happy to answer any questions you may have regarding the approaching danger,"* Certus said. *"If you would like to speak with him, please follow my men to the Abode. Otherwise, please begin driving to the Market. My men will escort you there. They can also provide a ride to either the Abode or the Market if that is what your family prefers. And as a reminder!"* he added, raising his voice again as several families gripped their weapons and shouted in defiance. *"The Third has read the minds of many of you here! I implore you not to forget what he can do with such knowledge!"*

Faces paled, curses multiplied, and though families shouted about rules and traditions, still, not a single Hunter made to attack Certus. A man shook his head with a revolted look before motioning to his family and leading them toward the Third's SUVs. Other families swore before steering themselves toward the cars as well. Several Traditionalists smirked at Phoenix and Copperhead before turning their backs to them and walking away. Copperhead snorted and shook his head in disbelief.

*"Cowards!"* Phoenix yelled, causing several families to halt mid-step. Fury burned alongside desperation within his eyes. *"All of you are cowards! You Traditionalists refused to let Blood Crow enter the Tournament for breaking the rules, and now you're running away when*

*the Third breaks one of the oldest rules in the entire history of Hunters?
And Contemporaries! Do you really think you're any better?"*

"*He's right!*" Copperhead yelled. "*Listen to your Lead! Come back
here, and stand your ground if you dare call yourself a Hunter!*"

Traditionalists lowered their eyes. Contemporaries stared at
Copperhead and Phoenix. Certus glared at them all. Phoenix gritted his
teeth as families began breaking away in droves. A few glanced back at
them as Copperhead continued shouting. But still the Hunters walked.

Bodyguards and Merchants accompanied the families as they
departed for the Tower or the Market. Even with the number of men
departing, though, the Third's army stood as vast and undefeatable as
ever. James shoved the words "we're doomed" out of his head. The crew
had to fight their way out, just like E had said. They couldn't let
themselves get caught. Not now!

"*Protect!*" a voice screamed.

Blood Crow's eyes widened as the crowds parted.

"*Steel Heart,*" she whispered.

Steel Heart ran forth with his broadsword in hand and planted
himself in front of the stage. Lion Paw pushed men and women aside as
he chased after him.

"*Steel Heart! Steel Heart, come back here!*" Lion Paw grabbed the
teen's arm. "*The Third has seen your memories. You cannot do this!*"

"*No!*" he shouted, yanking his arm away. "*Phoenix and Copperhead
are right. This is the Hunters' way, and these are our traditions!*"

His young face shone with pride as he thrust his sword into the air.

"*Do not forget! Protect! Protect!*" he shouted to the crowds. "*I will not
run away! I will not forsake our honor! Stand with me, Hunters. You must
not live to regret this night. It is the Hunters' way!*"

Courage began to shine through the fear that had darkened the
Traditionalists' faces as they watched Steel Heart wave his sword about.

*"Are you really going to let a teenager outdo you, you cowards?"* Phoenix screamed.

A man with graying hair raised his spear. *"I will not cower as the young sacrifice themselves. Protect!"* he cried. He and his family sprinted to Steel Heart's side.

More broadswords and spears appeared as other Traditionalists responded with a rousing shout of *"For life!"* James watched in amazement as one family after another ran to join Steel Heart.

*"Contemporaries! Are you going to run while Traditionalists fight?"* Phoenix raged. *"They're putting their lives on the line while you're tucking tail!"*

*"Yeah! Or are we the only Contemporaries with our balls left?"* Copperhead shouted.

A woman lifted her sword. *"Come on, you cowards!"* she yelled.

Fierce cries answered her as Contemporaries rushed forth and joined the Traditionalists. The remainder of the crowds looked at Certus again before departing. As the newly-formed army of Hunters began taunting Certus and his men, Lion Paw gave Steel Heart a beseeching look.

*"Lion Paw,"* said Steel Heart. *"These are our ways. You always told us that they're worth dying for. Was it all a lie?"*

Lion Paw's eyes found Blood Crow's. As her gaze begged him not to disappoint her more than he already had, something glimmered into life within his sapphire eyes. For a split moment, James thought he might prove himself to be brave after all.

Then shame fell over Lion Paw's face.

*"I'm sorry,"* he said. *"But my children in Reality. I'm sorry."*

Blood Crow closed her eyes as he turned and fled toward the SUVs.

# CHAPTER 18

# PROTECT

Steel Heart scrunched up his face and held back his tears as he watched Lion Paw flee. He swore. "*I'm sorry it took me so long,*" he told Blood Crow. "*And I'm sorry for not thanking you before,*" he told James. "*You helped me in that hallway and saved me from those blue particles. I should have thanked you earlier.*"

"*No. I should be the one thanking you. You protected me from that snake woman,*" James replied.

Certus lowered the microphone with a dull expression as the Hunters continued throwing insults at him. He waved his hand. Bodyguards and Merchants poured out of the remaining SUVs and began marching toward the Hunters.

Hope flared within James. Battle was about to break out, and when it did, the commotion would provide enough distraction for the crew to fight their way to their car. E cast another sharp look at Phoenix, who replied with a firm nod. He drew a deep breath.

"*Brothers and sisters!*" he yelled. "*Do not let the Third have his way with us! Show him the consequences of going against the Hunters' way!*"

Traditionalists and Contemporaries shook their weapons as they whooped and shouted. They turned in unison and pointed their weapons at the oncoming horde.

"*Bring them to the Market!*" Certus shouted.

Steel Heart let out a long and fearless cry as he charged at the Third's army with his sword. The Hunters rushed after him with screams that thirsted for honor. E's machete whirled through the air toward Certus. As he dodged her blade, she yelled, "Now!" and leapt upon the circle of men surrounding the crew. James thrust his spear through a Merchant's mouth as he joined the crew in a merciless attack. The Hunters clashed with the Third's men in a thunderous collision. Copperhead goaded his opponents as he cut them down. Phoenix shouted to him, and together, they blocked the blows of those who lunged at them and jumped off the stage to join the crew.

James hurled his spear into a Merchant's head and slashed open a Bodyguard's throat with a dagger from his belt. An endless stretch of enemies seemed to separate the crew from their car. He glimpsed Copperhead's family fending off the Third's men but knew that they could only hold them off for so long. He hurled his dagger into another man's head then aimed a new spear at a Merchant swinging a spiked bat at Lux.

"Watch out!" Blood Crow yelled.

James spun around to see a raging battle sweeping toward him. He shouted as a massive wave of Bodyguards, Hunters, and Merchants tore him away from the rest of the crew. He pushed and shoved the bodies that slammed into him, ground into him, threw him from side to side. The stage creaked and moaned then crashed onto its side. The screens wavered then toppled.

Something slammed into James's head. Sounds dimmed then sharpened again as his body hit the ground. He rolled to the side to escape the blow of a Merchant's crowbar. As the man lifted the bar again, James stuck his spear through his belly. The man fell onto his knees and grasped James's spear still lodged in his stomach. James jumped onto his feet, created a broadsword, and sliced off the man's head with a single stroke. The head dropped onto the ground, its eyes rolling back in its sockets, its vertebra exposed. James had never decapitated a human before. The horror and thrill of it was stunning.

He snapped out of his trance as Blood Crow screamed from somewhere in the distance. He spun around then gasped as vertigo pushed him face-down into the dirt. He touched the back of his head and looked at his hand to find blood glistening on his fingers. He grasped dirt with one hand, gripped his sword with the other, and dragged himself an inch across the ground. He stopped as vertigo rocked his vision again. He shouted as someone kicked him aside and ran past. His eyes fell on the Merchant's headless body. A memory blazed up within his mind, the memory of E in the Arena, pulling out a Merchant's spear from her stomach and sealing the wound with a fearsome cry.

James clenched his teeth as Blood Crow shrieked again. He dug the point of his sword into the ground and pushed himself up. He needed to find her. He needed to find Blood Crow and protect her!

He embraced the pain throbbing across his skull then dove into it. He harnessed the fury—no, the determination—he found within. He let out a cry that raked his throat raw as he fueled a strength he had never known before, a strength that scorched and purged and purified. His mind pinpointed the cracks in his skull then pulled everything tight. Blood stopped flowing down his neck as the pieces of his skull sealed back into one whole.

He parried a Merchant's blow with his broadsword then beheaded him. Following Blood Crow's cries, he cut through screams and bloodshed until he found her, at last, defending the car alongside Steel Heart and what little remained of Copperhead's family. Several of the windows had shattered. James thought of Phoenix as he raised his sword.

"*Protect!*" he screamed.

"*For life!*" families replied.

They charged forth with him. He hurled a spear into a man who jumped toward Blood Crow. Pain suddenly seared his back and ripped through his chest. Blood Crow screamed out his name as his legs buckled. He gripped the spear protruding from his chest and tried to breathe. Blood flooded out of his mouth as the spear was pulled out from behind. A foot slammed into his back and sent him into the dirt. As he rolled over, another foot collided with his cheek. He tried to lift his sword as a Bodyguard began spearing him in the stomach again and again. More feet descended upon him along with blades and spears. He choked on his own blood as he strove to fight back.

"James!" Blood Crow shrieked.

"No," he gasped as she ran toward him.

A Bodyguard slashed through her side, and Merchants leapt toward her as she fell. James's fingers scrambled over the dirt as he tried to flip over onto his belly and crawl to her. A Bodyguard drove her spear through his chest, pinning him into the ground. A Merchant lifted a sword, ready to take off his head. James clutched at the spear holding him down and wriggled and kicked despite the pain that burned him with every movement he made. Even as the sword swung down toward his neck, he refused to surrender.

"Traitor!" a voice screamed.

A massive sword whirled forth and split the head of the Merchant before he could behead James. A dagger shot into the head of the woman who had pinned him down. A body was tossed up into the air in the distance. A man stumbled into view, his arms full of his own guts. Blood spurted before his head fell from his neck. Those standing next to him spasmed before their heads toppled onto the ground too. Their bodies collapsed into a pile.

Kit.

His blood-stained body towered over all those surrounding him. His eyes burned bright like lightning cracking apart a night sky. Everyone staggered back as he raised his great, curved swords and roared with rage. He ran forth and swept up those surrounding James and Blood Crow in an unrelenting storm of slaughter that filled the air with cries of pain and terror.

E snatched a spear off the ground and hurled it into a Merchant aiming his daggers at Kit. Behind her, Copperhead and Honey shouted warnings to each other as they felled all those who rushed forth to attack Lux. Lux supported Phoenix as he helped him stumble forward. Even in his battered state, Phoenix continued stabbing enemies with his sword.

Blood Crow staggered toward James and yanked the spear out of his chest. He gasped and clutched at the pulsating wound then grasped her outstretched hand and forced himself to stand up again. They lurched forward together and ran several steps before Blood Crow collapsed with a shout of pain. She gripped her bloodied leg and cursed as he tried to help her stand up again.

He drew upon every drop of pain and anger he possessed, and again, he found an all-consuming focus. He cried out with the shaking desperation of a man who could not watch the destruction of those he loved as he sealed several of his deepest wounds. He gathered Blood Crow into his arms and bellowed another long cry of determination as he lifted her up. Blood continued streaming out of the cuts and holes he had failed to heal as he sprinted toward the car.

E shouted a warning. He saw the point of a dagger flying toward his head then Steel Heart as he leapt out of nowhere. The dagger plunged into Steel Heart's head.

"No!" Blood Crow screamed.

Steel Heart fell to the ground and laid still with vacant eyes that stared up at the full moon. James continued running as Blood Crow screamed again and again for Steel Heart. Glass dug into his arm as he reached through a broken window and unlocked the car. He threw the back door open and set Blood Crow down inside. He glanced at Snow's figure quivering under the blanket then yelled as two blades flew into his back. He spun around even as his legs grew limp, gripping the broken window as he tried to keep himself standing. He dropped onto the ground and tore out the knives as Bodyguards and Merchants ran toward him. Kit's daggers flew into their heads before they could reach him.

"Get in the car!" Kit roared at him.

James grasped the back seat and strained as he tried to haul himself inside. Blood Crow gripped his arm and pulled him in.

"Honey, Copperhead, get to the car! Protect it!" E shouted before sending another head spinning through the air.

Honey cracked open one last skull with her tomahawk. Copperhead pulled out his sword from the stomach of a Merchant. As they dashed toward the car together, a Bodyguard lunged at Copperhead. He shouted in dismay as his last family member jumped forward and took the blow in his stead. Honey cleaved the Bodyguard's neck, slapped Copperhead across the face as he reached for his fallen family member, then forced him to continue running with her. They reached the car and defended it as Kit and E ran to help Lux and Phoenix.

Kit sent teeth flying as he caved in a Bodyguard's face with a single punch. With his elbow, he shattered a Merchant's cheek then his temple. As another Bodyguard charged toward him from behind, he whirled around and hurled a punch that made the man spin around head-first.

He pulled the man back by his vest, gripped his hair, and snapped his neck in two. He grabbed Phoenix and slung him over his shoulder.

E shouted to Lux. They rushed forth together and began slicing out a path toward the car while shielding Kit, who defended them from behind. He rent the air with another terrifying roar as more enemies raced toward him. He tossed Phoenix aside and drew back his sword.

He slashed across a Merchant's belly and gutted him with his free hand before slicing across a Bodyguard's mouth once then twice. He gripped her neck. Her eyes bulged and bled as he lifted her up and slowly crunched in her throat. His hold only tightened as she swung her legs and beat her fist frantically against his arm. He threw her onto the ground, lifted his sword high, and roared as he slammed the blade down into her head. Her eyes, brains, and tongue exploded out of her skull.

All of his enemies turned and fled as he breathed in deep and roared once again.

He shouted at Copperhead and Honey to get in the car then yelled at E and Lux to join him as he grabbed Phoenix again and ran to the car as well. He flung Phoenix onto the floor of the backseat, kicked him so that he crumpled up into a ball, then jumped into the driver's seat. E skidded across the hood and leapt in next to Kit. Lux belly-flopped onto James and Blood Crow and tossed the keys to Kit. The engine roared into life. Honey slammed the door shut as Kit stomped on the gas. Other cars pursued them as he mowed down Hunters, Bodyguards, and Merchants alike.

"The dog and the Twelfth are in the back?" Kit shouted as the car jostled and jumped over bodies.

"Yes!" E said. "Bloom's family too!"

"Family?" he exclaimed, glancing at her.

The car zoomed out into the Desert. The engine revved to the brink of explosion as he pushed the pedal onto the floor.

"Hold on!" he yelled.

James grabbed a headrest. Kit swerved the car. They spun in a dizzying blur, blowing up a tornado of dust, before the white of the Desert vanished. The car whirled through dim light and humid air. Mud and water sprayed through the broken windows as the car slammed back down onto its tires and skidded across shallow waters. The group shouted as they crashed into a tree.

"Out!" Kit roared as he released his vice-like grip on the steering wheel.

He and E kicked open their doors and jumped out into the swamp. James yanked Blood Crow out of the car as Kit threw Phoenix over his shoulder again.

"Bloom!" E yelled.

Snow clung to Bloom's back as he and the other wolves leapt out of the car. James forced his crumpling legs to keep up with his will as he sprinted across the water with the others. Kit stopped next to the stump of a dead tree and furiously signaled for them to run through. They dashed into the exit one after another. James's feet sank into red sand as he ran out from the exit.

A myriad of stars speckled a sky that blended black, brown, and ruby. It was as if a giant brush had shaken diamond ink onto a burnt galaxy. Red sand dunes stretched on for miles all around him. Patches of blue ocean glimmered between the dunes in the distance. Dry desert bushes as well as small, shallow pools interrupted the sand every few yards. Some of the pools lay flat on the ground. Others lay embedded in the sides of the dunes like mirrors. Rows of misty, snow-capped mountains stood far away on the right. The pack sniffed the air feverishly as the group assumed a battle formation. Kit appeared last with Phoenix still slung over his shoulder. The wolves lowered their snouts.

"*We are alone*," Father said.

The crew groaned in unison.

James stumbled past several pools and bushes, kicking up sand with haphazard steps, before falling face-down. He rolled over and pressed his hand over a wound still sealing on his chest. Realization permeated his exhaustion as he continued gulping in the cold, crisp air. They had done it. He could hardly believe it, but they had actually done it. They had escaped from the Third.

Honey and Copperhead dropped down next to a large bush nearby. Lux didn't bother moving but simply let his katana fall from his hand and collapsed. E began examining Blood Crow's injured leg. Snow slid off of Bloom's back as Kit tossed Phoenix aside. He walked around the group as he scrutinized the dunes with keen eyes.

"Hurry up and heal what you can! We need to keep moving," he told them. "We're still in *the Iris*. We can't stay here for long."

The relief that had risen within James burst under the weight of Kit's words. Who cared if they had escaped from the Third? They were back in No Man's Land. They would be totally vulnerable if the Calf arrived now. They had to return to the moonlight as soon as possible before it was too late.

"I said hurry up!" Kit raged.

E stood up. Alarm bolted up within James as she walked toward Kit with quickening steps.

"We'll go to *the Mountains* next," Kit continued. "We'll lay low there then circle back to *Lapis Lazuli* and–"

"*You son of a bitch!*" E shrieked in Korean.

He jumped as she slammed her fists against his chest. He jerked his head back with a look that was as offended as it was surprised.

"'*Son of a bitch?*' Hey. Hey! *Stop hitting me!* You should be more grateful. I just saved all of your ... are you crying?" he exclaimed.

"That's right!" E shouted as tears rolled down her cheeks. "I'm crying. I'm crying, I'm crying, I'm crying! What are you going to do about it?"

Kit stared at her, open-mouthed, as she howled and pounded away at his chest again. The shock on his face slowly melted into a soft gaze. She hurled her fist a final time then stood back, huffing and puffing. He grinned and crossed his arms.

"Well, well, well. Look at how the tables have turned. Well, now you know, E. Now you know what it feels like when someone just disappears out of your life like that. Your mind really goes places, doesn't it? Doesn't it? Serves you right."

She stared at him, wide-eyed and shaking with indignation, before spinning around and stomping away from the group. Kit chased after her, looking both guilty and gleeful. Lux grabbed Bloom's mane as he lunged toward E.

"Bloom!" Lux said as Bloom dragged him across the sand. "Give them some privacy. Stop butting in. Hey, help me out here!" he told Copperhead.

He stumbled forward and threw himself on top of Bloom too. "Really? A Jackal? Didn't expect that from Black Fang."

"Hey, man. They care about each other. That's all that matters."

Sleet, Terrain, and Forest gathered near a pool. They muttered to one another and glared at Kit. Father watched E in silence.

"*Let go!*" E shouted as Kit grabbed her wrist. "*Let go!*"

"E," he said as he struggled with her, "stop being so difficult!"

"*I said let go!*"

"Calm down!"

"*Let go!*" she raged.

"*I can't let go!*" he raged back.

She glared at him, still fuming, then wriggled in his grasp as he forced her hand up. He pressed her fist over his heart.

"I love you," he said. "I love you, remember?"

The anger in her eyes wavered. The memory of E and Kit lying together on red silk flashed across James's mind. He glanced at Snow, whose expression reflected his own frustration and despair. He knew that she, too, wanted nothing more than to stop the reconciliation that was occurring right in front of them. But what could they do? Tell Kit to get his hands off of E when he had just saved them all and would continue to do so even as the night progressed? They needed him if they wanted to survive, and there was nothing they could do about it. Nothing. James gritted his teeth as the anguish of self-loathing burned within his heart. He should have taken his chances during the day. He should have talked more with E.

Kit sighed as he tilted back his head with an expression that barely suppressed his exasperation. He let go of E's wrist.

"By the way, how are you feeling?" he asked as he rubbed his eyes.

She flared up immediately. "How do you think I'm feeling? We just lost the battle!"

"Not the battle! I mean, you know." He hesitated then said, "*Tomorrow is Christmas.*"

Guilt smacked James upside the head as he remembered that E's father had died on Christmas Eve. More tears rolled down her cheeks.

"I'm fine," she said.

"Yeah, that's a lie," he said with a hollow smirk. He looked her up and down as concern overtook his expression. "*Why do you always say you're okay when you're not okay at all?*"

More tears joined those dripping off of her chin. Kit sighed again, looking more drained than if he'd finished fighting ten battles. He wiped away her tears. She buried her face in his chest as he wrapped her in his arms. A few moments passed as he shushed and cradled her. He gently lifted her chin. He looked at the ground then at her, and for a moment, there was nothing threatening or even charming about Kit.

Instead, he simply looked broken.

E blinked then nodded gently. Relief spread across his face. He sighed deeply and tightened his hold around her. He kissed her on the head then pressed his cheek against the spot that he had kissed.

"Thank you," he said.

"For what?"

He slid his hand up onto the nape of her neck. "For coming back to me."

Father snapped around first then Bloom then the rest of the pack.

"*Run!*" Father yelled.

It all happened in a split moment.

Spears flew into the wolves as Bodyguards rushed out of an exit and onto the sand. Certus shouted orders as more spears zinged through the air and pierced Phoenix, Lux, and Blood Crow. Copperhead scrambled back as Father gurgled at him to run. He dashed over to Honey, throwing a knife into a Bodyguard who aimed a spear at her as he went, and forced her to sprint up a sand dune with him. Kit cursed and lifted E off of her feet. She screamed and thrashed in his arms as he ran away and disappeared into an exit.

And throughout all this, James was running, running toward Blood Crow. She thrust her finger toward Snow, and he hated himself for knowing that she was right. The crew had lost. He needed to save Snow and escape.

He veered and sprinted toward Snow instead. He created a spear and hurled it into a Bodyguard. He flung another spear and another and yet another as men rushed toward him. He reached for Snow as Bodyguards grabbed her and wrenched her arms back. He dodged a spear, caught another that shot toward him, then threw it into a man's chest. The final spear that appeared in his hand remained in his grip as countless weapons plunged into his body.

Grunting and gasping, he fell onto the red sands, captured by the Third's men at last.

# CHAPTER 19

# THE HEAD MERCHANT

The body bag unzipped, revealing a domed ceiling that reached high up into the shadows. A green glow danced upon mosaic tiles of gold, white, and blue. James glanced at the steaming pool in which he'd once seen the gossiping Shamans bathe then again at the space above where he knew the invisible bridge stretched across the air.

He wriggled in the body bag as a Bodyguard reached down and pulled out the gag in his mouth. He spat blood in her face before she could touch him again. She wiped away the blood then slammed a punch into his cheek. She yanked him out of the body bag and threw him onto the slippery, tiled floor. He suppressed his cries as she tore into his many wounds with a series of kicks. After a final kick, she glared at him and walked away.

The chains binding his hands and feet clinked as he tipped over onto his back. He told himself to grow angry, to feel the injustice of the beating, to submerge himself in the pain thumping throughout his body. But his rage eluded him. He could only find more pain within his pain as his hopelessness fed an exhaustion that weighed so heavily down on him that he thought his bones might break.

He curled up on his side and swallowed mouthfuls of the thick, humid air. He stared again at the location of the invisible bridge. If only the crew were all up there and not down here. If only they had continued running across the sand dunes as Kit had planned. As Bodyguards threw Phoenix and Blood Crow down at the edge of the pool several feet away, James's thoughts floated away from the chamber and back to the red sands.

The wolves had been stabbed into submission before being muzzled, tied, and caged. The crew had been stripped of their belts, bound, and gagged before being shoved into body bags and tossed into cars. The wheels had jumped endlessly over uneven mounds before zooming out onto rough terrain. Though the darkness of the body bag had blinded James, he'd known that they were being driven to the Tower.

He had not, however, expected to hear the commotion surrounding the Tower. Only a moment of listening had been enough to tell him that the Hunters who had left the Solstice were still far from receiving any satisfactory answers for their forced evacuation. Their yells and curses had diminished only after the Bodyguards had carried the group up countless stairs.

His mind fell back into the present as Snow was thrown onto the ground in front of him. A Bodyguard dropped Lux down behind him and kicked him in the stomach. Metal scraped across the tiles as the Bodyguards pushed the pack's cages to the far side of the chamber. Sleet, Forest, and Terrain writhed and knocked their muzzled snouts against the bars. Bloom's eyes darted from crew member to crew member as he, too, banged his snout and strove against his restraints. Father alone remained still. His sharp, golden eyes followed the Third's men as they gathered up the body bags strewn across the ground and swept the group's blood into the drains. A man flung his broom aside.

"Why are we cleaning when they're just going to keep bleeding out anyway?" he complained.

"You know the rules. Try to keep everything clean," a Bodyguard replied in a monotone voice.

James caught the words "Hedonist's job" and "not paid enough" as the man crossed his arms and muttered to himself. He spat into a drain then did a double take at Snow. He grinned.

"Welcome back, Twelve! Did you miss us?"

Fear twitched on her face as the man clopped toward her. She began to squirm. James fought to free himself, to protect her somehow, as he saw the predatory glint in the man's eyes. He paused in his struggle as she suddenly froze. Determination slowly hardened her expression before shrewdness flashed across her face. James had seen that shrewdness within her before. It was the same sharp shrewdness she had wielded to ambush and read E. She remained cold and indifferent as the man squatted down next to her.

"Aw, come on. Say something, Twelve," he said. "Or Snow, right? That's what that skinny, little Guide of yours always calls you. You missed us while you were out there, scampering around, didn't you? Causing all this trouble for us."

Bodyguards kicked Phoenix and Blood Crow into silence as they shouted at the man to leave her alone. The man began flicking the back of his index finger against Snow's cheek. Rage spiraled up within James and blasted away his exhaustion. His mind pinpointed every injury on his body. His wounds wove swiftly together as the man continued flicking his finger.

"So, what was it like out there in the planes? I want to hear all about it. Did you finally get some action out there? Get one of those human-looking citizens to put a smile on your sad, little face? Everyone always says you're one of the few Shamans who wants to get rid of all the red-light districts in the claims, but I know you Shamans better than that. I bet you're a nasty little bitch under that nice-girl front you always put up."

"Hey," said the Bodyguard who had kicked James before. "She's still a Shaman. Just shut up, and help us clean. Leave her alone."

"Who cares if she's a Shaman? She can't do anything to me with her hands tied behind her back."

"What are you talking about?" said another Bodyguard. "She couldn't do anything before either."

"Yeah, what's she going to do?" said yet another. "Just look at her. And she's actually supposed to be a Shaman."

The man shared a round of sneers with his comrades then leaned down and hovered his mouth over Snow's ear. James coiled up on the ground. Snows tilted herself ever so slightly on her side. If she rolled suddenly and at the right angle, her hands would touch the man's boot. And, James knew, if she held on to him in the struggle that was sure to ensue, she might find a way to touch some of his bare skin. She might find a way to read him.

"You know, I really like Asian girls," the man murmured. "All of you are so small and soft but tight too, if you know what I mean. And submissive. Yeah, it's real nice how submissive you Asian girls are. Now that I think about it, I remember hearing from some of the other Bodyguards that you squeak like a mouse whenever someone surprises you." He leaned in even closer. "I can make you squeak all night if you want."

Pure, red fury colored James's mind, his thoughts, his whole being. He reared up onto his knees, shot himself forward, and sank his teeth into the man's neck. The man's screams, the crew's shouts, and the Bodyguards' commands all rang in James's ears as a swarm of hands descended upon him and grabbed his head and pulled on his body. He bit down harder. The man screamed louder. A Bodyguard swung a hammer into James's jaw. Spores of light popped in front of his eyes as pain radiated around his head. Snow shouted his name. The man's whispers replayed in his mind. Fury spiraled up within him once more. He tried to deepen his bite even as the Bodyguards pushed their fingers into his mouth and pried his teeth out of the man's neck. They threw James back and converged upon him with drawn daggers. He roared out the rage still burning within him and sealed his shattered jaw back into one piece.

The Bodyguards froze, clearly stunned, then spun around as the door of the chamber creaked open. Hunters' shouts drifted in as ghostly echoes before the door closed with a soft, reverberating boom. A hulking figure as thick as the many pillars standing in the shadows moved through the darkness toward them. The Bodyguards abandoned James and rushed to form a row. They straightened their backs as Certus appeared. His eyes fixed on the man whom James had bitten then swiveled onto James before staring at Snow. The man lifted his head higher as Certus walked up to him. He scanned the bite marks still healing on his neck.

He sliced off the man's head with a flash of his sword.

James exchanged looks of surprise with Blood Crow and Phoenix as Certus glared down at the man's body. The Bodyguards flinched as he lifted his massive foot and stomped on the man's head. He continued stomping in measured, rhythmic beats until his brains lay scattered across the ground in chunks of raw pulp.

"The Third has commanded it once, he has commanded it a thousand times. You will show the Twelfth Shaman respect!" Certus shouted. "And you will not lay your hands on a woman, the Twelfth or otherwise. Needless to say, this one"–he pointed his sword at the headless man–"is stripped of his title as a Bodyguard. Take him to the

Market! Give him to Bear or the Butcher, I don't care which one. Let them do what they want with him."

"Yes, sir!"

The Bodyguards hurried out of the chamber with the man's body and the remnants of his head. A figure slipped into the shadows before they closed the door. Bloom's nose twitched. He began heaving deep, rough breaths then slammed his face against the bars of his cage in a fresh fit of rage. Sleet, Forest, and Terrain erupted into muffled snarls.

"Will you guard them while I go to the Third?" Certus asked the figure in the dark.

The figure walked toward them with quick, sure steps. Realization rolled toward James, side-by-side with shock, swelling then slamming into his mind. A cold fury swept over him as his heart smarted with the sting of self-loathing. He had been an idiot. Such a dumb, naive idiot!

The figure emerged from the shadows and stepped into the wavering, green light.

"Kit!" Lux exclaimed.

Snow lifted her head. Blood Crow's mouth dropped open with outrage. Phoenix gritted his teeth.

"Go ahead," Kit told Certus. "I'll guard them until the Third comes."

Certus inclined his head in a slight bow before leaving the chamber.

Water dripped.

Bloom continued banging his snout against the bars.

"Kit," Lux repeated. "Kit, what are you doing here? Where's E? What going on?"

"I'll cut you," Phoenix snarled at Kit. "I'll cut you!"

Kit's eyes flashed. He glared at Phoenix then smirked. Placing his hands on his waist, he pressed his tongue into the side of his cheek then smirked again. He walked toward Phoenix. Fear seized James as he realized that nothing would stop Kit from taking off Phoenix's head or even from piercing his watch. But instead, Kit knelt down and pulled out a strip of rough cloth from a compartment on his belt. Gripping Phoenix's face, he forced open his mouth and shoved the cloth inside. He tied the ends tightly behind his head, grabbed his face again, and forced him to look up at him.

"The Third wants you in one piece, so I'll let things slide tonight," Kit told him. "But one of these nights ... one of these nights, Phoenix, I'm going to punch in your face so hard that they'll have to pick out parts of your skull from your brain, and you'll hit the ground before you even knew that I was there."

They glared at each other before Kit cast Phoenix's face aside. Blood Crow yelled and flopped about as he gripped her hair. He slammed her head down onto the floor.

"Bastard!" James screamed. For the first time in his life, he felt a murderous hatred that disregarded all morals and laws. All he wanted—all that filled his mind—was to tear Kit's hands away from Blood Crow and cut off his head. "Get your hands off her! You coward! Coward!"

Kit finished tying the cloth behind her head and stood up. James despised himself for the drop of fear that diluted his anger as he walked toward him. He flung all the threats and curses he knew to prove that he wasn't a coward himself. Kit kicked him onto his back then knelt down and placed his palm on James's nose. Slowly, he began to twist, pressing and grinding into his face a pain so excruciating that he never would have been able to imagine that such a pain had even existed. His nose snapped then splintered then collapsed entirely so that Kit's palm sank into his face. James didn't even know that he was screaming until Kit lifted his hand. He choked as he shoved a cloth into his mouth. Blood continued pouring out from his mutilated nose, soaking the cloth, as Kit tied the ends behind his head.

Snow began shouting threats to reveal Kit's name. He silenced her with a sharp slap across the mouth. He gagged her with a cloth before turning to Lux.

"Kit!" Lux said. "Kit. No, wait. Wait!"

Kit gripped his throat then tightened a cloth around his mouth as well. As he rose to his feet and turned toward Bloom, he drew a large dagger that glinted in the strange, green glow of the chamber. He walked up to his cage. Bloom stopped struggling but continued huffing heavy breaths as he glared up at him. A deep growl broke out of Father's throat as Kit's eyes widened.

"You have no idea how long I've been waiting to do this," he told Bloom.

He gripped Bloom's mane. The cloth in James's mouth smothered his screams as Kit yanked Bloom's head to the side and began stabbing him. Father and the other wolves thrashed in their cages. Phoenix teetered on the edge of the pool as he rolled about and tried to free himself from his chains. Blood Crow and Snow shouted into their gags as they, too, squirmed and struggled. Lux alone remained silent.

Kit released his hold on Bloom's mane. His head thudded onto the floor. As he gripped Bloom's ear, Father threw himself against his cage with such force that it screeched across the ground. Kit cut off Bloom's ear, flung it aside, then cut off the other. He reached deeper into the cage, grasped his hind legs, and dragged him closer to himself. He gripped his tail, slipped his blade under, and pulled up until his tail broke away from his body. Tears ran down James's face as Kit stood up again. His dagger quivered in his fist as he pumped air in and out of his lungs. His black eyes burned bright with his ruthless hatred.

Shouts filled the chamber as the door opened again. James numbly registered that the Hunters were getting closer. A woman was screaming about the honor of Hunters. Others were shouting about Steel Heart's bravery and their obligation to follow his example. The clamor silenced as the door closed. Bells chimed in the shadows, chilling James's heart. Certus guided the Third into the light and stopped near Phoenix and Blood Crow. The Third remained impassive as Phoenix tried to shout to him through his gag.

"I thought you were going to watch them, not torture them," Certus said as he frowned at Bloom's ravaged body.

"You're one to talk," Kit retorted. "And besides, both of you already know." His eyes bulged as he looked at Bloom again. "You know how this damn dog took my girl away from me!"

"Speaking of your girl, where is she?" said the Third. "Certus told me that you ran away with her."

Kit tightened his grip on his blood-stained dagger. "We agreed that I could keep her if I gave you the rest of them. We agreed that you wouldn't send her out into battle with the Red Calf."

"I remember," said the Third as he motioned for him to calm down. "I only ask because from what I've read, she's stronger than ten of my best men put together. I'd like to recruit her as one of my Bodyguards. A woman like that needs a good job."

Kit's black eyes flitted back and forth between the Third and Certus.

The Third sighed. "Or perhaps you'd like to keep her locked up in that apartment of yours every night like you did before and neglect her until she can't stand it anymore and runs away again?"

Kit glanced at Phoenix.

"And," the Third continued, "may I remind you that although you agreed to bring all of her crew here, you allowed Honey to escape with Copperhead. So, unless you'd like for me to cancel our agreement on account of your failure, I suggest you at least let me know where E is."

Kit sheathed his dagger then walked up to the Third and knelt down in front of him. "Please, feel free," he said.

The Third placed his hands on each side of Kit's head. The brightness in Kit's eyes dimmed.

"Excellent," the Third said a split moment later.

Kit blinked rapidly as he removed his hands.

"And again, Kit, I want to assure you that I am committed to forging a trusting relationship with you. I am very much invested in your future here. You have my word that I will not endanger E in any way. After all, it is in both our best interests to keep her safe. Now—"

The Third expelled a small sigh of frustration as the door groaned open. The sound of clashing blades rang throughout the chamber, announcing that battle had begun with the Hunters. James looked at the Third, expecting to see some hint of worry or, at the very least, alarm. But he saw only weariness as Snake Eyes scurried out of the darkness.

"Three, you called for me?" Snake Eyes said with a well-oiled smile.

"Yes, Snake Eyes. Please join us here," said the Third in a voice that was as tired as his expression.

The bells on Snake Eyes's wrist continued clanging as he strode over to the Third. His gaze skimmed over the crew and lingered on the wolves before focusing again on Three.

"Kit," said the Third, "I'm sure you're familiar with my Head Merchant, Snake Eyes?"

"Of course." He placed his hands behind his back and looked down at Snake Eyes as if he were vermin.

"Snake Eyes, are you acquainted with Kit?" said the Third.

"Well, yes," he said. His smile tightened. "As your Head Merchant, it's my job to know all the Jackals in the Market. So yes, I am well-acquainted with Kit. Or Kit the Cruel as he's often called," he added, glancing again at Bloom.

"Yes. Kit the Cruel, Kit the Cunning, the Charmer, and my personal favorite, Kit the Silver-Tongued and Golden-Handed. Quite an impressive resume, don't you think? Especially for someone his age."

"Yes," Snake Eyes said. His eyes swiveled between the Third and Kit before nervous laughter warbled out of his mouth. "I'm sorry, my liege. Is there something I'm not quite understanding here?"

"Yes, as a matter of fact, there is. Kit brought me the crew I've been searching for, the crew I had tasked you with finding. In return for his good work, I've made him my new Head Merchant."

Snow's gag muffled her gasp. James and the others stared. Snake Eyes blinked.

"I beg your pardon?" he said.

"You have failed me for the last time, Snake Eyes," said the Third.

Snake Eyes backed away. He shook his head and laughed again. "But, my liege. We have been partners for many years now."

"And it has been many years since you've proven to me that you are underqualified for this position!"

The chamber repeated his words as if to mock Snake Eyes. The Third huffed out a sigh then proceeded in a low, hissing voice as Snake Eyes continued staring at him with wide eyes.

"How many times must I remind you of the numbers? How many times will you fail to bring me what I asked? How many times do you think I will turn a blind eye to all the things I have seen so plainly in your mind with every reading?"

Snake Eyes's lower jaw shuddered. The Third sighed again. The anger on his face settled into sternness.

"I have spoken with the Tenth, and we have agreed that you will take Kit's place in Lavender as his Jackal. I can assure you that it is still a lofty position. Kit had worked his way up the ranks quite a bit already. As soon as the two of you are situated into your new roles, your first assignment will be to work together to shut down the forbidden fighting pit in the Market. I will have none of this 'Arena' nonsense anymore. Do I make myself clear?"

"Absolutely," said Kit.

"This ... I can't," sputtered Snake Eyes. "No. No! The things I've done. The things you made me ... I gave ... I gave you my mind. My life!"

"And I still have both in the palm of my hand!" the Third shouted. "I am giving you this one chance to walk away now, Snake Eyes, and I suggest you take it!"

Snake Eyes took another step back, wheezing for air as if he were in danger of suffocating to death. Consternation curdled into fury on his face. He created a broadsword and pointed it at the Third. Certus stepped forward. Kit smirked.

"Snake Eyes, think of what you are doing," Certus said. There was an ounce of genuine concern in his voice that surprised James. "Threatening a Shaman is grounds for permanent expulsion from the City."

"I will not leave the City. Not without his head!" Snake Eyes yelled. Froth bubbled up in the corners of his mouth as he continued wheezing. "Or have you forgotten that I was once a Hunter? I know how to fight. I know how to kill!"

Kit slashed off Snake Eyes's arms first then his head. The Third and Certus both sighed. They looked unsurprised but nevertheless disappointed that Snake Eyes had chosen such a self-sabotaging path. The Third massaged his temples as Kit dragged Snake Eyes's body over to a drain. He kicked his severed head forward as he went.

"I take it he's been beheaded?" said the Third as Kit walked back to him. "I can't imagine him shutting up otherwise."

"Indeed, my liege," Certus said. "Thanks to Kit."

"Yes, well, I was afraid that it would come to something like this," the Third muttered. "Go ahead and imprison him, and when all this is over, take him to one of the Runners. Make sure he's Run for free. He can consider it a part of his severance package."

The sounds of battle blasted the chamber as the door creaked open yet again. The Hunters' cries now carried a shrill and unbridled frenzy as if no amount of blood could quench their thirst for anarchy. The door closed, leaving only the sounds of marching feet and jingling bells.

"What is the meaning of this?" the Third said.

Bloom stirred first then Kit. The gag in James's mouth stifled his shout of surprise as an army of Bodyguards marched into the light. With them, chained and bound so that she shuffled forward with her hands behind her back, was E.

# CHAPTER 20

# WITH ALL MY HEART

E's chains clinked against the tiled floor as she and the army of Bodyguards came to a halt. Fear flickered in Kit's gaze as her eyes fixed on him. A broken sound escaped from her as she saw Bloom ragged and motionless in his cage. She pierced Kit with a look that demanded an explanation. He shook his head slightly. She glanced at the crew and the wolves as they burst into muffled shouts.

James yelled into his gag that neither Kit nor the Third could be trusted, that they had been working together all along. Kit took a small step forward and began mouthing silent words to her. She shook her head and mouthed something back. Behind her, Certus shifted the tip of his sword ever so slightly toward Blood Crow's watch. James's shouts caught in his throat. The others fell silent as well. Certus's message couldn't have been clearer. They were all to remain quiet. Any attempts to speak to E or to interfere with the Third and Kit's plans would result in a pierced watch. James bit into his gag, tortured by frustration, as Certus lowered his sword. A Bodyguard knelt before the Third.

"Forgive us, my liege. We had orders from Snake Eyes to come to you right away if we found one of the crew members you've been searching for. We caught E. She was in the Market, trying to access the underground tunnel again. She's standing right behind me. I brought as many men as I could with me to ensure that we'd bring her to you safely."

Displeasure drew the Third's mouth into a thin line. A few of the Bodyguards shifted their weight. Their eyes wandered toward Snake Eyes's headless body.

"It would seem that Snake Eyes failed to tell all of you that I had wanted her to be taken to one of the safehouses in Lavender if she were found," said the Third.

The Bodyguards stood still, clearly fearful of making any movements that would trigger the Third's wrath.

"My apologies, Kit," the Third said. "I know this was not a part of our agreement. It goes without saying that this will not happen again, especially given Snake Eyes's termination from his role as Head Merchant."

"It's not a problem," Kit said as the Bodyguards glanced at one another.

"How many of you did she take down before you managed to outnumber her?" the Third asked.

"Quite a few, my liege," said the Bodyguard, bowing his head.

The Third slowly shook his head from side to side. He pursed his lips as if he were mustering all the patience he possessed. Just as James thought he might explode and order Certus to stomp on Snake Eyes's watch, he sighed again.

"Leave her here, then. It's more trouble than it's worth to try and take her back now. Go, and help the others with the Hunters. Thank you all for fulfilling your duties."

The Bodyguard paused as he made to stand. The bells on his wrist jingled softly.

"What is it? You may speak," the Third said.

"They're rioting in the Market too, my liege. Looting. Vandalizing. The battle is escalating downstairs as well."

"Are we losing?"

"No, sir. I assure you we are not. And we're avoiding piercing any watches, just as you commanded. My only fear is that they'll start looting the upper rooms next."

"If the looting keeps them distracted, use that to your advantage. Use it to corral them into some of the rooms, even. Distract them, tire them, deplete their creations, then subdue them. Keep them away from the moonlight at all costs. That is your main objective. We must do what is best for everyone in the City. Now go!"

"Yes, sir!" the Bodyguards shouted.

The Third muttered to Certus as the Bodyguards rushed into the shadows. E continued glaring at Kit with a look that insisted on answers. James willed that she would somehow hear the thoughts that the group was screaming at her, that she would understand that whatever Kit had told her in the group's absence was a lie and that whatever came out of his mouth next would be a lie too. But even as desperation spiraled within him, his mind whispered, "Love is blind." Sorrow enfolded his heart as he answered himself, "And so is trust."

The Bodyguards opened the door.

A bullet whizzed through the air and shattered mosaic tiles in an explosion of blue.

The chamber erupted into chaos as screaming Hunters streamed through the door and lit up the shadows with ear-splitting gunfire. Kit and E dropped down onto their stomachs. The Bodyguards scattered and leapt behind pillars as they fired back at the Hunters. Certus threw the Third onto the floor and grunted as bullets flew into his head. As his eyes rolled up in their sockets, he twisted around and collapsed on top of the Third so that his huge frame hid him from sight.

The Third cried out to Phoenix, who rolled toward him and pressed himself against Certus's body as if he were a shield. Phoenix yelled to Blood Crow, who rolled over to them as well. James wriggled up to Snow's side and curled his body around hers. Lux squirmed toward them, ignoring James as he shouted into his gag to stay away, to protect himself. He threw himself in front of James and Snow then grunted as bullets thudded into his body.

"*Citizens! Look! There are citizens!*" a Hunter shouted.

"*Impossible!*"

"*Take them down! Take them down now!*"

Bullets zinged into the wolves' cages. They spasmed as their blood spurted and sprayed.

"*Oppa!*" E shrieked as bullets flew past Bloom's head.

Kit crawled swiftly over to Certus and dug his hand into a compartment on his belt. He pulled out a pair of night vision goggles and shoved it onto his face. He rolled toward the wolves' cages, created a machine gun, and opened fire on the Hunters, drilling away one moment then pausing the next as he aimed away from the Bodyguards. The Bodyguards ran from pillar to pillar as they continued shooting and clashing with the Hunters within the shadows of the chamber. They drove back those threatening to pour in through the open door.

E rolled toward Kit as bullets continued streaking through the air. He ducked behind the machine gun and created a sword. He brought down the blade on the chains binding her feet again and again until they broke. He hesitated as she lifted her wrists chained behind her back.

"Break them!" she yelled.

He gripped her hands and wrenched them up. Her arms snapped out of their sockets so that her hands lay above her head. He broke her chains with a single stroke. She jumped onto her feet and screamed with raw, bloodthirsty rage. Her dangling arms pushed back into their sockets. Her machetes appeared in her hands. Kit continued firing into the shadows as she sprinted forth and leapt into the dark. James heard the unmistakable sound of her machetes clashing with other blades.

"*Get her! Get her now!*" a man screamed from the shadows. "*You bitch! You think you can defeat us? We'll bring you down! We'll bring you down even if it's the last thing we–*"

He fell silent, and James knew that E had taken his head. Moments later, the door groaned and boomed closed. Something slammed down and locked. The bolt of the door.

"*Oppa!*" E screamed.

Kit's bullets thundered through the air as he swung his machine gun from one side of the chamber to the other. James curled himself tighter around Snow as screams rose up with the terror and dismay that only a massacre could create. Hunters and Bodyguards alike slumped onto the floor. Kit continued shooting even after the screams had stopped. A numbing silence followed his last bullet.

E ran out from the shadows and into the wavering green light. Kit threw aside his goggles and rushed forth to meet her. He grasped her arms as they stopped next to the pool.

"What are you doing here? I told you to stay home!"

"What's happening, *Oppa*? What's going on?"

"I'll explain everything later. Just go back. Stay where it's safe!"

"I'm not going back!"

"Stop being so stubborn, and listen to me for once in your life!"

"No, you listen! You're out of creations, and I'm staying here with you. I love you. I never wanted to leave you. I never wanted to hurt you. I love you!"

Kit stared at her as if she were the best and worst thing that had ever happened to him. He placed one hand on her neck and the other on her cheek. His hands shook despite his gentle hold.

"I'm never going to let anyone take you away from me ever again," he said. "And I'll be damned before I let the Third send you out to kill the Red Calf. I'll be damned before I see you die! I nearly lost my mind the first time I thought you were dead. I can't do it again. I won't!"

Panic shot up from the pit of James's stomach as E gazed at Kit with a stricken face. If she left right now, Kit would keep the group locked up and at the Third's mercy. And E. E would go back home and love Kit and trust Kit and live a slow death because of Kit. She would go back to the way things were before, but this time, Bloom wouldn't be there to save her and neither would anyone else. Someone had to warn her. Someone had to tell her the truth! Things couldn't just happen like this!

James looked at Phoenix and Blood Crow, but to his horror, he saw the Third's hands on both of their heads. Their eyes remained unfocused as the Third continued reading them. Snow squirmed and shouted into her gag. The wolves stirred feebly in their cages. Blood gushed from the bullet wounds in Lux's chest as he tried to call out to E. It was up to James and James only. He had to free himself from his gag. He had to tell E!

He began grating his face against the floor. The cloth in his mouth slipped on the blood still streaming out of his mutilated nose and traveled up his cheek. Kit gently stroked E's cheek with his thumb.

"Please," he said. "E, please. *Please, just go home for me.* I'll take care of things here. I always take care of things. You know I do. Just go, and leave everything to me. I'll come back to you!"

The cloth pulled taut against James's skin as he ground his face deeper into the floor. He yelled into his gag as his skin split open. The blood-drenched cloth slipped up to his temple, over his flattened nose, then finally, out of his mouth. He flung aside the cloth with a snap of his head, scrambled onto his knees, and inhaled.

"E!" James screamed with all his might.

The chamber multiplied his cry so that he seemed to call to her from the past, the present, and the future. Kit's eyes glinted. E looked at James.

"He's a liar!" he screamed. "Kit traded us so that he could become the Third's Head Merchant! Kit is the one who tortured Bloom!"

E looked at Kit. He avoided her eyes as he smirked and shook his head. He let go of her and began walking toward James.

It was over. James knew that it was. Kit would silence him then trick E into leaving the chamber. The crew was defeated. Kit and the Third had won. But that also meant that this was his last chance to say something that mattered, something that would convince her to do the right thing!

"I know you love him, E!" James screamed. "I know you do! But you want someone who protects your friends and rescues the weak! Someone who won't make you feel afraid and ashamed! Someone who'll love you back, and I mean really love you back! That's the someone you want, and that isn't Kit! You know it's not! Please, just save yourself! Save yourself!"

Kit knocked James onto his back with a kick that struck the air out of his lungs. He flung Snow and Lux aside. E watched, wide-eyed and still, as Kit positioned himself over James and pulled him up by his collar. He drew back his fist in what James knew would be the same sledgehammer-like blow that had pulverized Marcus's face all those many nights ago. He braced himself as Kit's knuckles sped toward him.

E's machete whirled through the air and plunged into Kit's back.

Kit spun around and stared at her.

There was more sorrow than anger and more fear than sorrow in E's eyes. She created another machete and assumed a battle stance. She was shaking.

Kit's eyes snapped onto the shadows. Bullets flew out of the dark and missed E's head by millimeters. The present seemed to slow into a limbo of decelerated movements as a small army of Hunters staggered forth. They continued perforating E's body with bullets in what James knew was a vengeful mission to fulfill their fallen leader's promise to bring her down. She covered her head with one arm and balled her watch hand against her body, unable to run, unable to hide, unable to heal fast enough against the barrage of bullets that would soon pierce her head or her watch.

Kit pulled out E's machete from his back. The moment accelerated into its normal pace as he hurled her blade into a Hunter's head. He sprinted toward her at full speed. Her eyes widened as her mouth opened into a shout. He launched himself forward and wrapped his arms around her. Crimson explosions burst from his head as bullets shot into his skull. The Hunters continued shooting as E and Kit fell into the pool with a resounding splash. Blood darkened the swirling and bubbling water.

Gunfire suddenly opened from above. The Hunters dropped onto the floor like puppets with cut strings. James's breath caught in his throat as he saw Zilch, Honey, and Copperhead standing on the invisible bridge. The tips of their guns flashed as they continued shooting at the Hunters. A Hunter's bullet struck Copperhead between the eyes.

"Copperhead!" Honey shouted.

His gun then his body fell from the bridge. Zilch dropped his gun as bullets struck him in the shoulder and the arm. Honey continued unleashing fiery wave upon fiery wave until only a single Hunter was left standing. The woman screamed as she shot wildly at the bridge. Honey shot her in the head and ushered in the silence of victory.

# CHAPTER 21

# GOODBYE

James's mind cranked and sputtered within his daze. Had Honey really appeared in this chamber? With Copperhead and Zilch? With guns and victory?

Zilch tied a rope to the invisible bridge then followed Honey as she slid down onto the chamber floor. She ran to the Third and kicked his hands away from Blood Crow and Phoenix. Both of them blinked then shouted with surprise as Zilch freed them from their gags and grabbed their ankles. He dragged them away from the Third's reach as Honey began digging through the compartments on Certus's belt.

"The keys should be in that one!" Zilch told her.

Snow raised her head at the sound of Zilch's voice and shouted into her gag.

"Snow!"

He ran to her, tore off her gag, and helped her to sit up. He threw his arms around her.

"Z! It really is you! Are you all right? What's happening? Talk to me, Z. Say something!"

"I'm fine, Snow. I'm fine," he said as he squeezed tears out of his eyes. "I rescued Honey and Copperhead from the Bodyguards when they brought them to the Tower. We searched for you guys until we found you here."

"Okay, but what about you? What about before? What happened to you after we left the Doors? I was so worried about you. You have no idea!"

"I would've gone to you guys sooner, I swear. But Kit caught me before I could get past the moonlight. He caught me, and he ... he tortured me!"

Snow stiffened as Zilch bit back his sobs. James closed his eyes, too exhausted to feel the full reach of his rage toward Kit. Honey whispered a triumphant "yes" as she pulled out a ring of keys from Certus's belt. She hurried over to James to unlock his chains.

"And I caved," Zilch said. "I caved and told him everything. I escaped into the passageways once they brought me back to the Tower, but I told him everything, and he and Three teamed up to capture you guys. I'm sorry. I'm so, so sorry."

Snow's face twisted into an expression that swore to punish Kit for what he'd done to her beloved Guide. James rubbed his wrists as Honey freed him. His fragmented thoughts merged together within his weariness.

"Kit tortured me and Bloom too, but he saved E," he told Zilch and Honey. He could hear the disbelief, the denial, and the acceptance in his own voice. "He saved her, and they fell into the pool. They fell—wait." He searched the chamber. Where was E? She wasn't sitting on the floor. She wasn't standing anywhere. Which meant—"E's still in the pool. She's underwater!"

Honey swore. Phoenix squirmed toward the pool, still powerless in his chains. James's mind reeled with a thousand questions about drowning and brain damage as he outran Honey and Zilch and prepared to jump into the sizzling water.

E burst through the water's surface and croaked for air. Kit lay draped over her shoulder like a great, slain beast.

James stretched his hand out to her.

"Take him!" E shouted, kicking and splashing as she struggled to maintain her hold on Kit.

James's anger glowed within him. He imagined shoving Kit back into the water and letting him sink to the bottom of the pool. It was only the desperation on E's face that made him grab Kit's arm instead.

Honey pulled E out and thumped her on the back as she coughed and vomited. James dragged Kit face-down onto the floor then flung his arm down in disgust. He hated that he'd had to touch any part of this monster! He swung his foot back as his memory replayed images of Kit slamming Blood Crow's head into the floor. He froze as he saw the bullet holes in his head.

It would have been E lying face-down on the floor if it hadn't been for Kit.

Zilch lunged. James grabbed him and held him back as he threw punches and kicks at Kit's body.

"He tortured me! He tortured me!" Zilch shouted.

"He tortured me too, Z! Just calm down!" James yelled even as he wrestled with the temptation to let Zilch have his way. He glanced again at the bullet holes in Kit's head then at the rest of his body lying defenseless on the floor.

What was the right thing to do here?

"Calm down?" Zilch shouted. "Calm down? Are you crazy? Get him while he's still down!"

They froze as E shrieked. The group watched her as she clutched her hair, stumbled back, and slammed a shaking fist against her chest. Her fingers scrambled around her stomach before squeezing into another fist. She stared at Kit with wide, unblinking eyes as she shook her head slowly from side to side.

"E," Honey whispered. She carefully set down the shackles she'd unlocked from her ankles and wrists. "E, it's okay."

E pushed her aside and staggered toward Kit. She swayed back and forth as if on the brink of explosion then screamed again. She swore as she began kicking him. James gripped her arms. She fought him with wild movements. Blood and brain spurted across the floor as she kicked Kit in the head. James drew her back as she broke down in sobs. He nodded at Honey, who promptly led Zilch away from them.

"E," James said. "E, it's okay."

He tightened his hold on her as she flailed.

"Don't tell me it's okay!" she screamed. "He lied to me! He lied to me again! And I fell for it. I'm a moron. I'm a moron." She curled up as she continued sobbing then drew a deep breath that clawed down her throat. Her soul seemed to splinter as she shrieked, "I hate him!"

She sank down onto the ground and pushed James away as he tried to comfort her. The blood from Kit's head spread across the floor like red watercolor and crawled into the fabric of her clothes. She leaned her forehead against her palm and continued filling the chamber with her sobs. James reached out to her again. Honey cleared her throat pointedly, making him pause.

"Zilch, go free the pack and wrap their wounds," Honey commanded. "I'll free the rest of the crew and chain the Third up. James, search the Bodyguards for bandages. They keep spares in their belts."

James stared at E again.

"James!" Honey snapped. Her frustration turned into sadness as she mouthed, "She needs space."

He despised himself for his own helplessness as he left E and hurried toward the fallen Bodyguards. His hands seemed to move on their own as he rummaged through belts and pulled out vacuum-packed bags of bandages. As much as he hated to admit it, Honey was right. Right now, his words would only weigh down on E's broken heart and fragment the pieces that Kit had shattered once again. There was nothing he could say to erase the pain of Kit's betrayal.

"Phoenix, what are you doing? Sit back down, and rest!" Blood Crow said.

James spun around to see Phoenix swaying on his feet. He began limping toward E. James ran to him, feeling equal parts annoyed, alarmed, and sympathetic. He caught Phoenix as he stumbled. He forced him to sit.

"No," Phoenix said as James ripped open one of the bags of bandages he'd scavenged. "Not me."

"What do you mean, not you? Look at you! Never mind the battle, all your wounds from the Tournament haven't even healed yet."

James groaned with frustration as Phoenix simply plucked the bag out of his hands and began dragging himself closer to E. He began scrambling after him then stopped as Honey signaled for him to leave him alone. He opened his mouth to argue with her before the truth silenced him once again. He couldn't help E, but maybe Phoenix could. After all, she regarded him with more respect than she did anyone else in the crew. The soft spot growing in her heart for him would definitely help too.

Phoenix finished pulling himself up to E's side and unraveled the bandages he'd taken from James. He was careful to touch as little of the white surface as possible with his grimy hands. He began wrapping a bullet hole struggling to close on her leg. She smacked his hand away and continued sobbing. He tried again. She smacked him away again then wrested the bandages away from him.

"E! Give them back," he demanded.

He spasmed suddenly and doubled up. E stared at him through her tears as he pressed his arms deeper into his stomach. A small curtain of blood fell from his mouth before he began to convulse. James cursed as he rushed over to him and lowered him onto his back. E looked at the bandages she'd taken then at Phoenix again as he grunted and snapped his head to one side. She knuckled away her tears and joined James as he tied Phoenix's wounds.

Honey knelt down next to Copperhead and examined his still body. She bowed her head and placed her hand on his shoulder in silent thanks. As she stood up, she winced and cradled the wounds she'd sustained in battle. James knew that her adrenaline was, at last, waning and that the pain of her wounds was beginning to overtake her. He watched as she gritted her teeth and stumbled toward Lux.

Despite the odds, the crew had, somehow, overcome all their enemies once again. But the night was still far from over. They had yet to battle the Red Calf. But how could they possibly battle the Calf in the state that they were in? Most of them could barely walk, never mind fight. And how were they supposed to escape the Tower to meet the Calf in battle when the Hunters' riots were still raging throughout both the Tower and the Market? Though James continued searching for answers as he and E finished wrapping Phoenix's wounds, he failed to find even a semblance of a solution.

E pressed her hand against her forehead again. She looked as if she was trying to keep her mind in one piece as a thousand memories and thoughts bombarded her. James hesitated, hating himself for what he was about to say. But he had to say it. E was their leader and their best fighter, and the Red Calf was getting closer to the City with every moment that passed. Despite the betrayal, despite the heartbreak, despite the unfairness of it all, she couldn't afford to mourn in this moment. They had to keep moving.

"E, we can't stop here." He paused as he continued wrestling with the desire to let her rest. He pushed out the words he knew would reignite the fire within her. "We have to fight. We have to win. We have to survive, remember?"

She tensed as if he had gripped her and demanded that she pull herself together. He looked away and waited as she wiped her eyes and set both hands down on the floor. After several moments, she exhaled and gave her head a sharp shake. Though he wasn't surprised to see determination flicker to life within her black eyes, he couldn't help but admire her.

"Help me get Bloom out of his cage," she commanded.

He grabbed the remaining bandages and hurried toward Bloom. He swallowed his nausea as he saw his severed ears and tail scattered across the floor. They carried him out of his cage and laid him down on the ground. More tears gathered in her eyes as she inspected the deep gashes that Kit had inflicted all along his body. She exhaled forcefully then tended to him with James.

Bloom's eyes slowly opened and traveled back and forth through empty space before finding her. The corner of his mouth quivered into a small smile. E's hands slowed then stilled as his stub of a tail twitched. She turned her face away from him.

"I'm sorry," she whispered.

Bloom winced as he lifted his head. He nudged her arm until she looked at him again. Tears streamed down her cheeks as his smile widened. Cartilage and fur sprouted from the base of his severed ears. His flesh pushed out bullets as his wounds stitched together at twice the speed. Father limped out of his cage, wrapped in the bandages Zilch had used to bind his wounds. He gazed at Bloom, sniffed a few times in his direction, then nodded to himself. He walked slowly over to the edge of the pool and slumped down onto the floor.

"*We must find a way back to the Blue Border. We must keep watch for the Beast,*" he told the group.

"*May I remind you all,*" the Third said suddenly, "*that the bounty I placed on you is still active?*"

The pack burst into low growls. James prepared himself for a verbal battle full of blackmailing and threats. The Third could only have the worst intentions for breaking the eerie silence he'd maintained until now. E stepped toward the Third but stopped as Phoenix stumbled toward him instead.

"*Any Merchant or Bodyguard who sees you will capture you,*" the Third said. "*The Hunters are still rioting in both the Abode and the Market. You must accept the fact that leaving this chamber is fruitless. You must remain here.*"

"*I know of a safe path out of the Abode,*" Terrain snarled. "*It will lead us directly into the Desert, so do not fret over us, Three. I assure you we can take care of ourselves.*"

"*Then you may want to consider the fact that I have stationed dozens of my men all along the Blue Border,*" the Third replied as everyone except Forest gave Terrain questioning looks. "*They will see you if you venture out into the Desert. They will bring you back.*"

"We are going out to battle the Calf," Phoenix said as he came to a stop in front of him. "We are going, and you can't stop us."

"You will do no such thing. You will stay here in the Tower, where you are safe."

"We have been through this before!" Phoenix exploded. "I won't let you take back the golden eye! I won't let your greed destroy anything else!"

"It does not matter what you will or won't allow! You are not leaving the Tower. End of discussion!"

"Enough," said Snow before Phoenix could shout back.

James turned to find her standing alone with her head held high. A firm resolve was emanating from her, cold and beautiful like her namesake. When she spoke, her tone was crisp and even.

"Three," said Snow. "You will call off the order to capture us, and you will cancel the bounty. You will also have all of your men withdraw from the moonlight immediately."

The Third sighed and shook his head, clearly tired of repeating his refusal to let the crew go.

"I don't care how many men you've posted," Snow said. "The Desert is massive. I doubt they'd even be able to see us once we're out there, never mind catch us. You might as well have them retreat so that more of them can help quell the riots."

"I would rather order more of my men to spread out in the Desert so that you cannot escape their notice," the Third said, his voice stiff with forced patience.

"And how would you do that? You need Certus's walkie talkie to speak to your men, don't you? Your hands are literally tied right now, so talking to your men is out of the question. And, of course, if you try to create another walkie talkie, we'll simply cut off your hands. It's not that difficult of a matter."

"Even so! My men will be sure to see you once you enter into battle with the Red Calf. After all, its darkness will be difficult to miss. Once they see it, they will be sure to capture you."

"Yes, its darkness is difficult to miss. We know that from experience. We told you before, didn't we, about how we barely escaped with our lives the last time the Calf attacked us? Actually, that makes me wonder if we'll even last long enough in battle for your men to capture us." She paused as if to let her words sink in. "Phoenix, we're going to go fight the Red Calf no matter what, right?"

"Right," he said, still glaring down at the Third.

"Even though we might die in the fight?"

"Of course."

"You moron," said the Third. "Does your life mean so little to you? What about your loved ones? Don't you care about what they'd do if you died?"

"My mother is a strong woman. She'd want me to die doing what's right."

"Neither she nor your father would want you to die at all!"

"Which is why," interjected Snow, "I propose a trade. Three, you will call off your search on us and make all of your men retreat from the border. In return, Phoenix will remain here with you in the Tower until the Calf is defeated."

Everyone tensed. The Third remained silent.

Phoenix sputtered incoherent words. "What?" he pushed out. "What–no! Snow, you can't just–"

"Done," said the Third. "I agree to your terms."

Phoenix gaped at his father. James lowered his gaze as the others stirred. So it was Phoenix. Phoenix was the one price that the Third was not willing to pay. Not for his sight. Not for his freedom. Not for all the Flowering.

The wolves exchanged confused looks, clearly doubtful that the Third would agree so easily to such terms. E glanced at Zilch then faced the wolves. James knew she would speak in Korean to protect the privacy of Phoenix and his father before she'd uttered even a single word.

"*He's the Third's only son,*" she told the pack.

Bloom and his brothers jumped then stared at her with wide eyes. Father shot out a deep sigh from his nose before nodding.

"I do have one requirement, though," the Third said, "and that is for one of you to keep in communication with me via walkie talkie. I will need to send my men out if you do not succeed in killing the Calf."

"Done," E said before Snow could reply. "You have my word that we will give you updates."

"Then please bring Certus's walkie talkie over to me, and press the top button so that I may speak to my men."

"Wait, wait, wait. No, wait. You can't do this!" Phoenix said.

E pierced him with a black glare. She marched over to him.

"E, no. This isn't fair!"

She kicked his legs out from under him. He landed on his back, winded and stunned, then curled up on his side and hugged his stomach. E plucked Certus's walkie talkie from his belt and knelt before the Third. Static sounded as she pressed the button.

"*This is the Third. I repeat, this is the Third speaking.*"

Several walkie talkies strapped to the belts of the fallen Bodyguards repeated his words from within the shadows.

"*I command all of you who are stationed at the Blue Border to return to either the Market or the Abode, effective immediately. Also, I am voiding both the search and the bounty on E and her crew. Do not approach her, her crew, or the wolves. Anyone who approaches them will face consequences. Spread the word, and continue to keep all humans away from the Blue Border at all costs. Have there been any signs of the Red Calf?*"

More static then, "*No, sir. None of us have seen anything all night.*"

"*Good. Then that is all.*"

Silence pervaded the chamber once more.

E stood up and closed her eyes as she took a deep breath in and a deep breath out. She balled her fists. Bullets popped out of her flesh and clinked onto the floor. All of her wounds shrank and sealed so that despite the blood and grime still covering her, she stood battle-ready. She opened her eyes again. The green glow of the pool danced within her black gaze so that the fire of her determination glinted like light on a moving dagger. All traces of heartbreak had crawled back into herself so that the trails her tears had left on her cheeks were the only remnants of her sorrow. She lifted her chin, ready to lead, ready to fight. She scanned the crew's many wounds.

"It's fine," said James as her gaze lingered on his nose. "I can fight. This is my only wound right now."

"We're good too," Honey said. She panted as she forced herself back onto her feet.

Lux clutched at his bandaged chest and nodded.

"Yeah. Just say the word. We're ready," Blood Crow said as she attempted to stand.

"You're not going anywhere," James snapped as she toppled back onto the floor.

"My leg is healed, James," she said stubbornly.

"You can't even stand up! E, make her stay. Talk some sense into her."

E didn't respond. Instead, to James's surprise, she hesitated before turning and staring at Kit. He didn't understand the apology that flitted across her eyes.

Her determination burned away her apology as she faced them again.

"I'm going teach you how to heal your wounds like I do. I'm going to teach you how to heal instantly," she told the crew. "But I want you to keep it to yourselves. I don't want the wrong humans finding out about this technique. Do you all understand me?"

Disbelief filled James first, then pride. She'd made up her mind. Despite the guilt he knew she felt and even the fear, she'd made up her mind to tell the others the secret which she'd kept for so long out of loyalty to Kit.

"Healing is more than just focusing," E said. "It's also about your emotions. You need to dig into your pain, find the anger within it, and fuel that anger. The more you do, the faster you'll heal. Or, at least," she said with the slightest hint of a sad smile, "it'll work better than just thinking about it and hoping for the best."

"So I just have to get pissed off, and I'll heal like you?" Lux said.

"No. You really have to feel it," said James.

E looked at him.

"You really have to feel the pain and the anger," he said as he walked over to Lux and Honey. "It has to be the only thing you know. And when you do it right, you get this crazy amount of focus and ... and power. It's a lot harder than it sounds. I've only been able to do it a few times."

He signaled to E to let her know that he would take over training Honey and Lux. She gave him a firm nod of thanks before walking over to Blood Crow and Phoenix. Doubt and confusion weighed down Lux's expression as James continued coaching them. As his eyes caught on Kit, though, anger twisted his face.

"That damn bastard," Lux hissed. "I trusted him!"

"Well, that is what you tend to do," Honey said, rolling her eyes.

"Trust isn't always a bad thing," James reminded her.

"No, but Honey's right," said Lux. He sighed and shook his head. Palpable disappointment made his shoulders droop as he told Honey, "I guess I can see why you're so paranoid of strangers now. I do trust everyone we meet. I ... I really am like a stupid puppy! I never even stopped to think things through."

James glared at Honey as she opened her mouth to release what he knew would be a torrent of scolding. She rolled her eyes again and clamped her mouth shut.

"I was rooting for Kit and E to get back together," Lux continued. "I thought he was so cool. Him and the Market. And I was pissed off at E when she wouldn't go back to rescue him. I trusted him over her, even after everything she's done for me."

Lux, then James and Honey, gazed at E, who was still busy teaching the others. The memory of her first night in the Market floated into view within James's mind. Her eyes had sparkled with amazement as she had walked through the streets at Kit's side.

"You're not the only one to fall for his charms," he told Lux. "He's good at catching people when they're vulnerable, and I'm sure he's had plenty of practice over the years. You've been going through a lot in Reality for a while now. It's easy to turn to a guy like him when life's hard."

He felt a stab of guilt as he realized that he'd never bothered to ask Lux more about the hardships he faced daily in Reality. Maybe if he'd been a better friend to him, he wouldn't have felt so desperate to begin with. James promised himself that he would be more attentive if they made it out of their battle with the Calf alive. Honey too. After all, she probably had to deal with her dysfunctional family still, and she clearly thought about her dead friend regularly. Did Blood Crow have any invisible wounds that ached within her too?

"Thanks," Lux said, though he remained downcast. "But that doesn't change the fact that I messed up. Like, royally." He heaved another sigh and scrubbed his face with both hands. "I should've listened to you, Honey. And I never should've been so quick to judge E the way that I did. I shouldn't have just written you guys off like that. But I really just wanted to escape from everything so damn badly."

Honey's annoyance began crumbling away as Lux pressed his hand over his eyes. She patted him on the back and murmured a few words of comfort. His sorrow deepened as he raised his head and gazed at E again. In that moment, James saw a silent promise shining in Lux's eyes. A promise to endure no matter how hard his circumstances. A promise that he would not allow desperation or naivety to lead him to trust an enemy again.

His gaze strayed from E to Kit. Anger reignited within his eyes before he spat "bastard" again. As he squeezed his eyes shut and grunted and strained, flesh crept over his wounds at a slightly accelerated rate. His healing, though, still remained far from reaching the near instantaneous rate that came so naturally to E and Kit. James continued encouraging him and instructing him.

"It's not working," Honey said after several moments. "You just look like you're constipated."

"Well, it's hard, okay?" Lux said, tossing up his hands. "I'm pretty pissed right now, but I'm new at this kind of healing!"

"Please. I've seen you get irritated more times than I can count in the past few nights. I know you can do better than that."

"Irritated is different from angry," said E as she walked over to them. "At least, it is from the kind of angry that I'm talking about."

She continued coaching all of the crew members with patient words and firm corrections. Bloom joined his brothers as they laid down next to Father and healed more of their wounds. Father opened one eye to look at him before resuming his focus. Blood Crow scowled and wrung her fists.

"Why isn't it working?" she said.

"I guess we're just not pissed enough," Lux said as he continued straining.

"Does it have to be anger only?" Honey asked, her body falling limp as she panted for air.

E glanced at Kit again. "I'm actually not sure. Anger is supposed to work the best, and it's always worked for me. I've never tried other emotions before, actually."

James studied his memories carefully. "I think other emotions might work. I noticed before on Halloween that Lux heals faster when he's happy compared to when he's sad. But anger does work the best as far as I can tell. I think wanting to protect others is good too, though. Well, actually, it was that protectiveness that triggered my anger before. Oh, and ... uh ... determination. So I think the need to protect works well and so does determination. The anger and aggression get mixed in organically. At least, it does for me. And, well, even if it isn't the best technique, I think it might be better than the seeing-red kind of anger too. Or just pure hate. I think there are long-term side effects to using that kind of rage all the time, even if it does work the best in the moment."

He couldn't help but glance at E. Surprise twitched on her face before she looked away. He didn't want to make her feel bad, but he didn't want hatred and rage to poison the others like they had poisoned her. Of course, he understood that anger was not only a powerful tool but also, perhaps, the most powerful weapon available to those who needed to survive dangers and hardships. But there had to be limits. Anger couldn't spiral into rage all the time. There was good to be found in the type of aggression that worked hand in hand with determination. And there was no way that some form of anger, or at the very least, aggression, couldn't accompany a fierce desire to protect loved ones and the innocent from foes. Anger in and of itself wasn't necessarily a bad thing but a vital ingredient in the formula for survival.

But diving into unbridled rage over and over again only eroded the self-control that preserved the integrity of the human soul. After all, how many times had he fought to bring E back to herself after she'd fallen into her own rage? How many times had she lost herself within her hatred and hurt the very ones she'd sworn to protect? How many years would need to pass before her soul would heal enough to let her control her anger fully? Many, he was sure. And he couldn't allow the others to meet the same fate.

"Well, maybe this will help all of you to feel a little more determined," Blood Crow grumbled. "We have to go out into the Desert again even though the Calf could come into No Man's Land at any moment. On top of that, I only have one creation left, and I'm willing to bet most of you are out completely."

"How many do all of you have left?" E said.

James's heart fell as the crew responded. He had three as did E. Snow had six, and Blood Crow had one. The rest had run out, just as Blood Crow had predicted. Acknowledging the crew's lack of creations, though, did seem to ignite a needed sense of determination, for everyone's wounds began to heal much faster than before. Still, many moments passed before shallow wounds sealed completely and even more before the deepest injuries stopped bleeding.

"Take a utility belt from a Bodyguard," E commanded as the crew tried to catch their breaths. "Get weapons, but choose ones you're familiar with so that you don't get confused in battle. Pack lightly, and don't get greedy. It'll only slow you down. Once we're all ready, we'll go out into the Desert using the path Terrain mentioned before. Blood Crow, create a car as soon as we get there, and drive us back to the moonlight as fast as you can."

"Shouldn't I create the car?" James said. "I have more creations."

"*You and the Twelfth must conserve your creations,*" Father growled. "*As I said before, the Last has gifted each of you with unique powers that are sure to prove pivotal during the battle. You must be prepared to do anything during the fight.*"

"And E is our best fighter, so I'll create the car. Don't worry about it," Blood Crow said.

"Good. Zilch, you'll stay here with Phoenix," said E.

"What? I can't stay here. Even Snow's going, and she's blind!"

"Snow has no choice. She's the only one who can get the golden eye out of the Calf."

"But–"

"You suck in battle! Do you really want a repeat of what happened at the Doors? I can't save you every time you fail to save yourself!"

Zilch crossed his arms and scowled.

"You'll come with us to see the passageway out into the Desert then come back here," E said. "When the battle is done, you can use the path to come get Snow. Understood?"

"Understood," he muttered. He touched Snow's arm and said, "I'll get you your weapons. You just stay here and relax."

He and the crew began rummaging around the fallen. Lux examined a large dagger rimmed with jagged serrations before adding the blade to his scavenged belt. James watched out of the corner of his eye as Phoenix stopped E in her search. He, Honey, and Blood Crow pretended to keep scavenging as they crept closer to the two.

"Are you really going to make me stay behind?" Phoenix said.

"A deal's a deal," E growled.

"But I should be out there with all of you! I should be fighting alongside you. I shouldn't be in here like some kind of ... of...."

Something softened in E's eyes. "You're not a coward, Phoenix."

He shook his head. "You don't understand. I'd given up on humans before I met Crew Blue. I thought I was fine on my own as a Roamer. But then we met, and I realized that I wanted to take a chance on humans again. I became hopeful again. I became myself again! And right now, I want to fight with you. Please. I can't stay here like this while you guys put your lives on the line. And you know I don't want to stay here with him any more than I have to!" he said, throwing a look of disgust at the Third.

"Phoenix," E said.

She hesitated then covered her mouth with both hands and whispered into his ear. He listened before jerking his head away from her.

"It's disgusting that he won't throw it away on his own initiative to begin with!" he spat.

She sighed. Phoenix looked away from the disapproval on her face. She whispered to him again. He stared at her as she drew back.

"You have to stay here," she said. "You know you do. I know you don't like it, but it's the only way. Besides, you won the Tournament for us, and you've been fighting without a break ever since. There's no shame in staying behind. You've done your part, and now, you need to stay." She paused then said gently, "That's an order."

Despair hung so thickly over Phoenix's face that James might have thought that E had ordered him to sacrifice his life for the crew and not to stay out of harm's way. Phoenix covered his eyes with one hand as he sighed. E's eyes remained soft as he swallowed and nodded.

"At least let me help you find the right weapons. Let me at least do that," he said.

"Actually," said the Third, interrupting yet again, "allow me to create some quality weapons for you, E, as well as for James and the Twelfth."

Suspicion lifted its snout within James and sniffed feverishly for danger. His fingers tightened around the dagger he had picked up as E and Phoenix approached the Third together.

"And why would you bother doing that?" she said.

"Even if I cannot persuade you to stay in the Tower, I would still like for you to have a fighting chance against the Calf. Also," he added, "I hate preparing briefings."

E blinked. Phoenix narrowed his eyes.

"If you create anything even slightly suspicious for any one of them, I'll consider our pact nullified, and I will go out into the Desert!" he said.

"Understood and agreed," the Third replied.

E signaled to James. He neared with his dagger at the ready. Two knives appeared in the Third's chained hands.

"From what I've read, James, you're quite good with knives. Please, take these. I assure you that their quality is superior to what you usually use."

James picked up the blades. Both were not only sharper than his usual knives but also lighter and, somehow, more comfortable within his grip. They were exactly what he would have wanted and, no doubt, what he would need for the upcoming battle. He brushed aside the speck of admiration that soiled his resentment for the Third.

"Nothing suspicious?" Phoenix asked.

"No," said James. "They're good. I'll keep searching for other weapons."

E nodded and, moments later, walked away with two machetes of such dark blue that, like an oil slick, they melted into black in the absence of light. Phoenix snatched up the two silver daggers that appeared in the Third's hands next and delivered them to Snow. Both fit in her small hands perfectly and promised to fly swiftly through the air with minimal effort. One by one, the crew members began stepping back into the light, their belts ready with choice weapons.

"Who would've thought that the Third would give up on the golden eye?" Zilch whispered to Snow as she climbed onto James's back. "How did you get him to agree to this?"

"I'll explain everything later, Z," she replied.

The pack joined the crew as E walked out of the shadows last. Bloom, though still missing the tip of his tail and half an ear, looked as well as James could have hoped for. Like the rest of the wolves, his wounds had stopped bleeding, and he trotted forth without a limp. E clipped Certus's walkie talkie to her belt then surveyed the group. James and the others nodded. Phoenix stared at the ground, his expression hard and distant. The Third remained silent.

"*Lead the way, then,*" E told Terrain.

The group followed him as he slunk off toward the opposite end of the chamber and disappeared into the shadows. E slowed to a stop. James halted alongside Bloom at the outskirts of the shadows.

"E?" he said.

Snow squirmed slightly on his back. He knew it was concern that made her tighten his grip on him.

E turned around and stared at Kit. Resentment and sorrow both swam within her eyes as they lingered on the bullet holes in his head. There were memories in her gaze too. There were promises, both broken and unfulfilled. There was all the history that lay between them, connecting them, whispering of a future that could be, a past that could not be erased. There were echoes of sacrifices he'd made for her and even the sacrifice he'd made in this very chamber. She took a step toward him.

Kit's fingers twitched then stretched toward her.

Her lips parted in surprise. Snow inhaled sharply as James prepared to throw his knife. Phoenix jumped to his feet. Bloom crouched down, ready to spring forth. Kit's head was still far from healed. Some of his brains were even scattered across the floor. He shouldn't have been able to move at all.

They stared at Kit for several moments, waiting.

But he remained motionless.

E continued gazing at him as if she wanted to say something. She turned around. She swallowed and placed a hand over her heart.

She breathed in and walked away.

# CHAPTER 22

# THE RED CALF

Terrain quickened his pace as he trotted up a sloping stone corridor. James tightened his hold on Snow's legs as the group followed Terrain. They had been traveling up an ascending passageway ever since leaving the chamber. James was sure that they would soon reach the Tower's peak.

"I still can't believe I didn't know about this path," Zilch muttered to Snow. "I've failed you. Again."

"Don't be ridiculous," she said. "The other Guides don't even know about any of the passageways, never mind this one. You should be proud that you discovered so many on your own."

"*The Twelfth is right,*" said Terrain. "*You are young, and the Abode holds many secrets. It would be impossible to uncover all of them so quickly. In fact, you may not discover all of them even within your lifetime.*"

"*Speaking of secrets, Terrain,*" said Sleet. "*When did you discover this path?*"

"*I bet it was when he was friends with the Third during the Last's era!*" piped up Forest.

"*Acquaintance!*" Terrain snapped. "*He was an acquaintance!*"

*"Yes, and during your acquaintance's lifetime, you would, on occasion, sneak off to the Abode,"* Forest said with a smile. *"You only stopped after he died. I remember!"*

A sigh shot out of Father's nose. *"So, that is where you were scampering off to."*

*"You knew that he was sneaking out?"* Forest asked, wide-eyed.

Father's glare followed Terrain as he flattened his ears and hastened his steps.

*"I am your father. That means I know everything."*

Terrain paused as the path evened out into a long corridor. Beams of moonlight shone through small holes that perforated the walls and ceiling, crisscrossing the dark space stretching on before the group. They followed Terrain through moonlight and shadows.

*"And speaking of knowing things,"* Father said to the crew, *"once we enter into battle, you must never look away from the Beast's dark eye. That eye is its main weapon, and whatever it fixes upon will be the target of its next attack."*

*"Will its attacks look like what we saw in the Keep or in the tunnels?"* E asked.

*"No. Those were aberrations, for the Beast could not control its darkness while trapped inside of Mother's heart. Now that it is free, its attacks will likely be in the form of black orbs as they were in eras past. These orbs are created from its darkness, and they will attempt to swallow the target which its dark eye fixes upon."*

*"Then our first objective should be to gouge out the Beast's dark eye, correct? So that it can't attack us with its black orbs?"* E said.

*"Precisely,"* said Father. *"Once that is done, the Twelfth can take out the golden eye without risking an attack."*

*"And taking out the golden eye will sever the Beast's connection to the Flowering once and for all."*

"*Yes,*" said Father. "*And once its connection is severed, we will be free to pierce the Beast's mark and kill it.*"

Snow adjusted her hold on James.

The golden eye. If Snow did manage to take the eye, what would the group do with it after the battle? Hide it somewhere, probably, but where could they possibly hide it so that it would stay out of the Shamans' clutches forever? Even if centuries passed, someone or something would find it eventually. And Snow. She wouldn't try to keep the Shamans' powers for herself, would she? No. She'd learned her lesson after what she had done to E back in the Keep. She knew now that power and pride were her weaknesses.

But then why did he still feel so uneasy?

"James," said E, "it goes without saying that you'll need to keep Snow safe until she can get to the golden eye. And Snow, you be ready to take that eye as soon as the chance comes."

"Don't worry. I'm ready," said Snow. She wriggled up higher on his back. "I'm ready to do whatever it takes. The dimensions are depending on it. I'm ready to die if I have to."

"I just said that you need to stay safe. We can't get the golden eye out if you're dead," E growled. She hesitated then said, "I'm trusting you to keep yourself alive, Snow. I don't want you dead."

James felt joy spring up within Snow as she lifted her head slightly.

"*Indeed. The only death we will be seeing is that of the Beast,*" said Father. "*To pierce its mark, we will need to hold the Beast down. As I explained before, it can instantaneously move its mark to a different location on its body. We must hold the Beast down so that we can find its mark and pierce it regardless of where it decides to hide it. This will be difficult to accomplish, to say the least, but with a group this size, I know that we will find a way to overpower the Beast.*"

"*So to recap,*" said E, "*we take the Beast's dark eye first so that it can't attack us. Then we take its golden eye to sever its connection to the Flowering. Then we hold the Beast down, find its mark, and pierce it.*"

"*Correct,*" said Father. He stared into the darkness ahead. "*And be prepared for anything. The Beast is cunning. One mistake, and you will pay dearly.*"

Terrain stopped in front of a dead end. "*We are here. Once we step through this exit, we will emerge in the Desert.*"

"Then this is where I'll leave you, Snow," said Zilch. He grasped her outstretched hand and kissed her knuckles. "Please be safe, my lady," he whispered. He exhaled to compose himself then glared at James. "Make sure she comes back alive, or I'll kill you myself!"

"Z," Snow said, her tone split between bemusement and disapproval.

"I'll keep you updated," E said, patting Certus's walkie talkie on her belt.

Zilch nodded. He ran back through the moonbeams crisscrossing the corridor. E stepped to the forefront of the group and drew one of her blue machetes, which glinted like moonlight turned into metal.

"James," she said, "once we're in battle, use the weapons from your belt first, and don't use any creations until you see an opportune moment. Once Blood Crow creates a car, it'll be only you, me, and Snow who have any creations left. We can't afford to run out early. And that goes for the rest of you too. The weapons on your belts are all that you have now, so use them wisely."

She paused then said, "Are you all ready?"

For a split moment, James saw the Red Calf in his mind and remembered that even the Last, with all twelve of the Shamans' powers, had failed to kill the Beast. If the group failed too, everything in both the

Flowering and Reality would be destroyed. Everything depended on the group. Everything.

The memory of Heri wishing him luck shoved aside the image of the Calf so suddenly that it was as if she'd somehow heard him worrying all the way from Reality and barged into his head to smack him back to his senses. She and the rest of his family were asleep right now, oblivious to the death and destruction the Beast could soon unleash upon them.

Determination incinerated James's fears. He looked around at the others, his crew, the pack, his family in the Flowering. He would rather die than allow the Calf to kill his loved ones. The group would succeed. There were no alternatives!

"I'm ready, E," he said. "I'm ready to kill the Red Calf!"

Snow's arms tightened around his neck. "That's right. We'll stop the Calf and put an end to its evil."

Resolve hardened the others' expressions.

"Well said, you two," said Blood Crow. "We will hunt down the Calf and banish it from the Flowering. We will not allow it to harm any more humans or citizens!"

"Yeah, we'll kill the damn Beast," Honey said.

"Yeah, we'll slaughter that cow!" said Lux.

Father snarled as the pack crouched down for the hunt. Though E did not smile, the pride that flared in her black eyes purged all remnants of fear lingering within James and, he knew, the others.

"Then let's not waste another moment," she said.

Blood Crow dashed toward the dead end and disappeared. The rest of the group ran through the exit, one after another. James gathered air into his lungs and courage into his heart before running too.

White dust puffed up from beneath his feet as he sprinted out into the Desert. He searched for the City and found it far in the distance.

They had more than half the Desert to cross before they reached the safety of the moonlight.

"Hurry!" E shouted as the last of the wolves leapt into the off-road SUV that Blood Crow had created.

Snow wrapped her arms and legs tighter around James as he gripped the roll cage and jumped into the car. As they zoomed toward the moonlight, he scanned the giant plateaus on his far left then the flat Desert land stretching on into the distance to his right. There were no signs of the Beast. No trace of its red, matted fur or its long, thin legs. The group would be fine. They would make it to the moonlight just like they had before.

They would be fine.

They would be fine.

The car shot past the tree of eyes. Something red emerged from the tree's trunk. Father snapped his head around.

"*Jump out!*" he yelled.

Snow clung to James as he launched himself out of the car. A large, black orb shot forth like a cannonball then froze midair as it swallowed half of the SUV. James landed feet first and forced his stumbling into sprinting as the remaining half of the car slumped onto the ground and skidded to a dust-billowing stop. Instinct spurred him to run away from the rest of the crew as they clambered onto the backs of the wolves. He looked over his shoulder as he continued running.

The Red Calf.

It stood crouched down on its spindly legs next to the tree of eyes, where it had lain in wait to ambush them. The golden eye shone upon its forehead beneath the Desert's dim light. Its dark eye fixed on him and bulged.

"James!" Father shouted.

A black orb shot toward James. Snow yelped as he sprang aside. The orb consumed the space from which he'd leapt then froze midair, still as death. He dared not look away from the eye even as his feet slammed back down onto the ground. He curved his trajectory and ran in an arc away from the moonlight. He had no choice. He couldn't head toward the City right now. He couldn't keep his back turned to the Calf's dark eye!

The eye followed him, throbbing again and again like a sick, black heart. Orbs shot forth and halted abruptly as they devoured the ground and air he left behind. His soul shuddered within him as he saw that each orb was the perfect size, a round coffin tailor-made just for him and Snow. The wolves skidded and scrambled around the orbs as they tried to reach him. Lux had seated himself on Sleet, Honey on Terrain, Blood Crow on Forest, and E on Bloom.

"*It wants* James *and the Twelfth!*" Father shouted. "*It wants their powers!*"

"*Forest, Blood Crow, get* James *and Snow to the moonlight!*" E shouted. "*The rest of you, follow me and distract it!*"

"No!" James cried as the group charged toward the Beast.

The dark eye palpitated as it swiveled about. The group scattered as orbs shot toward them at rapid fire. Each orb halted abruptly and remained still as it missed its target and swallowed land or air instead.

The Beast's neck suddenly cocked. It began to twitch and shudder even as its attack on the group continued. It stomped one hoof into the ground then another as its limbs cracked and lengthened. It grew until it was as large as the SUV it had destroyed.

Green fur and red hair appeared in James's periphery as Forest dashed toward him with Blood Crow seated on his back. She stretched out her hand. James reached for her. The eye fixed on her head and bulged.

"Look out!" he yelled.

An orb shot toward her. James leapt, Blood Crow jumped off of Forest's back, and Forest darted to the side. James continued sprinting as the orb consumed the space which Blood Crow's head had occupied just a moment before. She crashed onto the floor then flipped over onto her feet and raked her fingers through the ground as she skidded to a halt. She jumped onto Forest's back as he sped toward James again. Orbs shot forth and forced them to veer and zigzag away from each other. James fought through the strain clawing into his muscles and pushed his body to run past its limits. He needed to escape the Beast's line of sight. He needed to give Forest and Blood Crow an opening to reach him!

*"On the ground!"* Father shouted.

Orbs large and small exploded out of the Beast's eye in blurred succession. James flung himself onto the ground and pressed Snow flat beside him. White dust swirled as a chaos of black flew overhead and sprayed the distance.

What was happening? What was going on? Was the Beast trying to annihilate them all in one go? No. None of the orbs were aimed at the group, even though the Beast had been attacking them with such precision just moments ago. It was choosing to aim at something else now. But why and what?

Dust particles glittered down onto the floor as the barrage ceased.

Snow clung to James as he jumped back onto his feet. He frantically searched for the Beast through the haze and found it still standing near the tree of eyes. Its head hung low as it panted. Its dark eye swiveled and fixed on him. He sprang aside as the eye bulged.

But no orbs ensued.

Confusion flashed through his mind before hope lit up within him. Whatever that attack had been, it must have tired the Beast. Which meant that this was the group's chance to escape to the Blue Border all together! James looked away from the dark eye, ready to jump onto Forest and ride to the moonlight.

He froze.

Orbs of every size had created a massive, black wall that stretched out for miles to the left and to the right, blocking the group from returning to the City. They were trapped in the Desert. The Beast had cut them off from the moonlight, their only defense.

The Beast's bent legs pumped up and down as it turned away from the wall and faced the horizon. It swiftly scuttled across the white, jagged ground as it fled from the group.

"*After it!*" E shouted. "*Get it while it's still tired!*"

Forest sprang out from behind a cluster of orbs and dashed toward James as the others pursued the Beast. Snow's arms remained wrapped around his neck as he grabbed Blood Crow's hand and leapt onto Forest, who panted under all their weight. He veered toward the group to bring up the rear.

The Beast began to twitch and shudder again as it continued to flee. Its neck cocked before its limbs cracked and thinned. It shrank back to its original size and slowed its pace. James's heart pushed each beat into his throat as the group gained upon it. It may have cut them off from the moonlight, but he'd been right about one thing. Creating that wall had worn it out. It never would have shrunk back to a smaller size unless it was significantly tired, and judging from how much it was panting, the chase was costing it a good amount of energy too.

But it would eventually regain the strength it had used. The question was, how long did the group have before it did?

Blood Crow gasped. She jabbed her finger toward the Beast. "*I see its mark! It's on its back! The middle!*" she shouted.

James jerked forward as he poured his focus onto its back.

"*Where?*" Honey and Lux yelled in unison.

"*There!*" Blood Crow shouted, shaking her finger in frustration. "*It's bulging out right there!*"

The group lifted and stooped their heads as they squinted.

"*I see it!*" E shouted. "*Sixth vertebra on its spine!*"

Gasps and shouts rang out as, one by one, the others spotted the mark as well. James's eyes continued combing up and down the Beast's spine with increasing rapidity before he mentally slapped himself. He forced his eyes to rest on the Calf's sixth vertebra.

There. The mark. The Beast's mark. It was barely perceptible, just a sliver of shade brighter than its blood-drenched fur, hidden in plain sight. He never would have recognized it if Blood Crow hadn't pointed it out first. He doubted the others would have either.

And then the mark was gone. He hadn't even blinked, but it was gone. Gone, he was sure, to another part of its body, hidden away from the group. But they had all seen it now, which meant that when the opportunity came, they would need less than a split moment to recognize it and deal the fatal blow.

The Beast whirled around and faced them.

"*Scatter!*" E shouted.

James's grip on Forest slipped one millimeter at a time as Forest swerved and dodged an onslaught of orbs. One deadly, black rush after another pursued each wolf, driving them further and further away from each other. The pack halted with sprays of dust as the attacks ceased. Forest's sides vibrated against James's legs as he panted rapidly.

The dark eye roved over the group as the Beast heaved labored breaths. It breathed in deep and hissed out a long sigh. Its legs remained bent as it lowered its body and rested its stomach on the ground.

The Beast couldn't gather more energy while running away. It had to stop and rest!

"*Now!*" E yelled. "Honey, Lux!"

"Lux, let's go!" Honey yelled from the front of the group.

She raised her knife and pressed her knees into Terrain's sides as he sped forth from the left. Lux drew back his dagger as Sleet dashed forth from the right. Blood Crow and James bellowed a battle cry as Forest raced after Terrain from far behind. E drew two knives with one hand and gripped her machete with the other as Bloom flew straight forward like a speeding nimbus. Father galloped behind him, snarling with the rage of a gray storm cloud ready to rain down fiery hail.

"Lux, now!" Honey cried.

She hurled her knife. The Beast's foreleg shot up like that of a praying mantis to block her attack, and within that moment of distraction, Lux's dagger zinged through the air and thudded into its raw socket. The Beast screamed a human scream. Its eye swiveled and bulged. Terrain and Sleet carried Honey and Lux away from the orbs that shot toward them. Forest accelerated with a burst of speed. Blood Crow and James studded the Beast with knives and daggers from their belts. It shrieked again. Forest veered to the side as Bloom and Father ran up from behind. The Beast turned as if to flee then stopped. Suspicion jumped up within James.

"*Stay back!*" E shouted to the group.

She leapt off of Bloom and threw her knives as she twisted through the air. Her eyes flashed red and her blade, blue as she swung down her machete. As the Beast scrambled to the side to escape, Bloom leapt for its neck. The Beast crouched low then sprang over him. Father lunged with bared fangs. The Beast scurried to the side, barely escaping the snap of his jaws, as E jumped onto Bloom again. Bloom and Father leapt forward together, clawing and snapping their jaws. E's blue machete, swifter than her black, swiped again and again at the Beast's dark eye. The eye swiveled about in a frenzy, unable to focus, unable to attack. She threw daggers from her belt even as she continued slashing.

"*Surround it!*" she yelled. "*Wear it down more! Make an opening for Bloom and Father!*"

The group fanned out behind the Beast. It screamed as they hurled their weapons into its legs and sides. Blood Crow began to whoop and screech, using strange cries that she had surely used as a Hunter to disorient her prey. Her shouts electrified the crew's thirst to kill, and they, too, lifted up their voices with cries that hungered to finish the hunt once and for all.

James grabbed the Third's knives from his belt and threw them. The Beast grunted as each knife thudded deep into its flesh with the accuracy of a perfect weapon. He drew from Snow's belt as he depleted his own and sent each of her blades singing through the air. He hurled the Third's silver knives last. The knives flew forth, as swift and light as arrows, and studded the Beast's neck. The Beast stumbled and swayed.

E threw her last dagger and jumped off of Bloom, who lunged forth, quicker without her weight. He sank his teeth into the Beast's leg and yanked the Beast off of its feet. He jumped aside as Father leapt forward and bit into its dark eye. The group cried out in triumph as he growled and pulled and snapped his head from side to side.

"*I'll get its head!*" E yelled as she drew her other machete. "James, *Snow, get ready!*"

Forest sped forth. E and Bloom ran toward the Beast from either side. James grabbed Snow's wrist, ready to guide her hand to the golden eye. This was it. Father would rip out its dark eye, E would behead it, then Snow could easily–

Father's eyes widened. He released his bite and sprang back.

"*Back!*" he shouted.

A large, black sphere swallowed the Beast whole.

Forest swerved. E and Bloom jumped back in opposite directions.

"What," James breathed.

"*Retreat!*" Father yelled.

The group scrambled back. That sphere was made from the Beast's darkness, James was sure of it. Which meant that the sphere was impenetrable. Was that why the Beast had refused to run away again? Had it been gathering enough strength to create a shield that the group could never hope to destroy? And its dark eye. How were they supposed to see its dark eye now?

E and Bloom ran toward each other again. Snow twitched.

"E, back!" she shrieked.

E leapt back as an orb shot out of the sphere. Bloom swerved sharply and jumped to the side.

"Back, back, back!" Snow screamed.

E back flipped again and again and again then crouched low to the ground as the attacks ceased. James struggled then choked out air as he remembered to breathe again. Though he and the others stared only at the Beast's sphere, he knew that their focus, like his, had latched onto Snow. Bloom gave his head a sharp shake then ran to E. James found his voice again as she jumped onto Bloom's back.

"Snow," he said. "How?"

Her voice trembled as she whispered, "I can see it." She inhaled then shouted, "*I can see its eye when it's in its sphere! I can see what it wants to attack next!*" Her nails dug into his skin. "Honey! Lux!" she screamed.

Orbs shot out of the sphere in rapid fire. Honey and Lux pressed themselves flat on top of Terrain and Sleet as they fled toward the Desert's giant plateaus. The attack ceased, and for a heartbeat of a moment, James hoped that the Beast had tired itself out again. Dismay devoured his hope as orbs of every size exploded out of the Beast's sphere and flew toward the plateaus.

"Guys!" E cried out as the flurry hid Lux, Honey, and the two wolves from sight. "Bloom, let's go!"

"*No, stay back!*" Father yelled as he blocked Bloom from running to them. "*There is nothing we can do.*"

Self-loathing twisted E's face. She expelled a sound of anguished frustration then signaled for Forest and Father to follow her in retreat as the Beast continued building its giant, black wall.

"Our weapons," Blood Crow whispered to James. "All our weapons."

"I know. Don't freak out. It's fine," he said even as he fought to tame the panic writhing within him.

E had two machetes and three creations left. He had three creations too, and Snow still had six. But that was all the group had left to fight with now. They had thrown all the weapons they had gathered in the chamber in their last attack against the Beast.

The group halted as the barrage ceased. A new, black wall now stood behind a sinking screen of dust. It stood parallel to the plateaus so that one end met the curve in the crescent shape of the plateaus far off in the distance and the other end connected with the wall impeding the group from returning to the moonlight. Honey, Lux, Terrain, and Sleet were now trapped between the two walls and the plateaus.

"Blood Crow, James!" Snow screamed.

Orbs zinged out of the Beast's sphere. Bloom and Father sprang aside. Forest flattened himself onto the ground as Blood Crow jumped off to one side and James to the other. Forest wriggled toward Blood Crow as orbs consumed the space above him. Snow dangled from James's neck as he scrambled back onto his feet. Blood Crow leapt onto Forest's back.

"*Forest!*" Snow screamed.

Blood Crow clung to his fur as he dashed toward the horizon.

"Blood Crow!" James cried as an orb swallowed a chunk of her hair.

Father ran to James. "*Ride with me!*" he shouted.

He jumped onto Father's back as another explosion burst forth from the Beast's sphere and sprayed the horizon black.

"No," James said.

"*This way!*" E shouted. She led them further back.

"We can't just keep retreating like this!" James yelled as he tried to catch sight of Blood Crow. How was this possible? Creating even one wall had cost the Beast so much energy before. How could it create another wall already?

"*Be patient!*" Father said. "*The Beast will reappear!*"

Again, the bombardment ceased. Bloom and Father halted as they faced the Beast's sphere again. The right end of the new wall merged with the one that had trapped Honey, Lux, Terrain, and Sleet. The left end stretched endlessly across the Desert, leaving Blood Crow and Forest trapped on the other side. They were down not only in weapons and creations but in fighters too now. Even if they somehow managed to tear out the dark eye and the gold, how would they hold the Beast down to pierce its mark? All it had to do was shift to its larger size to escape from their grasp.

The sphere melted from the top down. The Beast's dark eye, still injured from Father's bite, drooped slightly out of its socket like the eye of a worn doll. Lux's dagger remained lodged in the Beast's raw socket, but the rest of the weapons the crew had thrown into its body had disappeared along with all the other injuries they had inflicted.

The sphere. It was the darkness of the sphere. The Beast had used its darkness to eat up all the weapons they had thrown into its body. Not only that, but immersing itself in the power of its darkness had allowed it to gather its strength rapidly so that it could heal and attack. Father leapt aside as the Beast's dark eye swiveled onto him.

But the eye failed to bulge as the Beast lashed its head from side to side in a futile attempt to dislodge Lux's dagger.

"*Now!*" E yelled.

Bloom and Father dashed forth. The Beast turned and scuttled away. It stopped short as it dug all four of its hooves into the ground and rubbed its knee against Lux's dagger again. E shoved her blue machetes under her belt and threw the spear that appeared in her hand. The Beast jumped aside a moment too late. It screamed as the spear plunged into its body. It buckled onto one knee.

"*You take left!*" E shouted.

Father veered to the left and Bloom to the right.

"James, spear!" E yelled.

Both James and E created a spear as they converged on the Beast from opposite sides.

"Now!" she shouted.

They launched their spears. As the Beast jumped back, E hurled one last spear. It skewered the Beast.

"Yes!" James screamed.

A sphere began to swallow the Beast then vanished as it sank onto its knee again. It tried to stand up. James threw a spear into its body and forced it to kneel once more. Bloom's feet whisked across the white tiles of the Desert as he pulled ahead with a burst of speed. James grabbed Snow's wrist again. Hope, joy, and relief all flooded him as E drew her blue machetes, sprang off of Bloom's back, and leapt high into the air. She plummeted toward the Beast's neck as Bloom leapt forth with his claws and teeth bared.

The Beast smiled.

A black sphere swallowed it whole.

E continued to fall, powerless to gravity. Bloom's eyes widened as he continued to soar toward the sphere. Father leapt forth.

In the split moment that followed, James knew that Father had forgotten all about him and Snow seated on his back. He had forgotten about E, the fate of the dimensions, and even himself. All he cared about was his son.

James gripped Snow. As he flung her and himself off of Father, he created a spear and hurled it into E with such force that the blow carried her past the Beast's orb and onto the ground instead. Father slammed into Bloom and pushed him aside midair.

"*Father!*" Snow shrieked.

Father yelped as an orb shot forth and swallowed half of his body. White dust enshrouded him as he thudded onto the floor. James grunted as he landed shoulder-first on the ground. Snow cried out as she lost her hold on him and rolled away. Bloom shook his head then snapped around and stared at Father's body.

E vomited blood as she forced herself to stand up again. She gasped sharp breaths before roaring and pulling out James's spear. They were both out of creations now. They were down to her two machetes and Snow's six creations. And Father. Father was as good as dead.

A thread of red-yellow saliva spooled down from the Beast's mouth as its sphere melted. It licked its lips as if to savor an exquisite taste. It had healed all of its wounds again, but by some miracle, Lux's dagger was still lodged in its raw socket.

Orbs zinged toward James as he scrambled onto his feet. He ran toward Snow then cried out as another stream of orbs forced him to swerve away from her. E sealed her wound with another roar as James dashed toward Snow again. The dark eye's gaze swiveled onto him.

"No!" E shouted.

She hurled the spear she had pulled out of her body. The eye turned away from James and fired an orb that ate her spear midair. The Beast shook its head and rubbed its knee against Lux's dagger.

"Bloom, get Father out of here!" E screamed.

Bloom bit into Father's nape and ran. Blood and guts spilled out of Father's halved body as he carried him into the distance. Another torrent of orbs blocked James from reaching Snow and drove him further out into the Desert. E ran toward the Beast with her machetes then leapt aside as the eye swiveled rapidly between her and James. The eye fixed on Snow. James screamed. E hurled her machete at its eye before it could bulge. The Beast ate her blade with another orb then rubbed its knee against Lux's dagger once more.

"James, get Snow!" E cried. "Run!"

He sprinted toward Snow again as E charged toward the Beast with her last machete. A sphere swallowed the Beast, and though James couldn't see the dark eye like Snow could, he knew that the eye had fixed upon E.

Snow created a dagger and threw it at the sphere. The dagger disappeared into the sphere's darkness.

"*I am the Twelfth!*" she screamed. "*I have the power to take your golden eye!*"

The orb meant for E shot toward Snow instead. She yelped as she flung herself aside. James continued sprinting as the sphere began melting away. The Beast looked at E. Snow let out a long battle cry as she created one knife after another and threw them blindly. The Beast fixed its focus on her then screamed and looked away again as E threw her last machete into its side. Empty-handed, she sprinted toward a spear still planted in the ground. The Beast thrust its knee against Lux's dagger and dislodged the blade at last. It blinked rapidly and shook its head as Snow's last knife bounced off of its leg. James screamed out his desperation as he ran faster than he had ever run in his life.

The dark eye bulged. An orb shot toward Snow. James launched himself in front of her. Instinct triggered him to reach out with his watch hand.

And, as he floated through the air, he thought of how he should have gone to more of Heri's dinners. He should have told her that she was the best sister he could have ever asked for. He should have told his whole family that he loved them. He should have told Blood Crow that he loved her too.

He closed his eyes.

"NO!" E screamed.

His eyes sprang open.

He saw the black orb flying toward him. He gasped as he caught the orb with his watch hand. He tightened his grip as he landed on the ground and skidded across the dry, jagged floor on his side. His arm vibrated as he pushed back on the orb. It burned cold as ice as it pressed deep into his palm. He could feel it struggling against him, burrowing and grating as it strove to devour him. He flipped onto his back, still pushing up as the orb pushed down.

He screamed as pain split apart his hand. E's and Snow's shouts grew distant. Darkness seeped out of his watch and spread across his hand in black rivulets that fragmented his arm and traveled up toward his neck. But even as the pain made his body, mind, and soul diverge and converge in turns, he continued screaming at himself that he had to fight, he had to win, he had to protect the ones he loved!

He drove himself deep into the fire of his determination and gripped the strength he found there. He burned away all fears, all doubts, all weaknesses. His hearing and vision snapped back into his control. The cracking pieces of himself pulled together. The darkness rushed back into his watch. He let out a cry that seemed to tear apart his throat as he dug his fingers into the orb. He forced himself back onto his feet then mustered all his strength. Twisting his body, he flung the orb aside. He spread his feet into a fighting stance as he readied his shaking hand to block more of the Beast's attacks.

But the dark eye was focused solely on Bloom and E. They were several yards away, running, swerving, and leaping as they dodged orbs and tried in vain to reach one another.

"James!" E screamed. "What's happening?"

"James! James, where are you?" Snow screamed from behind him.

"Stay there, Snow!" he shouted. "E, I can touch it! I can touch the darkness with my watch hand! I can block its attacks!"

Snow gasped. E's and Bloom's eyes widened even as they continued dodging. James hurried backward toward Snow's voice, his focus still on the dark eye, then stopped as her hands found his leg. He kept his watch hand at the ready as she clambered onto his back. He glanced at the ground for fallen weapons as he ran toward E, but it was no use. Orbs had consumed them all.

"We're out of creations and weapons," he told Snow. "We're still not close to getting to the Beast's dark eye, and we don't know how to hold it down. There's nothing we can use to pierce its mark even if we do."

An orb shot toward him. He skidded to a stop as he smacked the orb aside. Snow's arms tightened around his neck as he continued striking aside one orb after another.

The attacks ceased. The Beast snorted as it glared at James. The hatred in its dark eye barely masked its shock. James smirked and twitched his fingers to goad it. E and Bloom ran to one another as he struck aside another orb. She leapt onto Bloom's back at last. Orbs rushed toward Bloom and James in intervals. Bloom dashed from side to side as James continued striking.

Snow gasped. "Wait. We're not out. We're not out of weapons! E!" she screamed. "The tree of eyes! Your dagger! The dagger that Kit gave you!"

The memory of E sobbing beneath the tree of eyes flooded James's mind. The priceless dagger with stones of lapis lazuli. Kit's first gift to E. She had buried it among the tree's roots!

"Go dig it out!" he screamed as Bloom swerved away from another orb. "We'll distract it! Get that dagger so we can pierce its mark!"

He ran up to a motionless orb hanging in the air and gripped it. He spun then hurled the orb at the Beast. The Beast snapped its head toward him. Bloom dashed toward the tree of eyes standing black and jagged in the distance. A sphere swallowed the Beast so that the orb James had thrown disappeared into the sphere.

"James!" Snow screamed.

He deflected the orb that flew out of the sphere then charged, striking aside each attack as Snow shouted warnings. He balled his watch hand into a fist as he sprinted across the last few feet separating him from the sphere. He screamed out his determination as he slammed his knuckles into the darkness. The sphere shuddered like a building that had felt the first tremors of a great earthquake.

He began pummeling its cold, black shell, lost in his love for his friends and family, furious at the Beast for endangering them, desperate to finish this battle for good. As his knuckles splintered, he dug into his pain, fueled his determination, and healed his fist between each blow.

"*Come out! Come out, you coward!*" he screamed.

The sphere lurched forward like a charging ram. He seized the sphere and dug his feet into the ground. He tightened his hold and, with a strength that reached beyond his body and mind and drew from the center of his soul, he lifted the sphere high above his head. He roared out his will to protect as he threw it down.

The sphere shattered.

He lunged forward and gripped the Beast's dark eye with his watch hand and its neck with his right hand. He kicked its legs out from under it and slammed it down onto its side. He throttled its wet, slippery neck as it writhed and flopped and kicked about. It began to twitch and shudder. Its legs cracked as they lengthened.

"No!" James cried as his fingers stretched over its fattening neck.

"What's happening?" Snow screamed.

"It's shifting!" He knew he only had a fraction of a moment before it threw off his grip.

Snow pitched herself over his shoulder with a fierce cry. She grasped the Beast's wet coat as she fell upon it. The Beast convulsed as if she'd stabbed it. It stopped growing. James stared, wide-eyed.

"Help me!" Snow screamed as she dug her palms into its body. "We can make it shrink! I know we can! Just press down!"

He thrust his hands deeper into the Beast's eye and neck. He followed Snow's lead and pushed and pressed as if he were forcing the Beast back into a box. It moaned and flailed weakly as it shrank back to its original size.

"Yes!" Snow and James cried out.

He continued strangling it with his right hand as he dug his fingers deeper into its cold, dark eye. He tugged over and over again, trying to pry it out. The eye still drooped from its socket thanks to Father's bite, and he could feel it squishing around with every tug. But no matter how hard he pulled, he couldn't tear it out.

Realization hit him. It didn't matter. They didn't need to tear it out to get to the golden eye!

"Snow, reach forward! You can take the golden eye! I'll keep my hand over its dark eye so it can't attack you!"

She kept one hand pressed down on the Beast's body while her other hand scrambled toward its head. The Beast's thrashing grew more frantic.

"A little more!" he yelled. "To the left! Now to the right! The left! The left!"

Snow's hand jerked from side to side, an inch away from the golden eye.

"Further!" he screamed.

The Beast jumped up with a sudden burst of power that flung Snow aside and threw James onto his back. He barely managed to keep his hold on its eye and neck as it lunged for his throat. His arms shook as the Beast bore down on him.

"Snow!" he cried as it began to shift.

He choked on his own blood as the Beast stomped its hoof into his stomach. His vision diminished into a soft blur as it twisted its hoof deeper.

Snow grabbed James's shoulder. Her hand fumbled up the length of his left arm and onto his watch. The Beast froze as she gripped the golden eye. She gasped as the milky film of blindness covering her eyes vanished. She looked at the Beast with clear eyes the color of lapis lazuli.

She wrenched the golden eye out of its forehead.

The Beast screamed and lifted its hoof off of James. Bloom seemed to materialize out of nowhere as he dashed toward the Beast with open jaws. E's eyes flashed with a fire that towered up and reached for victory as she raised her lapis lazuli dagger. She launched herself off of Bloom's back and twisted high up into the air as he leapt forth. James snatched his hands away from the Beast and rolled aside as Bloom plunged his fangs into its dark eye. With the power that both Father and James had lacked, Bloom tore out the eye with one swift pull. The blinded Beast shrieked as it collapsed onto its knees. Bloom spat out the eye and leapt aside, and as the eye hit the ground, the entire Desert blackened like land that had survived an atomic bomb. Instinct struck James and, he knew, Snow and E. It connected the three of them as he and Snow threw themselves forward, gripped the Beast, and willed its mark to reappear on the vertebra on its back. The mark obeyed their will as E fell from the sky with a great war cry that echoed across the Iris. She plunged her dagger straight through the Beast's mark and into the Desert's black floor.

The Red Calf, along with all of its black orbs and its dark eye, disappeared.

# CHAPTER 23

# BY DAY OR BY NIGHT

J ames remained balanced on both elbows, halfway onto his feet. Snow's grip on the golden eye whitened. Saliva dripped from Bloom's dangling tongue as his stomach palpitated with rapid breaths. E stood up, gasping for air like a survivor of a shipwreck. All of them stared at the spot where the Beast had lain just a moment ago.

James stood up slowly. He gazed at the Desert, taking in the vast, black land that had been so white just moments ago. Something within him seemed to snap gently as Snow threw herself at him and wrapped him in a tight embrace. She began bawling into his chest. The thing that had snapped began to tremble, and before he could stop himself, he began crying too. The rest of the crew, now freed from the black walls, rode toward them as he wept out his relief, his exhaustion, and his disbelief.

They had won. They had actually won. They had killed the Red Calf. The dimensions were safe now. Humans and citizens were safe now. He swore to give Heri a hug once he woke up. E sheathed her lapis lazuli dagger then unclipped Certus's radio from her belt.

Static then, "E? E, what is the meaning of this? You agreed to give us updates! What's going on?"

A hollow chuckle shook James as it wandered out of his mouth. The Third sounded so angry, but how could anyone be angry over something as trivial as updates right now?

"We were ambushed as soon as we stepped into the Desert," E said. "We're done, though. It's done. The Red Calf is gone."

More static followed.

"And the golden eye?"

"It's gone too," she lied. "I ... I'm sorry, Three. I really am."

Static again.

"Well," the Third said. "That's that, then. No use crying over spilt milk. At least you are all safe. That's the important thing. Yes, that's the important thing."

"I'm going out there," Phoenix said in the background. "Zilch, let's go. Now!"

E turned the radio off and let it drop onto the black floor.

Something squirmed.

James yanked Snow to the side as E and Bloom jumped into battle stances. They stared at the red tendrils creeping out from where the Beast's dark eye had fallen on the ground. James lifted his watch hand higher as a grinning mouth sprouted from an elongating, red branch. A new tree was twisting out of the Desert's floor, a tree that was red instead of black and bore mouths instead of eyes.

A memory of Sleet emerged from the folds of James's mind as more mouths burgeoned. He had explained before that the black tree of eyes had grown from the blood that had spilled when Father and the Last had taken the Beast's eye. Which meant that this tree of mouths was growing from the blood that had spilled when Bloom had taken its dark eye and secured their victory. Bloom snapped his head around then ran toward the tree of eyes in the distance.

"Father," E said.

They ran after him. As the rest of the crew caught up, James grabbed Blood Crow's hand and jumped onto Forest's back. The group gaped at Snow as she ran alongside Terrain then jumped onto his back behind Honey.

"Snow, you can see!" Lux exclaimed as E leapt onto Sleet.

"It's the golden eye," Snow said, lifting it up. "It's because I'm holding it. The Shamans' sight lies within it."

"*So it is gone, then? The Beast is truly defeated?*" said Sleet.

"*Yes,*" E said. "*The Red Calf is no more.*"

Smiles began to spread across their faces then vanished as they neared the black tree. The wolves raised their heads in alarm. Father's chest sank in and threatened to collapse with each rattling breath. Most of his guts had fallen out of what remained of his body, and what the Beast had taken showed no signs of reforming. The crew dismounted as the wolves skidded to a halt. They all drew closer with the quiet steps of those who knew that they were approaching the dying.

Bloom nudged Father with his snout. His eyes rolled back into focus and roved over each of his sons before resting on E.

"*The Last,*" he whispered.

James's throat tightened. Father had completed the Last's final mission. The long wait was over. Both he and the Last could now rest in peace.

E got down on both knees then bowed deep and low in front of Father. James and the others maintained a unified silence as they bowed as well. He knew that this was their way of saying thank you, for no words could possibly thank this ancient and loyal Castaway enough. Their silence carried more meaning than any attempt to articulate their gratitude. As they rose to their feet, Father gazed at the golden eye in Snow's hands. A questioning look fought through the pain gripping his face.

Of course. Father's heart. They could use his heart to seal away the golden eye. It would be safe from the Shamans forever if it was sealed away.

But only if Snow chose to give up the eye.

She clutched the eye against her chest as she walked toward Father then halted mid-step. Uneasiness reared its head higher within James as her hands enveloped the eye, leaving only slivers of its golden surface visible. He hated his own suspicion. This was Snow, his surrogate little sister in the Flowering. She had just helped save the lives of everyone in this group and all the dimensions. And yet, he couldn't shake the memory of her lunging for E back in the Keep. Nor could he forget the jealousy that had possessed her in that moment.

She pressed the eye deeper against her heart then lifted her blue eyes toward the full moon. Longing radiated from her, longing for the sight she had now, longing for the life that she could keep if she simply opened the eye and took back the powers the Shamans had lost so long ago.

Then her grip on the eye loosened, and her longing faded like moonlight in the dawn. She bowed her head like a flower greeting a long winter night, and despite the relief that broke apart his uneasiness, James couldn't help but think, if only. If only.

"Guys!"

The group spun around as Phoenix and Zilch ran up to them. Zilch stared at Snow's eyes then sank onto his knees in disbelief. Her breath quickened as she turned away from him. She clutched the eye again, but James knew that this time, it was determination that had tightened her hold and not temptation. She knelt down at Father's side and held out the eye with both hands.

"*I'm ready,*" she said. "*I'll make sure that the greed of eras past will never consume the Flowering again. I swear it.*"

Father stared at her, wheezing halting breaths, before nodding. He turned his focus to Bloom. There was no hatred or resentment in Bloom's eyes as he held his gaze. There was only regret that despite all the hurt and the conflicts and everything in between, this was how their relationship would end. With no second chances, with no room for conversation. Death was more final than hatred.

Bloom shuddered with the cries he could not voice. Forest began to wail. Terrain shook violently then stilled before shaking again. Sleet closed his eyes as more tears joined the ones he had already shed. James watched his own tears fall onto the black floor as all around him, the crew wept as well. He put his arms around Blood Crow as she covered her face with her hands. She buried her face into his chest as he held her close.

Father gazed at each of his sons a final time before resting his eyes on Lapis Lazuli. Moonlight and memories filled his eyes, erasing all the pain. He exhaled a deep breath that carried the weight of finality. His eyes closed with the slow peacefulness of one falling asleep. He lay still for a moment then vanished, leaving a purple orb in his place.

Sleet, Terrain, and Forest pointed their snouts at the dim sky and howled. Bloom turned his head away from Father's heart. As E hugged him, he nuzzled her black hair and continued weeping. Snow picked up the purple orb, stood up, and stared at the Tower.

She sighed softly.

With a gentleness devoid of reluctance, she pressed the purple heart against the golden eye so that the two seemed to kiss. Father's heart immediately opened in a small circle. As the circle widened rapidly like ripples on water, the golden eye dissolved and reformed as a shrunken version of itself within his heart.

For a fraction of a moment, the golden eye hovered within his heart.

Then Father's heart closed around the eye.

Tears continued trickling down Snow's cheeks as a milky film slid over each of her eyes, blinding her once and for all. Father's heart fell from her hand as she continued weeping.

E picked up the heart. The group watched as she placed it in the cavity where Kit's dagger had lain then covered it with black earth. She pressed down on the layers with firm hands.

"The golden eye will be safe here," she said. "And even if someone does find it, there's nothing they can do. Father's heart will guard it forever. You did the right thing, Snow."

Snow nodded. She was still turned toward the Tower. James broke away from Blood Crow and walked up to Snow. He laid a gentle hand on her shoulder.

"Take me back, James," she whispered.

He knelt for her.

He wished that there was some other way, any other way. But they both knew that her place was in the Tower, where she would rule as a Shaman, and his place was out in the planes, where he and the others would hunt the moulded as humans were born into the Flowering to do. Grief consumed him completely as she climbed onto his back for what he knew would be the last time. The group stood still for a moment as they stared at the ground where Father's heart lay buried.

They began walking back to the City.

Each step James took seemed to grow heavier as they drew closer to the Blue Border. Losing Father and now parting with Snow. Both drowned all the joy that should have come with their victory.

The group stepped into the moonlight then stopped. In the distance, smoke streamed out from the Tower's windows. Bodyguards, some running, others limping, hauled bodies through the open front doors and laid them down on the ground. Remnants of the Solstice still lay scattered across the land between the Tower and the Market. Many of the Market's tents had collapsed. Fires burned, and black columns of smoke floated up toward the full moon. James could smell the smoke even from here.

But all the destruction hadn't been in vain. There were no signs of battle. No screams or bloodthirsty yells. The riots had been subdued. The Third had defeated the Hunters.

"Dang," said Lux. He shook his head as Bodyguards shouted to one another and tended to the fallen. "The Hunters destroyed everything!"

"They've had their revenge," Blood Crow said.

"Yes," said Snow. "But I doubt it'll be enough."

Phoenix glared at the ground. James could see the battle between anger and concern raging within his eyes. The Third had won against the Hunters, but how would he recover from this? The Hunters had destroyed so much of the City. And Snow was right. They would not forget his interruption of the Solstice nor their defeat at his hands.

But James supposed all that was the Third's problem now. There was nothing the group could do about it. This had been the Third's choice. Despite his hunger for power, he'd still chosen to protect his son as well as the lives of those in the City. James felt that he could almost forgive him for all the suffering he'd put the group through when he thought about it that way, but he was also fairly sure that he would take any opportunity to pummel the Third if the chance ever came his way.

E placed her hand on Snow's shoulder. "Are you sure you're ready to go back there right now? We can stay out here a little longer if you want."

"No, it's all right. I'm ready," Snow said. "I don't want to, but I'm ready."

Her arms unwound from James's neck. The sorrow he'd barely managed to dam welled up into tears again as she slipped off of his back and climbed onto Zilch's. It would be so strange to travel throughout the Flowering without her. He couldn't help but feel a pinch of jealousy at the thought that someone else was in charge of looking after her now.

"Thank you for taking care of her," Zilch told him.

James swallowed his sob. "Of course. No problem."

Tears continued dripping down Snow's face as he laid a hand on her shoulder and tried to speak. He cleared his throat and hung his head as he found that he could not.

"James," she said.

He squeezed her shoulder to let her know that he was listening.

"Thank you so much for everything. I'll see you in a bit, okay?"

He cleared his throat again and stepped back. Blood Crow touched his arm first then slid her hand into his. He gripped her hand before clearing his throat a final time.

"I'll miss you, Snow," he said.

"We'll make sure to come visit you," Honey said.

"At least twice a year," Lux declared.

E nodded. "At least twice a year. We have to. Snow is a member of Crew Blue."

Snow's face relaxed into a sad smile.

"We'll bring you presents," Lux said.

Honey scoffed. "What can we possibly give a Shaman that she can't find on her own?"

"I'm sure we'll find something," he said with a shrug.

"*We can meet in Reality too if you want, if it gets too lonely or if you need help,*" E told her in Korean after glancing at Zilch.

Snow's smile brightened a shade. "*Yeah. Let's do that, Unni.*"

E flinched. James chuckled in spite of his tears. "Unni" was an honorific girls used to address any other girl who was older by a year or more. It literally translated to "older sister" and signified respect as well as friendship. It was a heart-warming word.

E crossed her arms and huffed as she looked away.

"Should we do it now?" Snow asked Zilch.

He breathed out a long, reluctant sigh. "Yeah. I'm ready."

The group stared at them. E slowly uncrossed her arms.

"You go first, Z," said Snow.

Zilch glanced at the horizon that lay beyond the Blue Border then sighed again.

"*Goodbye*," he told E. "Your turn, Snow."

"*Goodbye*," she told her. "*And thank you all for everything*," she told the group.

"Be careful in there," E replied. "And remember that you're more than what they say you are. Who cares if they can see and you can't? You can still outsmart them all."

"Thanks," said Snow, her smile brightening another shade. "Now that you mention it, I think I'll tell the Bodyguards that I'm friends with the infamous E of the Arena the next time they annoy me. I'll just casually mention that she comes to visit me every once in a while too."

A small grin pulled up a corner of E's mouth. "Make sure you do," she said. "Oh, and...."

She drew the lapis lazuli dagger from her belt then took Snow's hand and wrapped her fingers around the hilt. Understanding twitched on Snow's face.

"Could you give this to the Third?" E said. "Tell him it belongs to Kit. And tell him ... tell him I don't need it anymore."

"Of course," Snow said softly. "It would be my pleasure."

She grasped E's hand then let go. Zilch worked his mouth into a smile before nodding at the group and turning toward the Tower. The group watched them until distance shrank them into anonymity. Blood Crow leaned her head on James's shoulder.

"She'll be okay," she said. "She isn't the same girl she was when we first met her."

"I know," James replied. And he really did. Snow no longer was the girl who fidgeted with her fingers and feared anyone who yelled at her. She was the Twelfth Shaman whom the Last had chosen to help defeat the Red Calf.

His eyes strayed to his watch. He'd hoped that with the Beast's defeat his watch would have assumed a normal form. But it remained a black, faceless circle, and he doubted it would ever change. The powers which he'd inherited from the Last were still within him as was the curse of the Beast. His watch had been doomed from the moment he'd eaten the eye in the blue box.

He inhaled deeply and looked up at the full moon. It hung in the sky, as huge and heavy as the first time he'd seen it the night he'd been born into the Flowering. His mind traced the memory of him tripping over the roots of the tree of eyes then hovered over the lapis lazuli box in his awakening dream. He opened the box and stared at the Beast's eye.

He still didn't understand why the Last had chosen him to receive the box. True, he had helped E and Snow to kill the Beast, but he still thought that E would have been the better choice. Snow too. Giving her all of the eye would have made much more sense than splitting it with him. So why had the Last chosen him?

Lux held up his watch. "It's time, you guys."

"Finally," Honey groaned.

Sleet pawed at the tears still streaming down his face then stood up. *"We will navigate through the Iris as much as possible while you are gone,"* he told E.

She nodded. *"We'll see you when we return."*

He led Terrain and Forest out of the moonlight. They stopped and turned toward Bloom. Bloom took a deep breath to steady his weeping then walked out of the moonlight as well. But instead of joining his brothers, he sat down and gazed at them as if to encourage them to go ahead without him. They stared back at him before trotting further out into the Desert.

Bloom's tail flopped from one side to another as he looked at the crew. They didn't need telling twice. One by one, they stepped out of the City. Phoenix inserted his hand into Bloom's mouth first, then Lux, then Honey.

"Wait," James said as Blood Crow placed her hand between Bloom's fangs.

His heartbeat accelerated at an embarrassing rate. This was ridiculous. He'd just battled the most dangerous citizen to have ever existed, and here he was, shaking at the prospect of asking out a girl. And they had already held hands and everything! E gave him a slight push forward. He yelled at himself to spit it out.

"If you're not heading back right away, you want to go catch a movie or something? I'll pick you up. Or, wait, of course I'll pick you up. We're all in the same ... uh ... yeah. What do you think?"

Blood Crow glanced at E, who smiled and looked away.

"That sounds good," Blood Crow said, blushing.

James laughed nervously as Bloom bit down on her hand. He hadn't realized how long he'd wanted to ask her out, and now that he'd done it, he felt both stupid for having been so slow to do it and proud for having done it at last. He strode toward the moonlight, feeling as light as if he had stripped off body weights. He stopped as he realized that E was still staring at the Tower. Bloom joined him as he returned to her side.

"You okay?" he asked.

She glanced at both of them then stared at the Tower again. James sighed. He recognized that look in her eyes.

"There's nothing wrong with moving on from someone like him. You're doing the right thing," he said.

"He saved me."

"Yeah, he did. And he nearly got you killed a hundred times over too and all for his own dumb reasons. You can't call that love. Or, at least, you can't call that true love."

She sighed and closed her eyes. Bloom licked her arm and shuffled his paws.

"I hate myself," she said. "We just defeated the Beast. We just lost Father. We just said goodbye to Snow. But all I can do is stare at the Tower. Why am I like this? Why am I so weak?"

"You are not weak," James said firmly.

He placed both hands on her shoulders and turned her around to face him. She glared at the ground, still filled with self-hatred.

"You were in it deep with him, and he took you when you were vulnerable. He always has. He manipulated you, and you cared for him. It'd be weird if you got over everything so quickly. Closure is a process."

She smirked without smiling.

He sighed. "All that matters is that he can't get to you anymore. You're safe now. You can move on. You don't have to deal with him anymore."

"Don't have to deal with him anymore?"

A vulnerable kind of fear that James had only ever seen within her memories joined the anger in her eyes.

"Don't have to deal with him anymore? I do have to deal with him! Don't you see? He's all I have left to deal with. He's in my head, and even though I want to forget him and all those memories, I can't, no matter how hard I try. It's all in the past, but I still can't act like it!"

James's hands slid off of her shoulders as he considered this for several moments.

"Well," he said slowly, "that doesn't mean you can't move on or that you haven't moved on already in some ways. I mean, you did leave him before, and you left him again tonight."

E's frown deepened. She tensed as if fearful of what he would say next. He gave Bloom a pointed look. He nodded in response then nudged E's arm and stared at her with an unblinking focus that could only signify a request for head scratches. She placed her fingertips between his ears and scratched fast and rough, clearly too distraught to realize how hard she was scratching. He winced as her nails raked deeper into his skin. She glanced at him then sighed before slowing her fingers into a massage that spread a smile across his face. James resumed as her shoulders relaxed. He spoke slowly, taking care to choose the right words. He couldn't afford to be tactless right now.

"I don't think we can do anything about the memories in our heads, especially the intense ones, so I don't think it's weird or weak that you can't forget. And just because it's in the past doesn't mean that it can't reach into the present. All of our experiences feed into who we are right now, so I think it's normal, you finding it hard to forget, I mean.

"But, well, I'm hopeful. I'm hopeful for the future. You're out of the City now, and you have Crew Blue. Things are different, and time fades everything, even our memories. The past is behind you, which means you've still gone forward, even if you don't feel like it. And E," he said as pride unfurled within him, "you really have come such a long way."

She stopped petting Bloom. Her gaze returned to the Tower, but James could tell that her focus had withdrawn into her thoughts.

"You know," she said, "maybe this is why the Last chose you to inherit some of his powers."

"Huh? What do you mean?" he said, wondering what she was talking about all of a sudden.

"Most humans would have blamed me or called me a moron for falling in love with someone like him. Or they would have said that it's my decision and used that as an excuse to do nothing. They wouldn't have bothered trying to understand. They wouldn't have bothered to do or say anything at all. But you saw, and you understood. You tried to help me, and you never gave up on me. You're still not giving up on me. The Last must have known that you were the friend who would turn me away from him for good."

"I just did what any decent human would have done. It wasn't anything special," he mumbled as he rubbed the back of his neck.

"Then why was no one able to do it before you came along?"

He opened his mouth then closed it. He wasn't quite sure how to answer that. Others, like Marcus and even Honey, had tried to talk to E and turn her away from Kit. But neither of them had seen her memories the way he and Snow had. And though Snow had held the knowledge of E's past, the trust she'd broken had prevented her from saying anything truly effective. In the end, only James, armed with his knowledge, friendship, and love for E, had been able to convince her to do what she had needed to do, and he had convinced her when it had mattered the most.

Of course, it all had come down to E making the decision for herself too. Everything he had done would have been useless if she'd chosen to ignore him. But he couldn't deny his role in her decision either. She, like all human beings, had needed help in order to do the right thing, and he, as her friend, had been able to give her that help.

"It's thanks to you that I even made it out into the Desert at all," E continued. "Kit would have convinced me to stay in the Tower or to go back to the Market. And you saved Snow. You threw yourself in front of her even though you thought you'd die. And Snow saved both of us from the Beast and sealed away the Shamans' sight for good. The Flowering is safe now thanks to the two of you."

"I guess that's true," James said as he gave his neck a few more rubs. "But don't be so modest. Snow and I both don't have your battle skills or your leadership skills. Us, the crew, the pack. None of us would have made it this far without you. You were always destined to lead all of us here. You were always meant to kill the Beast and put an end to everything. You were the key."

Bloom wagged his tail as he beheld E with pride.

"And you did it all with Bloom's help, of course," James added.

He responded with a humble smile.

"We all were destined to put an end to it," E said. "You, me, Snow, Bloom, the crew, the pack, and even the Third. None of us could have done any of this without the other."

James knew it wasn't false modesty. It was the truth. Defeating the Beast had not been the work of one but the result of many humans, citizens, and circumstances all playing out their own roles throughout the ages, for good or for evil. He was just grateful that the good had won despite the evil. Just one of the many evils could have easily ruined all of the good.

But the good had prevailed in the end. The good had won.

Relief warmed his heart and consoled the grief within him. He turned around and gazed at the Desert. Beyond the black and parched land, the horizon glowed with the beginnings of a sunrise. Golden light began filling the sky, soft and bright. So much vastness lay ready for them, so much space clear of hungry darkness.

So much freedom.

"Come on, E. Let's go home."

Bloom trotted out of the moonlight once more. Sleet, Terrain, and Forest halted in the distance and stared at them. E turned away from the Tower and faced the horizon. The golden light filled her eyes.

"Yeah," she said. "Let's go home."

She followed James out of the moonlight. Bloom gave her fingers a parting lick before opening his mouth. She placed her hand between his fangs. She was still gazing at the sunrise as he bit down.

James laid his hand in Bloom's mouth too. The full weight of his exhaustion fell on him as he allowed himself to accept that the long night was finally over.

"See you tomorrow night, Bloom."

He swept his tail twice across the ground then bit down. An image of his golden eyes floated in front of his mind as he slowly opened his eyes.

A clock was ticking. The heater rumbled into life downstairs. He lifted his hand and touched his cheek.

He was crying.

James wiped his eyes. His skin prickled as he sat up. Sunlight had brightened his bedroom and welcomed in the cold, winter morning. Phoenix's sleeping bag sat next to him, rolled up like a stuffed, blue burrito. Lux's sleeping bag lay open like a laughing mouth. His mother was banging pots and pans and turning the faucet on and off as she prepared breakfast. She was singing "Silent Night" on repeat.

Today was Christmas.

Heri's door opened then closed. Footsteps padded past James's room and down the stairs. In the living room, Heri and Lux were laughing and talking. Honey cackled as someone turned on the TV. James sighed deeply as Blood Crow greeted Snow with a hearty, "Merry Christmas, Sophia!"

The stairs creaked as someone climbed them. Heri's door opened again.

"Meehae?" Phoenix said from the top of the stairs.

James dared not move as he listened for her answer. A few seconds passed.

"Meehae, are you all right?" Phoenix said.

A few more seconds ticked by before E sniffed and said, "Yeah, I think I am. I will be." She sniffed again then said, "Merry Christmas, by the way. It feels weird to be celebrating like this, doesn't it?"

Phoenix breathed out a sigh that carried as much relief as it did weariness. "It is weird. There's still so much to process. But I'm grateful. I'm grateful that we're alive and that we're all together right now."

James imagined E nodding in the silence that followed.

"What about you?" she asked. "Are you all right? About Phillip, I mean."

The stairs squeaked. "I ... well...." He sighed as he chuckled. "I guess my dad does love me, just like you said. I have to accept that much."

Another silence followed.

"Come on. There's a feast waiting for us downstairs," said Phoenix.

The floorboards creaked as E walked over to him. James knew, somehow, that a small smile had formed on her face.

"It'll be nice to have good Korean food for breakfast," she said as she walked down the stairs with him.

"I still don't know half the dishes that are on the table," Phoenix said with an embarrassed laugh. "You'll have to explain them to me again."

Enthusiasm hopped up in E's voice as she began listing the names of the dishes and their ingredients. Her voice and Phoenix's traveled into the living room and blended in with the conversations of the rest of the crew.

James burrowed deep into his sleeping bag again. He would go down and join everyone soon, but before he did, he wanted to be alone for a few minutes. There was still loss. There was still pain. But just for this moment, at least, he wanted to feel the peace of knowing that he and all of his loved ones were safe and well.

His mind began singing along to his mother's voice.

All was indeed calm. All was indeed bright.

He closed his eyes and rolled onto his side.

He breathed in, breathed out, and smiled.

### *THE END*

**THE WORLD OF**
**EYES OF AWAKENING**
**WILL CONTINUE IN**
**BOOK 3.**

# A LETTER FROM THE AUTHOR

## Abusive Relationships

*Please note that this letter contains spoilers from*
Eye in the Blue Box *and* Tree of Eyes.

I loved the man who inspired Kit. I loved that man with all my heart. He was sharp, self-assured, and hard-working. He was my only friend during one of the most broken periods of my life. And what a life I'd already had, even back then. So many tears and screams and pleading and fighting had composed the years leading up to then. Surviving those years had drained my will to feel, to cry, to express any emotion other than anger.

How I wish I could remember how to cry.

How I wish I could have cried when I forced myself to leave him. Maybe a part of me wouldn't have felt so awful for so long if I'd gotten it all out back then.

I had loved that man with all my heart, but at a certain point during my time with him, I began to believe that he didn't care about me anymore. How could someone who cared about me treat me so horribly? How could he do and say the things that he did? This belief, along with the growing realization that I was, indeed, in an abusive relationship, caused me to leave as suddenly and unexpectedly as E left Kit. I experienced my first heartbreak then. I couldn't breathe properly for days, it hurt so much. They really do call it "heartbreak" for a reason.

For years afterward, I couldn't understand. I couldn't understand how genuine care and love could exist in an abusive relationship. So, I simply concluded that I'd been had. That I had meant nothing–absolutely nothing–to him and that he, therefore, must have meant nothing to me. He had simply used me and abused me, and it was a simple, black and white matter. I'd been deceived, and our feelings had been a lie. That was as far as I could process the situation at the time.

My terror of him probably contributed to my inability to process further. I'd grown to fear him while I was with him because his disapproval of me had become synonymous with my disapproval of myself. Even after leaving him, I couldn't talk about him, never mind process everything, because I was afraid that he would somehow hear me and become angry and disapproving.

There was the physical aspect too, of course, that contributed to my terror. There had been moments when his anger would flare or spiral out of control, and he would take his anger out on me physically. I imagine that the fear I experienced in those moments is similar to what an animal must experience before the hounds sink their teeth into it.

I grew so angry at him too, though. So, so angry. That bastard. His lies, the smoke and mirrors, the names he called me, the things he egged me on to do, the insecurities he put on me, the ways he'd sneer at the misfortunes of others. All his disrespect, his cruelty, his stubbornness, his pride. How could I have trusted someone like him? How could I have loved such a man? What kind of moron would love a man who had never even given two turds about her?

How could I have loved such a monster?

Writing these books unexpectedly forced me to confront all of my conclusions and all of my beliefs. In particular, I was forced to confront the memories I hadn't been able to process years before, memories that my mind–without my knowing–had blacked out. Maybe my mind knew that processing everything back then would have shattered me. Life had already been too much, even without him. Maybe my mind knew that simplifying and blacking out was the best and only way to protect myself at the time.

But when I began to write these books, I remembered.

I remembered the heartbreak in his eyes. How he dangled other women in front of me for a reaction after I left. How he pulled all sorts of stunts when I wouldn't give him what he wanted. How he had tried to talk to me again. His jealousy of the man who is now my husband.

Sitting on a bench in the park, his head on my lap and me grazing my thumb over the bridge of his nose. The lunches he brought me after seeing me eat raw tofu and kimchi due to lack of time and money. The night he demanded that I stop cutting myself and how I had, consequently, stopped. How he'd know I was distraught even if I didn't say it. The nights we spent at the arcade. How he cheered for me so that I could get over my phobia of games. How I whooped and cheered in his new car as he drove like a madman all around an empty parking lot for our pleasure. The way his face would light up at the sight of me. The hours upon hours we spent talking and drinking. The cold nights that were hot in bed.

The long text he sent me out of the blue. How he told me that he'd been thinking of all the things life had put me through and that he thought it was miraculous how good I had turned out despite everything. How he thought I was amazing. How those words were the nicest words anyone had ever said to me.

I remembered all the good times. I remembered all the mess.

How can care and love exist in an abusive relationship? Well, writing these books opened my eyes to the truth, and the truth is simply this: people can be really messed up, and the real world is rarely black and white. Good and bad can coexist, but at the end of the day, the good cannot simply replace the bad. It's love, but it isn't love. But I think it's important to acknowledge that there is some twisted form of love in such relationships because one of the biggest reasons I couldn't leave him was because I could see with my own two eyes that, in many ways, he did genuinely care, and I believed that love was worth fighting for.

People often tell victims, "He doesn't love you. You should just leave!" But it just doesn't make sense when you're actually in the relationship because there is good and there is care and there is love. Yes, abusive relationships come in all sorts of forms, and I am well aware that there are many relationships that are not like mine or Kit and E's. There are all too many relationships that have zero love and zero care, and the victim is quite literally a prisoner.

But in my case, I was able to leave only because I had come to believe that he didn't care at all about me anymore and, perhaps, never had. If I had known that there actually had been a bit of him that still cared, who knows? Maybe I never would have found the strength to leave.

I wish I'd known sooner that my leaving or staying didn't hinge upon whether or not he cared for me. It hinged on whether or not he really acted like it too. Not some of the time, and not just when he felt like it. But consistently. He had to act like it consistently. And if he didn't, then not only was it okay to leave, but it was pivotal to do so. My only standard couldn't be whether or not he cared. I had the right to need more. And at the end of the day, I shouldn't have had to be with a rotten egg who was capable of doing good. I should have been with a good man.

I don't beat myself up for failing to realize all this sooner, though. Or, at least, I don't anymore. Given how difficult my circumstances had been and how very alone I was, I thank God I was able to realize anything at all.

Other people will blame me, though. People blame victims all the time. When you can't just stop, drop, and roll away from the relationship, people often sum up everything in one simple phrase: "She's stupid."

But I'm not stupid. Despite years of family drama and financial hardships, I studied hard and graduated high school with a weighted GPA of 5.0. I went on to graduate with over a 3.9 GPA from one of the best universities in the state. After graduating, I figured out how to work my way up the food chain, even though no one in my blue-collar family could give me any guidance on how to navigate a white-collar world. I became a high-level executive assistant at a large and prestigious organization, where I ran alongside some of the smartest people in the city if not the nation or even the world, and those same people praised me regularly for my intelligence and work ethic.

I am not stupid, and other victims aren't stupid either. Victims shouldn't be blamed for being human beings who make decisions that any other human in that kind of situation would make. And besides, those who victim-blame are often the least likely to lift a finger to help out a victim once she does leave the one person who seems to care about her, so can you really blame her when she doesn't listen to those who blame?

For those who have been blamed. For those who have been abused. For those who are still hurting. I hope this book can comfort you. Even if it's just a little, that will be enough for me. We are victims because we are innocent and blameless. We didn't deserve it or ask for it. This was done to us.

But we are also survivors because we have fought and won our battles.

I hope my book can also help those who have never lived through something like abuse but still have the potential to understand. And even if it's not in the context of abuse, I hope you'll learn to care about the immense amount of hurting and suffering that exists in our world.

Maybe you don't have to learn how to dodge a dagger or throw a spear, but you can train yourself to try and understand the struggles of your friends, your family, maybe even strangers, even if it doesn't make sense to you initially, even if you've never gone through the same things yourself. Broken pieces often create a rough exterior that cuts into others.

Maybe you won't ever have to muster up the courage to slay a moulded citizen, but you can muster up the courage to speak the truth patiently and lovingly to those in danger of believing in a lie. Maybe you don't have to carry the burden of rescuing different dimensions from destruction, but you can weep with those who weep, even if it's an inconvenience to you. And with courage, empathy, and love, maybe you can play a key part in preventing those who are hurting from running back to the warmth of a fire that will consume them alive. You can play a key part in anything if you truly give that much of a damn.

Why did I choose a seemingly normal guy like James to be my hero? Because courage, empathy, and love are not normal. You don't find chivalry every day. James was always a knight in shining armor, even if he didn't seem like one at first. Anyone who fights others and even oneself ... especially oneself ... to help another is a hero.

I hope you can be a hero too.

I know you can be a hero too.

With all my heart,
Ann Yihyang Kim

# ACKNOWLEDGEMENTS

First, I'd like to thank my mom. It was only after you gave my books your vote of confidence that I truly knew that they were good. Thank you for all your feedback and for believing in me. Of course, there are many other things I should thank you for, such as raising me as a single mother. But to write out all the things you've done for me would take another book entirely. So, I will simply say for now that you are the best mother in the world, and I am blessed to have been born to you.

Second, to my beta readers. Brian and Tingwei, your input helped make *Eyes of Awakening* a much better version of itself than I could have possibly made it on my own.

To the EoA Reading Group. The ones who stuck it out 'til the end. The OGs. The true bosses. You guys read the entirety of *Eyes of Awakening* multiple times without ever expecting anything in return. Abbie, Albert, Alex, Jess, and Sharon, EoA simply wouldn't have become EoA without your continual feedback. There were so many times I was touched by your words, whether it was when I was reading about the tears you shed or your violent dislike or like of characters that I, too, violently dislike or like. The friendships we formed is one of the best things that came out of writing EoA.

Marina, thank you for all your encouragement and feedback and, of course, for these amazing book covers. It's a privilege to work with a close friend on such a meaningful project. Your partnership helped make book production fun, and I'm sure there aren't too many authors out there who can say that. Thank you for all the work you put into this, even in the midst of pregnancy, and for making the faces of my precious books so loveable.

# ACKNOWLEDGEMENTS

Albert, my husband and best friend. Who knew that one really, really late-night walk would blossom into a full-blown romance, which would then take us into marriage and beyond? On that fateful night, I learned two things: 1. Rabbits are actually rodents, kind of like rats. 2. You're kind of a really cool guy.

It's not an exaggeration to say that without you, I might not be alive. God sent you into my life at a point when I was drowning. A person can only swim for so long through so many storms before sinking beneath the weight of fatigue. You heard all my splashing, rowed through the waves, and pulled me out of the water. Thank you for loving me. Thank you for reading EoA approximately one billion times. Thank you for picking up all the chores over and over again so that I could have the hours I needed to write and pursue my dreams. Thank you for putting up with me when I'm being insufferable. I love you too.

And lastly, I thank God. Without the Father, I would not exist. Without Jesus, I would not have redemption. Without the Holy Spirit, I would not have guidance. When I became a Christian, I felt for the first time in my life that I finally had a sense of where I was supposed to go. I knew there were a lot of details I had to fill in along the way, but I felt like I finally had clarity. I finally felt awake. Thank you for Your love and Your mercy. I am nothing without You.

## ENJOYED *TREE OF EYES*?
## WANT TO SUPPORT THIS AUTHOR?

---

### · *Leave a review online*
*(Online reviews are **crucial** for a*
*book's success!)*
*Amazon, Goodreads, Barnes & Noble*

### · *Follow the author on Instagram*
*@annyihyangkim*

### · *Subscribe to the author's blog*
*ann-yihyang-kim.com*

---

## THANK YOU FOR SUPPORTING
## INDIE AUTHORS!

# ABOUT THE AUTHOR

Ann Yihyang Kim graduated with an English major and Korean minor from the University of California, Berkeley. After finding herself successful yet unhappy with her professional life, she remembered how much joy writing had once brought her. She subsequently wrote her debut novel, *Eye in the Blue Box*. Her short stories have appeared in multiple literary magazines. She lives in San Diego, CA with her loving husband and their rambunctious dogs, Max and Volk.

*ann-yihyang-kim.com*
*Instagram: @annyihyangkim*